~1981

THIS LAND FULFILLED

THIS LAND FULFILLED
by Charles A. Brady

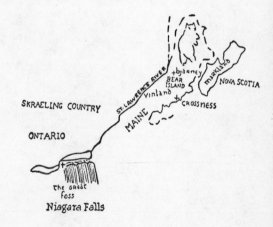

SKRAELING COUNTRY

ONTARIO

ST. LAWRENCE RIVER

BEAR ISLAND

bjarney

MAINE

vinland

MARKLAND

NOVA SCOTIA

CROSSNESS

the great foss

Niagara Falls

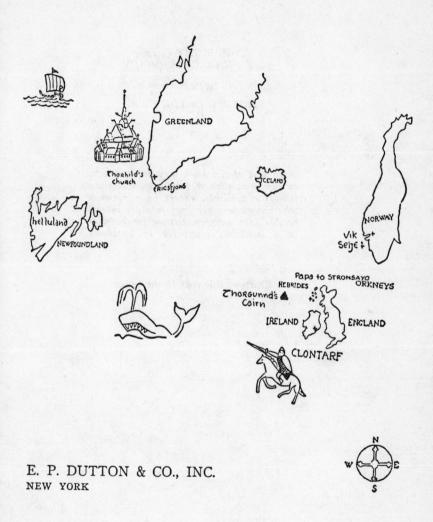

GREENLAND

Thorhild's church

Ericsfjord

ICELAND

NORWAY

Vik
Selje

helluland

NEWFOUNDLAND

Papa to STRONSAYO

HEBRIDES

ORKNEYS

Thorgunnd's
Cairn

IRELAND

ENGLAND

CLONTARF

N
W   E
S

E. P. DUTTON & CO., INC.
NEW YORK

Charts on title page by the author

FOR
ERIC LARSON
AND
KEVIN CHARLES

CONTENTS

THIS LAND FULFILLED

CHAPTER ONE

SAMAIN 1066

THE OLD QUEEN WAS THE LAST TO GO OF THE GREAT COMPANY which made the Vinland faring. Perhaps, since I am still alive, I should have said the last but one. But I, Thrand priest in voluntary exile on this eastern Irish shore that stretches between Dungarvan and Cloyne, do not count when weighed in the scales of the world. It may be that I should have counted somewhat, had I stayed content with what I was and what I had sixty years ago when I was still Thrand, son of that Thorberg Skaffhogg who built the *Long Serpent* for King Olaf Tryggveson. But a man pays no heed to such considerations when Christ calls him. So I Thrand, son of the greatest shipwright in all the northern lands, thane first of Olaf King and then of Leif the Fortunate, took service under the chieftain Christ at whose name not only all on earth but even the angels in heaven bow. I became a monk of the goodly household of Columcille's founding at Iona. Never, from that day to this one on which I begin to set down what passed many years ago on our great faring to Vinland, have I regretted that step.

Queen Grainne was very old when she died—over eighty as closely as one can make out. As it happens, I am nearer ninety than eighty; and, on the whole, men do not live so long as women. I cannot, therefore, have so very much longer to go in life. So it well befits me to write down what I remember of the great faring that men, in times to come, may hear of it and wonder. There is very much to write down and little time to write it down in. I shall begin, then, with the end which was Grainne's death day and the day on which the *Synnovesuden* sailed again into the west. After that I shall go back to the beginnings of it all which came about so many years ago now at the Yule feast in Olaf Tryggveson's court. I shall begin with the last day because it is a good place to begin with, and also because it was not the least wondrous of the many days I had seen as counsellor to the

Queen; and, before that, as confessor to her spouse, King Brian who was the grand-nephew of the High King, Brian Boru of Munster; and long, long before that as friend and comrade of the two of them in the days when all three of us were young.

Brian and Grainne had not always been King and Queen— though he was born into the royal house of Munster, one would not have thought, at the start, that things would so come to pass that one day he would sit a throne. Theirs neither was nor is a large kingdom, not even as kingdoms go nowadays in this dark half century since the men of Ireland laid to rest Brian the *Ard Ri* in the northwestern side of Patrick's Church at Armagh. There has not been a High King since the death in battle of Brian of Munster. There is such anarchy abroad in the land now that men fear there never will be another.

But, large or small, this kingdom is an important one, and one, moreover, that calls for much fighting to support it, for it commands the approach from the north and east to the fortress city of Cork. The High King's son-in-law, Cian of the Golden Cups, son of Maelmuadh, the old King of Cashel, gave it to young Brian after Clontarf—in those days all the chieftains called my Lord "young Brian" to distinguish him from his great-uncle, the High King, Brian of Munster, after whom he had been named. For, except for the High King's two ill-favored sons, Tadhg and Donnchad, whom the chieftains never trusted, my Lord Brian was the only one of the blood of Boru to come safely through that bloody shield-play at Clontarf.

Every year since that far-off day I say many Masses on the anniversary of Clontarf and whenever else I can, for victor and vanquished alike. For if the High King's forces fought there for freedom against slavery and pagandom, there was more than one of my close kinsmen in Earl Sigurd's host. It is never easy to live in times when men's allegiances are divided not only as between this King and that but also as between those gods who are many and our God Who is One. Forty years after that had King Brian, my young Lord, reigned beside Grainne, his Queen. Then, full of days and wisdom, he had gone to sleep beneath the white cairn on the headland. For twelve long years more Queen Grainne sat the throne alone. And now she, too, was going.

I knew when I saw her, lying among the pillows in her *grianan,* the moving leaf-pattern quick on the sun-warmed wall

behind her head, that Queen Grainne was going fast. I had seen
many men and many women die in my long day; and I did not
think that Grainne would last much beyond nightfall. We had
thought, when the sickness first began to run its dread course,
it was the wasting sickness which is a withering of the lungs.
As it turned out, it was worse than that. The disease that wasted
Queen Grainne's flesh on her delicate bones was the most terrible
of all diseases: the awful cancer which is under the sign of the
Crab. Cancer does not move as fast in the old as in the young.
It had its evil will of the Queen very slowly indeed—a good thing
for her waiting kingdom, if not for her whose every breath had
become a burden to her dear self.

Colman the leech was with her, just putting away into his
doctor's bag, the cupping-horn and the probe which he had used
to draw off the dropsy from the Queen's swollen legs. Grainne's
face looked drawn and wan on the pillows.

"She will not take her medicine this time," said Colman, dis-
tressed. "It would ease the pain more than a little."

"I do not wish the sleeping draught today," said Grainne,
opening her eyes. "Thrand priest and I have business to discuss.
I have not much time left to talk of business."

"But after?" said Colman eagerly. "Will you take it after you
are finished, Queen? When your business is talked out?"

"Perhaps," said Grainne with her smile that was quick to
come and slow to leave. It took a man's breath away once, I
remembered, even though it might not befit a monk to remember
such things. Yet why should he not? Why should I not? These
are things that should be set down. God made a woman's excellence and beauty as well as a monk's humility and sense of
wonder. So be it set down here by the quill of me, Thrand
priest, that, in the days of her glorious youth, Queen Grainne's
beauty was as much above the beauty of other ladies as a King's
tall white candle is above a tallow dip.

"No, Thrand," she said, when the doctor was gone and I, too,
strove to press the draught upon her. "No medicine. I shall
sleep the endless sleep soon enough. We have important things
to discuss, you and I."

I thought at first it would be something to do with her sons
and the disposition of the kingdom. But I was wrong.

"There is a strange ship coming to our shore, Thrand," she
said. "A Norse ship. I think it is one of those that fought with

King Harald Sigurdson's host against Earl Godwin's son last
month in the Saxon north. If what I saw in dream be true, the
ship is in evil plight. I want you to await it at the white cairn
on the headland with a troop of men. Take my youngest grandson, Cathal, with you. He is trustworthy and compassionate.
Above all things, I do not wish those men harmed. After they
are bathed and feasted, bring them to me in the council hall."

I was thunderstruck.

"In the council hall, Queen!" I said. "You are much too weak
to hold council."

"It will be my last council, Thrand," she said. "I have enough
strength left for that."

"But this ship, Queen," I said, still protesting. "How can you
know of a ship—for sure, that is? Dreams can beguile one, especially when one is sick. There is no news of a strange ship. Dis-
patches come through me since your illness. The shore warden
has sent none today."

"He cannot know of it yet," said Grainne. "But I know. I also
know that the men on board—there are few of them left after
the fighting—are almost spent. Be at the cairn by four o'clock.
They will not make shore before then."

Now no man, born and bred in the Norse lands, will deny
that there can be such a thing as second sight. But, though the
power is as widespread in Ireland as in Norway, Grainne had
never before given evidence of possessing this unchancy gift.
Could it be that, for the first time in her sickness, the Queen was
wandering in mind?

Grainne noted my perplexity.

"Never fear, Thrand," she said with a smile. "There will be
no trouble. Everything will come out all right."

The tide was changing now. The sea breeze, entering through
the lattice, stirred the many birds' wings that thatched the ceil-
ing of the Queen's *grianan*. It brought a fresh sea smell to our
nostrils. Grainne breathed deep of the salt fragrance. She sighed.
My heart began to quicken. It could not be, of course, but the
fresh wind smelled like that point in mid-Atlantic when, of a
sudden, the air tastes new because it is new, because it blows off
the New Land. The years rolled back. More than half a century
ran swiftly by me like the wake left by a long ship's prow.

"So you, too, remember, Thrand," said Grainne, watching me.

Yes. I remembered. I remembered her, and Brian, and Leif

the Fortunate, and his brother Thorvald, and the old Hunter who still followed Asa-Thor, and the crew of the *Mariasuden*. I remembered the red-skinned Skraelings and the grave on the headland that is Crossness forever. I remembered the dawns and the dusks and the great foss and the new smell of the forests. I remembered everything. That was our morning time and the morning of the world. It was evening now.

It was as if the Queen read my mind.

"Those days were magic, were they not, Thrand?" she asked; and her asking was more a statement than a question.

"Yes, Queen," I said.

"It is time passing makes the magic, I think," said Grainne softly. "Time passes and we remember how it was before. That is the magic. But it is a sad magic."

Something blinded me then. It was not tears only. It was light as well as dark. It is good to be a priest at any time. And some times are better than others.

"There is a magic that is not sad, Queen," I said to her. "If time is magical, timelessness must be even more so. We see them again, the loved ones. Forever are we what we were. Always remember that."

"I know," said Grainne. "I know."

"Queen," I said to her again after a pause. "I have one more thing to say before I go. I used to think, when I was young, that the dead grew dimmer in memory as time drew on. It is not so. Even in memory they grow brighter. If this is true in time, what will it be like in eternity where time is not?"

"Yes," said Grainne, pondering. "It may be as you say, Thrand. I, too, have noticed something of the sort as I grew older. It may be so."

She raised herself a little on her pillows.

"Now, Thrand," she said. "I have one more favor to ask of you, old friend. When I am gone, will you set down in writing for my sons and grandsons all that happened on our faring together to Vinland? It is not a little thing I ask. Yet it should be done. And you are the only one left to do it."

"Yes, Queen," I said. "I shall do it. I should have done it years ago if lesser things had not always pressed. But I have a favor to ask of you in return."

It was unfair, I know. But is one not always unfair to the

sick? Grainne knew what I meant. Her old eyes danced again
as they had danced in youth.

"Yes?" she asked.

"Take the medicine, Queen," I said. "It will be good for you
to sleep a little before the council."

Grainne put her two hands over mine as I raised her right
hand to my lips in leave-taking. It was a way she had in yore
days.

"No, Thrand," she said almost gaily. "Not even now will I
take my sleeping draught. You see, old friend, I may not chance
it. What if I did not wake? There are still guests to greet at
Grainne's court."

It came into my mind then that, though I might see her once
again, we likely would not talk together more, she and I. On
the threshold I raised my hand in salute.

"Farewell, Grainne!" I said, I who had not called her by her
first name in many years.

"Farewell, Thrand!" she said in answer.

There was a mist of tears before my eyes. Even so, I could
see the waves of pain passing over her dear face like heat ripples
quivering above a sun-warmed rock in midsummer.

As Cathal, Grainne's youngest grandson, and I marched to the
shore that afternoon, I had time to reflect on certain things. Not
for the first time did I meditate on the august mystery of suffering. How, I asked myself—foolishly, for well did I know
the answer—could God's love refrain from leechcraft when humans suffered as Grainne was now suffering? How could even
His omnipotence restrain His love from breaking through the
cruel wall pain raised? For it had to be omnipotence that re-
pelled His hero heart. The answer, of course—and every year
I understood it better and better—was that divine love is greater
even than divine mercy; that God so prized the freedom He had
given man that He would not even fetter it with that sweetest
of all sweet fetters, grace. Only once had He really intervened—
then when His Incarnation broke through the wall of time. There
is the breach through which all we sons of Adam and brothers
in Christ after stream. As for such lesser walls as the wall of
pain that now beat back Grainne's struggling soul, before midnight, I thought, her people's battering ram of prayers and the
chorused litanies of my praying monks would have pulled down

the last stone. There would be much grief then when the *caoine* would be raised for the dead Queen Grainne all the way from Dungarvan to Cloyne—and beyond, too, for Grianne had many friends among the other Irish kings. But it would not be hopeless grief as in other lands. Even in pagan days, as their old books revealed, these Irish used to call a death day the "day of birth."

This present business of the strange ship and Grainne's dream troubled me not a little. Granted the Queen had seen the ship or granted she had not, either way one had to humor her. But if she saw truly, this matter could be very dangerous. It had been a year of strange portents ever since the great comet had flashed across our April skies like a firedrake with its star-bright head and its miles-long tail of fire. I had been working then illuminating John's Apocalypse in gold-leaf and vermilion for the monks back in Iona; and I worked that frightening star into my book. Moreover, for a whole month and a week now the coastal waters had not been safe. Irish waters were still alive with the shattered sea-forces of that giant Harald Sigurdson who, for all his kingly ambitions, had gained no more of English soil than the seven feet his hapless carcass lay in after Stamford Bridge.

That battle had taken place five weeks before on September twenty-fifth; it was the day of Samain now. Since the day of Stamford Bridge—though so far we had only rumors of the happening—an even greater battle had been fought at the place the Normans call Senlac and the English Hastings. Duke William won there over the Saxon Harold, great Godwin's son. It comes into my mind now, as I write of far other things, that Duke William's victory means that something has ended and a new thing has begun, even as a new thing began on our Vinland faring. Men who come in after days will be able to tell whether I am right on this point or no. It seems to me I am. For good or ill, men do not stand still. For good or ill new things are always beginning.

The sentry was keeping his watch out on the headland at the *Finncairn na Foraire,* the White Cairn of the Watching, under which Queen Grainne's Brian slept his long sleep till Judgment Day. He raised his shield in greeting as we marched into sight. It had been a warm day for the last day of October. Now the air turned colder and the sea began to show an angry tooth. But I would not let the men light a fire on that headland where only

beacon fires were allowed, and they only in sign of invasion or
for a great burying such as we were likely to have in a day or so.
Grumbling a little, they huddled a little in the lee of the cairn
so that they could not be seen from the sea side. A cold mist
began to drift in across the chopping waves.

It is a strange thing. I have been a Christian for almost seventy years and a priest of Christ for over fifty of those. Yet
alien images still stir in my blood. I still see the faces of the
old gods everywhere I look. So it was now when I looked out
to sea on Samain. The clouds drifting in with the sea wrack
were women on horseback, Odin's battle-maidens riding the gray
sky. The waves showed white like the flashing manes of the
horses of that sea-god who is the son of Lir. Samain is a good
day for a soul's passing, perhaps, since both the gates of heaven
and the earth-doors of every fairy *sidhe* are open on this Eve
of the Feast of All Souls. But it is too cold a day and too eerie
for watching on a seashore for a ship that may not come and,
if it does come, like as not will not be welcome.

The mist had come down so heavily now that the ship, if it
came, would be close in shore before the most vigilant eye could
trace it. Above me on the cairn the sentry let his spear shaft
knock against the stone.

"There is a strange ship approaching, Thrand priest," he said
quietly. "I think it flies the ensign of Orkney's Jarl Erlend,
though, by the cut of it, it is not an Orkney craft."

"How many men?" I asked him, speaking low, signing to my
own men that they should be silent.

"No more than ten or eleven," said the sentry, "though it is
one of the long ships, not a *karfi,* and could easily hold many
more. It lists badly. The crew has a hard time working it."

They were fugitives then. Moreover, they had probably lost
two-thirds of their force somewhere between here and Stamford
Bridge. I had thirty in my troop, and the sentry made thirty-one.
Even if there were berserkers among the newcomers, we could
handle them easily. The problem now was to bring them to the
Queen's council room unscathed. It might prove all the more
chancy a problem in that these voyagers had fought beside the
men of Orkney who were the enemies of Grainne's folk ever
since the day when Brodir Jarl slew the High King, Boru, at
Clontarf.

"Hail them," I said to the sentry.

"Ship ho!" called the guard. His voice sounded strangely distant in the fog.

On the other hand, the strange ship was so close now one could hear the oars griding in the oar holes. Whoever stood in command on the deck had a little Gaelic, though it creaked as badly as his oars.

"We come in peace!" he said. "Will you let us stand in?"

"Say yes," I whispered to the sentry.

"Stand in!" called the guard.

We heard them shipping their oars then and casting the heavy mooring stone on the rock near the cairn. I did not let my men show themselves until everyone of the crew had set foot on shore. Then I stepped forward with my soldiers. If this had been war in earnest, this would have been a goodly maneuver. I thought that my old comrades in arms, Thorhall the Hunter and Thorvald Ericson, would both have approved; and they were hard men to please in matters of this sort. It was all vanity, of course. But, if a man has once been a warrior as I had, vanity dies hard in him, even though he be a priest. For to a man prowess in the grim game of war is like beauty to a woman.

But, if they had let themselves be trapped thus easily, the Northmen were prepared to give a good account of themselves now. Their corselets may have been hacked and battered. The swords that flew into their fists still looked very serviceable.

"It is a good ambush, Irishman," said their leader in grim approval. "If your head is white, it still remembers the ways of war. Now let us see if you can maintain your advantage."

The Norse leader was lean-hipped and broad-shouldered; young still, but weathered in storm and combat. His eyes were blue and his hair dark which is a combination one finds more often among the Norse, who have taken many Irish wives in their day, than among the Danes or Swedes; and most often of all in Iceland where Irishman and Northman have intermarried for close on three-quarters of a century. The fellow's accent, though, was Greenland through and through, not Iceland at all. It came into my old mind that somewhere, sometime, I had known someone very like this man.

"There is no need for fighting, Greenlander," I said to him at a venture; and the once familiar Norse words stuck on my tongue for I had had small opportunity to use that language these latter years. "I am Thrand, priest of Iona, counsellor to the Queen of

Dungarvan. In her name I invite you and your men this night
to feast and rest in her *dun*."

The Greenlander pulled at his lower lip a moment while he
pondered. Again a resemblance tugged at my memory. Whom had
I known who had just this trick of body?

"Very well, Irishman," he said suddenly. "We accept the invi-
tation. We go with you to the Queen as guests. Only see to it
that you do not break faith with us."

"We mean to break bread with you, not faith, Greenlander,"
I said sharply to him, a little nettled now. "And my blood is as
Norse as your own, even if my tongue halts after fifty years of
disuse."

"Your pardon then, Norseman," he said with a short laugh,
mocking me. "But tell me now—what is the name of this hospitable Queen of yours?"

"Grainne," I said very curtly. "The widow of King Brian of
Dungarvan."

"My grandfather knew a Brian and a Grainne," he said, musing a little. "Many times have I heard him speak their names
around the Yule fire. He is dead now. It was when I was a boy."

Even then I did not guess who this stranger chieftain was.
Nor did I ask his name, as courtesy required. For, in my folly,
I was still too angry. So, in silence, we marched off to Grainne's
dun. Fires and candles are lit early on Samain evening. Red and
yellow they gleamed through the wreathing mists as we drew
near. It was a comfortable sight. One would not have thought
death couched within awaiting his next prize.

The bath house was ready.

"The Queen will receive you in formal council," I said to the
Greenlander, "so soon as you have bathed and feasted."

When, after they had bathed and feasted, I led the guests
into the great hall where Grainne was holding her last council,
I saw at once that the Queen not only had on her diadem of
state but, what was even more significant, that she had dyed
her nails crimson as was the fashion with great ladies at the
Irish courts. It had not been Grainne's fashion for many years,
though. She had done it against the day of her burial, I said to
myself. Not once, since Brian's passing, had she sent her tire-
women for the berry dye. I remembered how, when he was laid

beneath the cairn, Grainne had stood out on the headland and raised her *caoine:*

> "*Alone shall I sleep now. No more shall I crimson my nails.*
> *Joy comes no more into my heart.*
> *For Brian my lord is dead.*
> *Fair was my lord among the men of Erin.*
> *White his limbs as white wood-shavings.*
> *Blue his round eye as sprig of woad.*
> *Fresh his shining mantle*
> *As grass above the green mound where god Aengus sleeps forever."*

The court was drawn up in full panoply: Grainne's guards and the captains of her *fiana* on either side the great entrance doors. Next the ranked nobles and pledgemen. Then, in strict order, the envoys, the visiting nobles from Leinster and Ulster, those hostages who were held in highest honor, the royal foster-lings, the Brehon judges, and the scholars. Her four sons, Conall, Cathach, Fionn, and Cormac, stood just in front of the Queen, her four harpers and two poets on her right and left. The lesser musicians and jugglers were ranked beside the litter where, pale and beautiful, Queen Grainne lay in front of her assembled court. Even as we entered the Greenlander, who was a man of great sensitivity, marked down the Queen's condition. He took me by the sleeve while we stood in the entrance, whispering the while.

"The Queen is ill," he said, moved. "Very ill. Why did you not tell me of this? We should not trouble her at such a time."

I had learned the foreigner's name by now. It was Thorvald Arneson. But even now, in my folly, it told me nothing, though it should have told me all.

"I did not wish to breach hospitality," I said. "And it was the Queen's will you should come. But it is true what you say. Queen Grainne is very ill. I do not think she will live beyond this night."

"She does me great honor," said the Greenlander. "I shall not forget it all the days of my life."

When he came opposite the dying Queen, the four sons made way for him so that he might approach. They did it with bad grace, though, for they were always at feud with the Orkney men. It came into my mind that, when the Queen died, there would be much trouble regarding these strangers. It was neces-

sary that they should get out of the kingdom at once—before
the night was over.

Thorvald Arneson raised his right hand in salute.

"Hail, Queen Grainne!" he said in Gaelic. "I am Thorvald
Arneson of Greenland newly come from the field of Stamford
Bridge where the Saxons beat us in fair fight."

Grainne gestured for the poet on her right to raise her a little
on her pillows. It was Mac Liag, the chief of her two poets, son
of that other Mac Liag who had been chief poet to Brian of
Munster, the High King, great-uncle of our Brian. The poet on
her left, a good poet, too, though not Mac Liag's equal, was
Mac Coise, grandson to that poet who had been chief poet to
King Mael Seachlinn, *Ard Rí* before Brian of Munster. As happened so often in Ireland in matters of this sort, the office was
hereditary.

"You are welcome, Thorvald Arneson," Grainne said, speaking in the Norse tongue she had learned so long ago in Olaf
Tryggveson's northern court. I would have thought she had long
since forgotten it. But she had not. "Are you not the grandson
of that Leif Ericson, the great Greenland *hersir,* who brought
Christianity to Greenland and was the first to make the Vinland
faring? If it be so, then I knew your grandfather in my youth,
and the great-uncle, too, whom you so strangely resemble. You
might be Thorvald Ericson come again."

Of course! If it had not been too unseemly a gesture for the
Queen's council room, I think I would have smitten my brow
before them all. I should have seen the resemblance at once. This
Greenland captain was the living image of Leif's brother, Thorvald Ericson, Thorvald the Skald who sleeps now under the New
World cross on the headland that is called, because of that, Crossness. So this was why Queen Grainne had seen that ship in dream!

"Yes, lady," said Thorvald Arneson, standing very straight. "I
am named for that great-uncle. Men who knew my grandmother
in the Hebrides say I resemble her, too."

"I did not know the lady Thorgunna," said Grainne very
gently. "But I have heard that in life she was most beautiful."

"So men say," said the Greenlander, bowing again. "I do not
know. She died long before my day."

"Tell me," said Grainne suddenly. "Are you a skald?"

"I am something of a skald," said Thorvald Arneson.

"Then," said Grainne, "I have a fancy to hear something of

that poetry before I go. My own poets, as it happens, are very good, though they know nothing of skaldship. Would you be willing, Thorvald Arneson—to please an old woman, say—to pit your skaldship against Mac Liag's bardship? I warn you he is a poet who has drunk from Odin's horn."

"If it please you, lady," said the Greenlander, "though nowadays I am more used to spear and oar than harp strings. Appoint what subject you wish. Only ask your other skald to lend me his harp for the contest."

Grainne spoke in Gaelic in the ear of Mac Coise who thereupon unslung the harp about his neck and, with a not very courtly gesture, it seemed to me, handed it to Thorvald Arneson. It puzzled me a little that Grainne should take up the time of her last council with details such as these. I think it puzzled Thorvald Arneson, too. But he was too much of a gentleman to say anything.

"I choose Love for my subject," said Grainne after a space, "because Love is the best of all subjects. Do you, Mac Liag, make your *rann* first, since Thorvald Arneson is the challenged and our guest, besides."

Mac Liag grinned a little; and well did I know why. He was in practice on that field of love, having courted Grainne's youngest lady-in-waiting, Eithne, for over half a year. Mac Liag was balding and beginning to be portly about the stomach. But, somehow or other, women always liked him.

I watched the Queen's eyes while her chief poet swept a practiced hand across the strings of his small harp. It was pitifully easy to tell that Grainne was sick unto death. But who would have guessed she was so old? To my own old eyes she was as lovely then as when Cúan Úa Lothcáin, in his day prince poet of all Irish poets, had called her fair as the fairy Etain.

"*Love,*" said Mac Liag, and I noted that his eyes taunted Eithne's where she stood among the Queen's ladies along the wall.

> "*Love is three times a robber.*
> *Like a robber he is daring.*
> *Like a robber he never sleeps.*
> *Like a robber he strips us naked in the night.*"

I nodded to myself when the *rann* was done. So the maiden still resisted the Queen's chief poet! Or, on second thought, did she? I thought Eithne's face turned crimson when the clapping went up.

It was a rule of the game in these contests that the poet who sang second should single out a key word from his competitor's last line and echo it in his *rann*. This way the scales were evened. The advantage of being second was more than counterbalanced by the difficulty. The Greenlander showed a careless skill in living up to the letter of these difficult regulations.

"*I love Love's robbery,*" he declaimed with a passionate sweep of his fingers across Mac Coise's sounding harp.

> "*Out of one darkness came we naked.*
> *Naked go we into another.*
> *Dear love, come to my naked arms, naked in your*
>   *naked night!*"

The applause rang loud in the hall of the Queen's council chamber, for the Irish nobles understood and admired the subtle daring of the Greenlander's reference. Speaking as a priest, I was not sure then—indeed I am still not sure as I write these words today—of the propriety of the thought. At first blush, it smacked of pagandom. At second—was it not but another way of speaking of the comfort of the Resurrection? Anyway, Grainne liked it. The red flamed for the last time in her pale cheeks. Her eyes were like stars. She looked as she had in Vinland long ago, on her wedding morning. She was raising her hand to declare her judgment when Mac Coise—and to this day I am not sure that her second son, Cathach, did not instigate the action—thrust swiftly in.

"Do not declare the judgment yet, O Queen!" he said quickly. "War is the second best of subjects, if Love is the first. I challenge this Greenland stranger to a test of *ranns* on war. And this time let him go first."

If we had not been in the Queen's council chamber, I think Mac Coise might well have challenged Thorvald Arneson to a more deadly duel than one with *ranns*. Even as things stood, he had breached the Queen's fair order. I had never liked the fellow and had so told Grainne more than once. But she would always keep him for his skill in song.

Luckily for all of us, if Mac Coise chose to show himself discourteous as host, Thorvald Arneson had no intention of being so as guest. Yet no man in the hall of council thought of him as in any wise a coward for his courtesy. He took a gold ring from his arm and presented it to Mac Liag.

"Never heard I a better *rann* on Love than yours," he said, "and I have been at Duke William's court where they know somewhat of *courtoisie*."

Then he turned to Mac Coise.

"As for your challenge, Sira Bard," he said, "I was of the vanquished at Stamford Bridge. So I have no heart just now for *ranns* on war. Godwin's son won over us that day, and well did he deserve to win for his men fought more stoutly than Harald Sigurdson's. But they told me this night at my feasting here that Harold Godwinson has fallen in his turn before Duke William on the field of Hastings. He was a good king. In honor of my valiant enemy, who is dead, listen to this end of the best of all losers' songs. In the end we all lose. It is good if we lose singing."

Thorvald Arneson had said that it was for King Harold of England he spoke the end of *Maldon*. But it was into the eyes of the dying Queen he looked while he cried out those great lines in the tongue of the Saxon that is not so very different from the tongue of the Norse:

> *"Hige sceal the heardra*
> *Heorte the cenre*
> *Mod sceal the mare*
> *The ure maegan lytlath."*

When he had finished, he sang them over in Gaelic to the assembled court, clashing his harp strings the while:

> *"Mind shall be harder,*
> *Heart keener,*
> *Soul higher*
> *As our strength ebbs."*

After that the Queen was silent for a space while she gathered her forces.

"Take this torque, Mac Liag," she said at last, giving her chief bard a circlet of twisted gold. "And you, Thorvald Arneson— how shall I thank you for your courtesy, for your skill, and above all for the great kindness that lies beneath your song? I have a thought on the matter. But before I gift you with your skald-fee, tell me this one thing—and put it not down to discourtesy

that I have to ask it. Is your ship still fit for sailing in? I want
you gone from my kingdom this very night. I think you guess
why I am so hasty in this thing."

It was not only Thorvald Arneson and his men who could tell
what Grainne meant. The whole court knew. In her kingdom
there were powerful enemies of all those connected with the men
of Orkney, the Queen's own sons chief among them. So long as
Grainne lived, her presence would protect her guests. But she
knew, and we all knew with her, that the Queen's might flowed
from her minute by minute.

"I will speak truly, Queen," said the Greenland chieftain. "We
were lucky to sight your coast. The keel is wrenched awry. There
is a gaping hole in our bottom stopped with no more than wadded
tow. Our sail is gone. Every seam needs calking. And, thanks
to the Saxon spears at Stamford Bridge, we are but few hands
to work a long ship. I think it would take us two weeks of dry
weather to ready the craft for sea. Even now, it is almost too
late in the year to set sail for Greenland. But set sail we must."

"You are enough in number to work a *knorr*," said Grainne,
musing.

"If it were a Norse *knorr*, yes," said Thorvald Arneson. "These
Irish coracles—"

He stopped abashed, flushing deep at what he had almost said.

"Oh," said Grainne with a wan little smile. "We build ships
well enough here in Dungarvan—well enough for Thrand, the
son of Thorberg Skaffhogg, anyway. And, priest though he is,
the son of Thorberg Skaffhogg should know a ship, if anyone
knows. But the *knorr* I have in mind is a *knorr* of *knorrs*. One
that has been to Vinland and back on the great faring Leif and
Thorfinn Karlsefni made."

There was a light now on Thorvald Arneson's face.

"The *Synnovesuden, lady?*" he asked, awed. "You keep Leif's
Synnovesuden yet? I thought the old ship was gone where the
songs and ballads go."

"I keep it yet," said Grainne proudly. "It is as good as new."

Yes, it was as good as new for all its more than sixty years.
Grainne—and Brian before her—had kept the *Synnovesuden* as
clean and trig as when it first came from the hands of my father,
Olaf Tryggveson's shipwright. That first faroff spring I came
to live with them, after my many years on Iona, I had been much
surprised to find the *Synnovesuden* still so shining fresh. Every

autumn it was duly rolled into its winter shed. Each spring it was brought forth again, new-tarred, new-painted, and new-calked. It was a goodly boat. Still, when all is said and done, a *knorr,* even such a *knorr* as this one, is but a *knorr,* after all—unless, as was true of this one, one has made the Vinland faring in her and received her as a bride-gift later. This comely craft, with the lady Synnove image rising from her prow, was like the sword a man bears to victory, or the dress a maiden stands up in to get married.

"Take out the *knorr,*" said Grainne to the captain of her first *fian.* "Take down the sail from where it hangs in the church. Give them both to have and hold to Thorvald Arneson. But first bring the Greenland chieftain before me."

She offered her hand to kiss to Thorvald Arneson. Gallantly he took it as it were the hand of his beloved.

"Your grandsire gave me a princely gift once," she said. "I give it now to you."

"It is a Queen's gift now," said Thorvald Arneson, kindling as he spoke. "It shall not be forgotten."

"Farewell, Thorvald," she said. "We shall not meet again in life."

"Farewell, O Queen!" he said, once more bringing his hand up to the salute. "I shall remember you in after days. My children shall speak of you and your great gift."

When he was gone, Grainne had Cathal, her best-loved grandson who had not been present at the council, summoned to her side.

"Take this ring-of-command, Cathal," she said, speaking to him swift and low, but not so low and swift I could not overhear. "Bear it, in succession, to the captains of my four *fiana.* Tell them they are to choose ten men apiece from each *fian* to escort me to the white cairn on the headland. Do it now, Cathal. I have a desire to see the *Synnovesuden* sail with the tide, and there is not much time left for either of us."

I knew well why it was Grainne gave the ring-of-command to Cathal and not to Cathal's father, Conall, or to one of Conall's three brothers. Her sons, because they were good sons, would balk her if they only knew this harebrained scheme—and for her own good. It came into my mind, for an instant, that perhaps I should tell these same sons of the Queen's foolhardy resolve. Then, for that I was an old friend, I kept my counsel. It was most likely that Queen Grainne would die there out on the headland. Was there a fairer place for a Queen to die?

It was quite clear now why Grainne had appointed the contest. The giving of the *knorr* could not be too bald. There would have been objections on her sons' side; and, on the side of the Greenland chieftain, great discomfort. The Queen's last act had been an act of statesmanship.

I went with Thorvald Arneson when the captain of the first *fian,* who had no Norse, took him to the church where hung the many sails Brian's and Grainne's warriors had taken in war. There were yews planted all around the goodly building, and around the cemetery as well. The trees made the church dark on the lightest day; and night had fallen some hours now. But the candles shone bravely inside. By their light Thorvald Arneson looked up at the looming sails, his helmed shadow and the shadow of the captain beside him both monstrous on the hanging cloths.

"It seems your King and Queen have done well in battle," he said, pulling at his lower lip in the way his great-uncle, Thorvald Ericson, used to have. "I take it these are Norse sails."

"Norse sails from Orkney mainly," I said. "But not all. They are Danish and English, too. More than one is Norman. Several are Leinster, for the Irish fight against one another as often as they fight against the outlander. They are like the Norse in that respect."

"Norse sails," he said again, his voice midway between interest and a kind of shame. "Well, why not? They learned their trade in the right school. My grandfather and great-uncle must have been good teachers. Which of these is the *Synnovesuden's* sail?"

"This one," I said, pointing it out to the captain of the *fian* so that his men might take it down.

I had at my belt another skald-fee for Thorvald Arneson: Mac Liag's silver harp in an otterskin bag. The Queen's chief poet returned the compliment of the massy arm ring with interest. This same impulsive openhandedness was one of the things I liked best about these quicksilver Irish.

The north star burned bright silver in a cloudless night sky when the *Synnovesuden* cleared the headland. A skein of late-flying migrant geese went over us, honking loud in the star-bright night. The moon, just rising, lay on the lightly moving

waters like a coat of golden mail on a warrior's breathing chest.
The tide was already at neap but no wave so much as broke
against the rock we stood on. Only a kind of froth lipped the rim
of the land, moving gently in and out as if the hand of some giant
sea maiden were casting a white embroidered cloth in and out, out
and in. It was so still Grainne's hair did not even stir on her head
where she lay back in the litter, watching till the *knorr's* white
sail glimmered, like a great moth, out of sight. Perhaps that was
why we did not know at first the Queen had died.

It was I who first saw she no longer breathed. By that time the
moon-mail on the wavelets had become a great silver moon-
buckler instead. Lying there under the autumn moon the dead
Queen might have been carved of silver herself. We covered her
with the great shield which the captain of her first *fian* always
bore in front of her whenever she went on processional. But before we lapped her in that comely targe, I had the captain carry
it to the water's edge and there strike it with his sword as was
the custom on that coast when a King or a Queen dies. The great
shield gave out a low humming moan when struck. As if in answer the water gave back a kind of melancholy roar and three
giant combers came rushing in from the outer sea to smash
against the rock.

"It is the three *tonns,* the three waves of Ireland," said the captain, moved. It also seemed to me that he sounded a little afraid.
"They mourn the passing of our Queen. It is always thus if a
royal shield is struck."

I knew the tradition of the three *tonns* of Ireland. But was it
really the three *tonns* of Erin that mourned for Grainne? Or was
it only that the tide had turned? A priest should know about these
things; but I could not tell. I copied down once from a Latin
book we had on Iona what an old Roman poet wrote on the passing of his lady: *Dryades ingemuerunt. The dryads grieved.* If the
sidhe of grove and tree made moan for a lady in Roman days,
why not these waves racing across three thousand miles of open
water from Vinland? All I know is that, looking down on
Grainne in the moonlight, it was as if I gazed on that sweet Valkyrie maid, all silver of face and hair and coat of warrior mail,
whom Odin, her father, cast into the enchanted sleep and ringed
with the magic fire. Grainne should rest now on the headland till
the day her Sigurd-Christ should come to take out the sleepthorn
from his shield-maiden and her mate, King Brian. The Queen's

torment was over at last; and I should have been glad thereat. But
my heart was sad, nonetheless.

Because King Brian slept under the cairn on the headland and
not in the *ruam* that was next to the church, we laid Grainne, too,
beside the sleeping king arrayed in her diadem of rule, her *findru-
ine* fillet, her silver sandals, light gold balls dangling at the ends
of her heavy braids, the silver shield still across her quiet breast.
The captain of her first *fian* bore her standard from the royal *dun*
which should no more know its mistress. At the proper moment
the trumpeters of the *fiana* blew their bronze battle-trumpets. The
assembled host raised the warrior-shout. And it was over. Then
her eldest son, the new King Conall, his brothers Cathach, Fionn,
and Cormac beside him, proclaimed the funeral games. Such
games, men said, had not been seen since the death of the Munster
Ard Ri. But I had no heart to look upon them.

I had far other things to do. I, too, had a funeral memorial to
build—to build with words. But this is not putting it quite right,
either. Again it comes into my mind that perhaps, because I am
a priest of Christ and a monk of the brotherhood of Iona, I
should not write down such things as I now mean to do. And
once again, as before, I answer myself: why should I not? There
are not many women like Queen Grainne these degenerate latter
days. It was the same God made her excellence and beauty Who
made my humility and sense of wonder. And there is another
reason for my writing, too.

For it is not the vanity of Queen Grainne's greatness—and, be
it never forgotten, she was a very great lady—I here set down;
nor yet the lovelier vanity of her youth and my youth and the
youth of Brian, her lord. No, even more than those things, and
they are not little, this is the tale of the great voyage we went. It
is the voyage that is, in the end, always the great thing. It is the
voyage men will one day remember when Brian and Grainne and
Leif and Thorvald are long forgotten. I beg of those men of
after years that, in their great charity, they will pray for the sin-
ful soul of Thrand Thorbergson, priest of Iona, who writes down
these matters that they may see and ponder.

CHAPTER TWO

YULE WITH OLAF TRYGGVESON

I CALL THIS FIRST PART OF MY TALE: YULE WITH OLAF TRYG-
gveson. For the beginning of our faring was at the King's great
Yule feast for the Greenland captain, Leif, whom men had even
then begun to call the Lucky.

It was a year or so after the time when first befell those joyous
tidings, the best after the conversion of Norway that were ever
heard in Norway and the outer islands, that Iceland had become
wholly Christian and that all the people had put aside the old
gods of the Aesir to receive the white Christ. It did not happen all
at once. For the old gods were strong in the land and in the hearts
of the Norsemen. But it happened.

Now here I must say some little thing about myself and about
how I became a priest, though this is not my tale but the tale of
the great Vinland faring. My father, Thorberg Skaffhogg, King
Olaf's chief shipwright, did not take up the new faith so early as
some others at Olaf's court. And, when he did, he kept up not a
few of the old usages. So it fell out that, as a boy, I was raised
heathen altogether. Even after my slow-of-counsel father came
over at last—I mind me it was at Pentecost in my eighteenth
year—we did not stop honoring the old gods in our household. I
used to grieve over this in my early days as priest. But it seems to
me now no bad thing, provided only there be no abomination, to
respect the past. It was Christ's way when he was young. At any
rate, it has helped me to understand much that would have otherwise been hidden. About Thorhall the Hunter, for example. And
many other things, too.

Now that I am become so old a man people have at last stopped
asking me why I became a priest. It was not so in the early days
of my priesthood. Then many men asked the question that is so
easy yet so hard to answer. It did no good to say it was because
I loved God because, in their hearts, even if they did not say so,

not a few among my questioners thought they loved God also, and
yet were they not priests. For a long time I used to put this question in return: why do you love this woman and not another?
That is the way with me, I would say. Only I love God even before women. It was an answer, after all, that helped me even
when it did not help them. To be a priest is to be a lover in a
measure far surpassing other mortal measures. If God ever calls
the heart, then the heart cannot rest in earthly things. I could say
no more then. I can say no more today. The roots of any love are
so delicate one dare not expose them to the air and light of everyday. But if anyone were to ask me that old question today, I
would put this question to him also: how much do you believe in
prayer? Above all else the world does not understand prayer. One
does not wrong the world by leaving it. One does not desert the
battlefield of life. One only uses other and better weapons—and
not for oneself alone, either. It is the lover's way always to give,
not take.

I felt this long before the call came to me. I felt it even when I
first looked upon the face of Grainne on that Yule Eve long ago—
if ever I had been destined to love mortal woman, hers was the
face I should have loved forever. But I get ahead of my tale a little, which is a bad thing for a teller to do. Long before I saw
maid Grainne, Brian was my friend.

Brian was younger than I by a good four years. It was I
taught him his Norse and his bowcraft. It was I first gave him
his great love of ships. He was my best friend at Olaf Tryggveson's court for all the difference in years between us, and for all
the greater difference that I was the son of a shipwright and he
Olaf's fosterling, the grand-nephew of a King and the grandson
of a King's brother. King Brian of Munster, he who was later
High King, was his great-uncle. After the death of young Brian's
father and grandfather in battle against the Leinstermen, King
Brian had sent the lad to be fostered by Olaf Tryggveson because, at that time two years before, Brian of Munster still was
on good terms with Sigtrygg, son of Amlaib Cuaran, the Norse
King of Dublin, and Sigtrygg, in his return, was still Olaf's more
or less faithful vassal.

But the wind was shifting now. Word had just come, carried
by Sigtrygg himself, that King Brian of Munster had broken
with Sigtrygg of Dublin because Sigtrygg had seen fit to ally
himself with Brian's mortal enemy, Maelmordha the King of

Leinster. King Brian had looted Dublin within the month. Meanwhile young Brian's position at Olaf's court trembled in the balance. My father, who was in the confidence of one of the King's counsellors, had told me of these troublous things and cautioned me to say nothing to Brian about them.

King Olaf had his own troubles. It was thought that, after Hakon Jarl died at the hands of the slave Kark, Olaf Tryggveson would be able to keep peace throughout all the northern lands. So he did in the main. But men grew restless all the same. There was unrest in the Faroes. The Orkney Jarls sent around the weapon-token. In addition, Olaf's prize policy of Christianizing the realms that owed allegiance to him fell foul of an unexpected snag. Greenland, where Eric the Red lived, continued to cleave to the old gods no matter what the King might do or say.

Then, in the fall before this present Yule, Leif, whom men now called the Lucky, Eric's son, sailed for Olaf's court after his autumn viking, and was there baptized. Now, to celebrate the Greenlander's taking of the *prima significatio,* which was the first step within Christ's church, the King appointed a great Yule feast.

I mind me still of that faroff day. My father, his corded arms stained with the gold and silver paint he was using to touch up figureheads on some of the dry-docked ships, called Brian and me to the doors of our long building shed. I laid aside the toy long ship I was whittling, and Brian put down the new bow he had been rubbing down to the clean grain.

"It's a brave sight, lads," said Thorberg Skaffhogg. "You'll see few braver in your lives if you live to be a hundred."

My father was right. I have seen some sights as brave since then, but none braver—not even the waking of Brian the *Ard Ri* after Clontarf. Yule Eve had set in bright and clear. The Vik Fjord was still open, which was almost unheard of at this time of year. To honor the Greenland guests the King had his lordly fleet drawn up in the harbor: sails set, oars raised, shields ranged in order on the shield racks. The broad striped sails were splendid in the December sunshine. My heart swelled at their beauty, for I had aided my father when he dyed them. The gold dragon-heads flashed bright at the crimson-painted prows. I was not alone in my pride, either. Though the men of Vik had seen the great craft many a time, they marveled anew now as the three chief ships drew up broadside along the quay. The *Crane.* The *Short Serpent.* The great flagship, the *Long Serpent,* with Olaf himself in full

chain mail serving as *stafnbui,* calling through a speaking-trumpet
to his warriors on the dock. They raised their shields. My heart
stirred again, this time for the King's splendor—for the North
has seen no greater King than Olaf Tryggveson.

"Hail, lord! Hail!" they said.

Then the son of Tryggve came ashore in the winter sunlight to
open his Yule feast for the Greenlander.

"I'd better be getting back to the King's hall now," said Brian,
carefully hanging the bow from two pegs on our workshop wall.
"But first a wager, Thrand. I lay you two to one there are as
many as twenty Thors among Leif's men."

My father laughed.

"Don't take it, boy," he said. "The odds are good. But you will
lose the wager."

It was an old joke of Brian's, one of which we never tired, he
and I. He used to say we Norse were all named Thor one way or
another. It was true enough that it was a little difficult for a foreigner to cope with this multiplicity of Thors, though it should
have been easier for Brian than for most. There was a temple to
Thor in almost every Irish city except those few small ones under
the control of King Brian of Munster. I had once set foot in the
great Dublin shrine myself.

"Stay close to me tonight," said Brian gaily as he left. "I'll
make shift to slip you some of the King's own ale."

They brewed good ale at Olaf's court; and I liked ale in those
days—it may be even a trifle too much. As cupbearer to the King,
Brian would be in a good position to offer me some of the very
best variety.

It's a long time ago now, that feast. But the pictures and the
colors stay fast in my mind, never running together and streaking
as do later memories. In an old man's mind yesterday is more
golden-lighted than today; and ours had been a golden yesterday. . . .

The clear weather did not hold. By dusk it had come on to snow
heavily. The thralls lit the pine flares in the King's great hall
where the long benches were set out with evergreen and holly
upon them, each man's byrnie, sword, spear, and shield hanging
within easy arm's reach over his head. By the time the warriors
were ready to sit down, the snow was deep enough so that it was
necessary to use sledges in order to transport the ale casks and the

birchbark panniers full of meat and bread from the bakehouses and breweries behind the hall. The later guests arrived on skis which added to the hubbub in the hall entrance: thralls jostling beggars and getting jostled roughly in their turn by the snow-covered jarls who were eager to get in and warm themselves by the bright fires.

It almost seemed to me as if, at Yuletide, Christ and Thor observed a truce. The Babe was born in Bethlehem and Asa-Thor drank Him a toast, letting the Child crook His fingers round the thunder-hammer as if it were a toy. The skalds sang the old songs with none to say them nay. Halfred Vandraedaskald, Olaf's skald, swept practiced fingers over his harp strings and called to the wassailers:

"*Hear me, ring-bearers!*
I sing of the son of Tryggve!
Hear me, givers of gold!
I sing of the spear-deeds of the openhanded ruler!"

Sitting beside my father at one of the tables open to the yeomen, I alone listened to Halfred who, defeated by the hurly-burly in the hall, shrugged his shoulders and put out an indifferent hand to where the women of the King's household were drawing strong ale from wooden barrels. It seemed to me, looking on, that Halfred really did not feel too put out. He knew the jarls would listen to him willingly enough later on, when their stomachs were not so clamorous and he rose, at Olaf Tryggveson's right hand, to chant the great *Lay of Bjarki* which the King loved so well.

Halfred liked women passing well; and, on the whole, they liked him as, for some reason, they seemed to like all skalds. I watched him playing with the fingers of the woman who drew the ale and it may be I was a little jealous. For words never came easily to my lips where women were concerned. If so, I was rewarded rather than punished for that sin of jealousy. For this was how I came to look on Grainne for the first time. It was then also that, for the first time, I found out what men really mean when they speak of the great beauty of women. The fire is cold in my blood now; and even then I never slighted Christ's service for the service of women. Nonetheless it was with me then as if sunlight had suddenly gleamed along the blade of a bared sword; as if I gasped for breath under the shock of icy water.

There was a new face among the women: a very beautiful one.

I could tell that she must be very new because Halfred the skald
did not recognize her. When he greeted her, in his lazily insolent
way, she stared through him until even Halfred the invincible had
to turn his head. I had heard nothing of a new woman. One thing
I could tell, though, from the white-bronze collar clasping her
white neck and the red-bronze belt that circled her slender waist.
Bronze was the Irish metal. The girl must be Irish and, judging
from the richness of those ornaments, most likely a chieftain's
daughter. Now that I came to think of it, I had been told and had
forgotten that there were women taken on the last autumn viking
against Ireland.

Halfred came behind the girl, grasping her suddenly by the
wrist. Catlike she wrested herself away and spat words out at him.
I could not catch them; but they sounded much like some of the
words Brian had taught me from his Gaelic tongue. It came into
my mind then, with a sudden pang, that in the old days such as
the likes of Halfred might have had his will of the beautiful captive, and no one to say nay. But ever since Olaf had turned
Christ's man, all foreign women were protected as jealously as if
they had been daughters of the King's own household. Looking
on her fairness now, Halfred did no more than make a wry face
and put out his hand elsewhere for another beaker of ale. It was
as if he wondered if there weren't something to be said for the
old ways, after all, for all the King's declaring for the new. But
my heart leaped a little as the maid turned back to her work. I
had never approved of Halfred Vandraedaskald. I was glad that
King Olaf's new customs would keep this maid inviolate from
such as he.

Halfred's and mine were not the only eyes that looked approvingly on Grainne, daughter of Rafarta of Clonmacnoise. It might
be said there was not a man's eye in the hall that did not linger
on her face for some short space at least. From where he waited,
tray in hand, for the beakers to be filled with foaming ale, I could
see that even the lad Brian—and as yet he had not looked with
much interest on women—admired the beauty of his young coun-
trywoman. (I have noticed more than once that Irish men are not
so forward in love as are the Norse. But women are forward
toward them to such a degree that perhaps this evens matters.)

Yes, the maid was fair to gaze on. Even in memory the wonder
of it takes me by the throat. Her crimson kirtle brought out the
surpassing fairness of her hair. Like pale gold it was, as fair as

the fairest braids of our blonde Norse maidens, and incomparably more delicate of texture. The soft-woven blue cloak she wore over the kirtle made her deep blue eyes look even deeper. Here, too, I said to myself, she was lovelier than our northern girls whose eyes were just as blue, it may be, but not so magically deep as hers. I would guess her age at seventeen. If I were right in this surmise, there would be no more than two years separating her from Brian. For a moment that thought laid a numbing hand on my heart. But only for a moment. Even then, I think, I knew inside that I had already given my heart away in far other bridal than this was like to turn out.

My father noticed the direction of my gaze.

"A beauty, eh, lad?" he said. I supposed he would call me lad when I was fifty.

"Yes," I said a little shortly.

"Olaf's men took her on autumn viking in Clonmacnoise," he said. "They say she fought like a she-bear. At any rate, she's under the King's protection now. So don't go casting sheep's eyes at the lass just yet."

I found myself worrying more than a little over what Olaf meant to do with her. Not that I questioned the King's intentions —Olaf Tryggveson was a Christian and a man of honor. But she had been taken on a raid, after all, and so was a prisoner of war, subject to the harsh rules that governed the disposition of slaves. Surely, I said uneasily to myself, surely Olaf would never make a thrall out of a chieftain's daughter. A hostage, yes. But not a thrall.

Brian was as good as his word about the ale. Every third time round he left a tall stoup on the board at my father's elbow. He was just doing this again when something unforeseen happened. A tall dark man, standing close to where we sat, nudged the boy's arm so roughly that the tankards bounced and clattered on the beechen tray. Brian, who could be hot-tempered on occasion, looked up angrily at him. The man wore a coal-black doublet and a Thor cut in soft silver round his neck. From his accent, it seemed to me, though I had not seen the fellow before, that he would probably be one of the Greenlanders who had come with Leif, not all of whom had accepted baptism. Otherwise he most likely would not have dared flaunt the Thor amulet, since for some time now the King had frowned on ornaments like these. His eyes were gray and piercing; his hair, too, wolf-gray. A sword-thrust scarred one ravaged cheek. When he smiled, a grin contorted his face like a spasm, while the eyes stayed cold and watchful. He was smiling now. I did not like him at first glimpse. It seemed to me that, all in all, Brian did not care much for his questioner, either.

"Who is the maiden, lad?" asked the Greenlander, jerking a thumb toward the doorposts. "The one under the Hárbard head?"

Now Hárbard was one of the many names for Odin—the Odin who, years and years before Christianity was even heard of in the Northland, had been carved on the doorposts of Olaf Tryggveson's great hall at Vik which was the hall of his ancestors before him. Brian looked where the Greenlander was pointing and I knew that suddenly, on this second look, he saw what had taken me but a single look to see. For he caught his breath, so breathtaking was her delicate beauty in the firelight that lit up the dark carved Hárbard beard and the fair hair that was now just beneath it. It was the Irish girl again. She had moved away from where I had seen her before.

"Come, boy! Answer me! Who is the maiden under the Hárbard head?"

The harsh voice grated in my ear. A hand of iron took Brian roughly by the shoulder. I was just starting up when my father's strong hand forced me gently but firmly down again.

"Steady, lad!" he said, speaking low in warning. "This is not the way to deal with a berserker."

"I do not like waiting for an answer! Speak up, boy!" said the dark Greenlander, this time shaking Brian by the shoulder.

For answer Brian struck the hand down from his shoulder.

"I am not your thrall, Greenlander! Nor any other man's!" he said, his own right hand stealing to the *ryting*, the long, bone-handled knife at his girdle. "I am willing to answer questions when asked by strangers, but only when they are asked in courteous manner."

I saw the odd spasm cross the Greenlander's dark, menacing face. He laughed a barking laugh that was not at all pleasant to hear.

"By Loki!" he said, still laughing. "A boy! A beardless boy to beard me! Well, beardless boys need lessons when they mingle with warriors."

The Greenlander raised his hand to strike my friend. The *ryting* leaped into Brian's hand in answer. The two faced one

another without speaking for a long moment. I put my hand on
my own knife.

"No!" said my father, speaking louder this time. "It is death to
breach the King's peace within the King's own hall. There are
better ways to settle quarrels than with bared steel."

The Greenlander's face began to work in an ugly way. He was
just taking a lithe step forward when another man spoke in his
ear.

"Remember whose court this is, friend Thorhall," said the second man in warning. "Remember, too, that Olaf is not overfond
of Greenlanders like yourself who refuse the white garment of
Baptism. Besides, this boy is an Irish fosterling of Olaf's own
fosterage. He is under the King's protection."

"Irish!" The man named Thorhall spat on the rush-covered
floor before Brian's feet. "So much the more reason to take the
peacock down a peg! I have no reason to love the Irish. It was
an Irishman gave me the scar I bear on my cheek. I had little
beauty to lose that I should owe an Irishman a face scar."

Flushing deep red at the insult, Brian took a long step forward
in his turn. But the second man now caught him by the shoulder
in a grip that looked every bit as strong as Thorhall's but kindlier
somehow.

"Easy, boy! Easy!" he said, speaking very low. "It would be no
fair match for a few years yet. Do you not know a wolf when
you see one? The saying is right: *A wolf is to be found where a
wolf's ears are.* Look at him again, boy! Do you not recognize
Thorhall Gamlason, he who was one of the Jomsburg vikings who
were loosed from the rope by Eric Jarl on the day when Vagn
Aakeson killed Thorkel Leire?"

Thorhall Gamlason! A berserker was one thing—but a berserker like this one! It was my first glimpse of Thorhall the
Hunter; and I have never forgotten it, though Thorhall has been
laid in howe these many, many years. I could see that Brian, too,
was sobered a little; that he looked now at the first of these two
Greenland strangers with grudging respect. He had not known
that this dark warrior was the famous Thorhall Gamlason who
had fought with the grim Jomsburg fellowship against Eric Jarl
at Halkelsvik and been one of the lucky twelve to survive that
bloody day.

I counted over to myself what my father had told me of Thorhall Gamlason. Because of the many times Thorhall had come off

victorious from the holmgang, men called him Holmgang-Bersi
as often as they called him Thorhall—but never to his face. *Bersi,*
one of the words for "bear," was Thorhall's secret name which
it was unchancy for others to use. As a matter of fact, he never
used it himself or suffered others to use it, in his presence, unless
the berserk fit was on him. For some time now he had been a
professional berserker, even as had been his father before him,
the old wolfskin berserker who had died at Hafrsfjord fourteen
years before this. Even as a berserker, Thorhall was a good deal
different from the general run of those fey fighters. He never
wore a bear-sark or a wolf-pelt going into battle, but only the
blue doublet which he kept for best, and which men feared his
wearing in time of peace. For, when Thorhall changed his customary black for his blue doublet, men knew it meant that he
wanted to fight. One would not call him quarrelsome, exactly. But,
whenever he fought in private feud, it was always to the death.
He never howled, foamed at the mouth, or bit his shield like other
berserkers. He fought in utter silence, except for a wolflike snarl
now and then; and he fought all the more effectively for fighting
in such silence. I have seen enough of men since that far-off day
to realize that Thorhall the Hunter was one mold of man. He
was the man who walked in darkness armed with iron weapons.
Thorvald the Skald was another kind of man; and Leif, his
brother, still another. I mean to say somewhat of these matters
later. Enough now to say that the world owes something to the
Thorhalls, though they bring more evil than good; and their
breed never dies.

Other things about him kept sliding into my mind. For I was
young then, and such things mean much to the young. Men said
Thorhall was a mighty swimmer, a mightier archer, and as good
at spear-casting as any warrior throughout the northern lands.
His sword was called Hvíting. He had gotten this famed weapon
out of a hero's howe where, men said, he had first wrestled the
dead barrow-dweller for it, while balefires burned outside on the
promontory. He had refused to take on the yoke of Christ with
Leif and the rest of his comrades. But this was not at all because
he feared the old gods overmuch. He preferred them, it was true.
But that was all. Nevertheless, on occasion, he was not even
loath to profane their shrines.

For example, he had looted Thor's wain once at Uppsala in the
land of the Swedish vikings—it was there he got the amulet of

soft silver he always wore about his neck. On the whole he really
believed only in his own might and main. *I matt sinn ok megin,*
as the blasphemous oath ran, which, before I turned Christian, I
had heard so many warriors take, and from Olaf Tryggveson, too.
But Thorhall always abode by the Warriors' Law of the Jomsburg fellowship that comrades should share all plunder; that no
man should speak a word of fear, however daunting the plight
he found himself in; that it was beneath a man's valor, when on
viking, either to shorten sail for bad weather, or sleep under
an awning while at sea, or bind a wound, however deep, till the
same hour of the next day after the wound had been received.

In after years, when men spoke of courage by the fireside, they
used to say that Thormod the skald had feared God, and Grettir
Asmundson the dark; but that Thorhall Gamlason had come from
his mother's womb incapable of fear. I think that was true,
though to this day I cannot tell how it comes about that there
can be men who do not fear God. But I must not brood so much
over the mystery of Thorhall Gamlason. There are other matters
to attend to than just this. We shall see enough and to spare of
Thorhall Gamlason before this tale of the great faring is done.

Brian and Thorhall still stood frozen, staring at one another
while the other of the Greenlanders looked at Brian, smiling a
little and pulling at his lower lip. That was a habit of his when
lost in thought. I was to see him do it more times than I can
count in after years. It meant that he was worried for all that he
smiled so blithely. But Brian could not know it then, of course.
On his side, he frowned at first. Then he, too, smiled in return,
bowed, and slipped his *ryting* back into its deerskin sheath. With
a kind of snarling laugh dark Thorhall, who had been waiting
motionless, stepped aside. The two of them, my father and myself,
and the men sitting at the nearby tables watched him stalk stiff-
legged to his appointed place at one of the long benches.

"Well, my rash young friend," said the second Greenlander in
his fetching outlander's accent. "You have come off better than
could be expected, I think, considering you are so young, considering you are so alone at Olaf's court, and considering the devil
you had to deal with. He is a devil, I may add, for whom something can be said. I would do much for Thorhall Gamlason, as he
would for me. But there is something else to be said in your
regard. Whether you know it or not, there are other complica-
tions for you since this week began. King Sigtrygg of Dublin

spoke his mind last night in the King's council. You have heard the news of what has been going on in your great-uncle's Munster?"

My father raised his bushy eyebrows at me in a way that meant he now thought we should have told Brian of King Brian's foray against Sigtrygg. Well, it was his doing, not mine. Had it been my decision, I should have told Brian at the very outset. Nothing I have seen since in life leads me to believe that frankness is not the best policy always.

Brian's face became troubled. I realized again how alone he must feel at this alien court of ours.

"No," he said. "What is the news from Munster?"

"No matter," said the Greenlander. "It is the King's business, not mine. He will doubtless speak of it to you in his own time and place. For the moment, remember these two things when next you are tempted to come to grips with such as Thorhall Gamlason. First: *it is a short road to ill luck in this world.* And: *bare is his back who has no brother behind it.* Remember, too, that no woman is worth a warrior's death—not even this little Irish Hlín-of-whitest-hawkland I saw you look upon so longingly even before Thorhall caught sight of her."

From the manner of his speaking it was easy to tell the fellow must be a skald—and a good one, to boot. I fancied myself a judge of skaldship; and I liked the Greenlander's figure for the Irish girl. Hlín was one of the names of Frigg, the wife of Odin. Hawkland was the place where the hunting falcon lighted after its flight aloft. In our northern countries that meant the arm and shoulder, not the fist as was the Norman fashion, and the fashion of the Irish courts where Brian had learned to fly the fleet birds of prey. The whole elegant phrase was a kenning for a white-armed girl. Brian must have thought it fitted the maid very well. He smiled back at the Greenlander.

"Perhaps," he said, still smiling, "perhaps you are right, though I do not think so. For this, as you may see for yourself, is a very lovely Hlín indeed. Anyway, I am most grateful to you. As for my having no brother to back me, that is not quite true. I have Thorberg Skaffhogg's son, Thrand, for my brother. But two brothers are better than one—will you be my brother? You, too, it seems, are alone at Olaf's court. My name is Brian, son of Cathach, son of that Mathgamain who was brother to King Brian of Munster after whom I am named. The King of Munster sent me here. I am Olaf Tryggveson's fosterling."

It could hardly have been news to the Greenlander. But he acted as if it were. He put out his hand in courtly greeting.

"I am Thorvald Ericson," he said. "Of Greenland. Nor am I altogether alone at Olaf's court, any more than you. I am brother to that Leif who is this night honored by the King."

It was the first time either of us had heard the name of Thorvald Ericson. But what impressed me more at the time was the fact that Brian was so proud to acknowledge our friendship, his and mine. There was a warm glow about my heart. I did not begrudge him a new friend so long as he never denied me. Nor did my father who was so many years better versed than I in the hard ways of the world.

The two of them, Brian and Thorvald, had moved on so that they were out of earshot now. My father looked at me, a crooked grin upon his face because, years ago when he had been a boy, a fishhook had gashed his mouth.

"Whew!" he said, wiping the sweat off his forehead. "It was touch and go, that. Well, all's well that ends not ill. Thorvald Ericson is a good man. Berserker or not, I would not have bet against him had it come to fighting between him and Holmgang-Bersi."

Something nagged at my mind. There was a question I had to ask my father.

"Tell me," I said to him. "Suppose it had come to fighting between Brian and Thorhall Gamlason, with no Thorvald Ericson to intervene—what would you have done then?"

My father laughed and picked up his ale tankard. He let the cool liquid flow luxuriously down his throat.

"A foolish thing, I am afraid," he said at last, patting the short knife at his belt. "But I have whittled men as well as ships in my day."

Then he became very serious again, and laid a hand on my shoulder.

"Listen to me, lad," he said. "Do not step between Brian and this new friend he has found. Thorvald Ericson is a man of price, if I am any judge of men. It will be well for Brian, I think, if he can call more than one man his friend in the time to come."

I looked over at the pair of them. Brian was not able to sit down with either new or old friend just yet. As Olaf's cupbearer, he still had important duties to perform. Later, when the toasts had gone round the board, perhaps he would be able to converse with all of us a little. For the time being he could do no more than escort Thorvald to an honored place on one of the long benches facing the King's high seat, and see to it that his tankard was never empty for very long. I lifted my own beaker, thinking the while on what my father had said and on how, in this one evening, Brian had added two more Thor names to his growing collection.

The great feast was gaining pace now. The King's chief groom had long since given orders for the eating and the drinking to begin. A herald, winding a trumpet for silence, announced that the peace of Christ's Yule and the Yule of Olaf Tryggveson, Christ's servant in Norway, had sealed the high hall against any letting of blood. That no thing with an edge to it might be used in the King's house for the next six days for any purpose whatsoever except to cut up bread and meat. That tankards were to be used for drinking, not throwing. That any man unfortunate enough to breach the peace of Christ and Olaf Tryggveson would be hanged and then spread-eagled on the outer wall of the King's bakehouse with a dead wolf beside him, like any common thief. The herald added, with grim gallows humor, that the King had a store of dead wolves pickled in salt, if the occasion should arise. A roar of laughter went up in the hall at that announcement.

There were over six hundred men feasting in the hall, without counting the servitors, the women of the King's household, and the jugglers and dancers who would do their tricks later on when the tables were cleared of all but the tankards—they would never be free of tankards any time in the next six days. Brian told me, in a breathing space, that he had seen as large a number dining together only once before, though his new friend, Thorvald Ericson, was a little less impressed. He said to Brian that he had seen eleven hundred drink of the Bragi cup in Iceland when the sons of Hoskuld laid their dead father in howe; and he had heard that Hjalti's sons had entertained fourteen hundred at one time on the days of their sire's funeral feast. Still, this was an impressive sight, at that, admitted Thorvald, adding that it did make some difference that it was one's own brother who was being honored in this high revelry.

When another lull came in the talking, I looked about the hall for Thorhall Gamlason. He was easy to find because of his black doublet, the only one worn there that night. The fellow was sitting on a back bench now, eating and drinking in silence, never speaking except when spoken to; and there were not many ready to speak to Thorhall Gamlason a second time. But I did not think he would make any more trouble this feast, judging by the cargo of ale he was taking aboard.

The scullion boys carried in the Yule pigs roasted whole, the ugly heads still on them, wrinkled winter apples in their gaping mouths. Other servants bore in long loaves of white bread with fresh golden crusts crisping upon them, and wooden troughs laden with blood-sausage that had been flavored with sweet-smelling marjoram and thyme. For six whole days this feast would last; and this was but the first day. Eyes glistening, beads of sweat standing out on their foreheads as the ale went round faster and faster, the jarls ate and drank, then ate and drank again till some of them began to loll back drunkenly against their benches and other some even rolled, snoring, into the aisles.

Sira Inge Skakkeson, the King's Chaplain, who was to say the first Yule Mass at midnight and so had to begin his fast, was not altogether pleased. Since I was to serve his Mass, he stopped at our table to make sure that I, too, would leave off drinking far enough in advance so that I would not break my eucharistic fast. I could tell, from the way he glared about the hall, that he thought there would be fewer of Olaf's lieges at midnight Mass than he had bargained for. Sira Inge had asked the King more than once that, whenever a feast preceded Mass, Olaf would command that men drink according to strict measure —that was, only from one drinking stud to another—and not let them throw down the humming contents of tankard after tankard without regard to the inset studs from tankard rim to bottom which regulated drinking, according to age-old custom, at the midday meal. But King Olaf, who had no intention of drinking according to strict measure himself, had always answered that a feast was a feast and that he did not intend to breach good custom. Sira Inge told me this all over again, grumbling away the while. He also said it was in his mind to ask the King once more when he could come near him. This, I could see, was going to be a hard task since the men did not care much for Sira Inge and kept jostling rudely against him if they met him in the way. I was afraid, too, that it would be no service to Christ to make these new and not unreluctant Christians think that Christ's servitors discouraged feasting when the priests of Thor had never done so. I told all this to Sira Inge; and he listened. For he respected my judgment on such matters.

Maybe I had drunk enough ale, and more than enough, too, for it came into my mind now and would not go out of it that Sira Inge, at least, did not have a Thor name. He came from Denmark originally where folk had been Christians a little longer than here in Norway. He was short and fat and the curling brown hair of his tonsure rim grew close to a pink scalp. Tonight I thought he looked more than a little like the Yule pig they made out of sugar at Yuletide for children here in our northern land. But he was a faithful priest, even if he did love his own will overmuch. I was to find out later that this was a priest's failing which, I confess, I have been hard put to keep down sometimes in my own self.

As it soon turned out, it was just as well Olaf's tonsured Chaplain kept his counsel on this especial matter. For the King had other plans. Brian bore him his huge drinking horn, and Olaf rose from the high seat to make known the beginning of the toasts. He was a kingly man, was that hero son of Tryggve. Even in physical frame I have known only one King larger than he; and that was the Harald Sigurdson who died at Stamford Bridge. But Harald Sigurdson never matched King Olaf in heroism or knightly prowess. I am glad to have seen the son of Tryggve in my day. I do not think his like will come again.

First—for that this was Yule Eve—King Olaf drank Christ's beaker. Then the heirship bowl to his dead father's memory. The third great bowl was quaffed in honor of that Saint Michael, the warrior archangel, who warded all Christendom with his heavenly tempered sword against the pagan and the forsworn. It comes into my mind now that, when I was a youth, there were more shrines to Saint Michael in the west and north than I see in these latter days. I am afraid men grow forgetful of their great angel friend. The fourth toast was downed in compliment to the Greenland guests, more particularly Leif who sat, still in the white baptismal garment he would wear for several days yet, on the King's right hand.

After this, as was customary, the vows began. King Sigtrygg of Dublin—I had not seen the son of Amlaib Cuaran before, and I looked with interest on the silken beard of which he was so foolishly vain—sprang to unsteady feet and vowed to bring King Brian of Munster to his rebellious knees, a vow which gave me a sudden qualm about my heart and, I noticed, made Brian, the Munster King's grandnephew, flush with shame and anger. For this, except for Thorvald Ericson's broad hint, was the first he had heard of his great-uncle's successful war against the Norse ruler of Dublin. I think it now occurred to him for the first time— and his young heart must have sunk further at the sudden thought —that, as Brian of Munster's close relative and Olaf's fosterling, his position could become very delicate indeed at this far northern court.

Next Sigvald the Tall vowed blood vengeance for his brother slain, in the outer islands, by Bue the Fat. Men had whispered that Sigvald had been somewhat laggard in taking up the feud; and there had been much slighting talk about his manhood. So this oath was very popular. One might say it did not square too well with a feast in honor of the birth of the little Prince of Peace. But old ways are stubborn. One must make a beginning somewhere. There was much of the old Adam left even in Olaf Tryggveson in matters of honor. Even then, as I sat there, I knew that one day Christ would have to wrestle Thor to a fall over points such as these. But the time was not yet. I am old now, very old. The time is still not yet.

After the meinie had shouted hoarse approval of Sigvald's vow, then Sigurd Svendson swore he would take ship for Orkney, in the spring, and there lie with Hallbera, Eyolf Valgerdson's dark-haired daughter, whether Eyolf liked it or not. King Olaf frowned at this toast, and was about to rebuke his liege man, for he did not like ribaldry where women were concerned, when his Chaplain, Sira Inge, who was not always lacking in wisdom and who could read the King's mind like his own Mass book, leaned forward and whispered in his ear that Sigurd was betrothed to Hallbera and that Eyolf, her father, had broken the betrothal which was against the laws both of man and God. So the King held his peace for the time.

It was left to Leif, son of Eric, to make the best vow of all— perhaps I should say the best vow of all but one. But I leave that to you to make up your mind on later. I say this without vaunting for, though I am concerned in this other vow, it is not of myself I speak, but of the vow and of God to whom my vow was made.

I looked carefully at the famous Greenlander when he rose to
his feet. I had seen Leif Ericson thrice before, but never so close
as this. He was not a tall man—Thorvald his brother was taller
by two good inches. But he was tall enough, at that. Close on
six feet, I should say: well-knit, clear-eyed, having a generous
breadth of shoulder, and a firm grasp. The golden hair swept
back from his brow in waves—there was red in it, as there was
red in the hair of all the children of Eric the Red of Brattahlith.
Here, I said to myself, was a kindly man and a resolute one.
Here was a leader of men.

But somehow Leif was a leader, and a hero, too, in a different
way from King Olaf or Thorvald Ericson his brother, or Thorhall the Hunter—always supposing one should ever call Thorhall
Gamlason a hero. I have thought much on this matter since, and
I think now that what I felt then lay partly in that these others,
even Olaf Tryggveson, belonged to the past and Leif the Lucky
to the future. For I lived in the kind of times my people have
always called an *alda-skipti,* a turning point in the history of
an age. A new thing was beginning; and Leif the Trader was
of it as his brother, Thorvald the skald, was not. Also, as I grow
older and older, I begin to see men more and more as huge
emblematic figures: as themselves and as something greater than
themselves which yet belongs to themselves. A young boy and
young girl are those lovers of the prime-time, my lord Adam
and my lady Eve. An old man is Abraham come again. A good
priest is Christ. I do not yet see Leif's shape clearly enough in
figure to say more than that he somehow stands for order and
organization. The men who come after me will know better than
I what it is I grope to say here.

But if I am right in thinking Leif a new man, the way he
now went about things was after the good old fashion of high
emprise; and that is a fashion I hope will never change. For the
songs will have to go on being sung. There will have to be Thor-
valds to make the songs; and Brians and Grainnes to make the
songs about. If these things ever come to pass, that such as they
will disappear, we shall be in a bad way indeed.

It had been expected that, when the time for making vows
arrived, Leif would bind himself over to making all Greenland
Christian, always excepting old Eric, his stubborn father; for the
King did not expect a son to go against his father in a matter
of conscience. And so Leif duly did while the meinie thundered

dutiful approval. But after that, while the exultation fit was still
strong upon him, the great Greenland chieftain went further even.
He called for another bowl and rose to his feet a second time.
It was now I first heard of the western land we later came to
call Vinland on our great faring.

"Listen, O King!" he called aloud, while the hall grew hushed
in expectation and the echo of his voice rang in the smoky rafters.
"I make still a second vow. There is another great land far to
the west—I have heard of it from the Irish monks and from
my father's friend, the trader Bjarni Herjulfson of Herjulfsness,
the only man of our northern blood so far ever to set eyes upon
it. But Bjarni did not land there, and I intend to land and, God
willing, settle. That land, O King, I here vow to claim for
Christ!"

Thunder rocked the great hall. This, the jarls said to one another, was like the ancient Volsung days when Sigurd Jarl slew
the dragon and men performed high exploit. Even Thorhall Gamlason sprang to his feet, shouting, though he shouted on Thor,
while the others shouted on Christ. Forgetting all about his great-
uncle and his own and his great-uncle's troubles, Brian dropped
on his knees before Olaf Tryggveson and asked to be let go on
the voyage with Leif the Greenlander. The King did not hear the
lad at first because of all the tumult in the hall. When finally he
did hear him, Olaf looked grave for a moment, as was his habit
when an idea came to him.

"Get up, my boy," he said in kindly wise, placing his hands
on Brian's shoulders. "We shall speak of this somewhat later,
you and I, when time and occasion allow. Meanwhile I shall keep
it in mind. It may well be things will so work out that you can go."

I had pushed close to the front now. For, as the vowings began,
a great thought had come to me. From where I stood, I could
hear every word Olaf spoke.

The King turned to Leif.

"Do you keep this boy in mind," he said, speaking low so that
not too many of those around him could overhear what he said.
But I heard nonetheless. "I have something to say to you about
him—later, perhaps, when we can talk without fear of interrup-
tion. Since the Munster King's attack on Sigtrygg, my vassal,
the Irish lad goes in some danger here—and not just from Sigtrygg's followers. I do not like his thus going in danger, for
he is very dear to me. Besides, if he is harmed, it will hurt my

parleys with his great kinsman. Do you think you can help me
in this matter?"

Leif bowed to the King.

"It may well be, Lord," he said.

Then he turned and looked at the boy with interest. I followed
his glance; and, looking at Brian through the eyes of another, it
was as if I, also, saw him for the first time. He was slender—
more slender than our Norse make, on the whole—but strongly
made. His curling hair was darker than most Norse hair; and
his skin whiter. He had eyes of intense blue. There was a proud
temper in the set of his mouth. It seemed to me that the Greenlander liked what he saw; that he thought there were the makings
of a good fighter here. If so, it was a good omen for Brian. Leif
had the reputation of being a rare judge of men.

Brian looked back at him, proudly, candidly, manifestly liking,
on his side, what he saw in Leif. Perhaps he would have said
something further to the great outland captain. But the time had
come for me to say out my say, too, before the King.

"I have a vow to vow, O King!" I called loud above the heads
of those few who now stood between me and Olaf Tryggveson.
"If God is willing to have me, I here vow to turn priest of Christ
and to serve Him in Greenland where there will be much need
of priests from this time on. It may even be that, if Leif is lucky
in this new voyage he has vowed, I may someday journey to the
new land to help win it all for Christ."

"By God!" said Olaf Tryggveson, moved—never had I heard
the King more moved. "That is a good vow! I will give five
marks in silver for your schooling as a priest that men in after
days may say that, after God's, Thrand Thorbergson was Olaf
Tryggveson's priest. It will be much to have made the first Greenland priest."

Was not that a good oath I took? Again I say I do not vaunt.
But it seems to me that one more priest for Christ weighs more in
heaven's scales than even the finding of a new land. To be a
priest is a great faring, too. I was afraid, though, that my father
did not think so. Over my shoulder I caught sight of him, his
eyes straining, his mouth open. I knew he thought I had drunk
too much. But, if so, it was not Olaf's good ale I tasted then. It
was that better drink the French *jongleurs* speak of when they
sing of the holy Sangraal which held that best of all good wine,
the wine of Holy Thursday which is our sweet Saviour's blood.

Then the giving of gifts began. The King took heavy gold rings from his arm for his skald, Halfred. He gave Frankish swords to his household retainers; and a new gold Mass cup to his priest, Sira Inge. Even the serving men got silver coins of Constantinople with the Greek Emperor's face upon them. For the thralls—right down to the old carline women who turned the heavy querns that ground the meal for everyday's bread—there were good bolts of red and blue dyed wadmal to be cut into holiday clothes. For each member of Leif's crew there was forthcoming one-eighth of a mark in pure silver and a great spear without barbs and inlaid with good silver at the socket. The ship's *stafnbui,* as became his position of responsibility and peril, got, in addition to the spear and silver, a saddle of Arab leather. For the King knew that, back home in Greenland, Leif's forecastle leader was a fancier of blood horses. Leif himself received a scarlet cloak lined with the finest fur of Arctic fox and ermine; a ring weighing better than six whole ounces in purest gold; a broadax all plated with silver; the sword Fjorsvafni—this was indeed a gift of gifts; and a huge Irish wolfhound.

I was standing beside Thorvald Ericson now. After my vowing, he had been the first to take me by the hand, in his generous way, and to speak words of congratulation.

"A good vow, Thrand Thorbergson!" he had said. "I wish you luck of it."

So the two of us were already fast friends by the time Brian found a chance to slip in beside Thorvald. Brian kindled at the sight of the kingly dog the retainers led up on his leash as the King's last present to Leif.

"Look!" he said. "How handsome the hound is! There is nothing like the Irish hunting dogs."

"Just as there is no one like an Irishman, eh, Brian?" said Thorvald Ericson, winking at me. "But you are right, I think. Do you know, Brian, I think Leif will give him to me. He knows I have always wanted, almost above all else, one of these great Irish dogs."

"Call him Bran," said Brian happily.

"Bran?" Thorvald raised sardonic eyebrows, grinning at me the while. "Why Bran? Because it is so like your own name, perhaps?"

"Because," said Brian, "Bran is a hero hound—the hound of Finn and Oisin who runs with them forever in the *Tir-n-an-Óg.*"

"The *Tír-n-an-Óg*," said Thorvald slowly. "Yes, I have heard
—what skald has not?—of your Irish Land of Youth. It is like
our own Valhalla, except that in your *Tír-n-an-Óg* the heroes do
more than eat and drink and fight forever. They also tell tales
and make love. I have thought more than once that I should
prefer the *Tír-n-an-Óg* to either Valhalla or the Christian heaven."

The Greenlander looked quizzically at the Irish lad whom he
had befriended.

"You know, Brian," he said. "You would make a very good
skald. It is easy for the Irish to become skalds, anyway. And it
is a pleasant life, that of a good skald. To sit on the King's left
and to get the *Braga-laun,* the skald's portion, from the King's
own hands—what could be more pleasant than that? Yes, and a
plentiful measure of the shining Fafnir-lair, too. Skalds have
been known to become very rich."

Brian shook his head at that, never hesitating for an instant.
He knew that the "shining Fafnir-lair" was a kenning for gold
because we had talked together of the *Niflung Song*; and the
Niflung dragon, whom Sigurd slew, used to couch on gleaming
gold. But I, who knew Brian like the palm of my own hand, did
not think that his heart was much set on gold. His heart, like
mine, was set on elsewhere.

"I have no wish to be a skald," he said, "though I respect
skalds. I have no great desire for gold, either."

"Oh, but there is much more than gold in a skald's life," said
Thorvald swiftly then. "Much, much more. There is the dragon's
blood, too. Dragon's blood is more precious far than dragon's
gold. Only a hero can taste dragon's blood. A hero who is also
a skald. When it comes upon the skald's tongue, then he understands the speech of birds and beasts. Is that not something, my
little Irishman?"

"It is something all right," said Brian. "But it is not what
I wish. I wish first to sail with Leif to the new land. Then to
have a ship of my own. And then to go back to Ireland, where
I came from, to serve my great-uncle, the King of Munster."

"Is that all?" Thorvald asked the boy with a grin. "No more
than that? Are you sure there is nothing more you wish—in the
way of another kind of gold, say? I mean the gold of the little
gold-haired Hlín you were so ready to fall out with Thorhall
over."

My friend, Brian, could not help blushing a little at that home thrust. But he still did not retreat.

"That, too, perhaps," he said. "But later on. So far I have not so much as spoken with the maid, Grainne."

"You have made thus much progress, then," Thorvald said, "that you know her name is Grainne. That is more than any of the rest of us have been able to find out. It has a comely sound, Grainne. Where did you learn her name so fast?"

"Mistress Gudrid told me," said Brian. "She who is Thorfinn Karlsefni's wife and who, so long as you Greenlanders stay here, has the first rank in the women's quarters. I asked her when I brought the cup to her. I had never spoken to her before; and some ladies might have thought I was overweening. But Mistress Gudrid is a very gracious lady. Tell me, Thorvald. Do you think they will make the maid a thrall? I would not like that fate for her."

"Nor would I," said Thorvald, pondering.

Then he went on talking, half to himself as it were, not taking the pains to answer Brian's question as to whether he thought Olaf's men would make the little maid a thrall.

"H'mm," he said. "That gives me an idea. You will forgive me, Brian, if I go away now for a little space. I have something to say to Mistress Gudrid apart. I shall not be long."

So Thorvald Ericson said something low in Mistress Gudrid's ear, pointing once to Brian and then to Grainne. It seemed strange to no one that he should speak thus familiarly to another man's wife although, in general, manners were inclined to be strict among us on this same head. For Gudrid was his and Leif's foster sister as well as the widow of their dead brother, Thorstein. Mistress Gudrid was a handsome woman in her portly way. The hair that curled under her embroidered coif was gray now; but it had been like spun gold not so very long ago.

Like her husband, Thorfinn Karlsefni's wife was a woman of decision. I watched her firm her lips, rise in her own turn, and go the high table where the King still sat feasting—Olaf Tryggveson always ate and drank like some hero in Valhalla. There Mistress Gudrid spoke briefly to Leif, and returned to her seat.

I think the time has come for me to say a word or two about Gudrid and her relations with the family of the Brattahlith *hersir,* Eric. Leif was bound to Gudrid by a double tie; perhaps one should even say by a triple tie. Not only was she the widow of his dead brother, Thorstein, but, in addition, her second husband, Thorfinn Karlsefni, the rich trader from Reyniness in Iceland's Skagafjord, happened to be one of Leif's closest friends. Moreover, Gudrid herself, who had been his father Eric's ward before she became his daughter-in-law, was closer than a kinswoman. She was more than a foster sister even. Leif and his brother, Thorvald Ericson, loved her like a real sister. As if she were truly a daughter by blood, old Eric had held her second marriage feast for her at Ericsfjord last winter; and the two families, theirs and Thorfinn's, had drawn very close together. So what Gudrid wished was as law to Leif. It might be that, in disposition, she wished mastery overmuch for a woman, but Leif and Thorfinn were masterful men in their own rights and knew how to cope with so spirited a woman. Leif listened to her now, smiled, patted her hand a little, then turned to the King.

"About the Irish boy now, lord King," he said, and my heart leaped at his speech. "I have been thinking on the matter. I do not think we need to confer as you so courteously suggest. I will take him with me when I sail in the spring. It also comes into my mind that, for quite other reasons, the girl, Grainne, will be in equal danger. Would you wish me to take her, too? She could wait upon my kinswoman, Gudrid. If it seemed necessary for decorum's sake, she could even sail in Thorfinn's boat instead of mine."

Though he had not thought on the matter, Olaf Tryggveson welcomed Leif's proposal. For the King did not have to be told what happened to a beautiful thrall attached to a chieftain's household. He knew all too well; and, as a just King and a follower of Christ, he could not have relished the prospect. It was true Grainne's hair would probably not be cropped, as happened to the other thrall women; and she most likely would not have to wear coarse white wadmal as a badge of perpetual servitude. It might even be better for her if these humiliations should be imposed. For he was afraid the warriors would fight one another for her possession so that the victor might take her to his lawless bed and there beget on her another line of nameless bastards. While her beauty lasted, she would be the death of men. A toothless old crone, she would end on the midden. All in all, it was not hard for King Olaf to make up his mind. He knew Mistress

Gudrid for a good woman and a Christian. She would protect the girl and be kind to her. In return, he could very easily see to it that she went into Karlsefni's household a free woman.

"Yes," said Olaf Tryggveson, slowly pulling at his long mustache. "It is a good disposition you propose. The boy shall go with you, and the maid with Mistress Gudrid—it matters not in which ship. Settle that among yourselves as you see fit. I shall give Thorfinn the six *aurar* which are the price of the girl's freedom, and I shall hold her freedom-ale at my own expense afterwards, before you and he sail away in the spring. As for the boy, Brian, I will give you somewhat more than the six *aurar* which are the purchase price of a thrall's freedom. He is my fosterling, and no thrall. He is a lad of the royal house of Munster."

Standing up before his carved high seat, the King drew himself to his full height. Skald Halfred swept quick fingers across the harp strings in token of silence.

"Lordings mine!" called Olaf over the clashing of ale horns. "The giving of gifts is not yet finished, it seems. Leif of Ericsfjord has just given me a gift: a subtle gift, a statesman's gift, one that cannot be weighed as silver is weighed for that it is so much more valuable than silver. I give him one in return. Though this is not the gift I wish to speak of—that will come later—I also yield to him my fosterling, Brian. And I give my new prisoner, the girl Grainne, to Mistress Gudrid, Leif's kinswoman and the wife of Thorfinn Karlsefni. Only I give them to Leif and Gudrid under different names than the ones they now bear. Let Brian henceforth be Haki, and Grainne Hekja."

Thorvald Ericson, who had gone back to his place by now, gave Brian a little shove at this.

"Go forward," he whispered. "And do you take Grainne with you."

Shyly the lad went forward to the high seat. On his way he spoke to Grainne, daughter of Rafarta of Clonmacnoise, for the first time. It is only looking back that one can tell what are the great moments in a life. This was a great moment. For it was the beginning of this pair's long colloguing together.

"Come with me now, Mistress," Brian said courteously to her in Irish, giving her the title that was in fact so far beyond the years she had yet attained. "It is best you do so. There is nothing to fear. I will be your protector."

Grainne did not flinch when he locked her arm in his and led
her before the King. I could see a delicate flush mantling under
her clear young skin. It began high on her cheekbones and burned
slowly downward till it was quenched in the more violent crimson of her scarlet bodice. Olaf put a kind hand on either young
shoulder.

"These are good children, Leif," he said, turning to his guest.
"You can use them as scouts in the new land to which you sail—
you and Mistress Gudrid, too, if Thorfinn Karlsefni and his wife
decide to follow you there. The boy will be a seasoned warrior
one of these days—the house of Boru breeds warriors with the
best. Meanwhile he is fleet as a red deer in some Scottish glen.
From what my men tell me, the girl is every bit as swift. At
least, she led them a merry chase over the Irish rocks until they
were able to catch up with her."

Looking on from where he stood beside me, Thorvald Ericson
jogged my arm and nodded his head in approval. Things were
going well, he seemed to say. I, as well as he, both liked and
understood this strategy of the King's—for it was manifestly
strategy, and no mere whim—in changing their names to Haki
and Hekja. It was going to be much better, in the immediate
future, if men did not think of the two of them as Irish. Even
in tolerant Greenland, where the quarrels of kings and the vassals
of kings meant a good deal less than in royal Norway, it would
be just as well.

"It's a good name, too," said Thorvald Ericson. "No need
for the boy to feel ashamed of it. Tell him that."

From his skald's treasure house of knowledge Thorvald was
remembering, even as I was, that Haki was the hero brother of
that valiant Hagbard who had been named after the name of
Odin. As for Grainne's new name of Hekja, what did it matter
what a maiden was called?

The King was not yet finished up there before the high seat.
Again, at a sign from Olaf, Halfred swept his fingers across the
singing strings.

"The King speaks, shield-bearers!" he called aloud. "Silence
for the son of Tryggve!"

Olaf raised his lion's head, as if thinking, before he spoke.

"I come now to that gift I promised," he said after a pause.
"One last gift I make to Leif of Ericsfjord. It says in the Christ
book that a laborer is worthy of his hire. So is a voyager worthy

of his ship. *Bound is boatless man,* we Vikings say in the Faroes.
My Leif is far from boatless. The boat he bought from Bjarni
Herjulfson and sailed here in is a good boat. Even so, I will
build him a better. Starting after Twelfth Night, in my shipyards
at Ladehammer, my master builder, Thorberg Skaffhogg, greatest
of shipwrights, will build it. Thorberg built *Long Serpent* for
me, the greatest ship in all the Northland. It needs as good a
ship to carry Christ to the new land. I ask but one thing of Leif
in return—that he let me name his new ship."

Thunder rocked the hall. My father preened himself as any
peacock at the mention of his name. Friends clapped him heartily
on the back, congratulating him on what must turn out to be
another fat commission. My heart swelled, too, for it was a
great thing the King had said about my father.

But it was close on midnight now, and time for the Christmas
Mass to begin. Olaf Tryggveson strode from his dais, his Chaplain, crucifix held high, going before him, myself tagging at
Sira Inge's plump heels, a surplice over my arm to be donned
before the ceremony began. As Sira Inge passed the long bench
where Thorhall Gamlason had never once left off drinking, the
sullen Greenlander spat on the floor after him. The King did
not notice the insulting act which was, when all was said and
done, a lucky thing for Thorhall. But Brian saw, and the boy's
hand tightened on Grainne's arm until the girl winced away from
him with a low cry.

I thought that gesture boded not well for any of us in the
future. But many things turn out better than they give promise
of doing in their beginnings. I minded me what Thorvald Ericson
had this night said of this same Thorhall Gamlason: that he was
an old wolf but a wolf for whom something might be said. A
wolf, moreover, for whom he would do much and who, in return, would do much for him. From the corner of my eye, through
the blue incense wreaths of the censer smoking in my hand, I
saw Thorhall follow our procession out the door; and, for a
moment, wondered if he had had a change of heart. It was the
ale that was in question, however, not any change of heart. The
fellow only wanted to relieve himself. We were still some way
from the marshy causeway when I saw the berserker trudging
back again from the midden edge where Olaf's privies were, his
ears sharp under the bright and bitter stars of late December.
Thorhall Gamlason looked an old wolf indeed; and, in some ways,

a sad old wolf. I think I began to pity him a little from this time
on. There is always something melancholy in fighting on the losing side—and something splendid, too, provided always one fights
hard and fair.

The snowstorm had lulled outside. The moon, just rising behind the oak trees, silvered the gilded dragon heads on the gables
of the tall stave church which Olaf Tryggveson had built a quarter
of a mile from his great hall at Vik. It was connected with the
royal buildings by a wooden causeway laid across a tussocky
marsh where the frogs sang loud on early summer evenings. We
stopped for a moment outside the church so that the King's procession, which had straggled on the road, might regroup itself
in more seemly wise. Brian took advantage of the little pause to
bring Grainne to my side.

"Here is another friend for you, Mistress," he said. "Thrand
Thorbergson."

The girl took me trustingly by my right hand. My heart yearned
at her candor and directness. I was glad that I had enough of
the Irish tongue to be able to wish her great joy of the Yule that
was just now beginning. Then our procession entered the church.

I do not think Brian had ever grown used to the wooden
churches Christian men had then begun to rear everywhere in
the north countries; churches that were so unlike the stone
churches of his great-uncle's Munster. But men must make out
with what they have. There was small wood in Ireland; and stone
for building was hard to come by in Norway. To me, as it happened, the wood churches were things of utter glory. For I could
remember the time, not so very many years before, when there
were only temples of Thor and Odin in our Northland. I have
seen the great minsters of Frankland and England since. Only
last year I watched with my own eyes the great fane Edward
of England had ordered built in London. Nevertheless, to this
day I think our Norse stave-churches handsome enough after
their quite different fashion, especially when the candles are
lighted for a feast day and the elaborate carvings of the walls
and pillars seem to come alive in the shifting mellow light: the
serpent moving under Sigurd Dragonslayer's sword; Sleipnir,
Odin's fairy steed, caracoling higher up.

An old fancy came again into my mind when Sira Inge girded
himself to preach his Yule sermon. I had thought more than

once that it was like a ship, really, this church of ours. When the wind blew strong, the high building creaked and groaned like a long ship in a storm. Wood took up the strain and gave before the squalls as stone would not. Whenever the high altar was lighted up, as it was this night, looking up at it from the floor of the church one almost thought one was sailing straight into a sunrise—a sunrise of shattering silver and gold and crimson. For, right behind the altar, where the church builders of Frankland are just now beginning to put colored glass, the King's painter, Eystein Breidskegg, had painted an enormous picture of Christ enthroned: Christ and His Mother and all His hallows who dwelt with Him now, as His thanes, in the high hall of heaven.

As I helped Sira Inge vest for Mass I heard King Olaf's English bell beat out midnight with its silvery tone that, on this night of moon and snow, sounded more silvery than ever. I gabbled my confession meanwhile, for Sira Inge had had no time for me before, what with all the shriving he had had in hand for Olaf and his jarls, to say nothing of the jarls' ladies who, if Sira Inge was to be believed, took shriving somewhat as a Christmas comfit, not a penitential sacrament. I learned then what life has since taught me again and again: that one must never judge a thing from the outside alone. This fat priest, at whom the meinie jeered if they thought the King was not watching, was both understanding and forbearing in his shriving.

Inside the stave-church all eyes were on Leif as, in his white baptismal garment, he knelt up toward the front, just behind King Olaf in his ermine mantle of kingship. Thorfinn Karlsefni and his wife, being Icelanders by birth, had taken baptism a year before when the faith of Christ first came to that land. Thorvald and the other members of Leif's crew, with the exception of Thorhall Gamlason, were to follow their leader into Christianity before the twelve days of Christmas were out. There was some little surprise, however, when Leif did not go to the communion table at the time appointed. It disappointed the King who had a shrewd eye for effect and who had intended that all men's gaze should be on the Greenland captain at this moment when, for the first time, he flung back his head to receive the consecrated bread at the hands of the priest.

I learned later—for the Greenlanders made no secret of it— that Sira Inge had forbidden Leif, only that afternoon, to approach the communion table until he had made good the wrong done Thorgunna, the Hebridean woman, who was with child by him. As it happened, Leif, who loved Thorgunna dearly, was most willing to acknowledge her as his lawful wife. He said he would set sail for the Hebrides in the spring and bring back his wife and child to Greenland. The babe, men said, was to be born this very month—indeed, might already have been born.

When the communion service was over and Sira Inge scoured the golden vessels, I stole a look at Grainne. The girl knelt, head bowed, praying, the candlelight golden on her golden hair. So adorable did she look there where she knelt that it seemed to me it was almost as if the Mother of God had come down from the painting above the high altar and prayed there in a blue cloak. I thought on how Grainne was free now from this day henceforward, and thanked the Mother of God who gave succor to all Christian maidens. Then, a little ashamed that I had not done so before, I remembered to thank her also for her great gift to the world that had ransomed all men from the thralldom of Lucifer—the great gift that was Blessed Mary's only Son Who looked down upon me now from where He sat behind the altar with His Mother and all His hallows in the pictured glory of heaven.

Brian had promised to wait outside for me after the service that all three of us, Grainne and he and I, might walk back to Vik together. So it was not really eavesdropping on my part, even though I shamefacedly felt it was, when I came upon the twain, where they awaited me under the bell tower, only to find that Grainne had been taken by a shaking fit and that Brian was hard put to comfort her. He had thrown off his warm cloak, which was of costly marten pelts sewn together, and had cast it over her trembling shoulders.

"No, Brian," she was saying to him as I came upon them, shaking her head in refusal and beginning to sob aloud. "I am not really cold. Take back your cloak. You will be chilled through without it."

But she went on shivering so pitifully that the boy's heart must have almost stopped in his breast. I know mine did. In the moonlight her face looked small and drawn into a little triangle of pure woe.

"What is it, Grainne mine?" he asked her gently, putting one arm about her.

The girl burst into a torrent of weeping at that.

"It has been so long," she said, sobbing louder and louder. "First there were the warriors. Then the chains in the long ship. And no one to speak to, for I have not yet the Norse tongue. No one at all, except a thrall here and there who happened to be Irish like myself. No one at all, until you spoke to me this night here in the King's hall."

A great wave of tenderness came over me as I looked on. I wanted to tell her that I would be her Norse tongue until she had one of her own. But it was Brian's place, not mine. Had not I, that very night, declared for another place than this? He touched the curls over her forehead where they coiled out under her coif. Then, leaning down very gently, he kissed her on the white brow, and on the cheek which was salt with tears.

"Do not cry, Grainne mine," he said very softly. "Do not cry. There is nothing to fear now. Here am I, and Thrand beside me. Nothing can harm you now."

After a time she stopped the great choking sobs that were rending her asunder, and dried her eyes with the edge of her kirtle. Glancing up at Brian again, she caught sight of the golden dragon heads on the stave-church gables glinting back the rays of the moon. The sight of their gaping mouths made her shrink suddenly in upon herself.

"Grainne!" said Brian reproachfully. "They are nothing but dragon heads on a church. Nothing more. All the churches in this land have such images upon them. They cannot hurt you. You must not be so timid."

"I know," she said, apologetically. "But why must these Norse have dragons everywhere? On their ships, on the backs of their chairs, on their churches? And how large the monsters are! And how small the blessed crosses against the sky!"

It was true enough, though I had never thought of it quite like this before. There were many more dragons than crosses on the stave-churches; and they were much bigger, too. I smiled a little ruefully at the thought. Thor, I said to myself, and not for the first time, was still strong in this land of mine. The King had very far to go yet before he would plant the cross of Christ on every rock and skerry in the Northland. And, once he had, how deeply would the new faith cut into the souls of these folk? Would they have done no more than merely exchange Thor for Christ? It would be a good exchange, in all conscience; but it would not be enough. But I placed my faith in the King all the same. Olaf Tryggveson was a resolute and valiant man. I thought he would prevail in the end.

A flake drifted lazily down to come to rest on Grainne's mantle. Brian saw it as soon as I did. He stooped to Grainne's ear where, shell-pink and small, it peeped out from under the blue cloak.

"Come now, Grainne," he said soothingly, as though to a frightened child. "It will not do for us to stay out so late on Christmas morning, the best day of all the year. What will Mistress Gudrid say of her new charge? Or Leif of his? See! Everyone has gone on to Vik now except the three of us."

Grainne looked up at us out of her blue hood, at peace once again.

"I will walk with you now," she said.

In the Yule night that would soon be Yule morning the snow began falling more heavily. It lay silver on Grainne's blue hood as the three of us walked home together, damping the delicate tendrils on her forehead, curling the darker lashes of her eyes. When Brian lifted the heavy leather curtain of the women's quarters for her, the girl pressed his hand gratefully and, with another look of gratitude, this time for me, slipped inside without another word.

There was no one abroad in the King's great hall when the two of us crossed it on our way to the bed-closet which I was to share this night with Brian. No one, except for a single man lying on his back, uncovered, on one of the long benches. With a start Brian recognized Thorhall Gamlason still dressed in his black doublet. Then, for it was very cold now with all the fires out, and because it was Christmas morning, he picked up a bear-skin from in front of the blackened hearth and made to cast it over the sleeper. At the first touch of the rug's edge, Thorhall Gamlason sat up quickly, hand on the heavy spear beside him. But, when he saw what the boy had done, he leaned back on his elbow, grinning. For once, that wolf's grin was not unfriendly.

"A bear's sark for a berserk, eh?" he said in that strange snarling voice. "Well, thank you, boy. But it is my whim always to sleep without covering. Still, what you did was kindly meant. So I thank you again. It may be we shall be good shipmates yet."

This time it was my turn to start. Shipmates! Of course. Thorhall Gamlason, who had taken the Jomsburg vikings' oath never to sleep covered except by the roof of a hall in winter,

pulled an oar in Leif's dragon ship. Now Brian, too, on the
King's own authority and Leif's pledged promise, would sail with
Leif in the spring. It gave me a queer turn to think that Brian
and Holmgang-Bersi, who hated all Irishmen, would be shipmates
together.

By Yule morning the snowstorm had set in in earnest. The
King's hall and all his outbuildings were sheeted over. Within
twenty-four hours it became necessary to tunnel paths from one
building to another. Olaf had had the foresight, despite the de-
ceptively clear weather of Yule Eve, to order his long ships pulled
up on rollers, after the review for Leif, and housed in the long
sheds at Ladehammer that were their winter quarters. So everything was snug and trig at Vik now. The granaries were full,
for it had been a good year in the fields. The roofs were tight-
calked against the wind and wet of winter. From now on men
could snuggle in, and furbish their war harness, and think back
on their autumn-viking and ahead to what the coming spring-
viking might bring.

The great Yule feast in honor of Leif went on for six whole
days. After that there were six other days of games and feasting until the twelve days of Christmas were out—and a little
better than out, too. There were wrestling matches in which all
the Greenlanders took part except for Thorhall Gamlason. No
one took offense at Thorhall's absence, however, for it was well
known he could not fight in play. And who in his senses would
wish to fight with him in earnest, saving for some affair of honor
when fighting could not be helped?

Almost every day the men played at *skinnleikr* in the great
hall with a ball made out of tightly rolled goatskin. In one of
these rough bouts Thorstein Thorskabit fell over the fireplace,
chasing the ball, and got his right leg crushed, which meant that
he would not be able to fare out on the spring-viking, if ever
again. So the King gave order that this especial sport be played
no more till spring, when men might go outside and disport on
the soft turf with less danger to life and limb. Thorvald Ericson
taught Brian how to play at chess with chessmen cunningly carved
out of walrus ivory. For my part, when I had the time, I taught
Brian the valuable art of binding stiff goose quills into the arrow
shaft with a greased thong. Mostly, when they were not eating
and drinking, the men tinkered with their war gear, replacing a

helmet strap here, whittling a bow there, fletching arrows whenever nothing better offered.

Over in the women's quarters Grainne helped Gudrid with her
weaving and sewing; and grew to love the generous-minded Iceland woman who was Thorfinn Karlsefni's wife. One of the bakehouse cats kittened at the end of January; and Grainne took
one of the kitlings—it was a white one, I mind me now—for
her own. The kitten followed her everywhere so soon as it could
walk. When Thorvald Ericson saw the two of them together
for the first time, he told Brian and myself it was like the goddess
Vanabride whose cart was drawn across the blue summer heavens
by a leash of white cats. Since Vanabride was one of the names
of Freya, goddess of love, and since Freya was the most beautiful
of all the radiant Vanir, I thought, though the thing was folly,
that it would not go amiss to tell Grainne what Thorvald had
said. The girl was pleased. I noted that every time she met Thorvald after that she gave the Greenlander a sidelong smile.

As for Thorvald in this same matter of Vanabride and the
white kitten, he was so taken with his own fancy that he made
a new lay about it. The next time King Olaf appointed skald-
competition, Thorvald used his Grainne lay and won the *Braga-
laun* over Halfred who up to now had gone unvanquished.

Only one thing darkened our winter. One sleety night, in late
February, a messenger came over the mountains on skis bearing
news from the Hebrides. He had picked it up on his winter faring
in Denmark. It had gone to Scotland first; then England, and
from there to Normandy. After that it had made its way through
the German lands to Denmark; and so at last to Olaf's realm.
On Yule Eve the lady Thorgunna had died in childbirth, bearing
Leif a son. On her deathbed she had asked those round her to
get this message to Leif of Ericsfjord: that, when he could, he
should tryst with her once more at her burial cairn.

Leif took this news very badly. He, who had never drunk to
speak of, now fell to drinking so heavily that Thorfinn Karlsefni
and Thorvald Ericson feared for his reason, if not his very life.
Once he went so far as to make an attempt on his own life. It
was Mistress Gudrid who saved him that time. A wasting fever
laid hands upon him at the end of one of these drinking bouts;
and it came into my mind that the lady Thorgunna was calling
him to her—I had heard of such things from my father. I had
seen men in frenzies for one reason or another many times be-

fore; but never for love. It seemed to me that the love of women, which is the source of all life and most beauty, could also be the most destructive of passions. Leif mended, though, at last, if very slowly. By spring he was almost himself again.

Even now, however, Sira Inge would still not admit Leif to the sacrament. The priest said he must go on pilgrimage first. For now he had another grave sin laid to his account. Because of him and of his lawless love the lady Thorgunna had died a pagan; and so another immortal being had been lost to Christ forever. I used to grieve much over this when I was young. It was a hard saying on Sira Inge's part; and I never thought to question it. But I grieve no longer. A learned monk, who had been taught his letters at the court of one of Hrolf the Ganger's sons and who had thereafter learned more theology than Sira Inge had even heard of, told me years later that there was no reason why the lady Thorgunna should not have a high place among the saved. Each year since I have been a priest of Christ I have said my Yule Eve Mass for her soul.

So the long winter wore on till spring while, in the King's shipyards at Ladehammer, the long ship that was to be Leif's grew like a living thing under the shaping hands of my father, Thorberg Skaffhogg—and under my hands, too, if it be seemly to mention this.

CHAPTER THREE

THE NAMING OF THE SHIP

NOW I AM OF THREE MINDS WHAT I SHOULD CALL THIS PORTION
of my tale. It deals with how we built, my father and I, the ship
Leif sailed to Vinland; and the building of that boat would make
a goodly name. It deals also with Leif's and Olaf's faring to
Selje isle in the Sognefjord where the holy maid Synnove's body
was found; and that was a goodly venture, too. But I have decided, though these deserve commemoration also, to call it: the
Naming of the Ship. There are other pens and better to write
about maid Synnove; and other ships as good as ours—none
better, though—were built at Ladehammer. But none before in
all our Northland—though not a few since—was ever named by
the adorable name she bore; a name that, barring the names of
the Three-in-One, is the name of all names most honored in
heaven and earth.

The war between Asa-Thor and the white Christ was much
in my mind that winter. I knew that, for all the King had done,
there were people who still held back in their hearts. Many men—
to be on the safe side, as it were—continued to sacrifice to Thor
and Odin on the sly, arguing, within themselves, that they did
not, on that account, scant their duty to this new and untried
God, Christ. Some of this clinging to the old ways was, I thought,
innocent enough, though Sira Inge never thought so. It seemed
to me there was no particular harm in setting out porridge for
the Yule Nisse on Christmas Eve; nor in maidens dancing about
the Fairy Oak and singing songs to the Queen of Elfland on
May Eve. But abominations were another thing again; and there
were plenty of these darker things yet trafficked in as well.

Witchcraft, for example, was much older in our land than even
Thor. It had strong roots and old—just how strong and old I
had occasion to find out quite soon. The Old Religion, as the
country folk like to name it, still draws people after it. So I do

not like to call attention to it even in this remote fashion. Nevertheless, since the happening concerned both Brian and Thorhall the Hunter, I set it down here in its proper place, albeit with some misgivings. I hope what I write here may not be held against me.

One cold night early in February—it was, I mind me, a fortnight or so before the coming of the ill tidings about Thorgunna —when the King was away in the mountains hunting elk with Leif, Thorolf Mostrarskegg, the steward at Vik, brought his mother, Gefjon, into Olaf's hall. Of all the Thor names Brian joked about, here was the one who made the most mischief; and his loathsome mother made still more. Gefjon was a witch who, men said, had learned her dangerous trade in the old days under Ragnhild Ericsdatter, daughter of King Eric Bloodaxe and of his evil wife, Gunhild. Gefjon had also, when a maiden, spent much time in the Orkneys where, even in these latter days, sorcery is still common. She owned a famous witch bag which she always carried, next the skin, around her withered waist. This had a healing-stone in it, a small inner pouch full of aromatic simples, and some moss that had grown out of a dead man's skull. People said Gefjon's *fylgja* was a walrus. Once, when Grim of Haddeby had a blood feud with her son, Thorolf, a walrus followed him out fishing, and Grim swore that the walrus had old Gefjon's eyes. I do not know about that. What I do know is that old Gefjon was the one thing my own mother ever feared. I remember that her nose waggled over her chin, and that the skin of her face was as mottled-pale as a toad's damp belly.

There are some other things that can be told about Thorolf Mostrarskegg's evil mother. She lived next to an elves' hillock where, three times a year, she performed the elves' sacrifice, sprinkling the mound with hot blood from a freshly slain black bull which her son, Thorolf, was careful to procure for her no matter how great the expense. She was known to own a Thorchair and a magic staff on which she rode on nights of storm— or so men said, at least. She could sing for a wind, and spin for a death. Her love potions were in great demand in the neighborhood of Vik, as were her dream riddlings. King Olaf had had her flogged once, although she was even then an old woman, because she had been found scrabbling in a new-made grave— when they came upon her there she had three green-mold human fingers in her hands which had belonged to the dead man. Thorolf tried to have this scandal hushed up; and the King said naught about it after the flogging. But everybody knew about it anyway. The most costly thing of all the eerie things she had to vend was a sleep-thorn. One had, they said, but to scratch an enemy sleeping with this thorn; and then he would never wake from that sleep unless old Gefjon herself took off the spell which she was usually willing to do for another costly fee. Men said it was part of the same thorn tree from which Odin had plucked the magic thorn with which he pricked Brynhild before that shield-maiden fell into the enchanted sleep whence Sigurd Jarl awakened her. But, for all her spinning of spells and the fees she got there-for, the old woman did not seem rich. Her house by the elves' hill was no better than a sty.

Gefjon had still another uncanny gift which used to be very much in demand in warriors' halls on winter nights when men's minds, darkened by Odin's twin ravens of thought and memory, turned back on what had happened in the past and forward to what was going to happen in the future. She was a *volva,* a prophetess. After Olaf took Christianity, the old woman feared to practice this prophesying openly. For the King had had several witches put to death for this very thing; and, above all else, he hated anyone who, like Gefjon, had ever had anything to do with his ancient enemy, King Eric Bloodaxe's vile wife, Queen Gun-hild. So it was a somewhat risky thing she and her son were doing this night in Olaf's hall. Thorolf Steward thought he was safe enough, however. His comrades, he knew, would scorn bear-ing tales, whether they approved or not. And the women of the household, some of whom would come this night, were always mad for fortunetelling. As for Sira Inge, he was away in Den-mark with Bishop Sigurd on whom he was expected to wait attendance once or twice a year. It is in my mind, as I write, that perhaps I should have put a stop to it. I would have, surely, had I been a priest. But I was not a priest then; and, as young men are like to fear, I feared overmuch that the name of tale-bearer would be put upon me.

Thorolf had made careful preparations for his mother's visit. He had had the *volva's* chair set up for her in the middle of the great hall; on it a cushion stuffed with the feathers of fresh-slain poultry, including three black cocks. Tables were set out at which the old woman, as was customary on these occasions, dined alone off a porridge of goat's kidneys and a tray full of the roasted hearts of a chicken, a capon, a cow, a pig, and a sheep. For some reason, it was necessary that the spoon she used be of brass and the knife hafted with yellow walrus tusk.

Whenever, as now, she attempted divination, Gefjon wore a dark blue cloak set with topaz and beryl all down the hem. There were glass beads about her scrawny neck, and on her gray head a hood of black lambskin lined with the skin of a white cat. Her magic staff, which she bore with her whenever she walked out into the world, had a great knob of massy brass upon it. Her shoes were of shaggy calfskin with long latchets, and at the end of each latchet a huge bronze button. Her gloves were of catskin lined with white cat fur, a detail which, when Grainne noticed it, made the maid shudder to herself and clutch the white kitten which never left her side. I did not care whether Grainne were bothered or not. It irked me that the girl had come at all after I had taken the trouble to warn her it would not be a seemly performance. Thorvald Ericson only laughed at me when I made my complaint to him. Did I not know, he asked me, that that was just the way to insure a woman's coming?

"But Grainne is a girl, no woman," I said to him. It was a stupid thing to say, and Thorvald Ericson took advantage of that opening.

"No?" he asked me, mocking. "Look at her again, little priest."

After old Gefjon had done with slobbering over her food, she asked that those women of the household, who happened to know the old incantation called *Warlocks All,* be brought before her that they might stand about her in a ring and, by their singing, lure the spirits of the dead to her. Some old thrall women were found who remembered the ancient ways. While they sang in their quavering carlines' voices, the *volva* closed her rheumy eyes and rocked back and forth, moaning a little, in her Thor-chair. After they were done singing, those men who wished to know the future and were willing to pay a silver penny for the privilege filed forward one by one.

Never opening her blue-veined eyelids, the *volva* put a clawlike right hand on each head in turn, and prophesied. It was the usual thing for the most part. Good crops for one man. A fair wife for another. A wound on spring-viking for still another—not a mortal wound, though, said the *volva,* nodding her old head. When, however, Thorvald Ericson came before the hag, her hand, of a sudden, trembled and fell nerveless to one side. A hush came

over the great hall. Thorvald smiled to himself a little, stepping
backward and setting his hands on his hips.

"Well, mother!" said Thorvald Ericson jauntily. "What do
you see for me?"

The *volva* still did not open her eyes. A shudder passed over
the old frame. The lambskin hood slipped back a little. With dis-
taste I noticed that her head on top was as bald as a hunting
eagle's. A vein beat in it like any wriggling blue snake.

"Death it is I see, Thorvald Ericson," she said at last in a
toneless voice. "Death by an arrow in a far land where you lie
out on a ness under a wooden cross. The man who kills you is
red-skinned with slanted eyes like a Lapp, and a single red feather
in his black hair."

The silence stayed unbroken in the hall. Overhead some snow
shifted on the roof. Thorvald Ericson tossed up his bone-hafted
knife and caught it by the haft.

"Is that all, mother?" he asked with a little laugh. "Then it
is little enough you tell me of what is to be. Since, in the end,
all men must die, it little matters where and when they bind the
Hel-shoes on my feet. No man gains more in life than the Norns
have granted him. For every man must die once, and no man
fights against his doom. So nothing matters. Nothing whatsoever—except that, for his manner of passing, a man's name shall
ever after be on all men's tongues."

Then, though he did not have his curved harp with him,
Thorvald Ericson raised his voice in strong skald-song:

> *"All, all shall the ring-bearer lose*
> *In the day when he feeds the eagles with his dark blood.*
> *All, all.*
> *There shall be nothing left.*
> *Not fire-of-the-flood, if he be a sea-king.*
> *Not dwarves-and-giants-drink, if he be a skald.*
> *Not white-breasted Hlin, if he be a lover.*
> *It is all one in the end.*
> *Ran's arms.*
> *A spear in Sarkland.*
> *A sword-thrust in his bed.*
> *All, all is lost, except for glory."*

I knew enough of skald-craft to be able to tell that fire-of-the-
flood stood for gold and dwarves-and-giants-drink for that mead

of Odin which was the gift of poetry. Ran, of course, was the sea
goddess who drowned mariners; and Sarkland the land of the
Saracens against whom the Varangians served the Emperor in
far-off Micklegarth.

Again no one moved in the long hall. No one even so much as
spoke when Thorvald Ericson was done. Only, after a long interval in which one could hear a dripping from those eaves where the
smoke-hole thawed the deep February snow, Thorhall Gamlason
called over to his fellow Greenlander.

"It is well sung, skald Thorvald," said Thorhall Gamlason.
"But one thing is sure in life—that Lady Hel will take us all to
her cold arms at last. It is well that, on that grim nuptial day, we
go to her embrace smiling."

The *volva* turned blind eyes in the direction of the new voice.
No one identified the speaker for her. But she knew him anyway.

"I have heard much of you, Thorhall Gamlason," she said.
"Come here that I may spae your weird."

Thorhall Gamlason the Hunter came at no one's beck and call.
He only stared insolently at Gefjon and did not stir from his
place.

"No, thank you, crone," he said. "I will dree my weird when the
time comes. Till then I do not need to know it. A man may go
smiling in the dark if he know not the outcome of his going. But
to know the future, if the future be ill—and in the end all futures
turn out ill—freezes the blood and marrow, as the sun freezes
into stone the she-troll caught out after sunrise. No. Do you
go your way and I shall go mine. I want nothing of your spaeing,
witch."

It was a home thrust that, about the she-troll. The *volva* grew
corpse-pale at Thorhall's insult.

"I will tell your weird anyway," said Gefjon, her thin voice
cracking in a rising keen of rage. "And little good will it do you
to know this fate, even as you say. For you, too, Thorhall Gamlason, will die abroad. What is more, you will die at the hands of
the youngest warrior in this present hall."

I think my heart turned over at that; and Grainne's, too, if one
could tell by the whiteness of her face. The youngest man in Olaf
Tryggveson's great hall was Brian. Thorhall Gamlason's glance
rested on him a long space before he spoke to her again.

"It may well be so, crone," he said at last, amusement in his
voice, not anger at all. 'It may well be that I am fey. Cubs grow

up some day or other; and it comes into my mind now that this one is a good cub. It may be. When first I saw the Irish lad Yule Eve, I thought my byrnie moved on my breast and that my shield sang on the wall. But till that same doom day comes—if it ever comes at all—we can be friends, eh Brian?"

"I should like to be your friend, Thorhall," said Brian from his end of the hall.

To my vast surprise, there had been actual liking in Thorhall Gamlason's snarling voice. It was, besides, the first time Thorhall had called Brian by name—and he called him Brian, too, not Haki, as Olaf's warriors had now begun to name him, even as the women now named Grainne Hekja. Truly had Thorvald Ericson been right when he told me there was something to be said for this gray wolf.

Then Thorhall Gamlason turned again to the *volva*.

"Old bitch," he said, taunting her cruelly. "Toothless old she-dog—do you whine naught but evil destinies? Death and wounds and—"

The *volva* broke in upon him, fury choking her.

"Not so, dog!" she said, answering his taunt in kind. "Not so, womanless one! Yes, womanless one who must lie every ninth night with the troll in the Svínafell! There is one lucky one here, if you wish to know. She is there! The girl in the plaid!"

Beside herself now, a hideous anger distorting her face, old Gefjon pointed a bony index finger to where Grainne sat in her plaid, a silver arrow which Mistress Gudrid had given her piercing her fair hair. The girl shrank back against the bench, terror and loathing in her blue eyes.

"You, too, girl!" said Gefjon and, though this time she spaed weal not woe, her saying sounded more like a curse than ever. "You, too, I see in that far land where the red men draw their crooked bow. But you bear life in your young flesh, not death like Thorhall Gamlason and Thorvald Ericson. You hallow that new land with life. You will have strong sons, girl, and die a Queen at last, full of years and wisdom, honored by all."

After that old Gefjon would foretell no more. So the evening did not turn out to be so successful as Thorolf Mostrarskegg had planned it would be. The Vik steward had some reputation as a brawler; and he thought now it befitted his honor to resent the deadly insult paid his mother in his presence. So he cast certain black looks at Thorhall Gamlason who only grinned back at him and said nothing. But when, next morning, Thorhall appeared in the King's hall in his best blue doublet, Thorolf Mostrarskegg, who knew only too well what that gay change of raiment betokened, thought better of his resentment and betook himself to his saeter hut in the upland fells where he stayed till spring was far advanced and men's minds had turned to other things. So the peace was not broken, after all, in Olaf Tryggveson's great hall. The King lost a steward, though, which, since Thorolf Mostrarskegg was not notably an honest man, was more his own loss than the King's. That was all the profit Thorolf got of his mother's trafficking in forbidden matters.

On my way out of the hall I came abreast of Grainne, the white kitten now wrapped in her shawl against the night air. Flakes as large as white goose feathers were falling. They tasted feather-cold on my tongue while I waited for her to go out the door first, a kind of anger quickening in my heart that the maid should have come at all after I had gone out of my way to warn her off.

"Well, Grainne," I said, and there was a niggling spite in my voice. "So you came after all. I trust it was well what you saw and heard this night."

I spoke to her in Norse, not Irish. It was not yet two whole months she had been at Olaf's court. But she was an apt scholar. Already she spoke as well as Brian for all his additional two years of practice—and better, too, since her tongue, being a woman's nimbler tongue, twisted around the unfamiliar sounds more skillfully than his.

Grainne was always quick to show resentment.

"It was well enough, Thrand," she said sharply. "Did not the witch woman say I should be a Queen?"

That angered me anew.

"Then let me be your counselor when that day comes," I said, bowing low in bitter mockery.

Old Gefjon had not read my fortune that night. But I heard it spaéd nonetheless, though I knew it not at the time.

"As you choose," Grainne said, sweeping out regally in front of me.

It has been no bad lot, that, to have been Queen Grainne's counselor for so many years. But the only thing I was sure of that far-off night in February was that, if the faith of Christ were ever to prevail fully here in the North, something would have to be done to counter such abominations as this of Gefjon's.

I think I knew even then that, while she and what she did were
debased, the instinct that drove men to consult her was a right
one. Men have to believe something always. I began to give this
thing much thought.

The difference between me and my father over my wishing to
go for a priest was mended in the only way such a quarrel can
ever be mended—by a compromise in which both sides gave in. I
agreed not to press my wish to be a monk until after I had first
made a voyage with Leif Ericson as far as Greenland and back.
On his part, my father agreed to object no further after that time
had come and gone. I still think I got much the better of that bargain inasmuch as what I yielded to him was not so very much of
a yielding after all. I wished with all my heart to make that
voyage—and beyond, too. For there was always the chance that,
afterwards, Leif would take me on his Vinland faring. At least
he seemed not at all unwilling when we talked about the matter. I
could ship as supercargo, he said, on the sailing to Greenland.
After that, depending on how satisfactory I showed myself, we
should see what we should see.

Meanwhile love grew between Brian and Grainne. Though it
hurt me to look on the two of them sometimes, it pleased me, too.
For I had made my own choice once and for all Yule Eve. Anyway, is not all love one? Is not that fire in the human heart kindled first in the heart of God? That flame burned brightest in the
Incarnation when Love first took on human flesh, and again in
the two-forked flames of Pentecost when the apostles' human
flesh was touched with the veritable Spirit of Love. However hot
it burns in its lesser way, love between man and woman is but a
goodly bed of coals after the glory of those two weal-fires. But,
if it can be a bale-fire burning to our ruin as the love of God can
never do, human love casts a lovely light all the same. And it is
easier to look on than the fire of divinity. As only an eagle's orb
may stare upon the sun at midday, so only the Son's eagle glance
may gaze upon the naked splendor of the Father and of that
Spirit Who, after the order of love, proceeds from both of them.
It is as if the eye of the flesh must look upon God through the
smoked glass of human joy; and the joy of human lovers is
human joy at its highest and dearest.

Since I was to leave his house so soon, I spent as much time as
I could in my father's shipyard at Ladehammer while Leif's ship

was building. Though I had helped him with most of the boats he had built of late, this was the first one for which he made me almost equal to himself as shipwright. We do not know what happiness is while it is still passing. I know now that those were days full of happiness. Even on Iona I was to know none more deeply satisfying. Indeed, so far as the labor was concerned, Ladehammer shipyard was not unlike Iona. I have but to close my eyes now and think back, and I can hear the thud of the wooden mallets and smell the fragrance of the chips curling under the plane.

By early spring the great ship was finished except for two things. One of these unfinished matters was the usual ceremony of giving the craft a name—it was a large *knorr,* almost as long as a long ship with twenty-five thwarts. The other was the quite unusual matter of the King's wanting to insert the relics of a saint in the crossbeams behind the stern post. They did this in Frankland and Britain now, I had prompted the King, with Sira Inge at my elbow to aid my plea. Of course, there happened to be a good supply of native saints in those lands. Saints were not nearly so plentiful in Norway with Christianity still in its infancy. But, I said, there was a way around this difficulty, too.

We had reached this stage when my father, Thorberg Skaffhogg, got wind of what was going on. He objected strongly to the idea; and Thorberg's opinion in anything affecting ships weighed heavily with the son of Tryggve. The situation was even more complicated than it seemed on the surface. For all his ardor for the cause of Christ, Leif, too, felt vaguely uneasy about the proposal; and, in the long run, Leif Ericson would have to have the final say. As for Thorhall Gamlason, whose opinion was listened to by Leif's crew, that gray wolf was in violent opposition. He even had a plan of his own, preferring, as he did, the hideous old habit of "bloodying the rollers," as it was called, by sacrificing a human life to the sea god and goddess, Njord and Ran. When he heard of this, Leif Ericson kept a sharp eye on his fellow Greenlander. He knew there would be enough bastards, and to spare, whelped this spring in Vik to admit of Thorhall's buying one of the unwanted brats and putting it to this unholy use—his own crew had helped out in the sport of breeding these despite all he could do to curb them. Leif said nothing to the King of this, however, considering it a matter between himself and Thorhall. Meanwhile, with the help of Bishop Sigurd, Sira Inge, and myself, Olaf Tryggveson made up his mind. He would get himself a relic and give it to Leif for the new ship. If the Greenland captain chose to reject this gift, well and good. But the King did not think he would so choose.

This business of the relic was mainly my idea, though I worked through Sira Inge and the two of us had taken what advantage we could of Bishop Sigurd's backing. The reason why I thought such a relic might be forthcoming was something I had overheard with my own ears when Bishop Sigurd visited Vik this past Candlemastide. I was in attendance on the Bishop when he told the son of Tryggve it had lately come to his ear that Norway, too, as well as Scotland, with its Iona, might have a holy island, the little islet of Selje where the holy maid, Synnove, fell asleep.

Selje lies some hundred miles south of Vik out in the sea north of Sognefjord. As I saw the only time I ever went there, it is a bird-haunted declivity of red rock facing a long gray mountainous coast with blue-black forests covering the sides of the great fells right up to the snow line. Brawling mountain becks fall like white lace down the long flanks of those steep mountains. Offshore, white breakers bare their teeth at skerries and headlands. Once a ship has run the dangerous gantlet of the outer roost, it is possible to rest at anchor in a broad bay cut off from the north by a towering blue wall of rock.

It was here, I heard Bishop Sigurd tell the King, that the holy Irish maid Synnove's ship moored on the north side of the creek men now call the creek of Heilagramannvik. She and the followers who remained faithful to her were fleeing from one of the fierce Viking kinglets of the outer islands—his name was not remembered, for this had happened very long ago—who would press himself in marriage on a maiden vowed to the bridal service of the heavenly King. These Irish voyagers had been driven hundreds of miles off their course by a fierce storm. It was here at Heilagramannvik, where they landed, that Synnove and her people lived out the short life left to them in the bleak caves of Selje, feeding themselves on fish and pulse. It was here they died when the roofs of the mountain caves came crashing down upon them on that dark day when Haakon Jarl and his heathen warriors landed on Selje which was within the territorial boundaries of the Jarl's possessions. Haakon, to do him justice, knew nothing of the maid except that she was a maid and trespassing on his land. It was his intention, once he saw her fairness, to ravish her. But Haakon did not get his will of Synnove. God would not suffer his holy virgin, Synnove, to be ravished and her liege men slain by pagans, choosing instead that they be dealt the cleanly death they died.

Remembering now how the King had appointed his spring Thing at Dragseid, which lies between the two fjords of Molde and Sogne near where Selje is, it came into my mind—and Sira Inge agreed—that there might well be holy relics lying on Selje, if a person were to look carefully for them. If the King required other arguments, it could be pointed out that his latest convert, Leif of Ericsfjord, still had laid upon him the penance of pilgrimage before Sira Inge would admit him to the eucharistic table. Here was a golden chance for the Greenland captain to become full Christian.

When I put all these things to Sira Inge, he jumped at the chance to propose them to the King. I waited on him when he spoke to Olaf. The time, I mind me now, was somewhere in the week before Palm Sunday.

"It might be done," said Olaf Tryggveson, musing. "If Leif is willing, that is. If we go, who among us knows what belongs to this matter of pilgrimage?"

Sira Inge stayed silent. For all the years he had been a priest, he had never gone on pilgrimage except with monks. He knew nothing of the ways of pilgrimage where kings and nobles were concerned. Then a thought came into my mind.

"Take the maid Grainne, lord King," I said. "She was born a Christian in a land where all go on pilgrimage. Besides, the dead Synnove was Irish. It would be more than fitting that one of her countrymen visit the holy isle."

"We do not know where the holy maid's body may be after all these years," said Olaf Tryggveson, still thinking.

"That is true, lord," I said to him. "But does it matter?"

"No," said the King in sudden decision. "Let the maid Grainne go with us to the Dragseid Thing. I shall take Brian also. It comes into my mind that I shall not see my Irish fosterling much longer, and I love him passing well. But the son of Eric must make his own decision. I will not force his will in any way."

As it turned out, Leif was glad to go for more than one reason. Besides this important matter of pilgrimage, it was clear that, once he weighed anchor in the spring, no one could tell when—or even if—he should see Norway and its great King again. Also, as he said to Sira Inge, he thought he would like to honor the great

King Christ, whose thane he had become, in as many ways as
possible. And, men said, there was no better way than to pay due
honor to His saints.

King Olaf set sail for Selje in the *Long Serpent* at the beginning of the last week in Lent. Leif was so weak he had to be
assisted on board. For, despite the mortal illness which had earlier
brought him to the very brink of death, the son of Eric had taken
no solid food, in this first of his long fasts as a Christian, except
for a little meatless broth and a crust of dry bread in the morning
during all the weeks appointed for fasting. Men said in later years
that there had never been such a fast in the Northland except once
only, when Kjartan Olafson fasted thus during the Lent before
the Easter when he married Hrefna Asgeirsdatter. Leif fasted so
hard and long partly because he was doing penance for his sin
toward the lady Thorgunna. But, I think, he fasted even more for
the human reason that he mourned her passing so. For the lady
Thorgunna had been passing fair and a most pleasant leman to
dally with; and he had treated her hardly while she lived.

The day we sailed forth to Selje in the *Long Serpent,* I had my
first chance to judge Leif's seamanship for myself. Just before
we were to leave Vik harbor, the wind fell. While aboard his flagship, the King left all decisions regarding seamanship to his
stafnbui who was as good a sailor as one found in the Northland.
This *stafnbui* now gave it as his opinion that there would be a
calm lasting several days. Olaf Tryggveson then gave orders to
go on shore again and try once more that evening. If the calm
still held, so that it looked as if it would be necessary to row all the
way to Selje, he would take, instead of the *Long Serpent,* the
smaller and more manageable *Crane.* Leif Ericson was a guest
aboard the King's *Long Serpent;* and his opinion had not been
asked in this matter. I saw him look up at the motionless sail.

"Do not give up yet, O King," he said to Olaf.

Then Leif called Brian to him and, in a low voice so that no
one overheard him but myself, instructed the boy to go ashore,
to climb the hill of Vik whence one could get a view of the open
sea, and to note if the wind blew outside the fjord. Leif told
Brian he would be able to decide this by the way the gulls were
flying. Brian obeyed. When he returned, he reported that there
seemed to be a kind of wind in the outer channel, even though
the fjord where the *Long Serpent* was moored remained calm as
an unflawed glass. Moreover, such as it was, the wind blew in the

direction of Selje. I marked how Leif smiled at the boy's account.

Leif's brother, Thorvald Ericson, who had come out into the fjord to see us sail, nudged my elbow.

"I think you will find, friend Thrand," he said with a little laugh, "that a Greenland captain can teach these Norse lobscouses something after all."

Leif came before the son of Tryggve.

"We may row out now, lord King," he said to Olaf. "There will be a wind outside the fjord."

The *stafnbui* who, no more than Olaf, had observed the byplay with the Irish lad was thunderstruck.

"Row out!" he said. "Are we, then, to row all the way to Selje?"

Olaf Tryggveson looked at Leif who only smiled again and said nothing.

"Row out!" said the King peremptorily.

Once outside the fjord, the *Long Serpent's* limp sail bellied into life with a cracking noise that echoed off the face of the cliff. It was as if the dragon prow had suddenly imped a drake's rustling wings.

"By Njord!" said the *stafnbui* to himself as I stood beside him on his platform. "This Greenlander knows his business!"

The wind held all the way to Selje. Thinking on this captain's title of the Lucky, it seemed to me that Leif's fabled fortune was at least as much great skill as good luck. I am afraid the *stafnbui* went so far as to put it all down to magic. But it was much better than magic. Knowledge is always better than magic.

Yes, he was a good captain, that son of Eric the Red.

The Dragseid Thing was held on Easter Monday. On Tuesday of Easter week King Olaf, with Leif Ericson, his skald Halfred Vandraedaskald, Brian, Grainne, myself, a party of his men-at-arms, a band of thralls from Dragseid, the Dragseid priest, and two Selje fishermen to guide, rowed out to Selje from the mainland in five of the Dragseid boats. It was Olaf's intention to land at Heilagramannavik where, the fishermen assured him, was the point where the Irish party had come ashore a half century before. But, as we rowed over the long swells, Leif's sharp eye marked where there had been a recent landslide in the western cliffs. Even from the boats it was possible to see, as we drew nearer, the white gleam of human bones amid the rubble of rock. So we landed

there instead in a boiling surf, and the thralls set to work at once
in the scree, grumbling a little over what they thought an uncanny
task, while the rest of our party, including the King, assembled
what bones they found in clean white cloths that had first been
blessed by the Dragseid priest.

For some reason—possibly because he thought it might frighten
the girl—the King did not wish either Brian or Grainne or myself
to assist in this part of the day's task. We wandered off together,
therefore, happy in our holiday, over the fallen rocks where the
bone sorting was now going on and up the steep slope to a cave
mouth which, half choked with fallen stone, opened out on the
wide Atlantic that creamed and broke in white surf-froth hundreds of feet below us.

It was warm in the golden sunlight of late April, though the
wind blowing off the high peaks still carried a breath of snow
with it. The fishing gulls circled, crying without cease in the salt-
fresh gulf of air and water beneath their and our dangling feet.
Huge white clouds drove over the sky, laying carpets of dark
blue and deep green here and there on the changing water floor.
A fresh water stream, running along the base of the hill up which
we had climbed, chimed under and over the far-off dull thunder
of surf. A single sheep grazed off to our left, cropping the fresh
green shoots that, in this tussock or that, thrust up their heads
through the paler winter grasses. The stream was still ice-cold
from the melting snow. But yellow had already begun to meal the
willow-bushes; and catkins were swelling on the lithe saplings.

Brian spread his sea cloak for Grainne to sit on in the cave
mouth. I watched her coin-clear profile, a little flushed now from
the spring sun, as the girl looked pensively out over the Atlantic.
Grainne was most beautiful, I thought to myself for the thousandth time, and growing more beautiful with each passing day.
It was strange to think on then; and it is stranger now when I am
an old man and she lies sleeping under the Dungarvan cairn. Life
was to teach me that most men know three women in their day:
the mother who bears them; the girl who awakens them to love
and beauty; and the wife who is mother, lover, and wife all in
one. I had known the first two of these now. Of my own will I
would never know the third. But these are the thoughts that come
later. Then I only knew that Grainne was beautiful with a beauty
that took a man by the throat and shook him till he was weak.

A sudden plump of rain drove a silver veil between where we

sat, almost as if suspended in air, and the outer sea where one
might see the sun still shining. Quickly the three of us retreated
into the cave. Inside it was not dank and musty at all, as one
might have expected. There was even what seemed to be a faint
and pleasing breath of new-dropped rose petals—though this
could hardly be, for the time of roses was some two months in
front of us. Nor was it altogether dark, either, as one might have
expected it to be from the outside. Instead, a faint radiance—
more like star light than sunlight, I still remember—gleamed midway between us and the back of the cave. Suddenly the hair
stiffened on the back of my neck. Grainne, too, must have seen
at the same instant. She gave a low cry.

A dead girl lay there in the cave—almost, it seemed, as if she
had just fallen asleep. I, who knew at once it could be no other
than the maid Synnove, dropped on my knees where I stood and
prayed. Brian, Grainne by his side, her breath coming in short,
quick gasps, ran to fetch the King.

Olaf Tryggveson came at once, toiling up through the scree
that littered the slope. I watched the mighty King look down on
the holy maid, as if he were Sigurd Dragonslayer and she the
sleeping Valkyrie, Brynhild, plunged into her enchanted sleep
from the prick of Odin's sleep-thorn. The smell of roses grew
even stronger now. This sleeping maiden had been dead for over
half a century, as man reckons time. Yet her fair body was as
incorrupt as if she had just that moment fallen to rest. We
were to see many wonders on our Vinland faring, I and the other
men of Leif's high company. But that is the moment I look back
on with most wonder. If God grants that one day I wake in
Paradise, I will know that maid's face again.

"Lift her on your shields," said Olaf Tryggveson to those of
his awe-struck retainers who had followed him into the cave. "Be
very careful of your holy freight. It is a great saint you bear—one
who shall be known through all the Northland."

The King turned then to Leif who stood now, silent, at his
shoulder.

"Well?" he asked. "What think you of this matter of the relic
now, friend Leif?"

"You spoke true, O King," said Leif. "If it be permitted, I will
have one of her tresses to be let into my crossbeams. But a tress—
no more than a single tress. I am not worthy even that much."

Standing there in the radiance and the smell of roses the King smote down his gauntlet on a rock ledge.

"By the splendor of God!" said Olaf Tryggveson, crying aloud. "I will build a church here—on this rock! The holy Synnove shall have such a shrine that all men shall come to see it, not alone from every fjord in Norway, but from all over Christendom beside. And you shall have a tress, Leif, for your ship. A very little tress, so that her great beauty be not spoiled."

As they bore the holy maid down the slope to lie in the church at Dragseid till the time her own shrine should be built, the poet-fit came over skald Halfred. He smote the strings of his curved harp and sang aloud:

> *"High and glorious the Vanir!*
> *High and glorious the Aesir*
> *Who have ruled our northern skies*
> *But rule no more!*
> *No man had speech with them or saw them*
> *In their remoteness.*
> *They were immortal, and they are dead—*
> *Dead before Ragnarok when the gods were to die!*
> *This maid was mortal; and she lives forever.*
> *Hail, holy Synnove, our saint!*
> *Hail, gold-tressed Hlín of Christ!*
> *Hail, Synnove the maid!"*

That is another day I mark with red in the private book of hours that I keep—the day I looked, for the first time, on the holy face of the maid who, though she came from Ireland, is the first of all of Norway's saints. I have prayed to her each day since then; and that is nearly seventy years agone. I do so now again, even as I write: *Holy Synnove, pray for me and for all men of northern blood that we may gaze upon your face in Paradise.*

It is time now to deal with the great matter of the naming of the ship.

Bishop Sigurd came to Vik for that naming. It was a warm day in very late spring when the boat was teased gingerly down the rollers and became water-borne for the first time. My father, who had been very angry when we first brought the relic home

from Selje, had not stayed resentful long. He drew his breath
in sharply now as the ever-new miracle of launching occurred.
On land this proud thing he had built, for all the grace it would
soon have, had been no more than a duck waddling on the squealing rollers. Lo, water-borne, she became a swan admiring her
arched neck in the sky of dark water which was the fjord mirror
on which she floated.

So taken was my father with the living grace of the new-
launched boat that he missed something which had gone on by
the water's edge in the very minute of the launching. But I did
not, for I had been waiting for it. Even as the boat had teetered
at the top of the runway, Thorhall Gamlason, in his blue doublet,
had stepped swiftly out from some trees where he had been lurk-
ing and made to cast a girl child on the greased rollers before
the ship. Leif Ericson, who must have half expected some such
move on his henchman's part, caught up the infant just as the
heavy craft came rocking down the wooden run. It was a near
thing. Leif himself might have been mortally hurt. As it was,
he stood there panting, sweat running down his face and into
his eyes. The rescued babe was like a little red frog in his arms.
Naked, it stared up at him and cried.

"What difference would it have made?" asked Thorhall sullenly, for once abashed by his leader's vehemence and by the fact
he might have been responsible for Leif's death. "It is only one
of Tora's dunghill brats, after all. Is not Ran more important
than a stinking bastard no one wants?"

Tora was a deaf and dumb girl who lived near the midden
and suffered terribly from the falling sickness. Once a year she
had a new child; and no one could name its father, Tora least
of all. Leif looked at this latest of her nameless children. It was
soiled with its own dung; and stank. Nevertheless, so gentle were
his cradling hands, he might have been thinking on his own and
Thorgunna's son who would by now be no older than this pitiful
little girl child. It was as if Leif's heart went out in a rush toward
the helpless thing. For the first time, I think, he had some real
inkling of what the following of Christ might mean for him and
for the world of other men.

He turned to Thorhall Gamlason, the child still cradled in his
arms.

"Thorhall," he said in passionate utterance. "I tell you this stinking child of Tora's is more precious to me—and to you, too, if you only knew it—than Ran and Njord and Odin and all the rest of the Aesir!"

Thorhall Gamlason's jaw dropped in surprise. But he said nothing in answer.

"I mean to take this child back to Ericsfjord with me," said Leif, not letting go of Tora's babe, "and raise it with my own children."

Still Thorhall Gamlason said nothing. Perhaps the thought came to him that Leif was this bantling's father. If so, he must have remembered what Leif was and what Tora, and so put aside the idea at once. He only looked on sourly while Leif handed the babe over to Mistress Gudrid that one of her women, who had a child at nurse, might foster it for the time.

But Thorhall the Hunter had not quite shot his bolt. Later that afternoon Bishop Sigurd would be rowed out to sprinkle the ship with holy water preliminary to the ceremony of its naming. For the moment it was sufficient that the King's Chaplain give a lesser blessing so that the new craft might not go unhallowed for a single instant. Just as Sira Inge was dipping his aspergillum into the golden cup of holy water I held up to him, Thorhall Gamlason, who had stood by glowering ever since his first rebuff from Leif, knocked aside the chaplain's hand and spat into the golden vessel.

Now you must remember that the priest, too, was a Northman. Ash-gray with fury, Sira Inge smote Thorhall heavily over the ear with the gold-encrusted mace he made out of the aspergill. The heavy but hollow truncheon shattered at the blow. Thorhall reeled, but did not fall. He only grinned and drew the long knife that stood ever at his girdle. Then Leif rushed between the two quarreling men, his own sword out of its sheath.

"Listen to me, Thorhall Gamlason," he said, facing the Greenlander. "For the last time have I protected you from the King's wrath. Put up your knife this instant, or you shall answer to the son of Tryggve for this sacrilege."

The cold fire slowly died out in Thorhall's eyes. Other men he would fight, and with a will; but not his captain, Leif. And it was that he loved Leif, not feared him. There was no one Thorhall Gamlason feared; and very few he loved. With a shrug and a twitch of his face he slipped back the knife, and stepped aside.

The loading of cargo went on all forenoon, and into the early afternoon as well. Thorfinn Karlsefni was to sail at the same time, in his own ship, Grainne with him to attend on Mistress Gudrid. Grainne was a free maiden now, by the law of the Northland, since Olaf Tryggveson had held her freedom-ale for her nine days before this, some weeks after the *Long Serpent* had sailed back from Selje. Brian's new sea chest, packed with his few possessions, was carried aboard Leif's ship with the sea chests of the other men. The sea chest I bore on board was not a new one. My father had used it before me in the days when he was not yet a shipwright but sailed on a trading *knorr* as far as Micklegarth. It was the more precious to me for that reason.

The corn and meal sacks were stowed well out of the way of the water so that damp and mildew might not work on them. The malt barrel was similarly protected—the Greenlanders raised their own malt, to be sure, but it was not esteemed so highly as the Norwegian variety. Costly gifts of horn and silver and crystal from the King were first rolled in cloth before being laid away in chests.

Leif had bought a brood mare from a horse coper in Vik; and a stallion which he wished to enter in the horse-fighting contests old Eric held once a year at Ericsfjord. These had to be blindfolded before they would allow themselves to be led on board to the stalls contrived for them with carefully piled bales of hay. The milch cow, however, which he had also bought made no objection. When these animals were safely on board, Bran, the hound, picked his way over the gangplank, tongue lolling, tail wagging, and lay atop the bales, watching the horses. Two huge millstones of hard cheese and three tubs of whey were brought aboard at last; as was a great pat of salted butter, kept cool by being surrounded with pannikins of icy water. The *knorr* Leif had sailed to Norway and which he had bought back in Greenland from Bjarni Herjulfson was loaded at the same time. A skeleton crew would sail this back to Ericsfjord where Leif, whose business ventures were growing apace, would find good use for it.

That afternoon the King, Bishop Sigurd, Thorberg Skaffhogg, and Leif were rowed out to where the new vessel rode at anchor on the choppy waves. Sira Inge and I followed in another dinghy. Bishop Sigurd, white beard frothing over embroidered vestments, wore his best miter and carried the jewelled crozier which the King of Saxony had given him when he first sent Thangbrand Priest to Iceland, Thangbrand being of the Saxon King's household. Olaf Tryggveson had on his gold crown of rule and a soft-rubbed silver byrnie, Leif the scarlet cloak the King had given him at his last Yule feast. Olaf's warships were all drawn up in the bay; and from their decks the people of the court looked on. Thorfinn Karlsefni's men lined his decks. Whoever could had squeezed onto the deck of Bjarni Herjulfson's *knorr*.

The time had come now for Leif to redeem his Yuletide promise and allow King Olaf to name this new ship. The relic had been let into the crossbeams, the Bishop looking on, only yesterday. It came into the King's mind now that the name he gave this craft should be a holy name.

"Call it the *Kristsuden*," he said to Leif, *suden* being our Norse word for ship. "Call it the *Kristsuden* after the Saviour Who gave His precious blood for our redemption. Or else the *Krossuden* in honor of the Saviour's Cross and of your own great Lenten fast. Or the *Synnovesuden* in honor of the holy maid whose tress now rests in your crossbeams."

"Why not *Mariasuden?*" I asked in a rush of words, though it did not become me to speak out so boldly in the King's and the Bishop's presence. "Why not the *Ship of Mary* after the name of our blessed Saviour's Mother?"

Bishop Sigurd nodded like one of the toys I was one day to see in the fair at Novgorod.

"It is a goodly thought, this one of Thrand's," he said in his gentle fashion. "It is a wonder no one of us thought of it before."

"I agree!" said the son of Tryggve enthusiastically. "Mary is the best of all earth's maidens. Let it be the *Mariasuden!*"

"I have no objection," said Leif.

"It is out of my hands," said Thorberg Skaffhogg, half sullenly. "But I go on record here before you all that I do not approve in any way. How can a name like the *Mariasuden* fit a ship that sails with a crimson dragon on its prow?"

The Bishop, who was a forbearing and a diplomatic man, broke the deadlock then.

"Priest Inge Skakkeson sails to Greenland with you in Thorfinn Karlsefni's ship," he said to Leif who had thought it better that Sira Inge take passage on a ship where Thorhall Gamlason would not have to be his shipmate. "Sira Inge is a worker in wood—

none better than he in all the Northland. He has made Marys
for me in wood for my cathedral church. Let him carve a Mary
aboard. Meanwhile the dragon head will do. The drake will be-
have itself, I think—is not Our Lady the lord of the dragon?"

After that Bishop Sigurd, Sira Inge and myself bobbing in
his wake, had himself rowed all round the long ship, blessing as
he went, and sprinkling the boat with holy water in the name
of the Father and of the Son and of the Holy Ghost. When the
Bishop had finished, Olaf Tryggveson stood up under the prow
and, with his sword, lightly touched it where the figurehead would
later be. The dragon was there now so that once again, as ever
in my memory now, the son of Tryggve seemed to me like the
hero Sigurd Dragonslayer.

"Thanks be to God," said the King, intoning solemnly, "and
to His Mother, the blessed Virgin Mary, and to the holy Synnove,
too, that this ship has now come happily upon the water without
let or hindrance, and without loss of life. Now do I give this
great ship over to the protection of the Virgin, naming it, by the
name of the Virgin, the *Mariasuden*, trusting that she, who is
God's own dear Mother, will keep watch and ward over it at all
times and seasons, prospering all its enterprises in the new land
to which it is bound till one day, in the fullness of time, when
all is accomplished, she brings it safe and sound again to Ericsfjord. In gratitude I give to Bishop Sigurd, who is the Virgin's
servitor here in Norway, a set of new vestments for his chapel;
and another set to the priest of Dragseid against the day when
the Synnove chapel shall be finished on Selje."

Next the King turned to Leif, handing him the sword with
which he had named the *Mariasuden*, the sword which, in ancient
times, the men of old had named Hrotti.

"This sword, friend Leif," he said affectionately, "shall be the
parting gift from me to you. For it comes into my mind now
that I am not likely to see you again in life. Let the weapon be
your comrade always. I do not think blade or point will ever pierce
your byrnie while this is by your side or in your hand. I ask
but one thing in return: that you keep faith with Christ Who
is your liege lord above as I am your liege lord here below. Do
you not only keep faith with Him, as becomes a faithful vassal,
but keep the faith for Him in Greenland and in the new land."

"I will, O King," said Leif. "For I believe Him of whom
you speak, and in Whose mighty Name I was baptized, to be

true God and King of heaven. If I do not see you more in this
world, lord King, farewell. But if the two of us are fated to live
longer, and if it is necessary that you send round the war arrow
to your lieges, in time of need send it to Ericsfjord and I and
the *Mariasuden,* your gracious gift, will be at your side with an
hundred men so soon as time and tide allow."

After the naming was accomplished, Leif had his crewmen
come aboard, except for myself and for the boy, Brian. I was to
attend Sira Inge with the holy vessels in the morning. Brian was
to stay on shore that night, by the King's express wish, that he
might be able to make his farewells to the King and the King's
household with whom he had now lived two years and more in
love and friendship. Leif had his rowers poise their oars so that
the King might see what a brave show the dripping blades made
flashing in the sun. Then the King, as was his fashion when he
was merry, ran on the oars and, standing on the ship's rail, cast
two heavy spears at once and did the dagger play for which he
was famous, wherein one sharp point was always in the air and
the King, without scathe, took the falling one by the handle. After
that they drank together for the last time from the one drinking
horn, Olaf Tryggveson and Leif, and embraced one another as
if they were brothers.

So went that valiant King, Olaf the great son of Tryggve, out
of the Leif saga; and, soon, out of the world altogether. He was
already fey, though he did not know it, on that day of the naming of the *Mariasuden.* For he died that autumn in his *Long
Serpent,* treacherously beset by the Danish and Swedish kings
and by the sons of Haakon Jarl who had an old score to settle
with Olaf Tryggveson. There was no time to send round the
war arrow. The ambush was well laid outside Svolder as the
King rowed home from crusade in Vendland. When Leif heard
this news in Greenland, he had many Masses said for the soul
of Olaf Tryggveson. Some men said, it was true, that the King
had not died at all but had swum in his armor to Vendland,
whence he would one day come again to Norway his kingdom.
But Leif did not believe this, though he would have liked to believe it. Nor do I, Thrand Thorbergson, believe it, either. These
things are always said when great kings die; but never yet has
one come again, not even great Arthur of the Britons who, men
fable, did not die but sleeps with the elves in Avalon. Nor, for
his part, did Thorhall Gamlason believe it. For there was not

much Thorhall Gamlason believed which he could not first see with his own gray wolf's eyes. But Thorhall mourned the King, if possible, even more than Leif did. For it seemed a pity to Thorhall Gamlason that a king so great as Olaf, the son of Tryggve, should have chosen Christ's heaven rather than the Valhalla of his fathers and of the radiant Aesir. So feel not I. But I know, at least, why Thorhall Gamlason felt the way he did. And I respect him for it. In his way—an old way that was passing —he kept faith with the gods.

On shore that afternoon and evening I went about with Brian while the Irish lad made his last farewells to the King and his other friends. He lingered longest of all over his farewell to the maid, Grainne, whom he was to see again so shortly in Ericsfjord, if all went well with Leif's ship and with Thorfinn's. But, whether the separation be long or short, time is tyrant over lovers. I thought Brian did well to snatch what victory he could from the enemy's devouring jaws.

The boy and girl sat together on the dock as long as the light lasted, watching the two dragon craft, Leif's and Thorfinn's, riding at anchor in the sunset which turned them both blood-red as the rampant serpents at their prows. As the dusk drew on, a little wind sprang up. It stirred Grainne's fair hair. It laid soft fingers on my mouth, enjoining silence in the presence of the mystery. It laid other more masterful commands on Brian's eager mouth. For suddenly, almost without realizing it, as if I were not even there, he had Grainne in his arms and was raining down kisses on her lips. The English bell spoke in the church of Vik. Then the wings of the sea birds, wheeling home, were all around us in the twilight; and I could hear nothing but the beating of my own racing heart.

Walking home to the King's great hall for the last time, the two of them plighted their troth, asking me to be their witness so that no one could later say they were not handfasted before leaving Norway. The red roses, climbing on the King's wall, looked a velvet black in the moonlight. But the white were as shining silver as if an archangel had just that minute stooped above their unfolding petals. The clean fragrance of the flowers was so strong in the summer night that ever afterwards, whenever I thought upon the time of that troth-plighting, I could smell again the smell of roses in the murmuring dark.

Early in the morning we were rowed out to the silent *Maria-suden* which rose and fell on the long dawn swells of the fjord. The awning was stretched over the sleeping men in their skin bags—over all but Thorhall Gamlason, that is, who lay out on the prow under the paling stars. He raised himself on one elbow now, grinning his twisted grin, watching Brian and me clamber aboard. Then the *stafnbui* roused the yawning sleepers who rolled up their sleeping skins and made everything shipshape while the breakfast was being made ready in a great iron cauldron near the mast. Two hornblowers, with long horns of rolled birchbark, then blew their *lurs* in signal that the time had come to cast off. A chill ran up and down my spine this first time I heard the *lurs* at sea. From that day to this, whether there are horns blown or not, dawnlight has sounded in my ears as if the gods were winding great *lurs* from Asgard.

The water made a little lapping sound around the dragon prow as Leif's men rowed out of the fjord—we would not hoist the red-striped sail before reaching open sea. Rapidly Vik fell astern. The King's great buildings dwindled to little toys. The shores grew narrower and narrower at the foot of the towering hills. The forest green of the fell slopes looked black as the distance increased. The higher peaks seemed grayer minute by minute, the snow fields whiter and whiter, the sky bluer and bluer into which the mountains reached.

As the men rowed, they raised their rowing chant to Ran and to the many drowned who sat now on her briny benches. Leif, lost in thought in the prow, made no objection. Thorvald Ericson led us, while we sang, with Thorhall Gamlason, fingering his silver Thor the while, in the van of the leather-lunged singers.

Thorvald Ericson gestured ironically to me from the prow as we swung into the song for a fourth and last time. Spray broke tangy in our faces. The *Mariasuden* shot like an arrow out of Vik fjord into the open sea. We were past the Trolls' Skerry now where, in his first days as King, Olaf Tryggveson had drowned Eyvind Kellda and his fellow warlocks. It was time to raise the sail.

"Raise the sail!" said Leif, making a speaking-trumpet of his hands.

The sail bellied out. The *Mariasuden* shook herself like a live thing, and fled before the following wind.

So come we to an end of that part of our faring which I call the Naming of the Ship. Thinking on the *Mariasuden* now and the Maiden Mother for whom she was named, it comes into my mind, after all these years, that, when I said I knew but two of the three women who waken men to life, I was wrong. For I knew another Lady early, and she a Queen. There is an old proverb in our tongue that unlucky is the lover of a Queen. And so truly it fell out with old King Brian, the *Ard Rí,* when he loved Gormflaith, Sigtrygg's mother. But it is not always so; and it fell out otherwise with me.

There is one Queen never plays her lovers false; and, saving her virgin honor, she has many lovers, that same Queen of whom I write here in the twilight of my years. She is fair as the moon, bright as the sun, terrible as an army set in battle array. The sun is her garment, the moon no more than her tirewoman, there are twelve stars in the crown on her head. She is the loveliest, lightsomest, winsomest Maid ever to play before the All Father in the courts of heaven. Yet her delight is to be with the children of men.

Centuries ago the Hebrew skald said it: *Many waters cannot quench Love. Neither can the floods drown it. If a man should give all the substance of his house for Love, he shall despise it as nothing.* It is true. I gave all the substance of my house for the love of that Lady's Son; and not once have I regretted it. There are many kinds of love, I know today. But all Love is one.

CHAPTER FOUR

NIGHT AT THORGUNNA'S CAIRN

AT FIRST WE OF THE *Mariasuden* DID NOT KNOW WHAT WAS
Leif's will in the matter of the lady Thorgunna's island, though
it was clear enough from the start that his homeward voyage
was somewhat roundabout. He said he wished to put in at the
Hebrides to see his little son by the lady Thorgunna whom Thorfinn's ship, with the necessary wet nurse, was due to pick up later
and carry to Greenland, after a stop at Thorfinn's place in Iceland. He said he wished, also, to cast a stone on Thorgunna's
cairn, which was a reasonable enough desire. But I was anxious,
nonetheless, because I remembered how, during his fever, Leif's
mind had dwelt on her command that he keep one last trysting
with her.

Leif had other arguments, too, which carried great weight with
Thorvald Ericson when his brother called him into counsel, with
myself to act as secretary—it was part of my work aboard the
Mariasuden to keep the log and the accounts inasmuch as I was
the only man of the crew who was also a clerk. Thorgunna, Leif
pointed out while I wrote his saying down, had been a heathen.
But, though Sira Inge thought that mattered, he did not think
God would refuse her His grace. She had had no chance, as he
had had, to hear of the merits of Christ. So Masses for the
repose of the dead lady's soul could not go amiss. If Sira Inge
would not do it, there were other priests in the world than he.
It was true there was as yet no priest in Thorgunna's island.
But there was one in Orkney, where he meant to leave the princely
sum of three marks in gold to pay for the Mass offering. First,
though, it would ease his mind if he might stop and pray himself
at Thorgunna's cairn. After thinking on this a little while, Thorvald Ericson agreed.

We made our Hebridean landfall three days after raising the
Irish coast. Leif moored the *Mariasuden* in the harbor at dawn

and went ashore with only me to accompany him. It was a very dangerous thing to do, since he had no way of telling how the lady Thorgunna's father, Orm Aslakson, would receive him. But Leif would involve no man of his crew in a danger of his own making. He meant to acknowledge the child, though. So that should make some difference. I knew without asking why he wanted me to come—but he asked me as a favor, he did not command me. I was as near as he could come then to a priest. For what Leif Ericson had that night to do he needed a clerk— one who knew how to pray, at least, however much or however little he chose to pray of his own will. For in those days, I mind me now, I yet prayed but little.

It was the night before this Leif had told me what he wished of me, asking me, at the same time, to say nothing of it to the others.

"You do not have to come unless you wish to," he said. "This trysting is my business, and no one else's. But, if you do come, I will take it as a great kindness. What do you say, Thrand Thorbergson?"

I meant to go as a last resort. But I thought it my duty to him to counter with a question first.

"You are bent on this trysting, captain?" I asked him. "I think it is unwise, perilous to mind, soul, and even, it may be, body."

"I am bent on it, Thrand," Leif said fiercely. "Not even pale Hel herself could keep me back!"

"I will go then," I said. But my heart misgave me even as I spoke.

Leif clasped my hand.

"I shall not soon forget this, Thrand," he said.

He looked strangely at my hand then.

"The lady Thorgunna had lovely hands, Thrand," he said, letting my hand go at last. "Tell me—how long before a hand turns to earth in the earth?"

"Do not let your mind dwell on such things, captain," I said to him. "It is not well for you."

I do not think he slept very much that night which was the night before we dropped our anchor stone in the Hebrides. I know I did not.

The next day went better than I feared it might. The old chieftain was glad to receive the man who, if things had turned out otherwise, would have been his son-in-law. He would have feasted Leif and all his company except that Leif would take nothing more than an oaten bannock and a sup of goat's milk. The lady Thorgunna's babe had thriven well under the care of her foster mother. There was a touch of Leif, I thought, about the child's mouth and eyes. The rest must have been Thorgunna's, though I had never seen her to tell for sure. The chieftain made no difficulty whatsoever about Leif's taking the bantling with him to Greenland in Thorfinn Karlsefni's boat. He was, if anything, more relieved than not. But there was another problem facing us, one Leif Ericson had not foreseen.

Leif had come habited as for a wedding in Olaf Tryggveson's Yuletide gift-suit and cloak of scarlet cloth. When it drew on toward evening, he told Orm Aslakson, Thorgunna's father, he meant to tryst alone that night out on Thorgunna's Ness as the promontory where the cairn was had now come to be known.

"I will go with you," said Orm Aslakson, stammering a little as he spoke, and I noted he had gone white around his lips. "We will take along ten men-at-arms."

Leif stared at him. The hair rose a little on my head.

"Ten men-at-arms!" he said. "Why?"

It came to me then in a thrill of horror that Orm Aslakson feared his dead daughter.

"Because," said the old chieftain, "men say that the lady Thorgunna walks of nights."

Leif Ericson sat very stiff and straight and white now on Orm's ale-bench.

"If you will permit, lord Orm," he said with the formality that belongs to the council hall, "I mean to keep this tryst alone."

"As you choose," said the old chieftain with a despairing gesture. "I think it most rash. But as you choose."

That evening, on our walk up the windy ridge to the promontory where the lady Thorgunna lay buried, Leif Ericson spoke his mind aloud. He told me he was not altogether convinced this story of Orm Aslakson's was true, though he believed that such things could happen. For he had talked with Olaf Hoskuldson, the father of his great Iceland friend, Kjartan Olafson, just after Olaf had wrestled the dead Hrapp at Hjardarholt and, in the morning, found his spear in that grim walker's barrow. But if it were really so that Thorgunna walked—a thing he would have to test for himself—Leif said he thought he knew the reason why she did so. He added that he also thought he knew how to deal with her disturbed spirit so that it would have rest again. One thing only consoled me as we talked. He spoke with love for the lady Thorgunna. I thought that, if love wrestled with hate, love would win. But I was not at all sure that it was hate moved the lady Thorgunna, either. Men and women have walked for love as well as hate. Nevertheless, the blood ran cold in my veins as I thought on these things. It is almost seventy years since that night. Yet I can still shiver when I think upon it.

I did not like the look of things about the cairn when we got there. There was a *Trollaskeid,* a fairy ring, near it—it seemed to me that Orm Aslakson had showed scant prudence in putting his daughter's grave so close to a place like that. Something would have to be done about that, I said. Leif agreed. He thought that maybe, for another mark of silver, the Orkney priest would also take ship for the Hebrides and sprinkle holy water over the ring. Orm Aslakson was still a pagan; but he was not hostile to priests. Meanwhile, Leif said, there was only one thing to be done. He must spend the hours of darkness on this ridge, waiting to see if Thorgunna would appear. If she did, he would tryst with her this one last time.

Though it was almost summer now, it was cold up there on the ness. I shivered when the sun dropped into the ocean. Leif shivered, too, and not from cold alone, though the air had grown chill enough at that. The two of us were weaponless, for Leif scorned to bear steel to a trysting with a woman, dead or alive. I had never been much for violence. Still it seemed to me, waiting, that a man felt naked without his sword.

"Shall I light a fire, Leif?" I asked him. "It would be easy enough. There is brush about here."

"No," he said tonelessly. "Sleepers in the earth do not care for fire."

That was true enough, I thought, and all the more reason why we should have one. But I did not say this aloud.

"Just a candle then," I said, almost pleading with him. "A holy candle blessed by Sira Inge last Holy Saturday. I have it here under my cloak."

Leif Ericson shivered again.

"Not yet," he said, his eyes afraid for the first time. "Later, perhaps. Yes, we shall need a holy candle later."

"How much later?" I asked him, my teeth beginning to chatter.

"When I walk out with the lady Thorgunna," he said, "do you stay here and light the candle and—if you are able—pray till my return."

We sat down then to wait till the moon rose, our backs against a rock—but not the rock of the cairn. Both of us wanted that cairn in front of us. The tide was beginning to flow back now. I could hear the brimming water lip the stone beneath our feet.

After we had sat together thus side by side for some time without speaking, the moon rose like some great silver buckler over the dead woman's cairn. Leif got to his feet then, and walked to the foot of the mound.

"Thorgunna!" he called in a great voice. "It is I, Leif. I come to tryst with you again even as you wished. I come at last to keep faith with you and with our son!"

The cry echoed off the cairn and was caught up twice more by the fjord walls in the bay below. It was as if great bodiless voices surrounded us up there, alone in the night, on Thorgunna's Ness.

Then there was silence again till Leif broke it with a second great cry:

"Thorgunna!"

And again, almost despairingly:

"Thorgunna mine!"

After that an odd thing happened. The moon went under a cloud so that I could not tell for sure whether or not a woman came round the corner of the cairn on the side farthest from the two of us. But it seemed to me one did. Certainly the Greenland captain acted as if one had. He moved swiftly away from my side till he was lost to sight in the night; and it sounded as if he were talking to someone as he went though, once again, I would not swear that, beyond a whispered murmur, there was any reply. At any rate, Leif was gone from the cairn a good long time.

"Leif!" I called after him.

There was no answer. Hand trembling, I struck a light with my flint and lit the holy candle. It made but a small gleam in that great darkness till the moon came out again and silvered the cairn and the running tide-race. Never, before or since, have I been so afraid. I was almost too afraid to be able to pray. I found myself thinking on the lady Thorgunna—if, indeed, it had been she who came to Leif's great cry. I was afraid of her;

afraid of her anger against Leif; afraid of her anger against all men. A great sorrow filled my heart, too; and a greater emptiness. It was as if I walked alone through desolation.

Leif Ericson came back to the cairn at dawn, even as the cocks started crowing in the steadings below the ness. His face was white and drawn. But his face was also peaceful, as it had not been when he walked away into the night. He said nothing; and I asked him nothing. In utter silence the two of us walked back between the silent houses that belonged to Orm's manor and to a spot on the beach just opposite the point where the *Mariasuden* rode at anchor in the growing light. Thorvald was waiting with a dinghy, to row us out to the long ship. He, too, spoke no word. But he threw one arm across his brother's shoulders as Leif Ericson clambered heavily over the gunwale.

The *lurs* were sounding on the deck of the *Mariasuden* even as we came aboard. From where I stood with Thorvald beside the mast I could see our captain in the stern looking out over the foaming wake our swift keel traced behind us. When his ship sailed stately past Thorgunna's Ness for the last time, it was as if the Greenland captain would call aloud to someone watching from that quiet promontory. He did not, however. Only his hand shot up, palm outward, in a gesture of farewell. Even as he did so, he caught sight of me watching him, and beckoned to me in friendly fashion, though I was troubled that he should have reason to think I kept any manner of watch over him.

"Thank you, Thrand Thorbergson," he said, speaking very low so that no one else might hear. "It is well with me now, and I think it is also well with her at last. I do not think the lady Thorgunna will walk again."

Our next stop was at the Orkneys where Leif left gold for Masses to be said for the lady Thorgunna's soul. It was there he also went to the sacrament for the first time. I think he was much quieter of heart after he had once taken the Eucharist.

CHAPTER FIVE

AT SEA

AFTER THAT NIGHT ON THORGUNNA'S NESS THE VOYAGE BACK
to Iceland was pretty much without incident. It had been a two
days' sail to the Orkneys. Then, with a stiff west wind blowing
against us, it was another five days to the Faroes. Three days
out from the Faroes, the south wind shifted round again, so the
men had to sit down to the oars. There were four more days
of this sort of heavy work before the wind broke again. After
two more days, we sighted Iceland which I had never seen before, nor Brian, but the rest of the crew more times than they
could count. The sea birds had begun to appear in force once
more. They were sea gulls mostly, and larger, on the whole, than
the gannets and fulmars we had seen off the island the Scots
call St. Kilda's. It seemed to me—and, when I asked him, Leif
Ericson said it was most true—that things grew bigger and
stronger the farther west we sailed.

The *Mariasuden* had favorable winds approaching this great
Atlantic island and made her landfall on the south, sailing westward by Reykjaness, and so round Snaefellsness and into Breida-
fjord. We rowed, then, a short way up the Laxá River to Budardal where Leif had appointed to meet his brother-in-law, Thorfinn
Karlsefni.

Thorfinn Karlsefni, delayed by the same contrary wind pattern that held up the *Mariasuden*—though Thorfinn had not
stopped in the Hebrides—arrived two days later. Sira Inge had
done his work well. The new figurehead—a tranquil Virgin, her
hood painted a bright blue—was ready when Thorfinn landed at
Budardal. When the time came to raise the new image on our
prow, Leif gave his crimson dragon as another present to his
friend, Kjartan Olafson, the Iceland chieftain, who said he would
place it on his best *dreki*.

A great crowd gathered to watch the setting up of the *Mariasuden's* new figurehead. When it was done, and our Blessed Lady

firmly fixed in place, people showed themselves, as might have been expected, of two minds as to that image. Barring Olaf Tryggveson's *Bison,* which had once touched at Breidarfjord with a present of Norwegian timber for Kjartan, they had never seen anything but a dragon or a *grima* fronting a prow. On the whole, though, they liked it. An old carline named Thurid, who had some small reputation as a spae-wife, went so far as to say it should prove lucky.

Grainne had a delicate powdering of freckles across her nose from the weeks of sun glare on the water. She blushed so when Brian admired the Virgin image that I took a second look at the wooden carving. Then I understood the reason for the girl's pretty embarrassment. Inge Priest had used her for a model. I could tell it pleased Brian very much when he finally realized what had been done. Not only had a priest-artist thought his Grainne worthy to sit for the Mother of God. Now he could look at the girl's fair face fronting the boat he sailed in every day during the long weeks and months when they would have to be apart.

Leif did not think it wise to tarry overlong in Budardal where a blood-feud had broken out between Kjartan Olafson and the Osvifsons. So Brian and Grainne were parted a second time since Thorfinn Karlsefni stayed behind to take care of the business he had on hand in the island.

The voyage from Iceland to Greenland, though far longer than any voyage I had yet made, was not so very long at that, as Leif's voyages went. For Leif had, more than once, sailed his ship straight from Norway back to Greenland without a single stop on the way. It was quite long enough, however, for Brian to get to know the ropes on board ship. He had three good teachers: Leif himself, Thorhall Gamlason, and Thorvald Ericson. Sometimes the *stafnbui,* too, whose name was Steinn the Far-Traveler, son of Thorir Autumn-Mist, helped the other three in the task of instruction.

For a start, the *stafnbui* showed Brian what he himself knew best: that was, how to serve as a good *stafnbui*. A *stafnbui* is the leader of the forecastle. In the case of our *Mariasuden,* he was the captain, really, under Leif. His was the most exposed position on the dragon ship if it came on to storm. He was also, on most ships, the leader in case of battle. But such was never the case on any ship Leif sailed in. There the *stafnbui* was captain only so long as fair weather held. If wind or arrow threatened, Leif Ericson always insisted on taking the place of greatest danger—Thorvald Ericson or Thorhall the Hunter would have preferred to say the place of greatest honor. But Leif Ericson did not think in terms of honor; only in terms of duty and of efficiency. And these are not at all the same thing, although, in the end, they may turn out to have the same results.

Leif's *stafnbui,* Steinn, happened to be famous for his skill in shaping wood—not as Sira Inge shaped it, to be sure. Steinn shaped it for practical use, not for beauty. Among other things, he showed Brian how to shape and splice a broken sail yard, if the need should ever arise.

Leif taught Brian the ways of navigation. How to estimate latitude by the shadow of the ship's side on the thwarts. How, at night, to steer by the moon; and by the polestar, too, although, when far north, the polestar could not be seen during the long summer daylight. The presence of birds, Leif explained, always meant the shore was near. One could usually tell how close the land was by the time of the birds' assembly. If, for example, petrels and boobies held their screaming meeting early in the morning and returned late, it meant that the ship was still quite far from land. If, on the other hand, these sea birds held their noisy gathering late and returned early, it meant that land was near. For, in this latter case, the birds must have slept on land instead of on the sea.

With a single square sail, such as our long ships carried, the *Mariasuden* could not sail close to the wind. She could make headway only with a following or with a quartering wind. If conditions were other than these, she either had to idle, waiting for the wind to shift into the right quarter again, or else take to the oars. Except under conditions of violent storm, which were always unpredictable, the best speed the *Mariasuden* could achieve —and she was a swift craft—was a little over six miles an hour; or, as mariners preferred to say, about six and a quarter knots. Voyaging along the coast, a full day's sail was reckoned at seventy-five miles for twelve hours. Out at sea, of course, these figures could be doubled. So the *Mariasuden* could travel regularly, with a little luck, one hundred and fifty miles a day. For Brian's benefit, Leif translated these sea mile values into land miles. It was quite easy to do. One had only to multiply by four, since one Norse sea mile was roughly equal to four Irish land miles.

Leif next pointed out to Brian that the *Mariasuden's* mast was, give and take an inch or so each way, in the neighborhood of some thirty-five feet high. By taking a sight from a point near mast-top, one could scan the horizon for seven miles around. If land loomed in the distance, it would add another seven miles to the lookout's span. So, except in a night storm, there was not much risk of a careful pilot's foundering on an unknown shore. Reefs, of course, were another matter. But, since reefs were always close to shore, the same rules of caution operated in their regard.

One of the most important things of all to learn was how to moor the ship from a rock skerry. While the *Mariasuden* was still riding at anchor in the River Laxá at Budardal, Leif had taken a hammer and chisel and showed Brian how to drive a five-inch hole in the face of a sloping rock, set in a mooring peg, and then loop the hawser over the top of the rock some two feet from the hole in order to take up some of the direct strain on the mooring peg. Anchors, too, were used whenever expedient. But, under certain conditions, anchors had an unlucky habit of making a ship swing, foul its line, and drag. The best way of dealing with this problem was to balance a prow anchor off midstream by a stern hawser attached to a mooring peg. That way there was double security.

In the long summer evenings, as the *Mariasuden* scudded before the wind for Greenland, the men told stories near the mast; and listened to Thorvald sing the ancient songs. Much to my surprise, I found that Brian could match the best of them with the stories he remembered from winter nights around the Munster peat fires of his childhood. I do not know now why I should have been surprised. For the Irish have always been great spinners of the web of story.

Leif's crew was mad for stories about magic islands lying far in the West. Brian had no fewer than five of these still bright in memory. There was a hero in each of them, driven on his quest by some overpowering desire. Maelduin sailed out to find his father's murderers. Bran sought a beautiful woman. MacRiala and his comrades hoisted sail to save certain condemned criminals who were their friends. The sons of Conall undertook their voyage for the sake of doing penance for sin. St. Brendan the Navigator—I liked his tale best of all because it was most like the tale I hoped to write on the parchment of my own life— sailed into the unknown West for no other reason than for the great glory of God. The name of the ultimate land to which these voyagers sailed was I Breasail. It ever fled before the following ships. But, if one could only land and throw a single burning coal upon it, then would it become fixed in the sea forever, and the great quest would be over.

"I would never do that," said Thorhall Gamlason unexpectedly after Brian had finished this fourth of his island tales. "First would I quench every coal in the sea so that the island would still flee before me forever and ever."

Though I had noted Thorhall Gamlason before this listening to Brian's tales of islands with the most rapt attention, he had not spoken out till now. It surprised me all over again that he spoke out with such utter vehemence.

"Why ever not?" I asked him.

"Because," said Thorhall Gamlason simply, "it is good for man to have some one thing before him that is not easily attained. Else wherefore live?"

"I do not understand that," said Steinn, the *stafnbui,* scratching his bald head.

Hooding his strange eyes the while, Thorhall gave Steinn a long level glance.

"No?" he asked. But there was no insolence in the question. "In that case I cannot explain it."

"I think I understand, Thorhall," I said to him after that. "For I, too, feel as you do."

And so I did. But I had found my ultimate island; and the name of that fair land to which I sailed was—and still is— Christ.

"I, too, understand, Thorhall," said Thorvald Ericson. "I understand. But I do not feel as either you or Thrand Thorbergson."

There was an abyss in Thorvald that nothing ever filled. I know now there are men like this. But Thorvald Ericson was the first one of them I had ever met. He was, besides, the one of them I liked best. I say Masses now for Thorvald Ericson who sleeps until world's end under Crossness.

As the long days drew on, I came to know this little commonwealth of ours with an exact and loving knowledge. Leif was the King, Thorvald Ericson, Thorhall Gamlason, Brian the nobles. I was the scribe and Steinn the *stafnbui* the steward of the little kingdom—I suppose, in the light of after years, one might say I was the priesthood, too. My crewmates, then, were the citizens who are the blood and bone of any commonwealth. After, on Iona, I was to learn somewhat of statecraft out of books. The *Mariasuden* was better than a book. The *Mariasuden* was what Bishop Augustine had once greatly called the Kingdom of Man. She was the Kingdom of Man in little; and she was very dear to me. No, I had no need for books on this head. I had seen it all written down in men's faces years before.

It was during stints of storytelling such as these I have spoken of, and over the cooking cauldron and ale beaker, that a man got to know his crewmates best. Counting Brian and myself, their number came to thirty which was one over the full complement of the crew that had sailed to Norway last autumn with Leif Ericson. It would have been two over had not one of Leif's best men, An Bramblebelly by name, married a woman of Olaf's court and, with Leif's free consent, been taken into the King's bodyguard by the son of Tryggve who was always on the lookout for strong young Greenlanders and Icelanders.

As the son of Thorberg Skaffhogg, I had to be better than a middling sailor. Besides, I had helped build the *Mariasuden;* so it could be presumed I knew something about ships, even if this was my first long voyage. Though Brian was not yet versed enough in seacraft to rate as a full-fledged seaman, Leif told me he had few worries for the future in the boy's regard. While I went over the lading with the Greenland captain our first night out from Iceland, Leif talked to me about the Irish lad. He said he thought another voyage or so, in late summer and early autumn, would season the lad sufficiently so that, when the *Mariasuden* sailed in the spring for the unknown land, he would more than fill An Bramblebelly's capable shoes. Thorberg Skaffhogg had built the *Mariasuden* large enough for fifty men. But, if it were at all possible, Leif meant to keep his crew list down to thirty so that he would have plenty of cargo space for the goods he would bring to his land-taking in the strange country.

Not counting Brian and myself, with five exceptions the ship's company were all hard-bitten Greenlanders and Icelanders, either

by birth or by adoption. In the case of Greenland, since the land
was so new, it was mostly by adoption. Hallbjorn Half-Troll,
Onund Trolleskog, Asgeir Aedikoll, Bolli Blacksark, and Hauk
Erlendson were all from Norway; and, on that account, were
known to their comrades as the Eastmen. Gunnbjorn and Floki
Ravenson had both been born in Scotland. Ari Marson, Rafn
and Steinof Humblepie were born in Ireland.

Tyrker, Leif's foster father, whom he dearly loved, hailed, on
his mother's side, from somewhere in the southern portions of
that great inland sea which the men of the southern lands called
the Mediterranean. On his father's side, no one knew whence he
derived. Tyrker had been a Varangian in the service of the Eastern Emperor and fought in Sarkland, which was why his friends
had long ago nicknamed him the Turk. Tyrker had no memory
of any father; and his mother had died in bearing him. So he
went nameless except for that nickname. Gunnbjorn, Floki, Ari,
Rafn, Steinof, and Tyrker all counted as Greenlanders, since they
had taken land there early and, by the time of the *Mariasuden's*
sailing, no longer knew any other country.

Except for Tyrker, all these were the lesser men of the crew,
serving for pay only. The other men, including Steinn Thorirson,
the *stafnbui,* Thorvald Ericson, and Thorhall Gamlason, all owned
shares in Leif's venture.

Of these others—there were quite a few new Thor names
among them for Brian to cope with—Thorgils Bollason was a
squat, dark-skinned man, bald-headed, and with protruding teeth.
He was a bit of a dandy, I remember, and kept two rich cloaks,
one deep blue with a white stripe, the other crimson, in his heavy
sea chest. His cousin, Bolli Holluson, who was also related to
those Osvifsons with whom Kjartan Olafson was at feud back
in Iceland, had long yellow hair which came down to his shoulders
in massy curls. He was of enormous frame, blue-eyed, hawk-
nosed, with beautiful hands that did not seem to go with the rest
of his great body, with his mighty shoulders and bull's chest.
Thorleik Eldgrimson was the oldest man on the *Mariasuden*—
fifty years, at the very least. His hair was iron-gray. But, despite
his age, he was as strong as any man aboard except for Bolli
Holluson.

Thord Thordarson, fair-haired and comely as a young girl,
was of slight build, a fact which did not keep him from being,
next to Thorhall Gamlason, the most expert swordsman of all

the crew. I shall have more to say of this same Thord somewhat later. For he was to play a very strange part indeed before our Vinland faring was over and done with. Thorbjorn Lambason, on the other hand, was as ugly as Thord Thordarson was comely. His black hair curled close to his round scalp like some warrior's from Sarkland; and his eyes were set too close together for comfort. He, too, was a fine swordsman, though not quite the equal of either Thorhall Gamlason or Thord Thordarson. Leif had told Brian always to give this man a wide berth. For Thorbjorn was the only person on board who made a point of never calling Brian either Haki or Brian, always referring to him, with a sneer, as "King's fosterling." Leif kept an anxious eye on Thorbjorn. He wanted no bad blood aboard the *Mariasuden* of any kind; and least of all bad blood in connection with such a nobly-born hostage as young Brian, grandnephew of the Irish *Ard Ri*. Since he could plainly see that this situation was Thorbjorn's fault, not Brian's, he even considered dropping Thorbjorn from the ship's rolls after this voyage was finished. I heard him say this to his brother, Thorvald Ericson.

There were two Thorsteins in the crew, distinguished from one another by their nicknames. Thorstein the White was compactly built with nicely corded arms and legs. His hair was so fair one could not see his eyelashes. Because of this fairness of his, he suffered terribly from the sun glare on the water, and so always wore a broad-brimmed hat while rowing that flopped about his ears and—as Thorvald Ericson once observed to me—gave him the look of a melting snow-troll that had been molded by laughing children and then caught in a February thaw. Thorstein the Black, on the other hand, had curly dark-brown hair and wore the scar of an old sword slash livid from jaw to jaw on his right cheek. That scar never tanned as the rest of Thorstein did. In winter, when the rest of his face was pale, it blazed an angry red. So, winter or summer, Thorstein the Black had a startling look about him. There were also two brothers among the crew, alike as twins almost with their red hair and freckles. Alf and Ornolf were their names. Both were nicknamed Laxfish. For not only were their faces speckled as any salmon's belly. They were, in addition, famous fishermen, capable of getting bites on their lines when, all around them, fish refused to rise to other fishers' bait.

One of the crew always wore his chain mail corselet. This

was not that he feared danger more than another man, but because of the fineness and the lightness of its workmanship of which he was very proud, as he was also proud of the silver-mounted ax in his sea chest. They were both pieces of his own working, as it happened. For this man was Leif Ericson's weapon-smith afloat and ashore. His name was Hunbogi Ale-Head, this latter nickname given him because, when his smith's work was over for the day, he could drink anyone he met under the table without showing the slightest sign of ill effect himself, beyond a slight thickening in his manner of speech which was not too apparent anyway, since Hunbogi Ale-Head rarely opened his mouth except to thrust a foaming tankard into it or to roar out a drinking catch that no one else could understand. Hunbogi was as important a man as a ship could carry. At times all had to depend on his weapon-craft, even such a peaceful trader as Leif was. Thorhall Gamlason, who did not ordinarily speak of things like these, considered it quite lucky to have such a one on board since a smith's trade was one of the sacred trades and under the express protection of Thor.

Sveinn Haldorson slept on the bench next to Hunbogi. Sveinn was red-faced and running to fat and far and away the jolliest man aboard. There was never any malice in him, though sometimes it seemed to Leif that his ribaldry went a little further than was really seemly. Viga-Thorlak, a clumsy bear of a man whose gentle nature belied his nickname of the Killer, lived up to that nickname in battle were not even Thorhall Gamlason's berserk fury went beyond Viga-Thorlak's weapon-madness. Bjorn Korekson and Thori Englandsfari rounded out the roster. Thori was a notable traveler who had been three times to Micklegarth and back. I do not think I remember anything noteworthy about Bjorn Korekson except that he was a pleasant enough comrade and pulled a strong oar on the right side of the ship facing the stern.

Those are many names, I know, to come on all at once. But that is just the way I came on them in the *Mariasuden*. As the days go by, they will become clearer in your mind even as they did in mine so long ago. Not all of them, though, for not all of them stand out clearly in my memory. And that, again, is very like life.

But they were a good crew, those men of Leif's, none better in all the Northland either before or since. When the shield rack was up or, in storm, with but an inch of planking between you and the arms of Ran, they were good comrades to have beside you. By the time the first bird couriers from Greenland came and perched on the gunwale, in token that the *Mariasuden* could be no more than half a day's run from Ericsfjord, I knew them all as well almost as any man could know another. For, like apples on the bough in a warm summer, friendships—and enmities, too, though we had little of these aboard the *Mariasuden*—ripened fast on shipboard.

These first birds to greet us were terns and bright-eyed mollie-mawks. The sea mews came a little later, bickering shrill; and after them the plovers. Three hours from our home harbor, the *Mariasuden* drove through a strong-swimming herd of seals which thrust up glistening serpent heads and watched after our swift wake. A breath of polar air blew down from the great northern icecap—I have not seen that icecap myself, but I have talked with those who have seen it. It was already midsummer now, but those layers upon layers of coolness tasted to me of never-ending spring. It was almost as if the farther we sailed, the younger grew the earth.

So came we to Ericsfjord where the great Greenland *hersir* had his steading.

CHAPTER SIX

ERICSFJORD

THE SHAPE OF WHAT WAS TO COME BEGAN AT ERICSFJORD where Eric the Red had established his manor finally after many tries elsewhere. It was a new thing I saw there seventy years agone. I do not think the men of Ireland and Norway, my two lands, know just how new even now. For the old lands do not change so quickly as the new ones. In part this is their strength; and, I think, in part their weakness, too.

I have lived long enough now to know that wealth counts for much in the affairs of men; and that wealth is reckoned in many ways besides the way of gold or of ring-hoards in the earth. More than this, the sources of wealth are always changing. There is a proverb now in use among Duke William's men that a man of spirit will go down one of these three roads: the road of the Church; the road of the King's palace; the road of the sea. Not all the men of Frankland would include the sea here; but Duke William's men are the grandsons of us Northmen. The saying means, of course, that power and riches lie either in the Church, or in the King's service, or in trade. I might say here, though it carries me from my tale a little, that I think it a great misfortune men can now find such wealth and power within the Church of the poor carpenter of Nazareth. I fear there may be trouble over this in time to come.

Now Leif's and Thorvald's father, Eric the Red, had chosen the way of trade and, in part, a way the Frankish proverb makes no mention of—and that is the way of land. There were no kings in Greenland. There were no kings in Iceland, either, it was true. But there were great nobles there; and the tyranny of great nobles can be even more oppressive than the tyranny of kings. There were no great nobles in Greenland at all, only merchant princes.

This shift had begun in the homeland many, many years before. In Norway mountain men had fought river men—the fierce *elvegrimer* of the border marches—and bested them. Then the men of the sea, headed by their great sea kings, had prevailed over both mountain and river men. The defeated nobles had thereupon retreated to Iceland, meaning to lick their wounds there and then try again until they had found that Iceland suited them better than Norway. So there they had made another kind of life, and a good one, too, until the time came for one of their own number, this same Eric of Ericsfjord who was now our host, to move on to the Greenland which he named. There was a saying now that in Norway one was a king's man and in Iceland a nobles' man; but that in Greenland one could be one's own man—always provided, of course, that one could succeed as a trader. Not all men had luck as merchants. The risks were great; and the labor hard, especially in the beginnings of this enterprise.

Men have begun to talk much, in these latter years, of a thing called history which is a chronicling of the great deeds that have been before. I think that, if one only looks closely at things, there are tides in history even as there are tides in the sea. Trade is one of these new tides that bear men into other roadsteads and other havens than the old familiar ones. My day has seen that tide bear power from south to north. It is not a simple matter, either. The warriors of Sarkland, who are all Christian men's bitter enemies, have played their part in this great shift by stopping the old sea routes over which the Roman dromonds used to ply with their rich bales of goods. The old harbors decayed: the harbors of Italy and Gaul. But from the Volga to the Shannon new harbors have been opened up with the men of the North in the van.

No conquest is ever other than bloody in its beginnings. Nevertheless, the more the trader's will prevails over the warrior's, the more peaceful this new way of conquest becomes. A warrior is for victory and glory at all costs; a chapman is for wealth and security if these dear commodities are anywhere available. The road thereto is compromise and reason. Even the most precious cargo must be second to the dictates of prudence. A new proverb began to be in men's mouths in those days: *Lading is less than life*.

Thorhall Gamlason spat when he first heard this saying; and Thorvald Ericson grinned his mocking grin. Still, slowly but surely, the new way has been winning. And this old Eric, master of Brattahlith, for all that his hot temper was a berserker's temper, stood for the new rather than the old.

In the end, though, some things do not change. The way of a man with a maid is one of them. The changeless lovers floating upon the tide of change are worth more than the tide.

This time Thorfinn's boat anchored within a few hours of the *Mariasuden*. Leif's ship, under my supervision, was already unloaded on Eric's wharf. Brian, who had helped in the hot work, was splashing about in the deeper water offshore to slake his thirsty body when Thorfinn's dragon ship came nosing close to the shingle beach that rimmed all Ericsfjord. As soon as his lookout's probing pole touched bottom, Thorfinn Karlsefni dropped two anchors, one from the bow and one from the stern, with no more splash than two large fish might make. For, what with Leif's *Mariasuden,* Eric's own long ship, an Iceland trader who had put into port only the night before, and twenty smaller *skutur* that plied in and out of the Greenland firths, there was no open space near the mooring rocks. Now that Leif had finished his own unlading, he was quite ready to move his ship out to midstream and let Thorfinn Karlsefni warp his in to a mooring stone that he might begin the work of his own unlading in turn. But the afternoon was already far advanced. Thorfinn preferred to let the heavy work wait till the next morning, when his men would be fresher. Meanwhile they might sleep on board in their skin hammocks one more night. As for Mistress Gudrid and maid Grainne, who deserved gentler treatment, Thorfinn said he would row them ashore in the after-boat to where Eric had appointed a woman's guesthouse.

While all this talk was going on about the night's arrangements, Brian, taking care to keep his nakedness well covered, swam over to where Grainne stood at the prow beside the serpent neck like some fair-tressed shield-maiden of old story astride a crimson dragon. In the lee of the ship's clinkered side, just under the prow, sun and water conspired together to make live green moving shadows on the planks. The shifting green lights playing over his ivory body as if he were god Aegir himself, Brian clung with one dripping arm to the prow hawser and looked up at Grainne. It seemed to me an odd shyness came over the two of them. I thought it was as if they were meeting for the first time—or even as if they had never met before. So are lovers' meetings ever new to lovers while they are still in the first fair flush of their glorious love.

In the end, Brian was the first to speak.

"Welcome to Ericsfjord, lady," he said formally.

I do not think it was altogether a jest, though he may well have begun to speak to her in jest. For the moment the strange woman above him must have seemed a great lady whom he did not yet know, not his dear Grainne at all. Then the girl smiled tenderly down at him, and the spell was broken.

"Greetings, Grainne mine," he said.

"Greetings, Brian," said Grainne.

There was no need to say more on either of their sides. But I, too, must needs salute the maid now.

"Welcome to Ericsfjord, lady," I called from the dock, my quill pen still in the hand which had just pricked down the last item of Leif's cargo. "We are happy to see you again, Mistress."

"Thank you, Thrand Thorbergson," she said.

There was a crescent moon sailing down the evening sky. It was no lovelier than the maiden, Grainne, daughter of Rafarta of Clonmacnoise.

Leif Ericson found out very soon that it was not going to be too easy to fulfill his Yuletide vow that he would bring Christ to Greenland. He had expected his father, Eric, to be the main stumbling block; and so it turned out. I mind me now of a proverb they still use in Ireland: *The hardest of all men to talk to is a Viking in his hauberk.* That was Eric of Brattahlith—Viking from the crown of his grizzled red head to his horny heel. He was taller than Leif and broader than Thorvald. Men said his dead son, Thorstein, was most like him in body. But I cannot say this of my own knowledge since Thorstein was some years dead when I first came to Greenland. This, however, I do know. If Thorhall Gamlason was like a wolf, this Greenland *hersir* was a bear: strong and not ill-natured, but terrible when roused. It was not wise, in Eric's regard, to forget that his first outlawing came about because he had killed a man—or that he had killed others since.

Nor was old Eric alone in his resistance to the things of Christ. Though it pains me to admit this, the Northmen were slowest, almost, of all peoples to take up our Saviour's sweet yoke. This was true even in Ireland where Patrick, Ciaran, and Brigid had lived and died. The first of the Irish Sigtryggs had come over more than three quarters of a century before this: and his son,

Amlaib Cuaran, went so far as to go on pilgrimage to Iona only twenty years before my coming to Greenland. But despite Amlaib's good example, the Norse in Dublin kept right on taking their battle oaths on the ring of silver and gold that was known as Thor's Ring and was still, within the last six years, dipped in the blood of human sacrifice. So there is no need to point the finger at Eric or to wonder that he did not take it at all kindly when he found that his son had it in mind to proclaim Christianity throughout Greenland, in the name of Olaf Tryggveson, at the summer Thing. Nor, though ordinarily Eric was the most hospitable of hosts, did he like housing a priest at Brattahlith. He never called Sira Inge by his first name, only by the name of Skakke which was his father's name and meant Wry-neck. Eric used to tell his friends, when Sira Inge's name came up, that, if this was the way Leif's famous luck was going, people could go on calling him Leif the Lucky, if they wished to. But, in that case, they would have to start calling his father Eric the Unlucky.

Now this was the state of affairs in midsummer. But Leif Ericson was every whit as tenacious as his stubborn sire. Mightily toiled he in the vineyard with Sira Inge, myself, and his foster father, Tyrker, helping him in especial. After his years in Micklegarth this Tyrker happened to have a strong devotion to Christ's Mother whom he always called *Leila Marien*—or that is what my ear heard him say—which was the Sarkland fashion of saying the Lady Mary, even as he had heard it in his youth. I think Mary helped us greatly in our work. Who more than she would want Christ acknowledged in a land that had not known him?

By autumn every chieftain on the island had declared himself and all his household for Christ, except for Eric, Thorhall Gamlason, and an occasional old thrall here or there who was too set in idea ever to change his ways any more. By the end of September we got an important new recruit. Eric's wife, Thorhild, who was the granddaughter of the great *hersir,* Wolf Squint, came over to the new faith and gave, moreover, twenty marks of silver and five of gold to build a church within two hundred feet of Eric's own hall. The old chieftain got into a frenzy at that. With timber worth its weight in precious stones in a treeless country like this Greenland, he thought it madness to waste all the prime wood he had stored for other purposes on the sills, crossbeams and uprights of a useless building that would, when

finished, be three ells broader and higher than any other building
in all Greenland.

I think now that Eric's real dislike of Christianity was not that
he loved Thor so much as that he loved Christ even less. He told
Leif and Thorvald and myself—for some reason he suffered me
as he did not Sira Inge—that he trusted more in the strength of
his own two hands and in the good steel of his sword and spear
than in either Thor or Odin. If he were to place all his trust
in a single god, he went on in his growling way, it might well be
Thor; but never would it be Christ who had never even bothered
to defend Himself when His attackers came out against Him in
the garden. But Eric did not really think one should place all one's
trust, one's *fulltrúi,* in a single god, no matter who the god might
be. Where, he asked us, would that leave the gnome who lived
in the thurse tree outside, near where Thorhild wished this foolish
church of hers to be? That gnome had come, in the beginnings,
with Eric's father from Norway to Iceland, and then with Eric
himself from Iceland to Greenland when the Thing first banished
him, almost nineteen years before, for killing Thorgest's sons.
Was he to renounce an old family friend like this one? Why, he
said, the lesser gods were everywhere: in trees; in waterfalls; in
warriors' barrows; even in old figureheads detached from the
prows of long ships. Did he not have a dragon and a *grima,*
from the head and stern of his first ship, set up over his hall door,
where they foretold the weather for him now, the dragon howling
for a north, the *grima* for a south wind?

Leif and Thorvald Ericson listened patiently to their father's
ramblings, though they must have heard all this many times before. It was true enough—I had seen and heard it with my own
eyes and ears—that the winds, soughing through the gaping open
mouths of dragon head and *grima,* made the painted beasts seem
to spit and hiss. But what of that? It would be the same, after all,
if they were no more than unpainted shingles set up there to flap
in the gusts of air. The gnome in the thurse tree was a different
thing again. As it happened, Leif did believe a little in that gnome
even as, I freely confess, I did, too—and still do, for that matter!
For I think there must be other orders of beings between God
and men than just the angels. But, again, what of that? If Christ
God, through His Father, did not will that the gnome have being,
then there would be no gnome, no Leif, no Thorvald, no Eric,
no Thrand, no anything. With Leif's consent, I explained this

latter argument carefully to Eric. But the old chieftain would not
so much as listen.

Then, at last, the real story came out—the story for which,
sitting in his high seat, old Eric had summoned this council. It is
an instructive story in more ways than one; and it taught me
somewhat of women's weapons which later did me good service
at shriving-time and on love-days when we priests strive to settle
differences between husbands and wives. A learned monk of Iona
told me years later, when I spoke to him of this matter, that he
had heard of the same thing Thorhild did in a play written by an
old Greek writer whose name no longer comes into my mind.

Old Eric had trouble beginning this tale. He tapped his fingers
on the armrest of his high seat impatiently and, I thought, more
than a little embarrassedly, before he could bring himself to speak
out.

"I have another reason for disliking your Sira Wry-neck," he
said at last to his sons, clearing his throat the while.

"Yes, father," said Leif forbearingly. "What is it?"

"He is ruining my married life," said Eric, shamefaced.

It took much to startle Thorvald Ericson. But that startled
him. He put down his ale cup, sputtering a little.

"Sira Inge!" he said. "You wrong the fellow, father! Why,
the priest is as chaste as—"

"I care not," said Eric sullenly, "if he be as chaste as the
gelded hog he resembles. What I object to is his imposing chastity
on me. By Thor! I will not endure it!"

"What do you mean, father?" Leif asked the old man then.
I thought his voice was patient, but somewhat puzzled now.

Eric the Red looked shrewdly at his two sons, paying no manner of heed to my presence.

"We are men, are we not?" he asked, as if probing them.

"I have no reason to think otherwise," said Thorvald Ericson
in his ironic way.

"Well," said old Eric. "There are certain necessities a man
has—you follow me, do you not?"

The *hersir* stopped again on that and waited for one of his sons
to answer.

"Yes, father," said Leif Ericson. I could see he grew more
puzzled every second. "What is it you wish to tell us?"

It came out in a rush then.

"Thorhild comes no more to my bed," said old Eric. "She says she will not sleep with me so long as I stay pagan."

Thorvald Ericson's mouth twitched. He pulled at his long lower lip. For his part, Leif never moved a single muscle.

"I think we may change that quite easily, if you so wish," said Leif to Eric.

"Do not think to come round me, boy," said old Eric, menace in his voice. "I shall never be a Christian. I will go on worshiping as I please—and, more to the point, not worshiping as I please, too!"

"There is no need for your turning Christian if you do not so choose," said Leif, seeing an advantage here. "Do you only give your pledge you will not try to stop other men from worshiping as they please. Then Sira Inge will tell our mother it is her bounden duty to be a wife to you again."

"The priest will do that?" asked Eric suspiciously.

"Yes," said Leif.

"Then I shall speak no more against the rule of Christ," said Eric. "Though I like it not that any priest should have such power over my bed—especially such a priest as Sira Wry-neck is."

After the Greenland *hersir* had gone grumbling off to his couch for the night, the two brothers stayed in the hall a space with me, neither daring to look the other in the face lest they break into a storm of merriment. I had difficulty restraining myself, too, though it was not my father who was in question. In the end it was Thorvald Ericson who first raised his head.

"How old, brother," he asked, "do you think our father is?"

The floodgates broke at that. Never have I heard men laugh as did those twain, Leif and Thorvald Ericson. It was as if the gods were laughing from Asgard over the walls the Jotunns built them. It was not seemly mirth, perhaps. But, then, neither are the doings of men always seemly.

At any rate, seemly or not, after this the Christianizing work went on apace with no one to say nay. Thorhild came back to Eric's bed. The old man kept his word to Leif, though he himself died as he had lived, the stoutest of heathens. I think no worse of him for that.

Though he did not expect this, Leif had a little trouble with his father over the Vinland faring, too. I suppose Eric had more than one good reason for not favoring his eldest son's voyage to the land that, many years before, Bjarni Herjulfson had seen. As he thought things over, however, he found himself changing his opinion. I think it came into his mind that, perhaps, things would go better in Greenland for him if Leif were now to take his preaching and his priest elsewhere, leaving Brattahlith in quiet for a space. He may even have thought that, if Sira Inge were gone, Thorhild might leave off her insistence on building this church so near the thurse tree where the gnome lived. Sira Inge, of course, was not going on this first voyage; but no one had yet told Eric that. He meant to come out with Thorfinn in his ship some time later.

What really tipped the scales in favor of the voyage was Eric's sharp eye for a business chance. Bjarni had described that far-off land as covered with greater forests than the eye of man had ever glimpsed before. However foolish his ideas about religion, Eric knew that his son, Leif, was a good sailor, none better in all the Northland. The shrewd old land-taker could foresee immense profits in a timber monopoly with every wood-hungry family in both Greenland and Iceland, where few trees grew, buying from him at far cheaper prices than Norwegian timber merchants would be able to offer, considering the expenses they would incur in the long transit between Norway and those islands. Much to Leif's surprise, though not to mine who had watched him debate this matter in his mind, Eric suddenly shifted his stance and began to favor the enterprise as eagerly as up to now he had opposed it. Moreover, he took it into his head that he would make one of the party on the *Mariasuden,* a thing that neither Leif nor Thorvald liked, for their father had grown much older than he knew.

Leif told his father some of his perplexities about Thorbjorn Lambason, the crewman who disliked Brian and called him "King's fosterling." Eric advised him to get rid of the man—but tactfully, so that there would be no hard feelings. He had a good countersuggestion, too. One of his own men—by name Illugi Tomcat—had been with Bjarni Herjulfson as cabin boy when Bjarni made his landfall in the unknown West. Illugi was sharp-eyed and intelligent. Why not take him along as a kind of pilot in Thorbjorn Lambason's place? Leif jumped at the chance and thanked his father heartily for it.

Another day, while the three of us were working over the *Mariasuden's* lading for her coming faring, Leif mentioned his difficulties in the matter of Thorhall Gamlason, including the prophecy old Gefjon had made in Thorhall's and Brian's regard which had come to his ears, though he had been away hunting elk with Olaf Tryggveson when the spaeing had taken place at Vik. Old Eric was by no means so sympathetic here. He liked Thorhall's sticking to the ancient ways. He admired his hunting prowess. And he was not the man to be daunted by a carline's prophecy.

"They do not make men like Thorhall any more," he told his son. "He is a wolf, it is true, as was his father before him. But you, son Leif, are in the plight of the captain the old skald wrote about:

> *'Once I had choice*
> *Of champions many—*
> *Now the wolf's pelt only*
> *Hangs on my hook.' "*

Eric took a long draught from his ale tankard, being careful to wipe the foam from his red-gray moustache before going on.

"It is an honest wolf, Leif," he said after a pause. "His coat will keep you warm in time of trouble, even if it may keep you a bit too warm, on occasion, in time of peace. Also, you will find he is not the less loyal that he remembers Thor. You will find you cannot guard against everything in life, Leif. Nor is it necessary. Time has more power to change things than has the human will. There is luck in that, I think."

So, in the upshot, Leif kept Thorhall Gamlason with him as the *Mariasuden's* hunter; and signed on Illugi Tomcat in the place of Thorbjorn Lambason who did not take this dismissal too much amiss. For Leif gave him two marks of silver as a parting gift; and Eric found a place for him on his boat, *The Gerfalcon,* which cruised Greenland's coastal waters, promising him, to boot, that in two years' time he could settle down as overseer on Brattahlith. Thorbjorn was well content on the whole. For he was nearing that time of life when men, at last, grow ready to quit the sea.

Brian went on two voyages before winter set in. One, a short one, on *The Gerfalcon* round about the Greenland fjords—Eric saw to it that Thorbjorn Lambason had land duties on that cruise. One, rather longer, to the Faroes and back with Thorfinn

Karlsefni. At the end of them, Leif judged him sufficiently seasoned to go with the *Mariasuden* in the coming spring.

Eric the Red's estate at Brattahlith was the largest and most
splendid in all Greenland. Both of his surviving sons, Leif and
Thorvald Ericson, lived with him on it; and his illegitimate
daughter, Freydis. So had the dead son, Thorstein, Mistress
Gudrid's first husband, until he died. Yet there was room, and to
spare. Eric's own house was reared on a slight rise near the shore,
facing the wharf and the mooring rocks. It was only three hundred yards from the little river that ran out of Ericsfjord. Behind
it stretched his hayfields and his one extensive field of grain, the
only grainfield so far in Greenland. For up till now the other
settlers had had neither time nor patience to nurse along a crop to
stubborn harvest in Greenland's short growing season. Eric's cattle barns contained no fewer than forty head of fat cattle. These
barns were of turf. But the farm buildings themselves were
reared, on foundations of stone, of seasoned timber brought from
Norway by way of Eric's old estate at Hvamsfjord in Iceland.

Eric had prospered much in the years since his banishment. His
wardrobes were full of freshly laundered linen, of woolen gar-
ments, of lustrous pelts of fox and marten. His cupboards were
stocked with spoons of horn and wood; with trenchers and tubs
and toggles and tallies for recording trading inventories; with
soapstone lamps and bodkins and belt hooks of bone; with shoes
of leather on wooden lasts. The seal and walrus hides were kept
in warehouses apart, because they smelled so rank during the
time of curing. So was the whale and walrus fat and the dried
fish. Eric had much store of gold, too; but not so much, at that,
as a man of his wealth in land and cattle might be expected to
keep. He always said—and I think he was right—that real wealth
was not to be measured in ornament or metal but in things to
eat and drink and clothe oneself in.

His boats plied regularly between Iceland and Greenland, on the
one hand; and between Greenland and Norway, on the other. He
sent an occasional one to London and Dublin; and, now and then,
to one of the Norse trading cities on the Channel coast of Frankland or up one of the Frankish rivers that flowed through the
lands of Duke Rollo's sons. At Dublin, in whose harbor the ships
of many peoples came together weekly, Eric did a thriving business with the famous trader known as Gille-the-Russian-merchant-

with-the-Greek-hat who was, in fact, neither Russian nor wore a Greek hat, though his headgear was outlandish enough, it must be confessed. I have since observed it is a great advantage to a trader to have something odd about him like this same hat of Gille's. It helps fix his wares in men's minds. But this holds true only for under-traders and middlemen, not great merchant princes like Eric and Leif, the son of Eric. They needed no gauds or gewgaws to set off their quiet authority.

The days passed and the summer waned. Both the people of Ericsfjord and Leif's men of the *Mariasuden* went about their different businesses, each after his own individual fashion. Day by day cheerful little Tyrker, Leif's wiry foster father, grew more and more bent until his back was curved like one of the bows men use in the Sarkland whence he came. Ari Marson became betrothed to a woman from Eric's steading—I think her name was Hallgerd but am no longer sure of this. Leif gave the betrothal feast for his man, promising to hold the marriage feast, at his own expense, after our return from the *Mariasuden's* great faring on which Ari had contracted to go. We had much mirth because of the feast for a week and more. This betrothal of Ari's was to have some consequences for our Vinland faring though, of course, no one could tell this at the time.

Thorvald Ericson took up with a woman on an outlying farm and got her with child by midsummer. There was not too much trouble over this. For the woman was kinless and, besides, Thorvald acknowledged the child, though he refused to marry the woman, saying with a laugh—and it was true enough, too—that others had fished that stream before and after him. Sira Inge was very wroth over this. But Leif defended his brother stoutly; and the priest could do nothing. Sveinn Haldorson laughed hard when this argument arose.

"Tell the priest," he said to me, "that one has to expect this sort of happening at sea, as the seal said when the harpooner lanced him in one eye."

Old Eric, Thorhall Gamlason, and Hunbogi Ale-Head went away for a few days around the time of Midsummer Night, without saying where they were going or, after their return, where they had been. It was suspected they had gone inland to a grove men knew of, there to sacrifice to Asa-Thor, especially since one of Eric's best stallions went with them and never came back; and it was well known that a man was supposed to eat horse-flesh during these Thor-feasts. But no one dared to question Eric on the matter. However, one good thing came out of this journey—if it be seemly to speak of good coming from anyone's misfortune. Old Eric had a bad fall coming back. It lamed him so that there was no further talk of his going with us on the *Mariasuden* when we should set sail for the new land. This accident of their father's took a great load off Leif and Thorvald Ericson's minds. It was not, of course, that they wished the old man any harm. But they knew that he would be a drag on the voyage they intended.

I served Sira Inge's Mass daily and, in conversation with him after, came to what, I think, was a goodly conclusion about my desire to be a priest. He agreed, after my return from the *Mariasuden's* faring, to recommend me to the Abbot of Iona through another monk he knew—a certain Richard called by us Norse *Svartmeistari* or the Black Scholar—who happened to be a fast friend of that Abbot. On his own side, Sira Inge was firmly resolved to stay at Ericsfjord, for the time being, to see to it that Eric's wife, Thorhild, did not flag in her intention to build the first church in Greenland. Then, when that was done, he pledged himself to come in search of us with Thorfinn Karlsefni, taking due care, beforehand, to bring out another priest from Norway to take his place in Greenland. I mind me now of this other priest, though I have not thought on him these many years. His name was Sira Roald; and the Greenlanders came to call him Roald the Long-Winded. So I suppose he could not have been overpopular.

My most important decision was easily reached—as it turned out, much more easily than Sira Inge feared when we first discussed the matter. He wished me to stay virgin when a priest even as was customary for religious throughout most of the western lands, although, so far here in the northern countries, marriage was still lawful for the clergy. Indeed there was a growing tendency for priests to be the sons of priests, a thing which Sira Inge regarded as a practice bad in itself and one fraught with danger, in addition, for the Church in the north. I agreed with him that this was a lamentable abuse. He said that the Pope had long had it in mind to do something about this situation, but that up to now he had not been able.

But I found no difficulty at all about this counsel of perfection which enjoins that brides of the Lamb stay chaste forever. Mar-

riage is for generation; and our Father, Who is in Heaven, is
an eternal act of generation not requiring, as men require, the
differentiation of sex. The first miracle Christ worked was to
turn plain water into wine at the marriage feast in Cana. Was it
in any way thinkable that Christ should have married after the
ordinary fashion of marriage? I did not think so; and Sira Inge
told me that both tradition and theology agreed it was in no wise
thinkable. His perpetual virginity enclosed, surrounded, and contained marriage even as did His Father's and our Father's pater-
nity. Christ *was* marriage; and so are we, His priests, after Him.
Yes, there had been another Marriage at Cana besides the one
consummated by the bride and groom who drank the miraculous
wine sitting at the table with the Master and His Virgin Mother.

From this time on, I looked with a different, a far gladder eye
on the joy of mortal lovers like Brian and Grainne who began
to be man and woman now, no longer boy and girl, and who, for
the sake of the law that governs love, now asked me to sit with
them in the long Greenland evenings so that they might not be
tempted to trespass on the Garden's bounds before the sacrament
of marriage should make them free of that same lovesome Garden. I say the Garden of design here, for only in the love that
moves between man and woman does fallen man still taste of
the bliss of that Garden which was in the beginning.

I began to see another thing, too. I began to see that God, our
great Husbandman, had appointed an economy in love as He had
appointed an economy in all other things—even, I dare say, as we
shall one day see, in Heaven itself. He, and we, His priests, with
Him, lay up goodly stocks to insure the earthly fecundity of
happy lovers. We are the salt to keep their dear flesh sweet against
the day when all flesh shall be glorified and no longer merely
grass to be cast into the oven of nature. We are the myrrh and
aloes that purify and render fragrant their mortal joy. We, too,
are Marriage. Meanwhile we walk in the Garden in the cool of the
day with that Father Who is the Maker of the Garden, and with
that Son Who is its Gardener, and with the Holy Spirit Who
sings canticles of joy from atop the Tree of Life which grows
forever in the Garden.

Yes, I was content watching love wax in Brian and Grainne.
I wondered about the new land much in those days. Would the
Garden there still flourish in primal innocence? Or would it, too,
be as we knew it in our sad elder world—lovely still in morning

and evening light, but with a canker coiled in the very heart of
the rose?

Leif and his men spent that winter getting ready for their
late spring sailing to Bjarni Herjulfson's unknown land. Thorfinn Karlsefni could afford to be more leisurely in his preparations. He would not sail until the following year; and, when
he did, he would take, according to the plan he and Leif laid
together, no fewer than three ships with him to establish a permanent colony. For it was to be taken for granted, if Leif did
not return, that he had made land-taking in the new world.
No one even admitted the possibility that, if we did not come
back, it meant, instead, that we had perished. That is not the
way to conquer in a new venture.

Leif's and Thorvald's half-sister, Freydis, had it in mind to
come out in her own ship during the interval between their sailing and the sailing of Karlsefni's three ships. But this part of
the venture was not yet settled among those three kinsmen. In
his heart, Leif Ericson would much rather that Freydis should
not come at all; and Thorvald Ericson agreed with him. For
the woman was a wanton; and, like most wantons, a confirmed
troublemaker, especially where men were concerned—though
women did not much like Freydis Ericsdatter, either.

Mistress Gudrid, as was her heedful fashion, used her time
well, weaving daily with her women. She finished one great tapes-
try of the Three Kings at the Crib of the Infant Christ; and
began another picturing the unsuccessful Suitors of Mary Virgin.
Grainne, who worked with her at the loom, became skilled in
this delicate handicraft. With her own hands she wove, as a
present for Leif Ericson, a great banner, with a raven on it,
to fly over Leif's first house in the new land. The ground was
of yellow. On it the bird of Odin was picked out in raised black
thread and had angry red eyes. This banner would be flown
only on days of festival. Or else during battle in which case,
by the way the banner's folds hung, the defending archers would
be able to allow for the angle of wind deflection when they
launched their arrows.

Grainne's white kitten was grown a fine white cat now, with
kittens of her own over whom Leif's great wolfhound kept close
guard as though the kitlings were his own shaggy puppies. Thorvald Ericson made three new songs for the Yule feast we spent

in Greenland—it was the second Yule feast the Irish maid had
spent out of Ireland; and she was a little sad on the first day
of the feast, thinking of the mother and father she might never
see again.

Thorvald also made a smith's song for Hunbogi Ale-Head
who, here as in Norway and Iceland, was the busiest man on
the manor in winter, forging spearheads for the shaft sockets,
soldering new handles on the shields which their owners then
polished till a woman could see to comb her hair in the burnished
surfaces. The new pointed shields, which the grandsons of Duke
Rollo had lately brought into fashion in Frankland, were just
coming in a little, for the first time, here in the North. Some
of the younger men fancied them greatly, though veterans like
Thorhall Gamlason and Hunbogi himself continued to keep to
the old round shields. But Hunbogi was willing enough to smelt
anything whatsoever, if the demand were only heavy enough to
warrant it. Whatever he made, round shield or pointed, long
lance or thrusting sword, a fighter could feel secure with one
of Hunbogi's weapons. Leif's armorer never stinted materials.
The only thing he ever jibbed at was cheap pinchbeck work like
the battleaxes that had a steel edge annealed into the iron of the
blade. His axes were always hammered of one piece from head
to edge without a weal to turn the cutting edge.

Sira Inge showed himself unexpectedly forbearing in a way
that helped lessen some of Eric's rooted rancor toward him.
Eric had carvings on his high seat, on his pillars, and on his
bench supports; carvings of which he was very proud—it was,
as a matter of fact, over these same ornately worked bench supports he had first fallen out with Thorgest in the affray which
cost Thorgest the lives of his two sons and led to Eric's banishment from Iceland. Eric prized these carvings above all his other
possessions. But they had begun to deteriorate of late, and no
one in Greenland knew how to put them to rights again. When
Sira Inge heard of the difficulty, he set to work, with Eric's permission, with a loving hand—and this despite the fact the carvings were of Thor and Freya and Njord as well as of Sigurd
Fafnirsbane—touching up this faded one with a bit of paint,
repairing this broken other with a cunningly carved piece of
wood that could not be told from the original, oiling the whole
with a special oil he had learned to compound back in Norway
with which to treat the wooden carvings in the new stave

churches. I have observed many times since then that, where a man's heart is in question, as Sira Inge's was bound up with this love of his for carving, he will grow much more lenient than might otherwise have been expected. It comes into my mind, and not for the first time, that love is the answer always where men fall out at odds.

Eric's manor of Brattahlith had one great curiosity on it that neither Brian nor Grainne had ever seen before—for there were no bears left in Ireland—nor had even I seen the great beasts in such profusion, though I was Norway born and bred, and there are many bears to be met up with in our Norwegian mountains. Old Eric had a fancy to keep bears in cages made of saplings wattled and interlaced: one of every breed of bear men knew of, and two if they could be secured. He paid hunters to bring him prime specimens from the inner areas of Greenland, from Norway, from Permia even. The prize piece in his collection, at the moment, happened to be a great white bear, full grown now, with a snakelike neck, which a Norwegian trader had brought him as a cub some years before, having found it floating on an ice floe beside its dead mother.

Now Thorhall Gamlason liked to spend what time he could around the cages. For bears fascinated him almost beyond all else. Brian went with him several times. On one occasion Thorhall Gamlason told him in my hearing—what Brian knew already —that his secret name was Holmgang-Bersi, or the Bear-Duelist. Thorhall also told Brian something Brian did not know: that his *fylgja,* who came to him in sleep and who was sometimes seen by others, too, was a great bear.

"But a brown bear, Brian, with a huge muzzle," Thorhall said, perplexed. "Never have I seen one like it—nor one so big. Perhaps it is only a dream bear."

"Or perhaps you will meet one like it in the new land," said Brian very suddenly, as if convinced, he knew not how or why, that Thorhall really would meet such a beast in the country to which we were sailing.

"It may be, Brian," said Thorhall, still shaking his head. "I do not know. But this I do know. I should like to meet a bear like that, if only once."

Thorvald Ericson liked the bears, too, especially the white one which, to his skald's eye, was like some spirit of the snow. On the night before our *Mariasuden* finally sailed from Greenland

for the new land, Eric of Ericsfjord gave a great feast. When
the time for storytelling came, Thorvald Ericson stood up before
his father's high seat and told the tale of an Icelander he knew,
Audun of the West Firths, who gave all he owned for just such
a white bear as Eric's, because he thought that never in his
life had he seen such beauty and such wonder commingled before.
After that Audun gave this same beast, which was his heart's
desire, as a free gift to Sveinn of Denmark, his liege lord, and
would take nothing in return, though he was penniless after paying for the great beast, and though Harald of Norway had offered
a king's ransom for the bear.

"By Thor!" said old Eric, smiting his own huge bear's paw
down on the table till the tankards rang like bells thereon and
Mistress Thorhild looked with pursed lips at her husband. "That
was a gift of gifts. The men who came before us knew how to
live and act. I think this tale should always be held in memory
so that men, hearing it, should know that, one day in the past,
a Northman acted as a man should act!"

Thorvald Ericson bowed to his chieftain father.

"It shall so be held, lord father," he said gravely, "so long
as I shall live to tell it."

Now that Thorvald Ericson has slept so many years on Crossness, I wonder if there are others left, besides me, who still remember his story of Audun of the West Firths and the kingly
gift he gave? I hope so. For it is a good story.

After the feast was over, I went with Brian and Grainne out
on the wharf just across from where the *Mariasuden* rode the
little rocking waves, tugging at her mooring stone. Steinn the
stafnbui was on deck. He waved to us across the water. It was
late, very late, as I could tell by the movement of the stars.
Soon should I serve Sira Inge's dawn Mass; and then, with
the tide, we of the *Mariasuden* should be away on our great
quest.

Brian was thinking of time passing, too. He put one arm
around Grainne's waist and gently turned her head upward until
she looked into the stars above. They were below her feet, too,
mirrored in the black moving water. I mind me now how I fixed
my eyes then on the drowned stars in the fjord.

"It wants but three hours till dawn now, my Grainne," Brian

said. "We have not long to speak to one another before the parting."

"So short a time as that!" said Grainne softly. "How can you tell it is so short?"

For answer he cupped her face in his two hands and turned it slowly upward once again.

"See!" he said. "See! The Bear's muzzle tilts upward. At midnight it rested on his left paw."

Grainne looked at the skyey Bear. Both of them, Brian and she, were mirrored in the star shine that faintly lit the water at my feet.

"Will there be the same stars in the new land, Brian mine?" she asked.

"Some of them will be the same," he said. "There will be new ones, too."

"So long as the Bear is there," she said. "Then I can watch for it every night the sky is clear and know that you, too, my beloved, will be looking on the same star I look on. It will make us closer to one another that way."

"I think the Bear will ride with us to the new land," said Brian, kissing her.

I moved farther off along the wooden planking of the wharf, leaving those lovers to the celebration of their mystery. The stars paled as the dawn came in. Gullinkambi, who is the cockerel of Valhalla, crowed from the world's rooftree all too early that last morning. It is ever so with lovers. The *Mariasuden* waited, and the quest, and the new world beyond the quest. But themselves are all the world and all the quest two lovers want.

Old Eric the Red, though he could have been called Eric the Gray now, was standing on the dock that morning, Thorhild beside him, when the *Mariasuden* sailed on its great faring. It came into my mind that the old chieftain looked bent and forlorn, leaning there on his great staff—for his midsummer fall of the year before had left him very lame. This *hersir* had been most gracious to me and to Brian and Grainne, too. I should have liked to do something to show my gratitude. But it was always my wont to think and Brian's to act. On a sudden impulse, the Irish lad slipped from our marching rank to kneel before Eric and to say, even as he made his farewell:

"What would you from the new land, lord?"

The old man was touched by the boy's graciousness. He looked vaguely round his manor, his eyes red-rimmed and rheumy, until the animal cages caught and stopped his wandering gaze.

"Bring me a new bear, boy," he said, patting Brian's shoulder as he spoke. "Of a kind I have not seen yet. That is what I have come to love best in life these latter years."

Brian stood straight when he got to his feet.

"I will, lord Eric," he said, saluting the *hersir* of Ericsfjord. "I shall bring you such a bear as you have never seen before."

We had already heard Mass. So there was little to keep us now as the tide swelled and the breeze freshened. After Sira Inge had blessed the *Mariasuden* and her crew—all but Thorhall Gamlason, that is, who stood aside disdainfully—Brian kissed Grainne where she waited, wistful in her blue kirtle, a nosegay of spring flowers for him in her hand: a nosegay of primroses, violets, lilies of the valley, their clean fragrance bound together by fresh leaves of the whin.

"Till another spring, Grainne," he said, stooping over her, not trusting himself to say more, for the tears were close to the surface in his eyes as well as in hers. "Till another spring when you come to me again in Thorfinn Karlsefni's ship. Sira Inge will sail with you, if all goes well. It may be we shall be married then in the new land and hold our bride-ale there."

Grainne's blue eyes were bright with unshed tears. But she held them back till the *Mariasuden* was down the river and well into the fjord outside. She had neither time nor room to say farewell to me. I waved mine to her where she stood, still not weeping, but not far from weeping, either, by Mistress Gudrid's side. As the wharf dwindled in size behind us until the people on it were but toys in a blue distance, I saw Thorfinn Karlsefni's wife stoop over the girl and fondle her hair. She was a goodly mistress, that wife of Thorfinn Karsefni's. She was one of those of whom not much is said in life. But life could not get on without such as Mistress Gudrid was—and her good man, Thorfinn Karlsefni, too.

Once out in Ericsfjord Thorvald Skald picked up the oar beat with his harp song that was not really his alone but had been contrived of old to fit the push and pull of the long oar. I think the beginnings of our northern word-music lie in that creak and pull of the long blade in its tholepin.

"Over the whale's way," Thorvald Ericson began in the sea-farer's song that is old beyond men's memory.

> *"Over the swan's road*
> *Fare we unfearful,*
> *Fare we and bear we*
> *Foam-feathered oars . . ."*

Everything was provided for, but the Norn sisters wait not on man's will. Even as the *Mariasuden* was passing by the last Greenland headland we would see for many moons, something happened that Leif Ericson had not bargained for. Ari Marson, who had been moody all winter ever since the week Leif had held his betrothal-ale—though all of us had thought this fit of his would pass once we were out at sea—rose from his rowing bench and flung out an arm toward a farm on the tip of the passing promontory. The other rowers turned to look at him, not missing a single beat, not speaking.

"It is his betrothed's farm he says farewell to," said Thorvald Ericson, speaking low in my ear. "Her father died last week. Ari said to me at last night's feast that it could be his, if only he had not bargained with Leif to sail to the new land. I fear me he has repented that same bargain."

It was as if Ari were talking aloud to himself, standing there on the shifting deck planking.

"Fair are the slopes where my loved one lies," he said aloud. "Fair are the hayfields under the sun—fairer than I have ever seen them. Whose hand shall mow them this autumn, if mine does not? Who shall lie with Hallgerd, if I do not? Shall I sail off thus, and Hallgerd stay behind?"

As if in answer to his call—though she could never have heard him at such a distance—a woman came out on the headland and waved a red kerchief to the passing ship. With a hoarse cry, Ari Marson hurled himself headlong into the water from his bench, swimming strongly to the shore. Stunned, all we, his crew mates, dishonored with him in his dishonor, watched him go, still not speaking. With one oar off beat, the ship wavered a little on course. Never pausing to consider what he did, Brian, who had not yet been assigned an oar, slipped into Ari's place; and the missed beat was restored.

Thorvald Ericson said something to Leif who had looked on silent the while. Leif nodded. Ari's going left him but twenty-nine men to row, not counting myself or Thorhall Gamlason, who ordinarily had other duties to attend to, though we could fall to right willingly in a pinch. So be it, Leif seemed to say to Thorvald. He watched the boy pulling stoutly beside Thorhall Gamlason who, when he rowed as now, had been Ari Marson's bench partner. Brian would do, I knew. A few sore muscles tonight and tomorrow; but within a week he would notice nothing amiss. The lad was slim. Nonetheless his muscles were tempered by youth and wholesome living. I would match him in a week against any oarsman aboard the *Mariasuden.*

It seemed that Thorhall Gamlason thought much as I did. As they rowed in comradeship side by side, he spoke to Brian.

"You are really a free man now, Irishman," he said, grinning his wolf's grin. "Doubly free. And free, besides, by the rule of the sea which is even above the gift of the King. We are not like the southern galleys Tyrker fought against in Sarkland with the Varangians. There slaves row the ships; and their ships stink of servitude. Once any man has pulled an oar in a long ship, here in the North, he is ever afterwards a free man. But there is another stink in my nostrils today—the stink of a Norseman who has forever lost his honor. Ari Marson is worse than a slave. He is a coward. I would kill him on sight, if it would not dishonor me to touch such vermin."

Brian did not answer. Instead he seemed to give his whole mind to the oar so that, on this first stint, he would make no mistake and call down the mirth of his comrades. But I knew he thought long and gladly on what Thorhall had said to him. It is a good day in a man's life, the day he comes of age in deeds, as Brian had just done.

It was true, too, what Thorhall Gamlason spoke of freedom. I remembered that law of the North of which he spoke; and a thrill of joy played up and down my spine as the *Mariasuden's* timbers gave to the rhythmic swing of the rowers. While I looked on the lad, he rowed as if the heart would break out of his laboring chest, the air sobbing raspingly in his overtaxed lungs. Then, of a sudden, I knew that Brian had gone one step beyond weariness into a realm of mystic release where spirit and body for once were one. For the first time in his life, I thought exultantly, this boy began to be as a man is meant to be. For it had happened to me, too, years before, when I first rowed one of Thorberg Skaffhogg's *skutur.*

A plump of cool spray broke salt across our faces. The wind was freshening.

"Sea ho!" called the *stafnbui.*

Leif Ericson raised his right hand, Thorvald Ericson standing at his back, his harp hand on the strings ready to change the tune.

"Break out the sail!" Leif called to two men at the mast. I mind me now they were two of our Eastmen, Onund Trolleskog and Bolli Blacksark, good sailors both.

It was done as Leif commanded. The sail broke out at the mast. The Mary figure bowed, obedient to the wind's bidding. We were at sea. The great faring had begun.

Behind us lay Greenland, Iceland, Ireland, the outer islands, and the old homeland where towered the fjord walls and the high fells. Ahead lay the streams of Ocean, the Gates of the Sun, and the shores of that new land which so far only Bjarni Herjulfson and Illugi Tomcat had seen of all the sons of men. Should we, too, see them in our day, we comrades of the *Maria-suden,* with the Blessed Virgin at our prow and, let into our crossbeams, a tress of the holy Synnove to hallow our going?

CHAPTER SEVEN

NEW WORLD LANDFALL

WHAT IS IT DRIVES MEN LIKE OURSELVES ON A QUEST SUCH as this one of the *Mariasuden?* One might say gain in the case of Leif Ericson, great Greenland trader that he was. But it could not have been the hope of gain alone, not even in his case. Besides, what had I, Thrand Thorbergson, vowed priest, to do with gain? Or Brian, grandnephew of the Irish *Ard Rí?* Or Thorvald Ericson? Or Thorhall Gamlason? No, it is something far other and stronger. Something like the instinct to beget; like bird flight in the autumn; like salmon swimming upstream. Something drew us. There was a land waiting to be fulfilled, though I would not be so bold as to say, looking back, that we fulfilled it.

It will always drive men, I think, this thing whatever it is— to the edge of great Ocean Stream, and beyond. As we floated, becalmed, in a sea of dream stars, it came into my mind one night that man would not easily leave off his questing after what lay just beyond his reach. Why should he not even, one day, make a flying ship and voyage among the stars themselves?

In after years, when men asked me—as they had a habit of doing, many men, for it was not soon forgotten, that faring of ours—how long the first voyage to Vinland had taken, I used to answer, and truly, too, that the *Mariasuden* had been on the sea for a month and a half altogether, from early in June when we rowed out of Ericsfjord, to sometime after mid-July when Leif first made his New World landfall. But, before we sighted Vinland, we had seen and gone ashore on two other lands and on one great island. And much had happened in between, too. Such as the great storm. And Illugi Tomcat's illness. And other things, too, that I could not very well talk of, though I thought upon them often enough, and still think upon them now that I am grown old. Private things. Things that had gone on in my mind and in my heart. Things that even now, so many years after, I think it better to keep to myself even though, in the last years of her life, I sometimes brought myself to speak of them to Queen Grainne and she to me, in turn, of the undiscovered spaces in her own heart. Yes, we enclose within ourselves far lands no other eye but God's has ever seen, we men and women of this earth . . .

That first morning out at sea, Leif did not let the boatswain shake Brian into wakefulness quite so early as he roused the others. He said to me, in explanation—though no explanation was necessary—that he knew the lad would be stiff and sore from his first real stint at the oars. So Brian, rolled in his skin hammock near the afterdeck, did not wake till the bright sun of morning smote full upon his face. Then, judging from the look of surprise with which he greeted everyone about, it must have been as if a great cock crew in his ear, as, of course, it had. For, as Thorvald Ericson laughingly said, when he gave the boy the breakfast Ornolf had kept hot for him in the iron cauldron, was not the morning sun a golden cock indeed? The cockerel of the gods in fact, Gullinkambi, the Golden Comb, whose trumpet-shrill crowing—or so men used to say, at least—would wake Odin's warriors to battle on the day of Ragnarok. Meanwhile, went on Thorvald Ericson, still laughing, Odin's rooster awakened sailors every dawn. For every day's beginning was Ragnarok to a sleepy seaman.

It was reasonable in human nature to expect that there would be a little bit of grumbling that first morning about Brian's having full crew rank without having served any sort of apprenticeship. Not on his own account, to be sure—there was no personal objection anywhere to the Irish lad whom all his fellows liked well enough—but because he was so young. Thorhall Gamlason, who grew to like Brian better day by day, and Thorvald Ericson together quickly scotched that discontent. What other recourse had Leif had? Thorhall Gamlason asked reasonably. After all, he had not arranged for Ari Marson's desertion. It was a great piece of luck for the *Mariasuden* that Brian had turned out to be so strong and willing as he had yesterday showed himself. Otherwise they would have had to parcel out Ari's work among themselves—would they have preferred to stand extra watches when all this could be so easily avoided?

Then, in his turn, Thorvald Ericson pointed out that the great skald, Einar Tambarskelve, was but eighteen years of age when he first went before the mast in King Olaf Tryggveson's *Long Serpent*. Yet such heroes as Ulf the Red, who bore the King's banner when Olaf went into battle, Kolbjorn the marshal, Vikar of Tiundaland, and Haavard of Orkedal did not scorn to sail with Einar. After that, there was no further complaint on the men's part about Brian's age.

The good weather held for three full days. The second day out from Ericsfjord Brian took the helmsman's after-midnight trick for the first time, spelling off Thorhall Gamlason who rolled himself into his sleeping bag, when relieved at the tiller, and went to sleep without a word. I watched with Brian for the first hour to make sure he knew what he was about—for it is one thing to be taught a skill, even by the best of teachers, and another thing to carry it out oneself.

There was no moon yet, but the stars were clear whether one looked up at them where they burned steady in the heavens, or down at their trembling reflections drowned to starboard and larboard of the *Mariasuden's* swimming keel. Brian was steering by the North Star by the light of whose steady beacon he kept the ship on course. It came into my mind that, since this star by which we steered pointed toward the Bear, it was possible that Grainne, too, watched as we did at this moment—always supposing, of course, which was not likely, that that sensible woman, Mistress Gudrid, let her stay up this late. It was Orion Brian watched in between, on my advice, and I watched with him, keeping my eye fixed so steadfastly on the great star cluster that it almost seemed as if the sky Archer's bright bow of stars grew larger and larger in the breathing summer night. I felt, on a sudden, as if I could reach up and pluck it down from overhead.

Then, like some round viking buckler, the maiden moon rose silver from the silvering sea. In a short space the water, which had looked like molten silver when the moon first rose, became a looking glass unclouded even by so much as a single breath from the unseen giant holder who held it up to view in the palm of his great hand. I could hear the lad beside me catch his breath at the peerless beauty of the sight. Locking his tiller carefully, so the ship would stay on course by herself a little while, Brian softly picked his way by the sleeping men in their skin ham-

mocks to the prow of the *Mariasuden* where stood Inge priest's
carved Virgin wearing Grainne's lovely face. Looking down into
the water mirror, Brian saw Grainne gazing back at him. I left
the boy there looking down, and went back to my sleeping bag,
the ship on course, the sea still, confident that nothing could go
amiss. It was a mistake, though not a fatal one. It was a mistake because Ran is sleepless, if men sleep.

The boy could not have realized how long he stood there,
tranced. But it must have been much longer than he knew—or
than I knew, either, for I did not wake at first. But, as Thorvald
Ericson turned over in his sleeping bag, drowsy as he was his
trained eye noted that the North Star was by no means where
it should have been, if the *Mariasuden* were still on course. So
he sat up abruptly, as he told me later, and looked at the tiller.
There was no one there. Then Thorvald's eye caught sight of
Brian dreaming in the prow. Quietly, so that he should waken
no one, Thorvald made his way forward to the figurehead. The
boy did not even move till Thorvald laid a hand lightly on his
shoulder. Then he started like a guilty thing. It was then I woke
as well, so that I heard what Thorvald had to say.

"Brian lad," said Thorvald, whispering, but a whisper carries
far across still water when no one even breathes but Aegir. "It
is not well to desert one's post at any time—above all, at night.
Leif will not like it, if he wakes. And what if Ran wakes first
from her moonlit sleep and stretches out her arms to catch the
comrades you betray? Have you a net to take Ran in, friend
Brian, that you moon-gather thus on watch?"

As always, Thorvald Ericson's tone was light. But there was
reproach beneath the banter all the same. I was glad for the boy
that it was night so that Thorvald Ericson—and Thorvald Ericson was the kindliest of men—could not see him blushing. Or
me, either, when I thought upon it, for it was my fault every
bit as much as Brian's. Thorvald followed Brian back to the
abandoned rudder, the two of them stepping gingerly by their
sleeping companions. Then the skald fit seemed to come over
Thorvald a little, as it generally did whenever he thought on
Ran and those nine white daughters of hers who were the nine
great waves that swam in the sea.

"Listen!" he said to Brian, still speaking low. I listened, too,
rearing up on my elbow out of the *huthfat* which is what a
sleeping bag is called in the northern tongue. "Listen! Ran is

asleep and breathing lightly as she sleeps, her white breast going in and out. But Aegir, her jealous husband, knowing the sea's fickleness, never sleeps. Hearken to him, ever turning his ocean mill! No matter how quiet the day or night, that sea quern of his is never still. Always it turns under Aegir's hand."

It was true. Underneath the lapping and sucking about the *Mariasuden's* lower strakes, one could hear a far-off humming like the tiny roar that lives in the sea shells that are the many ears of the sea god, Aegir.

"We ride Ran's daughters now," went on Thorvald in his skald's way. "And, like women in love, they like it and sustain us. But take care that the tables be not turned. Take care that Ran's daughters, turning jades, ride not us."

Thorvald Ericson went back to his skin tent after that, leaving a chastened Brian at the tiller, leaving me—for it took my fancy so to muse—to think on that Ran and Aegir who were the Norse god and goddess of the sea; and on great Manannan mac Lir who was the Irish god of Ocean Stream. Bran, the dog, who had wakened when Thorvald Ericson did, slipped a cold nose and warm lolling tongue into my dangling hand. I caressed him while he panted next my bench. The great hound did not go back to sleep again. The two of us, man and dog, sat there, side by side, without moving, till Gullinkambi, Odin's cockerel, once more voiced his hero-crow in the whitening east.

It is good, now I am old and dawn brings only cold and creaking limbs, to think upon those other dawns when blood ran hotter in the veins of youth. But dawn now also, as it has these many years, brings me the Mass. Not even again to hear Gullinkambi's crow over the *Mariasuden's* mast at sunrise would I yield up my Mass as priest.

So Ran held her hand that time. But not for long.

On our fourth day out the weather changed for the worse. Gray clouds hung over the sea; and a drizzling rain began. Leif's luck changed a little, too. Ilugi Tomcat, who had taken Thorbjorn Lambason's place, fell sick of a sudden. The ailment, as he told us between violent bouts of pain, was of long standing and utterly disabling for the time it came upon him, although in between these onsets he was as hale and hearty as the next man. The cause of the sickness was that Illugi suffered from the stone so that, at times, he found it hard to pass his water. Whenever the condition became acute at Ericsfjord, Eric had used to send a messenger to Hafgrimsfjord where lived a leech named Sveinbjorn. Sveinbjorn knew how to ease the pain with drugs and hot compresses; and, after a day or so, Illugi would be all right again. Or so it seemed, at any rate.

But Leif Ericson had one great worry in the matter, he told me and his brother Thorvald, taking the two of us aside a space. Sveinbjorn leech had once told Leif privately that Illugi would never really be cured until he was cut for the stone. The leech had wanted to do this for some years; but each time he proposed it Illugi was unwilling. Then he had showed Eric, Leif, and Eric's *stafnbui* what must be done if the pain should ever come upon Illugi when they were at sea or else in a place where there was no leech. Sveinbjorn had said the danger point would be reached when the sufferer began—if he ever did, that was— to swell like an ox that had lain dead for a day under a hot sun. That would mean, if it happened, that Illugi would surely die if he were not operated on within twenty-four hours after the first onset of the swelling. For the two years preceding the *Mariasuden's* sailing from Ericsfjord, Illugi had not been bothered in any way; and men thought his trouble had gone away for good and all.

Unfortunately it had not gone away for good and all. This present attack was the worst one Illugi had ever known. On the sixth day out from Greenland he began to swell, even as the leech had said he might. His face, arms, and legs turned a bluish color. The men of the crew looked questioningly at Leif. Even remembering what he could of Sveinbjorn's instructions, Leif's heart must have quailed at the thought of what he had to do. But he steeled himself to do it all the same. When did I ever see Leif Ericson at a loss except that one time at Vik when he grieved for the death of the lady Thorgunna?

"Make a hot fire under the iron cauldron," he said in a low voice so that Illugi might not hear but Hunbogi Ale-Head might. "I must try to do what the leech said had to be done if things should ever come to this sore pass."

While Hunbogi made the fire ready, Leif tried to get the sick man to take some beer that the drink might ease the agony of what he was about to do. But Illugi was much too ill to keep anything down now. At the very sight of the beer he turned his

head away and began to retch. Then, though there was a heavy
sea running which made steady footing difficult, Leif had Illugi's
bench mates stretch him out on a sea chest before the mast. By
now Hunbogi Ale-Head had hot water in readiness and the knives
heated even as Sveinbjorn leech, who had learned his trade from
an Arab doctor in Sarkland, had instructed.

"This will hurt, Illugi," said Leif, placing a cool hand on the
sick man's fevered forehead. "It may even hurt a great deal. Cry
out, if you have to. But do not move. I do not want my hand
to slip. Bear but a space. Evil is uppermost now, it may be. But,
since neither good nor evil endures for more than a short space,
it follows that good must be close at hand again."

"I will not move, Leif," said Illugi, smiling faintly. "Nor will
I cry out. I would not listen to Sveinbjorn leech back at Ericsfjord when he said I should be cut. So I will dree my weird in
silence. Did I cry out when Eric took the spearhead from my
back the last time we twain went a-viking to Caithness?"

The mention of the spearhead gave Thorhall Gamlason an
idea.

"Give him a spearhead to bite on," said Thorhall. "Thus did
we at Jomsburg when this kind of thing came to pass."

"I do not need a spearhead after that fashion," said Illugi,
shaking his head. "If it has to come to spearheads, I wish them
on the end of a thrusting shaft, the spear shaft in my hand."

"Among the Varangians," said little Tyrker, craning over his
foster son's shoulder, "the *hakim* put men to sleep, before they
used the knife, by speaking low to them the while they made
them fix their eyes on a bright mirror. Shall I try that, Leif? I
have watched the *hakim* often and know somewhat of their art."

"There is no time any more for any of these things," said
Leif, the sweat beginning to stand out on his forehead. I grew
afraid that his heart began to fail him more than a little now
that the time had come to do as Sveinbjorn leech had showed
him.

First Leif felt the bottom of Illugi's swollen stomach, just
above the groin, where he had been told was the bladder neck
through which the urine had to pass. There was a hard thing
there all right, even as the leech had said there would be. It
moved a little as Leif's fingers probed it. Despite himself Illugi
groaned at the touch, and the sweat broke out clammy on his
forehead.

"Quickly, Leif," said Thorvald Ericson at his brother's elbow. The hard mass moved again under Leif Ericson's fingers. He pushed it as far down into Illugi's penis as he could, then tied a waxed fish line above it so that it should not move back. Then he tied a second piece of line in front of the hard mass. After that first groan, Illugi did not stir again. But he shut his eyes.

"Thrand Thorbergson," said Leif to me, speaking very low. "This is a fearsome thing I have to do. I want you to chant the *Pater Noster,* as the monks do, while I use the knife."

I did as Leif requested. Sira Inge Skakkeson had taught me another prayer to use in time of great need—the *Alma Chorus Domini* which was a list of more than fifty kennings for the name of God arranged in the kind of verse the Romans called hexameters. I chanted it aloud in a strong voice now, beginning:

> *"Agnus, ovis, vitulus, serpens, aries, leo, vermis,*
> *Os, verbum, splendor, sol, gloria, lux, et imago . . ."*

Then Leif deftly made a lengthwise slash with his *ryting,* and took out two stones. He held them up to view. I mind me now that, of all those men, only Thord Thordarson turned his head away like any woman. The rest of the crew crowded round to see.

"See, Illugi!" said Leif Ericson. "Here is what caused all the trouble! But two small stones!"

Even now Illugi Tomcat did not open his eyes. But he smiled a ghastly smile.

"Two only, friend Leif?" he asked in a croaking voice. "The proverb has it: *All good things come in threes.* Look again!"

Sure enough, there was a third stone—a much smaller one— just above the first thread Leif had tied. It yielded to his probing now, and Illugi was content. Then Leif poured in the hot oil that Hunbogi Ale-Head had provided for the purpose. As he did so, Illugi gave a long sigh and opened his eyes.

"Now I will take the beer," he said. "It is dry work, this stone-gathering."

"So say we all," said Svein Haldorson roughly, taking up an ale-horn in his turn. "I am hungry, too. What say you, *stafnbui?* Shall we eat early this day? As the saying goes—and it is a good saying—*To the grave with the dead, let the living munch their bread!*"

Leif Ericson laughed aloud.

"Svein is right," he said to Steinn the *stafnbui.* "Give instruc-

tions that there be double rations issued in honor of Illugi Tomcat's stone-gathering."

The swelling began to go down almost at once. By nightfall
Illugi's color was better also, for his flesh was sound. He mended
so swiftly that, within a week, he was as good as new.

Illugi's bench mates made a joke about it. They began to call
him Illugi Geld-Cat, insisting that his tomcatting days were now
over perforce. This worried Illugi at first till Leif, who thought
the joke had gone far enough, told him that he had no reason
for worry on this score. He would live to beget many a little
viking yet. After that the men went back to his old name; and
it was necessary to find another source for our laughter.

There are those, I know, who will say it is indecent to jest
about such things. But I think otherwise. Perhaps it would be
so for angels who are pure spirits without bodies. But we are
men with blood and bowels. Laughter cleanses as any purge. It
is hard, unchanging, masculine, and, like song, one of the oldest
of things.

The first land we saw was the land which, as it happened,
Bjarni and his shipmates had come on last. It answered to
Bjarni's description as Leif had heard him give it; and Illugi
remembered the coast outlines, too. It seemed, from what we
could see of it, a forbidding land of rocky caverns and ice-covered
fells, like the dead land where Utgard-Loki lay bound, the prisoner of the gods, in his cold cave. In those old tales the land
of Utgard-Loki was full of treasures—of gold vessels guarded
by dead warriors, huge hounds, and terrible Jotunns. Looking
on this blighted landscape, I thought to myself that there might
well be dead men and evil giants here; but I would wager there
was little treasure to be picked up round about.

Leif Ericson gave orders, nonetheless, that the *Mariasuden*
should sail in close, and that he and five others—Thorstein the
Black, Thord Thordarson, Thorgils Bollason, Bjorn Korekson,
and myself to keep the log—should go ashore in the afterboat.
Bjarni had not done this long years before. But Leif thought it
should be done. It was true the land did not look promising for
much. Still, he said, first appearances were quite often deceiving.
Things might be very different inland.

As it turned out, we might well have spared that effort, except
that, as captain, Leif dared overlook nothing. The land was bare

of grass as far as the eye could see. Inland were great snow-covered fells and glaciers flowing slowly down in enormous sheets of ice. Though it was already high summer, the icy breath that came off those slopes made us shiver. Otherwise, all the way from the sea to the foothills of the high fells was nothing but one great sheet of rock. Leif Ericson looked at the five of us and laughed.

"Well," he said, still laughing. "There is not much for us here, it is plain to see. We have now gone Bjarni one better by setting foot on this land. But much good has it done us! Let us name it now, and go elsewhere. For a land must have a name regardless."

"What can you name it, Leif?" Thord Thordarson asked him with a shrug, letting his spear socket sink into a rock crevice, then twisting the shaft about contemptuously. "There is nothing here worth naming so far as I can see. There is nothing here but flat stone."

"Then let us name it the Land of Flat Stones," said Leif, never giving over his laughter. "It is a dull name. But it suits a dull land."

When we got back to the *Mariasuden,* Leif instructed me, for that I was skilled in writing, to set down the new land's name as Helluland, the Land of Flat Stones. So Helluland was it called. But, for our own part, we took no land in that barren place where stood the ice sheets and the lofty fells, lifting anchor, instead, and setting forth again in the morning. There was plenty of fish there, though, it should be noted. The fishing brothers, Alf and Ornolf, caught several score of large fish which were broiled that night. So the *Mariasuden* got some good out of Helluland. We ate well, at any rate, off that Utgard-Loki coast, which, so far as I know, was more than Bjarni Herjulfson had done.

Leif Ericson sailed the *Mariasuden* down the eastern side of Helluland which turned out to be an island greater than any we had yet known—some among us, though, argued that Greenland was the greater, but I could not tell—till we came to its south-western corner where he once again gave orders to put out to sea. After sailing three days and nights, we came to a second land. This, too, said Illugi Tomcat—he had gone back all the way to being Illugi Tomcat now—was a land he had earlier seen

with Bjarni. So Leif directed Steinn the *stafnbui* to set the
Mariasuden's course as close to shore as it was safe. Then he
put out in the ship's boat for the wide beach in front of which
he had cast anchor. He took four different men with him this
time: Bolli Holluson, Steinn the *stafnbui*, Thorstein the White,
and Thori Englandsfari. I, of course, as record keeper, went with
him every time.

This second landfall of ours was far more promising than
Helluland, though Leif still thought he should fare farther before he made his first land-taking. It was level and thickly
wooded, with broad stretches of white sand gently shelving toward
the sea. It seemed there would be safe harborage for many ships
here. This particular beach where we had come ashore was, as
I judged, as long as a mile and, perhaps, a little over, even.
Some of the lordly trees were as tall as a hundred feet in height,
with spreading limbs and huge round boles. Old Eric, Leif said
with a little smile to Steinn the *stafnbui*, would lick his bearded
lips over such a stand of seemingly inexhaustible prime timber
as this was. But, even so, he said, it was not in his mind to
claim it just yet. If necessary, we could always return. But he
did not think it would be necessary. It was in his mind that
even better things might lie ahead of us.

"Let us name this land and go," said Leif to us five. "Let
us name it Markland, which is to say, Forestland, in accordance
with its qualities."

Even as Leif was speaking, the wind changed sharply. The
great trees groaned and bent over our heads. It was a northeaster,
and it was blowing in the same direction we were now going.
So Leif gave orders straightway that we hurry back to the
Mariasuden as swiftly as we could in order to take advantage
of this unexpected windfall of ocean air before the welcome
breeze should blow itself out. So hurriedly did we leave the
shores of Markland that I did not even have time to set its name
down in my chart. I took good care to enter it, later on, though.
And, if I had not remembered, Tyrker, who knew a little Runic,
would have reminded me speedily enough. For, when he was not
drinking—which he did once or twice a year until he fell dead
drunk—this foster father of Leif's was the most careful of men.
I spent what time I could spare teaching him to set down words
in the Latin characters that are so much more serviceable than
the rune scratches and slashes which were all he knew till then.

Later on, in Vinland, I made other copies of this chart. I have one with me now. I look at it often. It is a magic key to the locked chest of memory.

The northeaster did not blow itself out. Within a matter of a few hours, as so often happens at sea, it had even become too much of a good thing. The *Mariasuden* scudded at breakneck speed before the following wind till, at nightfall, Leif Ericson ordered the men to take down the sail and the mast, in addition, fearing that the wood might snap in the rising gale. A little after dark, rain set in in torrents. The sea was so high now and the wind and rain so fierce that it had become impossible to hear Steinn the *stafnbui's* shouted orders. Never, Thorhall Gamlason shouted to me through the white stinging spindrift, though he had been at sea for a quarter of a century nearly, had he seen so violent a storm. Then, without warning, as was her evil wont when angry, Ran claimed a victim from among us men of the *Mariasuden.*

Thorstein the White's sea chest broke loose from its lashings and rolled to the starboard side of the ship where, the next time the *Mariasuden* pitched, it burst open and Thorstein's belongings clattered to the streaming deck. The ship righted itself in the trough of the next wave. But Thorstein's things were already afloat in the raging water that swirled and foamed over the floorboards. It was clear to all that, as the *Mariasuden* rose on the next comber crest, some of them would wash overboard. With a hoarse cry Thorstein the White raced to starboard to salvage what he could of his little treasures. The downrush from the wave crest took him off his feet as he teetered, hands scrabbling at the topmost strake. Then he was swept away into the raging water.

There was nothing anyone could do about it. Thorstein the White was a powerful swimmer. Had he been stronger at swimming than Breca the Bronding or Béowulf the Geat, it still would not have availed. Ran would not stay her hand. Nothing human could live long in that boiling sea. Nor could we, his comrades, so much as launch the afterboat. One long cry, and our deck fellow was gone.

Though it was a little early in the season for this kind of storm, it was clear that we were in the path of a hurricane; and that the *Mariasuden's* only chance to come through in safety

was to stay afloat until the mighty wind had passed over to
blow itself out somewhere hundreds of miles away from us in
the outer sea. So Leif Ericson, who was the most cunning of
captains, gave orders that everything aboard be lashed even
tighter; and that we men cling as best we could to mast foot
and floor board. He knew that, if the *Mariasuden* were to drive
upon a skerry or a hidden reef, we were sure to founder; and
nothing could be done about it one way or another. Luckily, so
far as anyone could tell, land was many miles distant from where
we now fought against the storm.

In a lull in the wind blasts Thorhall Gamlason, salt riming
his gray wolf's beard, nudged me in the side.

"Well, priest that shall be," he said, grinning his crooked grin.
"What think you of greasing the rollers now? Things look a
little different on a night of storm at sea than they do on dry
land with no wind blowing—eh? It is all one to Ran. She will
have her life willy-nilly. But Thorstein the White is a heavy
price to pay, I think, for the life of Tora's dunghill bastard."

Meanwhile, at the mast, Leif took counsel with Thorvald Ericson, his brother, and Steinn the *stafnbui*.

"We have done all we can," said Steinn when Leif asked him
what further could be done. "It is Ran's hands, and the hands
of Aegir now."

"There is no Ran, Steinn," said Leif very angrily. "There is
no Aegir, either. There are only the Three-in-One Who sit in
power on high, Christ's Mother with Them, and all His Hallows."

"We had better call on Them, then," said Thorvald Ericson
grimly. "It is clear it is out of our hands."

"That is a priest's task," said Leif. "There is no priest aboard."

"Though I like him not overmuch," said Thorvald Ericson in
answer to that, "would we had Inge priest with us—or some
priest, at any rate. I could do with a priest for more reasons
than one. For one thing, I sorely need a shriving. There was that
maid I lay with the night before we sailed from Erics—"

"There is a prayer against shipwreck in this new faith we
have taken upon us?" asked Steinn, interrupting Thorvald Ericson.

"There is a prayer for everything in our new faith," said Leif
simply.

"Pray it for us then, captain," said Steinn.

"Unluckily I do not know it," said Leif.

Nor did I. Sira Inge had never taken pains to teach me that prayer, if, indeed, he knew it.

There came a sudden respite in the pounding of the storm. The wind continued to howl all about the *Mariasuden,* and the waves were as awesome high as ever. But, for the moment, there was no wind overhead. At first I had a wild hope that the worst was over. Then I remembered that there was said to be a core of quiet in every hurricane. It must be that we now had reached this heart of storm. It was as if we were on the hub of the wind wheel. Though just beyond us the spokes still turned at dizzying speed, it seemed almost as if the hub were still.

So far there had been very little lightning and thunder. Now balls of blue flame stood outlining the tiller, and on the shield rack, too, till the *Mariasuden* appeared sheathed in fire. I had heard of these fire balls from my father, Thorberg Skaffhogg, though I had never seen them with my own eyes before. I knew now—and my heart sank at the thought—that this stillness was but for the moment. When the *Mariasuden* moved again out of the storm's heart, things would be worse than before.

"Pray that prayer against shipwreck for us," said Steinn the *stafnbui* a second time.

"But I know it not," said Leif Ericson, almost despairingly this time.

He wrinkled his brow in thought. He had been a Christian for so short a time, I said to myself. There was so much to learn; and, to my shame, I could be of no help here. But Olaf Tryggveson had been a good teacher, especially on matters where the lore of Christ and that of the sea came together.

"There must be a vow," Leif Ericson said slowly, still thinking hard. "And every man on board the *Mariasuden* must be in that vow. So the King said when we talked together in Vik."

Leif Ericson looked over at the listening men who waited on his smallest word. The great stillness kept on within the ship and about it for a little space. But the outer roar began to be louder. The storm was coming back now. Like the Midgard serpent it was putting its deadly tail into its mouth, and the *Mariasuden* with it.

"Well?" said Leif Ericson to us. "Will you vow with me?"

"We will vow with you, Leif," we said to him, one after another, myself and Brian in the van, for the Irish are always quick when it comes to prayer.

But there was one who did not take that vow. Thorhall Gamlason said nothing. Only, his crooked grin became fixed like a wolf mask drawn over his face that gleamed with brine in the bluish light.

"You, Thorhall," said Leif, staring at him. "Will you vow along with the rest of us?"

"It depends upon whom you make your vow to," said Thorhall, staring back. "If it is to Asa-Thor you make your vow, yes, and with a will. There is no use in vowing anything to Ran now. We lost our chance there the morning the ship was launched and we did not anoint the rollers with human sacrifice. Now she is angry and will not hear. But Thor is mightier than Ran in every way. Is not the Lord of the Hammer the Lord of the storm as well?"

The roar of the returning wind became much louder. Suddenly I felt myself growing so angry at Thorhall Gamlason that a red mist of blood seemed to come before my eyes. It was in my mind to take up a heavy oar and brain Thorhall Gamlason with the rowing end. But, in the end, I restrained myself.

I think Leif Ericson was, if possible, even angrier than I.

"Asar-Thor is lord of naught!" he shouted. "Of nothing I tell you—nothing whatsoever! There can be no question either of Thor or Ran here. We Christian men make our vow to the one true God—to the Three-in-One Who sit on high in power!"

Thorhall Gamlason set his long jutting jaw.

"Then I do not vow, Leif," he said evenly, not raising his voice. "Unless I vow to Thor—and even then in my own good time. My mind is free, and nothing will force it. Nothing. Neither Thor nor Christ."

There came a growl from the crew at that speech. They cast black looks in plenty at Thorhall Gamlason. I had never seen them dare to cross him before. It seemed that in this wrestle between Christ and the old gods my comrades had chosen their side.

"Vow without Thorhall, captain," said Steinn the *stafnbui*, the fear of death by drowning staring in his eyes. "Surely one man standing outside the vow can do no manner of harm. To whom make we the vow?"

"To Almighty God," said Leif Ericson, "and to Christ, His Son, and to Christ's Holy Cross, and all Christ's saints. And first we must recite aloud—you after me—the seventy-four names of God as Olaf taught them to me when I was baptized."

Then, while the sea's sullen roar and the roar of the wind deepened moment by moment, Leif Ericson called on the seventy-four names of God; and we of the crew after him. Haltingly he went at first, then with a rush till, as he reached seventy-two, his tongue began to falter once again. At last, with a mighty effort, he brought out the seventy-third, but the seventy-fourth, which I had heard was the highest name of all, would not come no matter how sorely he tried.

"You leave one out, my brother," Thorvald Ericson urged him, and there was great trouble in his voice. "The highest name of all—you have not named that yet."

"I know," said Leif Ericson with a groan. "I have forgotten. Do you remember it?"

"I never knew it," said Thorvald. "Olaf never so much as uttered it in my presence, so there was no way of my knowing it. I know some names of God, as becomes a Christian who is also a skald—the ones you have already named among them, although I could not say all of them back. And I believe what the Apostle Paul says, in the Epistles, as I have heard Sira Inge read them, that there is no name of all the names of earth higher or holier than the name of Jesus. But what you and Olaf call the highest name I never knew."

Just then Bolli Holluson cried aloud, as if in fear, and pointed to the prow.

"Look, captain!" he said, his voice high.

It was indeed a strange sight. A cluster of the fire balls, like a crown of soft light, rested on the head of the figure which Inge priest had carved for the *Mariasuden's* prow. It was as if a great Queen leaned from the ship over the storm waves, commanding them. Or as if a Valkyrie soared in flame through a night of tempest. Even Thorhall Gamlason was shaken at the sight.

"It is either Vanabride," he said to himself, but aloud so that I could hear him. "Or else one far greater than Vanabride. In any case, this Mary of the Christians is a very great lady."

"A very great one indeed, Thorhall Gamlason," I said grimly, for I was still wroth against him. "And greater than you know."

"I believe it," he said, still shaken. "But I will not vow all the same."

"We have been granted a sign," said Thorvald Ericson in Leif's ear. "Do you make your vow to Mary Virgin. Her name, at least, is easy to remember."

And then, as if he, too, were, like Thorhall Gamlason, speaking to himself, Thorvald added low:

"And, for a skald, very hard to forget!"

The storm was back in full force now. Leif had to cup his hands and shout till the veins stood out on his temples in order to be heard above the tumult of the wind and waves. The *Maria-suden* bucked and reared in the wave troughs like a mare gone mad.

"I vow," crief Leif trumpet-loud, "I and my crew together with me, a Mary image in pure silver to be set up in my mother, Thorhild's, church, at Brattahlith. Now do you vow, too, O crew!"

"We vow! We vow! We vow what you vow, Leif!" we all cried, one after another.

Fat Svein Haldorson shrugged his broad shoulders. I remembered that it had been said that he inclined to Asa-Thor a little—not so much as Thorhall Gamlason, but enough.

"Why should I not vow?" he said to me. "A woman's counsel is bad, maybe. But he who does not take it is mad, since a man's is even worse—though I would not want my old woman at home to hear what I just now said! I take the vow then. I am for this Mary over Asa-Thor."

"Listen!" said Steinn the *stafnbui,* holding up his right hand for silence.

There was a new and disturbing quality in the storm's roar now. I thought, at first, that the roaring sound had become more clear than before; and somehow—I knew not why—much more menacing. Then, almost in the next instant, I realized what the new sound must be. It did not belong to the storm at all except in so far as the storm could be said to have increased it. It was a sound one could hear on the calmest day with no wind blowing —the terrible sound of waves breaking over a sunken reef. The *Mariasuden* was driving straight toward a line of breakers.

The crew of the *Mariasuden* rushed to the oars even before Leif gave the order. It was dangerous what we did now; very dangerous. We might lose some of the precious wooden blades in the surf that seethed white on every side. But, with breakers so close in front of us, we had no other choice but to tumble the

oars pell-mell out of their lockers and thrust them into the oar
holes in the strakes. We must pull against the wind and surging
sea with all our might and main, with every straining sinew. Or
we died within minutes.

But Thorhall Gamlason, though none pulled a stronger oar in
the *Mariasuden* than he, did not sit down to his bench at once.
First, standing tall and gaunt there in the wind and buffeting rain,
he threw back his grizzled wolf's muzzle and shouted a berserker
shout.

"It is fate that rules a man's life," he called into the storm,
"and not his own comings and goings. One may not live forever
—and it is far better to die with honor than to go on living in
shame. Nevertheless, life can be sweet while it lasts. So I make
my vow to you now, O Thor, my patron. It seems we did not
score our ship-runes deep enough while we still had time. But
nothing is impossible to Thor. Asa-Thor, Lord of the Hammer!
I call upon you now! I, Thorhall, man of the Jomsburg vikings!
I offer you sacrifice! I offer you my dearest treasure. I offer you
yourself!"

So saying, Thorhall Gamlason plucked his amulet from where
it hung about his neck. Even as he did so, I realized for the first
time what a splendid thing that ornament really was. It would
have fetched a king's ransom in the great London or Paris fairs;
or even in the greatest of all great fairs, the Emperor's bazaar
in Micklegarth. Surrounding the central image, which was a little
Thor cast in purest silver, each single hair of the god's curling
beard as separate as if it were real hair, not metal, hung many
even tinier Thors. They clashed together faintly now as Thorhall,
bounding to the prow beside the figurehead, swung the beautiful
trinket in his hand before flinging it into the boiling sea. I could
hear those little gods jingling in their flight through the foam-
flecked air; and I knew how much it must have pained Thorhall
to lose all that beauty. Just as the costly talisman entered the
water, there came a thunderclap that almost broke our eardrums.
Lightning flashed in the same instant like a crooked sword of
flame. One of the fire balls came to rest, for a long moment, on
Thorhall Gamlason's shoulder before it disappeared. Then, one
by one, the fire balls went out till the *Mariasuden* was left in pitch
darkness. The rain came down more heavily than before. The
spindrift stung as savagely as ever. Nevertheless, it seemed to
me that the storm's intensity was lessening.

Leif Ericson thought so, too, for he urged us to increase our oar beat a little. Slowly did we begin to make some headway against the force of the waves that battered us on every side. The breakers' din was noticeably farther off now. There was a chance, I thought, that we might win through, after all.

Hours later, the morning dawned spear-gray in the east. The rain had finally fallen off altogether now, and the wind gone down. The seas, though, were still mountainous. But it seemed to the *stafnbúi,* and to me as well, that the crests were smoothing out more than a little. Steinn indicated to Leif his belief that it would be safe to turn their course around for a while and go with the waves toward land, always taking due care to brake the *Mariasuden's* speed with the oars so that we might not run upon the reef.

All in all, I thought Leif had reason to be content. Taking stock, he found that we had lost but three oars altogether, plus Thorstein the White's sea chest. The mast was still in one piece, and the mast block. Cautiously Leif had the men step the mast again, though he still did not order them to raise the sail.

The loss of Thorstein the White was, of course, another thing. We comrades of his had liked him well; and he, in his turn, had always showed himself both a good companion and the best of sailors. I was always glad afterward that Thorstein had been one of those to set foot on Markland. It would have been a pity for him to have sailed so far and touched naught at all of the new land he had risked his life to see.

Thorhall Gamlason—and Leif Ericson was in no mood to say him nay—then set about carving a rune-stick with Thorstein the White's name on it—hurriedly, for he did not know whether or not the storm might return. When he had finished with his hasty task, Thorhall opened his own sea chest, took out some wadmal, and wrapped the rune-stick carefully in it against the time when it might buried on shore.

"When next we land," he said to me and Brian, "I will bury this rune-stave so that Thorstein's name will be in no danger of getting lost among the many nameless dead down there where now he serves out his time on Ran's rowing-benches. It is important that a comrade do this for a comrade in his time of need. I would want it done for me."

A thought seemed to cross Thorhall Gamlason's mind at that.

He stopped in his roping of the sea chest and looked questioningly at the Irish lad.

"Would you cut a burial stick for a comrade in such a case?" he asked him.

"Of course," said Brian, never hesitating. "If he wanted it, as you do. Even though I do not believe in runes, I should cut the stick for you, Thorhall."

The old crooked smile played over Thorhall Gamlason's face then.

"But I forget," he said to Brian. "You are to kill me on land, are you not? Or so the carline wife, Gefjon, said back in Vik. I would need no rune-stick in that case—only that the Hel-shoes be bound upon my feet. Would you take care of the Hel-shoes, too, Brian?"

I felt a chill at the base of my spine. I did not care for this sort of joke at all—always supposing that it were a joke. It might not be, either. One never knew with Thorhall Gamlason.

It seemed that Brian did not like the grim jest, either.

"Stop it, Thorhall!" he said angrily. "Gefjon is a troublemaker. Pay her no heed."

"I pay her no heed, Brian," said Thorhall Gamlason, quite serious once again. "The woman is an evil bitch, I know. But she may have seen truly for all that."

The chill mist that had settled earlier over the ship in the gray dawn began to lift. Gullinkambi was very late this morning; but it seemed now that his golden *lur* would soon be sounding. The blood warmed a little in our tired veins. Thorvald Ericson took out his crooked harp, tautened the strings which had gone slack in the storm damp, and raised a rowing song.

"Hup!" said the rowers, salt spray cold on their bearded lips. *"Hup! Hup! Hup!"*

Even now Leif was afraid to hoist sail. Under the oars of the rowers, the long ship, our Virgin ever stooping from the prow as if she were blessing the waters, plunged heavily into a wave trough. The cold mist was almost gone now.

Leif Ericson put up a hand for quiet. We rowers feathered our oars and waited.

"Listen!" said Leif.

There was a dull thunder somewhere in front of the *Maria-suden's* prow. Then Gullinkambi crowed his proud crow at last; and the sun broke through the last cloud. The morning light changed from gray spear to gold horn. As far as the eye could reach, green breakers creamed on long white strands. Overhead the sky was as blue as a chieftain's flag. A great rainbow arched over this new land like Bifrost, the rainbow bridge of the gods that stretches from Middle Earth to Asgard. As the ship fled swiftly down the green slopes of the combers, it seemed to me that I, too, was a god—a god of morning time in the company of other gods, entering the *Tír-n-an-Óg* on the colored bridge of the gods.

But Ran, who never sleeps, was not done with the *Mariasuden* yet. Racing in from outer ocean, faster than the *Mariasuden* could sail, came Ran's ninth daughter, a great beam sea smashing over the roped and fenced cargo in the waist, breaking amidships, and fore and aft as well. There raced, in her fleet wake, another of her deadly sisters, surging heavily over the whole ship so that the freight floated loose, as well as three more sea chests, and so would the afterboat have done except that Steinn the *stafnbui* was able to get his hard fists on it and hold it back from the swirling maelstrom of water. By now, however, we were well through the breakers. A third wave from outer ocean, not so heavy as its two sisters but heavy enough for what it had to do, smashed across our listing gunwales. At the same time the *Mariasuden* struck on a hidden reef. There was a rending noise. The ship shuddered like a stricken thing; and was still again.

"Row! Row!" shouted Leif Ericson. "Before the waves come back! Quick! There is not much time!"

Our eyes bulged from our heads then with the great effort we put forth. It was touch and go for a long minute. Then, with a scraping sound that made my heart bleed for this ship of ours, the *Mariasuden* freed herself from the reef's fangs and shot into a calm patch of water on the safe side of that raging roost of sea. North of the shore—we would be in its lee in a few more strong strokes—lay a large island.

"Pull for the island now," said Leif Ericson, "and cast anchor off it for a space. I wish to look at the keel before we go any farther."

When we had cast anchor, Alf, who was a good swimmer, went over the side to examine the keel from below—from above it seemed as if the keel were sprung, but things sometimes looked different from below. It was even as Leif Ericson had feared, however. The rock had strained the keel timbers sorely. Before

we set forth to ocean again, the *Mariasuden* would need a new
keel. It would be safe for the time being, though—especially if we
were going up the river and into the lake from which the river
flowed.

Leif Ericson went ashore on the island with Thorvald Ericson,
Thorhall Gamlason, Tyrker, Brian, and myself. Gleaming dew,
though the forenoon was already far advanced, lay heavy on the
grass of that isle. Brian touched his fingers to the grass-blades,
then put his fingers into his mouth, and tasted the dew. I ate of
it, too. Never, I thought, had I tasted anything so honey sweet;
yet it did not cloy as honey did, either. Again the thought came
into my mind, half seriously, half in play, that this same western
island might be in truth the beginning of the *Tir-n-an-Óg*.

Shielding his eyes against the sun, which shone full now, Leif
Ericson looked his fill at the long white beaches of the mainland.
Never, he said to me, while I poised a new quill over my writing
block, never had he seen beaches so beautiful as these.

"I will call this place *Furthustrandir,*" he said after a long
pause, "for that the beaches are so fair. Set it down duly, Thrand.
This, our third landfall in the new world, shall be called Wonderstrands."

Then Leif Ericson knelt down and crossed himself, as did the
rest of us except for Thorhall Gamlason. We had been a long
time coming, we men of the *Mariasuden,* and, at the latter end
of our voyage, the danger had been very great. But Mary Virgin
had granted us a good voyage all in all. Leif said the *Ave Maria*
over to himself even as Sira Inge had taught it to him in the
speech of Rome; and then again aloud in our homelier Norse
tongue:

> "*Hil dig, Maria, fuld av nåde,*
> *Herren er med dig.*
> *Velsignet er du iblandt kvinnene*
> *Og velsignet er dit livs frukt, Jesu.*
> *Hellige Maria, Guds Mor, be for oss syndere*
> *Nu og i vår dödstime. Amen.*"

Then he got to his feet again and looked at us others.

"We will fulfill our vow," said Leif, "when we sail, God willing, back to Ericsfjord. A silver image of the *Jomfru* Maria to
be set on the Lady altar in my mother's church at Brattahlith. It
comes into my mind also that, if we win through to Greenland

again in the *Mariasuden,* I should like the artist who makes the
image to cast the face after the goodly fashion of Inge priest's
carving of our figurehead. Then we should have our *Jomfru* both
at sea and home in the church. For my own part, I intend to give
the *Jomfru* Maria something more as well. I will send a candle-
stick of purest silver to be placed in her *Mariakirken* which is
a-building now at Vik, the first in all the Northland. It has been
a long time and a hard one, this sailing of ours from Greenland.
Through the grace of Mary Virgin we have come safely. I only
wish the great son of Tryggve had lived to hear of this feat."

Thorhall Gamlason, who had been listening all this while,
hooded his strange eyes now, the crooked smile again upon his
face.

"You think it was the *Jomfru* who helped us in the storm?" he
asked Leif Ericson. "It may well be, for I see now she is a Lady
not without great power. All the same I think it was my patron,
Thor. And why should it not have been the two of them? Also,
when it comes to the giving of silver images, I am ahead of the
rest of you. Have I not given my silver Thor back to Thor?"

"It was not Thor!" said Leif Ericson angrily.

"No?" asked Thorhall Gamlason insolently. "Perhaps not. Perhaps it was Leif's luck all the time. For luck, too, is a kind of
god. Who can tell?"

"By God!" said Thorvald Ericson uneasily in my ear. "I am
grateful to the Blessed Lady. But there is something in what
Thorhall says all the same. Who can tell, in the end?"

Not for the first time, nor the last time, either, I found myself
surprised by this wavering of the Norsemen in this matter of
faith which came so easy to the Irish. It seemed to me they all
wavered in their faith—all, that was, but Leif and Olaf Tryggveson. I, too, I am afraid, have been among the waverers in my
day. But never Brian. The Irish are like quicksilver in other
things. In this thing of the Faith they are like iron.

It was Brian who picked up skald Thorvald's gage.

"Who can tell?" he said indignantly to Thorvald Ericson.
"Why, it is as clear as water! Anyone can tell!"

"Water can be clouded, my Irishman," said Thorvald with a
light laugh. "But I will not argue with you, Brian. For you it is
very clear. You are, I think, among the lucky ones."

Before we rowed back to the ship, Thorhall Gamlason buried
the rune-stick carefully where no wandering animal was likely

to dig it up again. Tyrker helped him, spading the mossy turfs
with the *ryting* at his girdle. When Thorhall was finished, he
knocked the loose loam from his hands and looked up mockingly
again at Leif and Brian. But not at Thorvald Ericson. In his
heart of hearts, I know that Thorhall thought that Thorvald
Ericson believed about as much—or as little—as himself. And he
was right.

"Who is to tell about this, either?" was all that Thorhall Gamlason said.

Then the six of us rowed back together in amity to the *Mariasuden*.

So did we make our first landfall in the place that after came to
be called Vinland. I come next to how the fair land got this name.

CHAPTER EIGHT

LEIF'S LAND-TAKING

I KNOW NOW THAT IT WAS NOT THE GARDEN, THAT NEW LAND we came to in the *Mariasuden*. For we sons of Adam are not fated any more to gaze upon that Garden in our lifetime, though some of us have been promised sight of it in the time that lies beyond. But it was very lovely nonetheless. I sometimes think that first Garden, which we lost so long ago, could not have been much lovelier.

After our visit to that Isle of Honey, Leif Ericson took up his anchor and sailed into the broad sound that lay between the island of the sweet dew, where we had buried Thorstein the White's rune-stick, and a great ness that ran out northward from the land. He told us in a few words why he did not think it prudent to trust too long to the damaged keel. Then he spoke somewhat about his land-taking. I know that Leif wished this first land-taking to be both seemly and auspicious—auspicious because, in matters such as this, he liked to cling to the old ways of his fathers; and seemly because, as was true of many of his fellow *hersirs* in Iceland and Greenland as well as in the outer islands of what, till the coming of Duke William, men liked to call the old Norse Road, Leif was a kind of artist in conduct. Sira Inge Skakkeson was an artist with knife and color pot. Leif painted his paintings in deeds.

Leif told us he thought the keel would bear well enough, if the sea stayed as calm as it now gave promise of staying. Even so, it was his resolve to land somewhere no later than nightfall; and to refit the damaged keel within two weeks at the outside.

So the *Mariasuden,* with Leif Ericson at the tiller and Steinn the *stafnbui* taking soundings at the prow, sailed west past the ness. By the time we had rounded the cape, it was ebb tide; and, even though the tide was a neap tide, there was danger the ship might run aground. We waited till the tide should turn again,

rocking gently off the inlet of a small river that ran out of a lake,
a little distance inland, into the lagoon where now we rested, and
so to the broad sea that glittered under the morning sun. Leif
had us dip a bucket into the water where the river flowed into the
bay. It tasted cool and sweet. So, that we might not waste time
during the wait, he ordered the men to clean out and refill the
water casks.

It was possible, from where we lay, to see two of the three sea
chests which had gone overboard when the great waves smote the
Mariasuden; and the greater part of the lost cargo, too. The
things were stranded on a sandbar between us and the shore. Leif
directed three of the men to go over the side—it was so shallow
now one did not even have to swim to the sandbar—and secure
what could be salvaged of these goods. As it turned out, the cargo
was almost dry already, except where the bottom part still lay
under the water line. As for the chests themselves, the hasps
had held; and, though the goods inside were wet through and
through, they could be easily dried out. But there was an accident
when the second chest came over the gunwale. It fell heavily on
Thori Englandsfari's left leg so that the bone broke and the leg
itself was twisted awry with the toe pointing where the heel
should be by rights. Leif Ericson set Thori's limb in splints and
contrived a wadmal web so that later on it would be easy to carry
Thori ashore.

When, at last, the flood tide came surging back, it lifted the
Mariasuden on it. The breeze had freshened, too, so that it was
possible to use the sail. Very carefully, for he was favoring the
injured keel, Leif and the *stafnbui* eased the ship into the little
river.

Once we were in the river, it seemed as if the trees marched
down to the edge of the water and there made a shield screen of
green boughs so thick it looked as if an arrow could not go anywhere between them. The sun burned hotly on the green moving
shield of the flowing water. At one point, as the ship glided along,
we passed a small clearing where the deer came down on delicate
hoofs to drink. Three of the fragile-limbed animals raised their
heads when the *Mariasuden* went by, and looked on our ship with
great liquid eyes. One of them was a great stag with spreading
tines—a true lord of the forest, I said to myself, using his power
wisely and well. For up to here the birds had been singing and the
squirrels chattering overhead. But quiet spread out all around

where this wood king drank. It was as if the lesser beasts were his court and they waited in silence till their good lord was done. None of the deer showed any fear at all and, before the long ship was round the next bend, the gentle beasts had gone back to their lapping in the mirror pool that still trembled and rippled from the passing of the cleaving prow.

Thorhall the Hunter gestured to the drinking beasts.

"You saw them, Leif?" he asked. "I could take one with an arrow—easily. It is almost too easy. Either this is a manless world or the beasts are trained to come to a keeper's call. Whatever the reason, they show no fear of man."

Leif Ericson put a staying hand on Thorhall's arrow arm.

"Not today, Thorhall," he said, "even though our meat supply runs low. These animals are so beautiful and so trusting. I cannot bring myself to let them be killed on our first day in this new land."

"As you say," said Thorhall Gamlason. "It is folly not to take them when the chance presents itself. Yet I, too, feel the peace and beauty of this land."

Said I not that this son of Eric was a man among men? He knew when to rule, which is a great wisdom, and when to be ruled, which is an even greater wisdom. Now he chose, for a space, to be ruled by this land he had even now come to.

Now Leif Ericson had something very important to take care of before he cast anchor in the lake. This was something that had been done by all Icelanders and Greenlanders making new landfalls ever since two years before the battle of Hafrsfjord, when King Harald Fairhair established his dominion over all Norway. It was the great *hersir*, Ingolf Arnarson, who had first brought the custom to Iceland. Sailing westward to escape King Harald, Ingolf, somewhere off the south coast of Iceland, threw into the sea the carved posts of his high seat. Where the tide bore them up on the shore, there made he his home.

Leif Ericson's own high seat pillars, with the feats of Sigurd Dragonslayer graven upon them, were stowed with the rest of the cargo in the *Mariasuden's* waist. They alone had not washed overboard when Ran's daughters struck the ship out beyond the roost; and that was considered a very good omen. Now Steinn the *stafnbui* and Tyrker, working hand in hand, unlashed them; and, with all the rest of the crew watching him, Leif cast these adrift from the prow. Bobbing and turning as they went, the pillars he had borne with him from his drinking hall in Ericsfjord slowly but surely made their uncertain way to shore.

The posts touched shore at last on a little beach with the great forest at its sandy back. The pillars could not, it seemed to me, have found a better place—though I suppose I should account this business of the casting a great foolishness. But I do not; and there's an end of that. With a long sigh of satisfaction Leif Ericson turned away from the gunwale where he had been watching and looked up at the sun. It had been, I judged, more than ten hours since we had left the island of the sweet dew. The sun was westering. It drew on to evening now.

"We will go ashore for the night," said Leif. "Tomorrow I will make my land-taking, and we shall begin to build."

Thorhall Gamlason, since his Jomsburg oath forbade his sleeping anywhere but on a ship in sailing season—unless, of course, he was hunting far afield—stayed aboard the *Mariasuden* to guard it, with Tyrker to relieve him in the night watch. Leif Ericson sent an outpost ahead, Onund Trolleskog commanding, to scout the shore and the trees close to shore for signs of other men. Onund's party returned with the news that they could discover no tokens of life other than the tracks of many animals and the droppings of birds. Then, six at a time, our weapons loose in our hands, carrying our leather sleeping bags slung round our necks, the crew of the *Mariasuden* went ashore for the first time since Ericsfjord. It was necessary to make an extra trip for the heavy iron cooking cauldron; and another one for Thori Englandsfari who was let down over the side in his net of wadmal. Bolli Holluson and Thorstein and Black together took him after from the boat, one on each side, and carried him ashore while he sat across their cradling arms, a hand about the neck of either of his jesting bearers.

There was no dearth of salmon—very large ones, too, larger than we had known before—in both the river and the lake. Alf and Ornolf, with myself to aid, set out lines and caught a mess of the great red laxfish for supper. While they fished, Alf and Ornolf talked. Not of the new land, however, as did their comrades. They talked, instead, of the many sea creatures they had taken elsewhere in a lifetime given over to fishing. Ling and haddock and whiting. Keeling and mackerel and conger eel. Sole and skate and turbot. Lobster and cockles and oysters, too. And—best of all, they said, for the sweetness of its tender flesh—the meat of

the small caain' whale that haunted the Faroes. As they went on
talking, I felt a hunger come upon me for the whale flesh, which
used to be the greatest delicacy on Thorberg Skaffhogg's table
back in Ladehammer, and I asked Ornolf if he thought we might
sight whale in waters as warm as these. Ornolf said he thought
not, on the whole. But Alf did not agree with him. So we talked
about this matter a space while the silver-mailed catch grew ever
higher in our wooden pails.

When supper was over—and we drank deep of the Norse beer
in our casks—Leif Ericson ordered the fires stamped out except
for the burning turf that was always kept smoldering, afloat or
ashore. Then he appointed a guard to stand watch this first night
in the new land. Gunnbjorn Ravenson, Steinof Humblepie, Thorgils Bollason, Viga-Thorlak, Thorleik Eldgrimson, and Bjorn
Korekson were on that first watch. They were to keep watch, two
at a time, turn and turn about, for a stretch of two hours, for
the six hours left before daylight. Brian and myself, for whom
Leif had other plans on the morrow, were left out of the draw;
as were Thorhall Gamlason and Tyrker who kept their own watch
aboard the *Mariasuden*. We twain were to help Leif with his land-
taking. He wanted us to be very fresh for that.

Hours after his camp had fallen asleep, I noted that Leif Ericson stayed awake in his skin bag, staring into the darkness where
nothing moved now but the little night things overhead and
underfoot. Except, now and then, a sentinel leaning on his spear.
Or else a great white owl calling from a tree. I could not fall
asleep myself at first. Once what seemed to be a demon, so shock-
ing was its echoing mirth, laughed out on the dark lake. Holding
my breath, I listened to that high-pitched laughter, heart racing
in my breast. Leif Ericson, hand on sword hilt, had sprung to his
feet. Then, as something dived in the water, he relaxed again.
The sound, I would wager, came from no human throat. But I did
not think it came from any devil's throat, either. Most likely,
judging by those water noises, it was a new kind of fishing bird.

As I lay awake in the darkness waiting for the morning, it
came into my mind that I wished Leif had brought Sira Inge with
him on the *Mariasuden* instead of leaving him behind for Thorfinn Karlsefni to bring with him in the spring. It was a selfish
thought, of course, since Inge priest had chosen to stay in Greenland, of his own free will, until Bishop Sigurd should be able to
send another priest to that priestless land. But it would have been

fitting, nevertheless, that a priest should have sanctified our first
coming to this beautiful new place; that a priest should have
blessed our houses even as they were a-building. Also—this was
a private reason on my part—in the years during which I had
been a Christian I had grown strangely used to and dependent
upon the pleasant habit of the Mass.

But even a captain and his scribe must sleep in the end. In a
little while Leif Ericson, too, slumbered with his men. Once again,
out on the dark lake, the fishing bird uttered its unearthly cry.
The two sentinels shivered and drew closer together. But Leif,
though he turned over in his skin bag and muttered something,
did not wake again till Gullinkambi shrilled his morning cry in
the east. Nor did I, once I had dropped off into my own dream-
less sleep.

Next day, between sunrise and sunset, Leif Ericson made his
land-taking according to the ancient practice of the Northland
that lies beyond men's furthest memories. I accompanied him,
bearing my writing tablets. Brian came with the two of us, inasmuch as land-taking called for swiftness of foot, on the markers'
part, and the Irish lad was by far the fleetest man on board the
Mariasuden.

At dawn, with his own hands—even as was called for by the
changeless ceremony—Leif built a huge fire in the iron cauldron.
Then, taking a blazing brand from it in his right hand, with Brian
to aid in this part of the work, he set forth over the land, making
a chain of fires. It was the law that had come down to Leif from
his fathers that a *hersir* might claim as much land as he could
stride over, fire in his hand, in a single day between dawn and
dusk. Along with the land rights went the accompanying rights
of grazing, sealing, whaling, hunting, and fishing. From what I
could see, gazing round, those rights would amount to a great
deal. The rich resources of this land seemed inexhaustible. So
thick and green were the grasses that cattle, when Thorfinn
Karlsefni should be able to bring them, would never want for
winter fodder. We saw tracks of deer on every side. There were
game birds, too, that could be stalked with a bow even as one shot
grouse in Scotland and the Orkneys.

Leif Ericson first went right and left along the shore for a
considerable distance in either direction, before striking inland.
When we turned away from the open beach, then, it proved to

be hot work among the trees and brush. Leif and Brian had to be very careful not to fire the dead branches that choked our way— I had the easier task by far here, for it was my part to follow in their wake, recording. There seemed to be trails here and there which, though we were quite glad to use them, made Leif more than a little uneasy. For, as he explained to us, if these paths could have been made by animals coming down to drink in the lake, it was equally possible that they could have been made by the shod feet of those far more dangerous animals called men. We would have to be on the lookout, he said. Natives of any given land rarely regarded newcomers as friendly.

A little before sunset Brian, who had been walking a few paces in the van, stopped suddenly short and put up a warning hand. I halted in my tracks. Without a word, Leif Ericson loped silently to the boy's side. In the soft loam alongside the trail there was the clear print of a naked human foot. It was, moreover, fresh. I would judge it had been made within the hour. Like animals in peril, we all of us froze into immobility. But nothing untoward moved in the bushes along the trail; and the birds did not leave off their singing in the sunset.

"Take cover, Brian," said Leif, speaking low. "Thrand, stay where you are."

For I was already in a kind of cover, behind them and a little to the left.

Quickly and quietly Leif and Brian stepped off the trail, being careful to leave no marks where the soil was soft, and behind a screen of low growing trees. Even as they did so, Leif quenched the torch in his hand, which meant that there was now, by custom, an end to his land-taking. It was well we had acted so swiftly. A minute or so later—no longer, certainly—a man came stepping along the path we had just left. He was stark naked except for a breech-clout about his loins. There was a red feather in his oiled blue-black hair. His skin was copper-colored. His eyes slanted in his head; and he carried a bow—a crooked bow not unlike the bows Tyrker had described as the bows he knew in Sarkland. His nostrils were twitching a little as if they smelled the burning pine knot Leif had just put out. Never had I seen such a man as this before. It came into my mind, though, that our Lapps had black eyes canted tiltwise like this strange man's. But Lapps are small. This man was as tall as Thorvald Ericson; and Thorvald Ericson was not a short man.

Stealthily, so that he should make no manner of sound, Brian slipped the crossbow Hunbogi had fashioned for him from his back and sighted it at the red warrior. The man was, at most, no more than ten paces from him. He could not miss. Brian's eyes sought those of Leif, questioning. Leif Ericson shook his head.

Leif Ericson was ever for peace. If he would not suffer Thorhall Gamlason to take a deer the day before, he would not have Brian slay a man today. But I thought that Leif had another reason besides his real desire for peace. Where there was one man like this one, there were sure to be others. Perhaps many others. The crew of the *Mariasuden* were brave enough. But they were far too few to fight the bowmen of a whole new land. So Leif and Brian and myself waited there beside the new world trail, not speaking, till darkness fell. Then very quietly, still not speaking, but swiftly, too, so that we should be away from the place before the moon rose, we made our way back to the beach.

The coming of the strange warrior meant that Leif Ericson's land-taking fell short by a few acres of what it might have been had the red man not come walking down the forest trail to where we wished to plant the last stakes of possession. But I thought the son of Eric was more than content. As it was, he had taken enough land—and to spare. It would, he said, laughing, to Brian and me, more than last out his lifetime.

"I would not speak of this red man to anyone," said Leif Ericson, as the *Mariasuden's* camp came in sight once again, an orange moon just rising over the ship where it rode at anchor— for the night had turned breathless hot. "Not yet, anyway. My brother, Thorvald, I shall tell, of course, and Tyrker. Steinn, too, I think. But no one else. Above all, do not speak of it to Thorhall Gamlason. Thorhall the Hunter is too bloodyminded to be trusted with such knowledge."

It was a mistake not to tell Thorhall Gamlason, one of the few Leif Ericson made in this new land. He should have remembered that Thorhall was the *Mariasuden's* hunter, and, so, well versed in signs and footprints. As for not telling someone about something, that was a game Thorhall could play as well as we. We soon found that out.

So ended Leif's land-taking in the new land. But a question rises in my mind about this land-taking. Can one take land anywhere? Or does one only offer oneself to the land and let the land take him?

Another notion comes into my mind, too, about this matter of land-taking, now so many years after the summer day I helped Leif Ericson in his first new world land-taking. I think that even then the idea of landholding was growing a little weaker among these men of the ship. It is true that this is not so with Duke William's men who have just now come into England and are ruling there; nor with these Irish among whom I now live. But they are men of the horse and men of the castle. They are not men of the sea. These men of the sea are restless and like to count their wealth in goods, not acres. They do not feel, as landsmen feel, that land should never pass out of the hands of the family; that the children of one's son must be begotten in the same bed as the children of one's father; that all the members of the line must, in the end, sleep in the same barrow so that the men whom the earth has nurtured may, in their turn, nurture the earth.

Here, too, in this change, I think I saw the beginnings of a new thing, the end of which lies many centuries in the future. For good or ill? I do not know. No one, I think, knows.

Next morning we began to build those cabins which of old we Northmen have always called *buthir*. Thori's leg healed nicely though, from this time on, he halted a little in his walk. The *Mariasuden* was drawn up on the shore and turned over on her side so that the keel might be replaced under Hunbogi Ale-Head's and my supervision. We used a new kind of wood for this, Hunbogi and I. A hard wood, good for ships, of which Leif had no experience but which, for want of a better name, he called *mosur,* since it was something like the maple wood one called *mosur* back in Norway.

Afterwards, because our ship had come near foundering nigh the promontory, the injured keel was set up on that cape's end for a memorial. Leif Ericson said that we should call it Keelness henceforth; and I set this down in the log. This was the same keel Thorfinn Karlsefni saw when he came in the spring. Leif had as yet, however, no manner of name for the new land, which chafed Tyrker more than a little. For Tyrker had a tidy mind which fitted all things into individual compartments as into chests. He complained of this to Leif. But Leif only smiled and said that a name would come along in good time. I was more patient than Tyrker. I knew that a land, like this one we had come to, is as a beautiful woman who cannot be forced against her will.

As it happened, I had a name to set down before the time summer was out; and it was a name of Tyrker's own finding, too,
though it was Leif who really gave it, as he had given the other
names on our faring. Tyrker had been out with an exploring
party one day in the misty time that wavers between summer and
fall, and had strayed off by himself so that, when the party returned, he was not with them. Leif had no time to grow anxious
about his foster father before the little bandy-legged southern man
appeared again, his mouth purple-stained, his hands laden with
blue grape clusters, gabbling excitedly in that speech of Sarkland
which he had known long before he had learned Norse. When
Tyrker recovered himself somewhat, he handed over what was
left of the grapes to Leif.

"Grapes! Grapes!" he said, beginning to speak once more in
his oddly accented Norse. "Vines upon vines of them! Never
have I seen such miles upon miles of grapes, Leif! Vineyard after
vineyard! We can press them for wine now. Then, this winter,
I can drink of the blood of the grape again, as a civilized man
should. For this cold northern beer has always lain uneasy on
my stomach."

Tyrker spat out the grape seeds in a kind of ecstasy. Thorvald
Ericson, who had once fared to Rome, suddenly found himself
thinking—as he told me later, knowing that I had a fancy for
such images—of a statue he had seen in that old city. It was
called a satyr, he said; and it was of a stocky man, like Tyrker,
with goat horns on his forehead and goat hoofs where his feet
should have been.

"Grapes!" said Tyrker again, as if singing to himself. "Grapes
for good red wine!"

"We will press your grapes for you, *fóstri* mine," said Leif
Ericson affectionately to the queer little man whom he loved so
dearly. "And since there are so many grapes about here, let us
call this fair new land of ours the Land of Wine."

So Vinland was it set down in the book I kept. Autumn drew
on and the wine was pressed in the Land of Wine. Thorhall the
Hunter, who had a taste for wine as well as for ale, found a
delicious game bird with a fan tail and red wattles which it puffed
out when angry. The great fowl proved to be better eating than
chicken even; and it went with wine as well as with beer or, for
that matter, with anything else.

As for the red warrior with the feather in his hair, Leif Ericson saw no more of him or of his kind; nor did anyone else among us so far as I knew. Gradually my fears in the warrior's regard went away again. As time passed, I was more and more inclined to believe that the warrior had come alone from somewhere far inland, and that he had gone back to his home, wherever that might be, without sighting the *Mariasuden's* camp.

I had with me a very precious thing which Sira Inge Skakkeson had given me the night before the *Mariasuden* sailed away on our Vinland faring. It was a treasure he himself had been loath to part with; for he had got it on Iona and there was not another like it in all the Northland and none better even in the length and breadth of Frankland where there are so many costly things. It was a book, ornamented by hand in green and vermilion and gold and silver leaf, of the Letters of St. Paul. There was one of these —*Romans 8, Verses 18-23*—which became very dear to me that summer and fall in Vinland. For I thought it said what I used to feel when I looked upon the beauty of living things:

> *For the eager longing of creation awaits the revelation of the sons of God. For creation was made subject to vanity—not by its own will but by reason of Him Who made it subject—in hope, because creation itself also will be delivered from its slavery to corruption into the freedom of the glory of the sons of God. For we know that all creation groans and travails in pain until now . . .*

I mind me now I took a kind of perverse pleasure in thinking that here, in this new land, that revelation had been fulfilled and that this land already enjoyed the freedom of the glory of the sons of God. It was not so, of course. Yet it was partly so, too.

Meanwhile the land had a name which is part of a land's fulfillment.

So we made ready for winter in the new land of Vinland, enlarging our cabins, felling trees for firewood, curing deer flesh, building a long shed on the shore—like the sheds I knew at Ladehammer—to keep the *Mariasuden* safe and snug from the northern snows.

CHAPTER NINE

THE BEAR

WHEN A MAN SHIPS FOR A LONG VOYAGE ON A SHIP LIKE THE *Mariasuden,* something happens to him. His other country, the land one, retreats in his mind. The ship he sails becomes his country. However, now that we had made our settlement in Vinland, that other sea country began to ebb a little for me in its turn. I found that Vinland was becoming my country in a way in which not even Olaf Tryggveson's Norway had been. It is not altogether true what one of those old Romans says—they spoke of him on Iona—that in travel one changes one's skies, not oneself. One may or may not change oneself—I cannot tell about this. But this I do know: new skies can change a man. They did me, at least; and Leif; and his brother, Thorvald Ericson; and Brian; and most of the crew, too, though I cannot really speak here for that old wolf, Thorhall Gamlason. Speaking for myself only, I know that, day by day, I became more fulfilled, as it were. Perhaps Thorhall Gamlason did change a little, at that. He found a god that satisfied him. Only, as other men have done before him, in the end he killed his god. And that, I think, changed him most of all.

If the great-tined stag we saw drinking on that first day was the forest lord of this far wilderness, I think Thorhall Gamlason might have said that a bear was its god. This is unholy talk, maybe, for a priest of Christ to set down. But it is not I who think all this. It was Thorhall Gamlason. Nonetheless I know why he felt as he did. For, with my own eyes, I saw more than a little of this matter: and with the eyes of others even more. One might even say that, in part, I saw through the great Bear's eyes and smelt through his moist nose. But I shall have to explain about all this in its proper place. Only one other time did I ever traffic with the unknown powers; and that, as you shall see, was in Dorrud's house on that Good Friday which was the day of Clontarf. I would not do it again. It is fraught, I think, with spiritual danger. In Dorrud's house, to be sure, I could not help myself. I did what I did of my own free will, that day in Thorhall's cabin.

Autumn brought one great surprise to those of the *Mariasuden's* crew who, like myself and Thorvald Skald, liked to look on lovely things. The trees died more gloriously in this new land than they do elsewhere. There are no trees at all to speak of in Greenland; and only scrub growth in Iceland. In Norway, Scotland, Ireland, and the outer viking islands, the autumn trees are sad ladies in yellow gowns. Here they are gods and warriors burning, like great Balder, on funeral pyres of many colors. A Vinland forest in fall is like trumpets blown for the day of Ragnarok. Especially about our lake mirror was it beautiful where the still water gave back magical reflections of the tree warriors in their funeral splendor. I liked to walk with Brian round this lake's looking glass, the lad talking of Grainne as we did so, our feet scuffing aside the bronze and crimson mounds of fallen leaves. It was, Thorvald Ericson said to me one day in wonder, like the shield-maiden Brynhild's magic fire-wall of painless flame or some soundless war horn wound by hero Sigurd.

As October drew on, Tyrker's wine was at last ripe enough for drinking; and the little man made the best of his grape-discovery. He began one of those bouts that, two or three times a year, left him senseless at the end of every evening, and no more than half alive during those days when the drinking fit—it lasted a fortnight usually, then went as suddenly as it had come—was on him. Tyrker bothered no one at these times, sitting alone with a drinking horn in one hand and humming over to himself, in minor key, one of the weird tunes he had brought with him from his Sarkland birthplace.

Nevertheless, Leif told his brother Thorvald, he felt that he had to speak to him. Tyrker was setting a bad example. He did not want the other men getting into the habit of this aimless heavy drinking so long, at least, as the autumn weather still held. There was still very much to be done; and not too many hands to do it. Remembering the red warrior of last July, Leif, without saying why he did so—but we knew, Brian, Thorvald, Tyrker, Steinn, and I—had the camp fortified on all sides, including the water side, with earthworks and a double stockade. Later on, in the long winter nights, he said he was quite willing that the drinking regulations should be relaxed—though he thought that the men should keep from swinishness at all times. All this was a matter of course; something that the crew of every long ship took for granted. But another fact made it necessary to husband the precious casks of strong ale. The malt and hops supplies we had borne with us in the *Mariasuden* were fast dwindling. They could not be replenished until spring.

Speaking of spring, Leif told his Vinland council that he had come to an important decision about spring. As soon as the sea was navigable again, he meant to take the *Mariasuden* back to Greenland. He had thought, during last spring when he and Thorfinn Karlsefni first talked this matter over, that Thorfinn would be able to make his way to the new land unaided, merely following, as Leif had done, the information given the two of them by Bjarni Herjulfson and taking with him, even as Leif had done in Illugi Tomcat, some member of Bjarni's old crew— several of these had settled down on farms in Greenland. He knew now, he said, that this plan could not work. The new land, from all that he could see, was so unbelievably enormous that Thorfinn Karlsefni, good sailor though he was—and Leif told us proudly there was none better than this Icelandic brother-in-law of his—would have no more chance of finding the *Mariasuden's* settlement than he would of turning up a pin in a haycock. It would not be so difficult with a map. So Leif intended to carry copies of my charts with him to Greenland. Then, if brother Thorfinn's three ships became separated from the *Mariasuden* on the westward crossing, they should be able, God aiding, to make their way to the lake island by themselves.

Leif also said he would take as few men with him as possible on his eastward crossing. This would leave more space free for cargo in the *Mariasuden*. We needed some cows and a bull. Some chickens. A few sheep, too. Also many seeds of different kinds. It was clear, he said, that this new land would bear grain more easily than either Greenland or Iceland—or Norway, either, for that matter. It should also do well with barley for brewing malt; and with hops, too. After this year, he hoped, we would not have to depend on a long and perilous ocean voyage for our beer. In addition, he would try to secure a store of the best malt. If the winds drove him anywhere near the Orkneys, he intended to put in at Papa Stronsay, which was on the northeast side of those

islands, where a hermitage of Culdee monks malted the best
barley for beer in all the Northland. Aside from the fact that
there were several Norse religious among these Irish hermits, he
knew they would be glad to sell a fellow Christian like himself a
supply of this barley as well as some seeds for planting barley
in the new land.

Meanwhile, though, he concluded, the waning beer supply would
have to be looked on with a jealous eye. And Leif's tipsy foster
father, Tyrker, as a senior member of the camp, was going to
have to set a much better example than he was now doing. So,
with a weary sigh, Leif Ericson spoke to Tyrker early one evening before the wine had him altogether under its strong spell.

"You are too old, *fóstri* mine," he said reproachfully. "Too old
for nonsense such as this."

But little Tyrker had a good answer for that.

"Odin, the All Wise," he said, hiccoughing the while, "is much
older. And does not Odin live by wine alone?"

Svein Haldorson was about at the time. He hugged himself
helplessly at Tyrker's drunken reply.

"I could not have done half so well," he said to me, laughter
rumbling in his huge belly.

Even Leif could not help but laugh as he looked down into
the merry eyes and shrewd brown face of the *Mariasuden's* satyr.

"Yes, *fóstri* mine," he said, still smiling. "That is true enough.
But, remember, you are not yet as wise as Odin."

Tyrker had an answer even to this.

"Maybe I will be, Leif," he said, swaying a little as he stood.
"Maybe I will when I have drunk as much wine as Odin the All
Father. You must give me more time—and much more wine—to
prove myself."

Their conversation turned out better than Leif Ericson could
have hoped for, at that. Tyrker was as drunk as ever again that
same evening. He did not start off again next day, however. In
fact, he did not once set drinking horn to lips again until the
Yule feast began two and a half months later.

Men have their own reasons, always, for drinking as Tyrker
did. I had often wondered what Tyrker's was. It was not the sort
of question one comrade asks another. He never told me, either.
So there is one of the several secrets I never managed to find out
while I lived in Vinland.

Brian helped with the digging for the earthworks and with the felling of trees for the stockade. It was easy to see that this new land agreed with him. He did not need grapes as Tyrker did. The wine of every morning was heady enough for youth. His shoulders broadened and his chest grew greater. He gained something over an inch in height so that he now stood taller than Leif Ericson but something under Leif's brother, Thorvald. Looking on him these piping autumn days, the thought came into my mind that Brian was no longer a boy. He was become a man; and a strong one, to boot. I did not think that any one of the crew could equal him in bodily strength now except for Leif himself, Bolli Holluson, and Thorhall Gamlason.

Brian was as much stronger than myself as an eagle is than an owl. I have not said this before for fear of shame in my own eyes. But it might be said with truth that I looked not unlike that latter bird of Minerva. It was an owl's curving nose and an owl's staring eyes, at least, that stared back at me from the pannikin of morning water into which I daily dipped them. Well, we cannot all be eagles. And an owl is not altogether lacking in good qualities, either. Or so I used to say to myself in those days of my youthful vanity.

Thinking a second time on Brian's strength of limb, I decided that Thorvald Ericson could probably equal the lad, too. But only when the battle-light shone in Thorvald's eyes. In between these times he was inclined to be languid, preferring to toy with the strings of his crooked harp, writing down new *rímur* which he would later sing to our assembled company at night. When it came to shield play, however, no man aboard the *Mariasuden* could best Thorvald Ericson.

During those days Brian spent more time with Thorhall the Hunter than with Thorvald the Skald. Thorhall Gamlason had much to teach a willing disciple; and Brian found, on his side, that he had a great love of the hunt. As it happened, these same autumn days were Thorhall's busiest time. Like all good hunters worth their salt, he abode by the ancient game rules that enjoined one might take no squirrel or hare in the summer months, and no doe or female bird at any time.

It came into my mind as I listened to him tell Brian the laws of the hunt that if Thorhall Gamlason had a real religion, it was this same business of hunting which he had learned, as a boy, among the Finns and the Lapps of the northern tundras. One of

their shamans had taught him how to dance, before a hunt began,
for the animals he wished to take. If the animal he chanced to
kill was a lordly one—a great stag, for example, with spreading
antlers, or one of the mighty new world deer with a blunt nose
curling over to meet a broad lower lip and horns that were to
other deer horns as was the oak to other trees—then Thorhall
would decorate the dead beast, bow before it, and say:

"Forgive me, my brother—for I am your brother and I grieve
much for killing you. It is only that I am poor and need your
flesh for food, your skin for covering. I am poor, my brother.
That is why I kill the brother I love."

Thorhall kept the horns of the greater animals he slew hanging
on the walls of his cabin—not for vainglory, he explained, but to
honor the forest princes these horns had once belonged to. There
were ways of preserving the heads, too, he said, but the Lapps
had never taught him these arts, insisting on keeping some of
their secrets to themselves. He also carved in walrus ivory little
images of the animals he hunted. He had done a seal, a deer, a
walrus, an aurochs, a mountain lion. Though he never sculpted
anything but animals, I accounted him an unusually fine artist;
and I am sure that Sira Inge, who was very knowledgeable in
such matters, would have done the same. While he worked, crooning over to himself the while a little song one of the shamans
had taught him, polishing and repolishing with loving hand, it
seemed to me that Thorhall Gamlason was doing something quite
other than just carving the image of a beast. It was almost as if
he were bringing the animal and himself together in some kind
of mystic union; as if he were wooing, even adoring the dead
beast by making a copy of it. Yet this was the same man—and
not without justice, either—our captain thought of as bloodyminded! Truly was the heart of any man a subtle and a complex
thing!

There was one animal Thorhall Gamlason never hunted—
though he often stalked bears and some men went so far as to
say that he could talk with them. Not for nothing was one of his
several names Holmgang-Bersi, or Bear-Duelist. The bear—or,
to be more exact, *a* bear—was his spirit-double and came often
to him In sleep, particularly on the eve of great occasions such
as battle or holmgang or some unexpected access of good fortune.
Thorhall called this spirit-bear his *fylgja*. Brian told me after
that he had heard of something like these *fylgja* among his own

people where they were called fetches. Since I have lived in Ireland I know that *fylgja* and fetch are something alike but by no means exactly the same thing.

I explained then to Brian what I knew about *fylgja*. They were more often women than animals. When he was evangelizing in Greenland in the winter before we set sail in the *Mariasuden,* Sira Inge Skakkeson had told the Greenlanders that each man who became a Christian got a *fylgjuengill,* or guardian angel, all his own. Thorhall Gamlason, who had once heard Inge priest speak on this, had told him with a laugh at the time that he would even consent to being baptized if Sira Inge could arrange for St. Michael to become his *fylgjuengill,* saying that the warrior saint would make a welcome change from the bear *fylgja* of whom he was becoming somewhat tired. Scandalized, Sira Inge had answered that St. Michael was the archangel who stood first before the throne of God. Still laughing, Thorhall had gone off again, saying he knew how it was—in his own religion one could hardly expect to deprive Odin of his wisest wish-maiden. All the same, I had wondered at this time if Thorhall had not been a little more than half-serious when he made the offer. I always thought that Sira Inge, had he been a little quicker of mind, might have easily bought Thorhall Gamlason's allegiance by promising him St. Michael as a patron even if he could not harness him for him as a guardian angel.

Brian began speaking to Thorhall Gamlason about bears because he had his own ax to grind in this matter. He needed Thorhall's assistance, if he were to fulfill his parting promise to Eric and bring home a new kind of bear to Ericsfjord. Looking back, I was not at all sure that Eric had been utterly serious when he made the suggestion, or if now he would even remember it. But there was small profit in saying such a thing to Brian who intended to fulfill the pledge on his side right up to the hilt.

Brian well knew that Thorhall Gamlason's principles permitted him to take a cub, so long as the cub was not injured in the process; and so long as, afterwards, the cub was reared honorably in a chieftain's household. Thorhall Gamlason did not brook, however, that any cub he caught be taught tricks to tickle the throats of thralls and fools. That, he used to say contemptuously, was the work of a juggler, not of a great prince among animals like my lord the Bear. Not for glee nor for gold would he suffer such cruel japery where he could stop it; and he usually could stop it,

too. In the early days of his hunting career he had challenged
more than one man to bloody holmgang over this same notion of
his. Nowadays no one would think of infringing Thorhall Gamlason's wishes in the matter.

Brian, of course, had no such intention in mind. I was with
him on the day when he told Thorhall Gamlason what he wanted.
Thorhall listened, first putting down the bowstring he was waxing
before the fire in his cabin where, in the dancing light, the great
horns spread greater shadow tines on the rough walls. It was
after the middle of November now, and growing very cold.
There was a little snow on the roof of the *Mariasuden's* shed.
Inside the long chill building, where the boat was housed, hoar-
frost glistened on the tarpaulin which hooded the long ship over.
The sailing season was finished with. So, till spring, Thorhall's
Jomsburg oath allowed him to sleep elsewhere than on deck.
Even now, though, most nights he slept in the shed wrapped in
his skin bag and without a fire. He always chose to work in his
cabin, however. One does not carve well with numbed fingers.

"I have no manner of objection to this enterprise of yours,"
Thorhall said at last, after pondering the matter for some time.
"Eric treats the bear folk well, I know—I have taken more than
one cub that still waxes honorably fat and full-grown in the cages
of Ericsfjord. But, if this enterprise of yours is to be according
to honor, you will have to accomplish the deed yourself. I can
do no more than show you the way to a likely cave mouth. Now—
or early next month at the very latest—is the time to try this
feat. The bear people go into winter quarters now to sleep away
the dark months. It is the best time to take a cub without blood-
shed which is a thing I will not brook. You are willing, Brian,
under these conditions I have laid down?"

"I am willing, Thorhall!" said Brian eagerly. "It will be the
greater exploit."

"Good!" said Thorhall, setting aside the bowstring and rubbing
his hands. "Let us get down to business then. I think I can lead
you to where lairs the largest of all the bear folk—there is a
great male there, a female, too, and two cubs. It is several days'
journey from here—perhaps as long as a week, even. We shall
have to leave almost at once, before the great snows come. I have
not seen these bears with my own eyes. But I have seen their
tracks. And, once, I was close enough to smell their musky smell

in the dark. One does not easily forget that smell once one has smelled it."

There was a faraway look in Thorhall Gamlason's eyes. He picked up a piece of walrus ivory and began to work it into the shape of a great bear.

"I have heard of bears like these," he said dreamily. "The Inuit people, who touch at Ericsfjord in their skin boats, have told me of them. They grow as high as nine feet tall and weigh as much as fifteen hundred pounds. Their strength is matchless even among bears. The Inuits say they can carry off the largest of deer without any trouble—by which, I now suppose, though I knew it not then, the Inuit mean a deer such as this one for which we have no name as yet."

Thorhall Gamlason gestured with the hand which held the ivory toward a pair of huge antlers on his log wall. Later on we learned to call these huge deer moose which was the name the Skraelings gave them.

"The Inuits never try to hunt these mightiest of bear," said Thorhall Gamlason, going back to his shaping of the mimic ivory bear. "It is too dangerous—and they worship it, besides. Speaking of these tracks I have seen, I did not think these greatest of bears ever came so far south as this. I am sure they do not as a general rule. Probably there is just this one family in all the region. It lives no more than a week's faring northward of us. We shall have to get Leif's permission for our journey, of course. I do not think he will mind."

Far from minding, Leif Ericson was very pleased. He liked this fast friendship which had sprung up so unexpectedly between Brian and Thorhall Gamlason. His father, Eric, he said to me, had been right in counseling him to keep the dour Jomsburger with him in the *Mariasuden*. He also said he began to think that Gefjon's prophecy had been a malicious wish, no more—by which I learned, what I did not know before, that Leif had been worried about the witch-woman's spaeing of ill.

So, with Leif Ericson's entire blessing, Brian and Thorhall Gamlason got ready for their quest of the bear. They waxed extra bowstrings, fletched arrows that were sharper and heavier than ordinary, made sure that their own furs were well sewn at the seams, plumped out their leathern scrips with strips of dried deer meat in case they should run into a streak of bad hunting on the way, saw to it that their flints were in good striking condition. Thorhall Gamlason also took along his heaviest spear as well as a famous ax of his which he honed till it was sharp on a gray whetstone shaped like a little man. This same ax was double-edged and fashioned like a halberd. Many a warrior, back in the days of the Jomsburg fellowship, had gone to his last night's rest under it. Thorhall insisted that the two of them carry shields, even though the added weight would make walking more difficult. He said that the reason for the shields would appear in good time. In addition, Brian brought along the crossbow from which he was never parted any more.

I wished, the day they set forth, that Leif had said nothing of witch Gefjon's prophecy which had almost passed from my mind. Now it made me a little anxious to think of these two faring forth together alone. But Thorvald Ericson scoffed at my fears when I mentioned them to him. He said he would answer for both Brian and Thorhall. So I plucked up heart once again.

I come next to a part of my tale that I find strangely difficult to set down. Up to now I have told of nothing—barring a few things my father recounted of the past—I did not see or hear with my own eyes and ears. Now I must tell of things which I did not see myself with the eyes of the flesh, even though I saw them—aye, and heard and smelt them, too. Of all the qualities men seek after, because they are the qualities that belong to God, I think I seek after God's truth first, and only then after His goodness and His beauty. From this standpoint of truth, I think that what I set down now is true enough—there is no difficulty on this head. Only—and near seventy years afterwards the thing still troubles me—I am not sure the way I took to see was lawful. Thorhall Gamlason, as it happened, was the cause of my seeing thus. This is the way it all came about.

It was our first Twelfth Night in the new land—just twelve days, as it happened, after Thorhall Gamlason and Brian had returned from their quest after the bear. I was in Thorhall's cabin with him and Brian, my writing tablets in hand, questioning them closely about what had gone on so that I might have a record of this feat for Leif's log. Thorhall, who had been licking his wounds since the two of them came back, was, I remember, at his carving again. I still mind me how he put down the ivory he was shaping and looked at me, as if measuring my mind.

"You like to see all things clearly, do you not, Thrand?" he

asked me after a time. "As I like to hunt, and Thorvald to make
poetry, and this Irishman of ours to make love. Well, if you are
willing, there is a way to see as clearly as if you had been there—
more clearly, perhaps, for in this way you will see through many
eyes. It is a little dangerous, maybe, but not too much, I think.
The shamans taught it to me when I learned the hunting dance
among them. Do you wish to try it?"

"What must I do to try it?" I asked him in return. "Is it anything against Christ's law? If so, I cannot consider it."

"Not that I know of," said Thorhall Gamlason. "Judge for
yourself."

He set a wooden bowl before me on his table, and poured into
it some powder with a bitter smell. Then he took down from the
wall a deer's thigh with a hole pierced through it, put one end of
the hollow bone in the bowl and the other at my nose, and invited
me to sniff the stuff into my nostrils.

"There is another way," he said. "Another way than this. One
may also eat the gods' flesh while it is still fresh. This powder is
already three months old, and I am afraid some of its virtue has
already ebbed away. But to eat the gods' flesh, unless you are
very practiced in it, is perilous. This way is safer. Besides, I can
get no more till spring. What do you say, Thrand?"

"Just what is this 'gods' flesh,' as you call it?" I asked him,
not yet satisfied.

Thorhall Gamlason barked out his wolf's laugh at that.

"That is my secret," he said. "I say no more. Do you not ask
me more."

As he said, it was his secret; and it is just enough that a man
keep his secret, if he can. I found it out, nevertheless, later on
during the next summer.

"I would not do it, Thrand," said Brian suddenly to me.

Thorhall Gamlason turned to him good-naturedly enough.

"Not even to see the maid Grainne?" he asked mockingly. "It
would be easy to arrange that, you know."

"Not even to see Grainne," said Brian with a flush. "Not even
then would I do it."

"No, Brian," said Thorhall Gamlason, and I thought there was
a touch almost of unwilling admiration in his tone. "You would
not. Nor would I press you. You Irishmen stay always to the
beaten path of your gods. Nor will I press Thrand, either."

Thorhall Gamlason made then as if to put away the bowl and

deer thigh; and the gods' flesh, whatever it might have been, with them. But I was tempted above my strength now. Like the just man, who falls seven times daily, I fell.

"I will do it, Thorhall," I said on a sudden.

"As you choose," he said, lifting one shoulder in a shrug. "But first smell this."

Thorhall Gamlason picked up a bear pelt, which he had lying over a wooden bench, and put it to my nose.

"My lord the Bear," he said by way of explanation, "sees through his nose. So shall you in a little space."

The bearskin was musky to the smell. I sneezed three times before he took it away.

"Good!" said Thorhall Gamlason, satisfied. "Now snuff up this gods' flesh of mine!"

I did as he bade. The bitter-smelling powder stung my nose. Except for that, nothing more happened at first.

"Sniff again, Thrand," said Thorhall Gamlason, watching me closely.

This time I found myself rocking from side to side as I have seen my father's Lapps rock at one of their festivals. And I began to see things.

"What do you see, Thrand?" asked Thorhall Gamlason.

"Colors," I said thickly, my tongue feeling fat in my mouth. "Colors such as we know in this world—only much, much brighter. Other colors that I never knew were. Pillars and palaces like those Tyrker speaks of in Sarkland. Jewels. Strange flowers and—"

"It is well!" said Thorhall Gamlason. "Listen now!"

He began to talk of the beginnings of their journey, his and Brian's. And, just as he talked, I both heard and saw. I was there. I saw through both Thorhall's and Brian's eyes. Knowing what I know today, now that I have been a priest of Christ these many years, I would not try this thing again. But, perhaps, in my heart of hearts, I am not altogether sorry that I did it this once. I think even Sira Inge might have been tempted in my place—but Bishop Sigurd never. Perhaps this is one reason I never became a Bishop, nor wished to become one, either.

The day Thorhall and Brian set forth from camp, it came on to snow a little in the forenoon. Not very much at first, but Thorhall did not exactly like the leaden color of the sky overhead. The low-hanging heavy clouds foreboded much snow at this time of year. They made good time, however, on their journey out to the place where Thorhall had seen the bear tracks. As luck would have it then, though they had struck due north all the way, they had outpaced the snow; and the tracks were still visible. They led, an additional day's journey northward, to an island on a lake much smaller than our lake where Leif Ericson had set up his Vinland settlement. Thorhall Gamlason made a wry face when he looked upon this island.

"This," he said to Brian with a humorous shrug, his dry voice ringing in my ears though I could not have been there to hear—and yet I was—"is something I had not foreseen. It will add a whole half day to our expedition—and we can ill spare a half day at this snow time of year. If it were only three weeks later, we could walk over on the ice dry-shod. But then, if there had been snow, we should never have picked up these tracks—for fate never shuts one door but she opens another. As it is, however, we shall have to make a raft. There is no other way out."

It took all the time Thorhall said it would to fell the trees for the raft, then lash them firmly together with some dried vine withies. So late in the season as this, such a raft as this one was an utter necessity. Even if it had been warmer, Thorhall and Brian probably could not have risked swimming. The arms they had to ferry over were too heavy for that. By the time their raft was done, the apple-green of a clear December afternoon had yielded to the dull embers of a winter sunset. I say December, and it was December when I saw it through their eyes—yet on the calendars of men it already read January!

"We had better camp on this side tonight," said Thorhall, glancing toward the island that was already dimming in that chill dusk. "I think we want broad daylight for what we have to do. There is another thing to consider, too. Although, in a way, I am akin to the folk of the bear, I have no mind to spend a night at too close quarters with those furry cousins of mine. After all, the worst blood feuds are known to take place within families."

Next morning, very early, the two of them poled their way across the shallow lake. It was clear enough where the bears they sought laired—there could be no other possible place for them on that rocky skerry than in a cave, on a sheer cliff side, under an overhanging rock. Now there were two ways up to this cave mouth. The first was by a narrow path leading to the entrance.

This first way was fearsome enough to look upon. For, besides what a man would find inside the cave, below the path he took lay nothing more than a straight drop of a hundred feet or so to a beach of shaly rock, promising death to anyone who lost his footing. This was the way the bears themselves used. But Thorhall Gamlason did not intend to use it. He said to Brian that, the way the wind was blowing, it would carry their hated man scent to the hibernating animals. He added that he did not think the drowsing beasts had been in hibernation long enough to have been plunged into their deepest winter sleep. Most likely, they were still one quarter awake—to the point, at least, where they would still be alert enough to pick up a human smell. He said, in addition, that he did not suppose Brian would find it over pleasant to face two full-grown Inuit bears who had awakened to discover him in the very act of filching one of their cubs.

So Thorhall Gamlason proposed that they use the second way instead. Not being eagles, Brian did not see, at first—nor did I, looking through his eyes—how the two of them would be able to do it. When one looked closely, the face of the cliff recessed slightly some ten feet or so above the entrance; but off to one side so that it was not in a direct line with the cave mouth. A kind of air vent—easily large enough for a man, even for a man carrying off a bear cub, but not for a full-grown bear—opened into what Brian supposed must be the back of the den. Of course, depending on the size of the cave, it could just as easily be the middle. But it really did not matter either way. Aside from the fact that they could not tell from without just where the bears were sleeping inside, Brian did not see how he or Thorhall could ever reach the smaller hole if, as Thorhall insisted, they might not even set foot on the path the bears used. He put his objection to Thorhall Gamlason a second time. Thorhall only laughed.

"There are more uses than one for good axes like mine," he said to Brian. "Watch me! But first do you stretch yourself out in this hole by the foot of the path, and cover yourself with your shield in case either the father or mother bear awaken at the noise I will have to make getting up, and make a rush down the path. Better the father than the mother in such a case, though I do not expect either animal will necessarily awaken. If, however, either of the animals does rouse and make a rush for it, the shield will protect you from the first onset. Before the bears can re-group for the second, we will be off on our raft. With the cubs inside, they will not follow us. And we will not stay to argue with giants like these Inuits."

Brian's eye measured the distance between them and where the raft was drawn up on the shale beach. It was no more than sixty feet surely. Thorhall's estimate of the probabilities was, he thought, right. Even allowing for bears being the strong swimmers they were, the two of them should be able to make their escape easily enough. Even if only one bear stayed with the cubs, once they were on the other shore it should be possible to keep the single animal at bay with long bow and arbalest until it got discouraged and shambled back to the lair. Brian did not think that, for all his principles, Thorhall would balk at fighting a purely defensive action.

"You understand about the shield now, Brian?" Thorhall asked him. "A pity, for once, that we do not use the long pointed shields of Frankland. They are not so good to wield when it comes to battle play, perhaps. But they cover more when one lies down in a ditch to hide from bears."

"I understand about the shield well enough," said Brian, lying down to show him. "What I do not understand at all is how you mean to fly without wings."

Thorhall Gamlason did not even bother to answer. Instead, he took his long ax-halberd, swung the crook as high overhead as he could reach by jumping, until it caught in the cliff side, hauled himself up the shaft like a cat on a pole, and so to the crotch of a dead tree alongside, where he perched, grinning down at Brian. Then he reached that long ax over and down to his fellow.

"Thus did we of the Jomsburg fellowship when it came to scaling walls," he said, hardly panting from the effort. "Now do you the same. There is room and to spare up here for two. But first wait for a minute or two to make sure the beasts do not awaken. It would never do to have the two of us treed and the bears baiting us beneath."

Sheepishly Brian got to his feet, out from under the shield, and took hold of the ax-haft. If he was not nearly so skilled at this new game as the older man, he had the strength and agility of youth to balance the scales. It was the work of a few moments only for him to clamber up to Thorhall Gamlason. Like most other tricks, it was an easy enough trick once one knew how to do it.

"Now," said Thorhall Gamlason, speaking lower as if he feared he might be overheard. "You must go the rest of the way alone, Brian. It is your feat; and so honor dictates and the laws of your might and main. Once you reach the airhole, let down the axe to me again. You will not need it coming back—coming back is always easier—and this way I will be able to cover your rear at either entrance, depending on which one you decide to come out by. If it is in any way possible, I would leave by the hole again— I think it must be far and away the safer. If it is not possible, however, I can join you at the cave mouth quite easily. Only make sure that the cub takes no hurt whichever way you think it better to leave by."

For the first time, Brian felt a little resentful that Thorhall Gamlason set so much upon the cub's welfare. Then, swallowing his irritation, he looked up at the hole above him; and I looked up through his eyes. It seemed a sickening distance away. He did not so much as dare to look down the cliff. Then, without saying anything more, the lad began his climb.

It was at this point I began to see out of a bear's eyes and to smell through a bear's nose. There is much about all this I cannot explain; and this, perhaps, was the strangest thing of all. I found I knew something about those bears that I could not possibly have known—something that even Thorhall Gamlason, whose *fylgja* was a spirit-bear, did not know. Yet more than ever do I believe—yes, even today—that what I came to know was true: about the bear's name; about where he came from; about the red Skraelings who hunted him before we did. Moreover, it was a very odd thing to be both bear and man, both hunter and hunted at once; to be both killer as well as what he killed.

I asked Thorhall later how it was I came to know so much about what had gone on before he and Brian set foot on that skerry. He said he could not tell me why but that this kind of thing often happened to those who ate of or smelled the powder he always called "gods' flesh." He added, almost with a touch of jealousy, I thought, that I must be a very good scryer.

Thorhall Gamlason had been right about one thing. The bear family had numbered four in the beginning. What he did not know, however, was that it numbered four no longer. The mother bear had lost her life in a Skraeling trap, drawn to that fatal snare by a cunning Skraeling trick after the time of hibernation had already begun. It had been the Skraeling intention to take either her or her mate alive to be the living totem of their people which was known among the other Skraeling tribes as the people of the Bear. I make so bold as to call these red warriors here Skraelings; for that was the name we later came to give them because of their habit of screaming in battle.

To this end, then, with burning pitch-pine knots had the Skraelings smoked the two sleep-dulled full-grown bears—the cubs, luckily, being under the air vent, had not even awakened—out of their den and toward a deep pit dug at the other end of the island from the place where Thorhall Gamlason and Brian had beached their raft. The tribe's magician, who was to keep the bear in trust for the rest of the Skraelings, had directed the plan in person. It had been a good one, too, as Thorhall Gamlason later said. But, like many another good plan, it had miscarried in the end.

Owing to the ferocity of the fight both bears put up—the female within the confines of the pit into which she had tumbled, the male on the pit edge—three Skraeling warriors had died and the she-bear, too. The Skraelings, after that, had been able to draw the dead bear out of the hole so that they now had a prime pelt, at any rate, to dress their priest's lodge with. But they could do nothing whatsoever with the frenzied male; and they knew nothing of the two cubs sleeping back in the cave.

Now, ten days after the death of his fierce mate, the old male bear, silver hair flecking his brown fur, was still not quite asleep. He had no worries about the cubs' food; for even now they had not wakened. But it took a long time for the agitation to die down in his own turbulent bear's heart. It would not take very much to rouse it again, either.

Thorhall Gamlason was right about two other things. Old Silver, as I came to think of the giant bear in my own mind, was from the north where the Inuits are; and these Inuit bears are the greatest of all bears far and away—greater, even, than their huge cousins, the grizzlies, whom we also came to know a little later on. He really should not have been so far south as this. As a matter of fact, the journey southward which was responsible for his straying into Vinland had actually begun several lifetimes before his own in the days of his great-great-great-grandfather. Year by year, the wandering family sired by that particular roving Inuit ancestor had kept moving farther and farther south from their original island home, slowly making their shambling way from one feeding ground to another.

It was Old Silver himself, and his giantess of a mate, who had first entered this Skraeling country where we had made our settlement. They and these two cubs were the last of their line since, for some reason or other, Inuit bears do not flourish well in these warmer climes. More than once it had come into Old Silver's dim bear mind that it might be a good thing to move back into that north country whence, decades before, his great-great-great-grandsire had come. But that was before the death of his mate in the red man's gin. It was much too late for anything of that sort any more.

Old Silver lay now in the musky lair—I smelled with his nose and thought with his brain—his small eyes dimmed with drowsiness, his usually keen ear clogged with the delicious deafness that always came with this same winter drowse, his sensitive nose conscious only of the grateful warmth which, like some other fell or fleece, now lined his cave of sleep. So he did not hear the climbing noises the two men things made on the side of his cliff; or, if he did hear them somewhere faint and far away, they did not disturb him. But it was another thing altogether when a man's head poked in through the air hole above the sleeping cubs; and a man's frame climbed down into the den.

Something woke then in the bear's numbed brain. It remembered the painted warriors and the bee stings of their spears. A red sun of dawning anger began to burn away the kindly mists of sleep. The bear growled deep in his throat and stood erect, towering gigantic into the roof of his cave. The man thing was climbing back toward the vent now, a slumbering cub in its arms. Old Silver put up a taloned claw and tore the man thing's shoulders. The flesh came away with the wadmal and the deerskin. There was a smell of hot fresh blood in the cave. At that, Old Silver went mad with the familiar lust for blood. He began to roar thunderously.

When Brian first heard that awful growling, he looked back from his climb; and, as he did so, his heart turned over with a sickening dip. His arms and legs became like water. He dropped the cub which went right on sleeping where it fell like some tight-rolled ball of fur. It was as if a troll had reared behind him; or the Grendel monster Thorvald Ericson had sung about at Olaf Tryggveson's court. The monstrous head, set on the blunt and

massive neck, was a snarling mask of horror. The muzzle slavered.
Brian was so close—now I was Brian and Old Silver at one and
the same time—that he could feel the hot breath of the giant beast.
What he did not feel at first—though he heard the rending noise
as the great claws tore through his clothes and into the flesh
beneath—was the searing pain that, of a sudden, went through
him like a flame. He put up a hand to ward off the next blow.
The creature cuffed at him with its gigantic paw. He heard the
bone snap in his left arm which fell useless at his side. With his
other hand he reached for the *ryting* at his belt and sank it up
to the hilt in the bear's furred chest. The long blade might have
been a pin in a girl's hair for all Old Silver seemed to mind. He
began to roar once more. The noise became deafening. Brian saw
the cavern begin to spin round like a child's top. His eyes blurred.
He was afraid that, for the first time in his life, he was going to
faint. It came into his mind, with wonder more than fear, that
now he would never see the maid Grainne again.

Old Silver raised his terrible right paw to strike again. It would
be the last blow he would need to strike against this puny enemy
who had dared to invade and profane his winter lair. But he did
not let his oak-heavy forepaw descend. Something was making
another noise at his back. With unbelievable speed and agility
the huge bulk wheeled and faced the cave mouth. Another of the
man things was standing at the entrance, calling him. Yes! Calling
him!

"Bear!" it called—and I called with it. "Great bear! Greatest
of bears! My brother!"

Or was it a man thing? It looked like a man, hairless and
forked, smelling of the obscene man smell. But it spoke so that
a bear could understand. There was something about it that, to
a bear's groping mind, seemed almost bearlike itself. Old Silver's
musk-mazed brain was like a musty earthern cave stored with
remembered sights and sounds and smells; with comfortable
memories of animal warmth and honey sweet on the rolling
tongue and fish cool in plunging waterfalls—with the man part
of me I found myself wishing, at that moment, that I could stay
a bear because a bear knew sensuous delight such as no man
could. Then this desire passed, and I looked on and heard again
as a man, yet never leaving the bear's mind, either.

In some strange way now Old Silver's slow mind seemed to
plod back in time and to recognize something akin to itself in

what could not conceivably be akin. Or could it? I felt Old
Silver's slow mind become more confused. Then the man thing's
odd unbearlike voice, speaking again—and this time to the other
man thing, not to Old Silver—broke the odd spell. For all that
this man-bear was a kind of brother, the bear knew that it was
also an enemy.

"Brian!" called Thorhall Gamlason. "Brian! Climb out now
while I am holding his attention in the cave mouth!"

Brian tried to get to his feet. It was impossible. He was too
faint. The faintness kept on coming over him in dizzying waves.

"I cannot, Thorhall," he said faintly. "I have lost too much
blood. Save yourself now. It is too late for me."

At the sound of the hated prey behind him, the great bear went
mad again. Snarling and spitting, he turned, one giant paw upraised for a final crushing blow against his wounded first antago-
nist. With the speed of lightning, the man in the cave mouth
thrust at the bear with his heavy spear. But there was death in his
heart and dust in his mouth, as he did so. For Thorhall Gamlason
knew that in slaying this bear—if slay him he could, instead of
being slain—he was slaying his luck. Worse than that, he was
profaning his own hunter's inmost sanctities by this shameless
invasion of the great beast's winter sanctuary. Yet he did what
he had to do. He was blood-brother to this bear. Was he not even
closer blood-brother to this stricken friend on the floor of the lair?

Even as the deadly spear entered his back, drinking deeper of
his life's blood than Brian's *ryting* had, Old Silver turned again
to the cave mouth to grapple with this more dangerous and more
treacherous of his two adversaries. At that, the man thing, with
the strange bearness—what other word will do but *bearness?*—
moved in close to the bear's enormous chest, striking repeatedly,
as he did so, with a long knife in his hand. Coming to close grips
this way, Old Silver clawed the traitor's back, scoring it terribly
so that the white bone lay bare beneath, hugging the man thing
tight to him till he heard the rib cage crack in the dreadful embrace. The bear's strong jaws were near the second man thing's
throat now. Dropping his useless knife, the man thing gripped
the animal by the ears and, with a berserker's strength, tugged
back the glaring head until his throat was clean away from the
yellow teeth. There was a sucking noise from the gaping spear
hole. Blood bubbled and gurgled in the great wound. Bear's gore
and man's commingled ran down on the rock platform before the

cave, making the footing slippery. Those straining enemies tot-
tered once on the brink of the precipice. Then, still locked in one
another's death grip, they fell from the edge.

Barely conscious now, bleeding and lightheaded from his fearful loss of blood, Brian crawled to the cave mouth through a
slippery trail of his own, Thorhall Gamlason's, and the great
bear's red arterial blood. Three feet away from the entrance, he
could crawl no farther. A nausea fit came over him. He vomited
and lost consciousness. When he came to again, the cave was still
empty except for himself and the two cubs who, wakened by the
mad fury that had caught up their warm lair, now whimpered
a little and rocked back and forth uneasily where they were lying
in the back of the cavern. There was no sign of either Thorhall
Gamlason or the bear. Brian could not tell how long he had been
unconscious. He wondered if both the wrestlers were dead. Then
he heard a scrabbling noise on the path outside. Something was
coming up the path in the half light. Something that crawled on
all fours even as a bear crawls.

The hair lifted on the back of Brian's neck—as it lifted on mine
there where I waited with him in the lair that was, at the same
time, Thorhall Gamlason's Vinland cabin. It came into the lad's
mind that it must be the bear who walked like that. There was
no escape for him now for, in his great weakness, he could not
climb; and the cave mouth would be blocked by whatever was
crawling up the path. Besides, there would be no honor but, instead, great shame in saving his life after Thorhall Gamlason
had laid down his own for him. There was one thing he could
do, though. He could sell his life dearly, even as Thorhall had
done; and as Leif and Thorvald Ericson and Tyrker and Steinn
the *stafnbui* would do. Fumbling about on the cave floor with
one groping hand, Brian found the *ryting* where Thorhall Gamlason had dropped it.

The scraping noise continued on the ledge outside. It drew
nearer and nearer; and now Brian could hear the sound of labored breathing as well. He set his back against the cave wall and
waited. A figure appeared in the cave mouth, gigantic in the
dusked frame of rock. The knife clattered to the cavern floor from
Brian's nerveless fingers.

It was Thorhall Gamlason on his hands and knees, grinning at
him through a streaming mask of blood, his wolf-gray hair dark-
matted and clotted with other blood from a rent scalp. It was

Old Silver who had landed first in that toppling fall, Thorhall Gamlason atop him, to the shale below. The fall had broken the bear's spine as well as driven the spear in his back straight through his heart and out the other side so that it even grazed Thorhall Gamlason's right breast. Except to paw once weakly and bewilderedly before his nose, the great beast had not moved after that.

"So," said Thorhall Gamlason, getting to his feet at last, and swaying back and forth there in the cave mouth. "We have two bears for Eric now, it seems—eh, Brian? Not just one. But I have killed my luck. I have saved my brother, Brian. And I have betrayed my other brother."

But Brian did not answer him. He had fainted dead away.

Thorhall Gamlason stared broodingly at his unconscious fellow. As a matter of fact, he was not so very far away from a loss of consciousness himself. It had been touch and go there, more than once, whether he would not faint, even as Brian had. His back pained terribly now where the Inuit had clawed him down to the bone. There were two ribs staved in in his chest so that breathing had become difficult. But, as a new wave of mortal sickness surged over him again, Thorhall Gamlason took hold of his blood-fouled beard with both hands, clapped it into his mouth, and bit down hard on it until the nausea had passed. It was an old Jomsburg trick; and it usually worked. When the dizzy fit passed off once again, he spoke aloud, although there was no one there to hear him.

"Blood nights are the hottest," he said, croaking from a parched throat. "Would that I had some of the *Mariasuden's* good beer by me—or even some of Tyrker's wine. Or would, at least, that the lake down there were a few paces closer than it is."

Then, lurching as if Tyrker's wine and the *Mariasuden's* beer were all too close at hand, Thorhall swayed down the slippery path again. There was so much to do; and he felt so sick and faint. He would have to bring water in his helmet for Brian. Then, after they had been well washed, the lad's wounds would have to be closed with deer sinew; and that dangling arm must be splinted so that the broken bone would knit straight. Besides all this, he would have to skin the bear before the wolves found him; and, while he was about this latter task, cut away enough bear steaks to keep himself and Brian alive for the time they would have to spend recovering in the cave. From the way his fellow looked,

Thorhall Gamlason was afraid this might be a long time—even if he lived. He was not sure he was going to live. He did not like the waxy look about Brian's nose; or the shallow way the lad was breathing in his swoon.

Thorhall Gamlason cocked a weather eye at the gray sky overhead. It would come on to snow very heavily soon—he was sure of that. That was going to make walking much harder for the two of them, especially for Brian who would have no reserves of strength. Well, if necessary, he said to himself, he could build a sledge for the injured lad. The hibernating cubs, which were much too heavy to carry, would have to be drawn on a sledge, anyway. As it had turned out, there were two cubs to care for, too, not just one. Two Inuit cubs. They would be the crown jewels in old Eric's collection. There could be no doubt of that. But he, Thorhall, had paid dearly for that prize.

As Thorhall Gamlason toiled up the rocky path with his second helmetful of water, the first flakes came floating lazily down. By nightfall, though by then he stumbled with weariness, he had finished the skinning of the bear and the quartering of its meat, besides bringing wood into the cave for fire. It was well he had finished with the bear so quickly. Soon after dark the wolves found what was left of Old Silver.

Sitting bleakly in the cave beside his unconscious comrade, Thorhall Gamlason heard the animals snapping and quarreling among their carrion selves out in the snow that had already begun to be quite deep. The flakes arrowed past the cave mouth like the shafts that had snowed death so thick and fast at Halkelsvik when Jarl Eric's men slew the Jomsburg fellowship. Because he was weary almost unto death, Thorhall Gamlason had not intended building a fire this first night. Listening to the wolves bicker without, he thought now he had better, and at once, in case he fell asleep before Brian wakened and was able to keep some kind of watch in his turn. He knew that wolves would stay away from naked flame when nothing else would daunt them. Fighting against the overpowering desire to sleep that kept overcoming him, Thorhall Gamlason arranged the brush and kindling and struck a seed of fire out of his flint.

The fire drew nicely under the air hole. If it had been day, I knew that the Skraeling scouts for the wandering war party which had taken the she-bear in the pit would have been sure to have seen the plume of smoke. But the fire had died down by morning.

And, before Thorhall Gamlason again roused himself to rebuild
it, the war party had pulled up its stakes at last and moved on far
enough so that it could no longer see the telltale stain against the
winter sky.

In the morning, Brian still did not waken. Thorhall Gamlason
began to worry in earnest now. He set the cubs closer to his sleeping fellow for the sake of additional warmth; and walked down
the path to the raft. It was time to build the sledge. The snow
was almost three feet deep by now; and still falling heavily. He
would have to fell another large tree over on the mainland for the
sledge—there was only scrub on the bears' skerry—and float it
over to the island before this third night fell since he and Brian
had first seen the bears' cave.

For long days and nights Brian moved between life and death.
There was a great wound on the top of his head which Thorhall
had not noted earlier. It was the main reason, he supposed, why
the lad had not yet woken up. The bear's taloned paw had dealt
him a terrible knock there—it was the greatest of luck that the
blow had not been mortal at once. Thorhall Gamlason washed
and closed the wound as carefully as he could; and forced water,
between times, through his comrade's jaws. Brian stirred and
moaned whenever this forced drinking took place. But he never
came to himself all the way; and not once did he open his eyes.
Within twenty-four hours fever raged in him. He babbled wildly
in delirium, never once recognizing the grim warrior who kept
vigil by his side.

So it went for a whole week. On the eighth day the fever
finally broke. The lad's head was cool again. Thorhall Gamlason,
who had experience in these matters, knew that his comrade would
live now.

The *glamourie* worked by Thorhall Gamlason's powder began
to weaken in me. I heard the fire crackling on the cabin hearth instead of many miles away in that cave on the bears' skerry. I also
heard Thorhall Gamlason's voice—his today voice, not his yesterday one—speaking. It said:

"Sniff again, Thrand Thorbergson. Sniff of my powder once
more."

I sniffed; and, on the instant, the cabin walls retreated. I was
back in the cave again where Brian was just waking from his
eight-day deathly swoon.

The first thing Brian saw when, at last, he really wakened for the first time was the bear cubs slumbering by his side. There were red embers in the fire Thorhall Gamlason had built under the air hole; and, in the cave mouth, a curious pearly light he found hard to place. Brian sat up on one elbow in order to see better. Immediately one of the sick waves he remembered having surged over him before he first fainted washed into his brain again, and he fell back, heart pounding, fetching his breath, it seemed, up from the very roots of his being. The cave was very quiet. There was a musky smell of bear all about. Brian found it pleasant just to lie there and not think.

After a space he again tried to get up. This time he made it. His head, once he managed to sit up, stayed clear long enough for him to make out the reason for the pearly gleam. The cave mouth was almost choked with snow; and the flakes kept on falling heavily as if they would never stop. Brian watched them come down for a time with a strange sort of childlike pleasure. It was so warm and snug inside this cave; so cold and bleak without. He thought that, if it had to come to such a thing, he would not even mind spending Yule here in the cave. Never had he felt so secure, so at one with himself, so utterly contented. The cubs at his side had something to do with this good feeling. He began to think he knew why Thorhall was the way he was about animals. The thought came to him then that, when the opportunity offered, he would tell Thorhall he knew all about that now. Brian wondered mazily where Thorhall could be. The effort of thinking so hard only left him the drowsier. He sat up again. But his head still felt like a pig's bladder blown up for a child's game. In a little while he fell asleep once more.

The next time Brian awoke, it was night again. The fire was still redly alive, but the pearly gleam had gone. This time he could see Thorhall Gamlason in the mouth of the cave. The Jomsburg Viking stood, leaning on his long spear, looking out on the darkness and on the falling whiteness in the darkness. Against the shifting curtain of ever-moving white that was the snow the spear shaft looked black and the spearhead gray. A sudden wave of liking for the lone watcher went out from Brian to the sentry in the cave mouth. Brian had made no manner of sound. Yet, almost as if he had been called by name, Thorhall Gamlason turned his head and grinned at him. Somewhere outside in the night went up a long-drawn bay.

"Wolves," said Thorhall Gamlason by way of explanation. "They fight for what is left of the carcass of the bear. In the beginning there was plenty for all. Now they fight for the remnants."

Again the eerie cry was raised. Brian shivered. He no longer felt warm and comfortable. It was as if, with the wolf's howl, the night and cold had come into this cave where he lay wounded. The cave itself seemed a troll's den again, as it had when the great bear loomed, snarling, over him. The sleeping cubs now struck him as savage and enemy things. Brian thought on Fenris, the Midgard Wolf, who would one day consume the gods in his black maw even as the long gray wolf shapes outside now devoured the rest of what had once been a bear. He thought, too, on the Fimbul Winter which, Northmen said, would be forever at the end of time; and on the swallowing of the sun when man should be no more.

A fearsome thing came then into Brian's mind. He remembered that the old heroes, Sigmund and Sinfjotli, had run in the woods as wolves. Perhaps Thorhall Gamlason was a shape-changer even as they. Perhaps he was a bear underneath. Had he not seemed to speak to the bear during the time he fought with him? Brian shrank back against the cave wall as far as he could away from Thorhall. Either this was a nightmare through which he was now living, one begotten of bright-eyed fever which would vanish with the fever. Or else—but, in the very act of again breathing the monstrous idea to himself, he remembered that Thorhall Gamlason had killed the great beast in his defense. And he was ashamed.

Thorhall had come all the way into the cave now and was busying himself about the embers.

"Here is melted snow to drink," he said over his shoulder. "And a bear steak to follow once the water has gone down. I wish we had beer."

"I am not hungry, Thorhall," said Brian, still ashamed of his wild suspicions.

"No?" asked Thorhall, the old wolf's grin very wide upon his face. "I think you will be in a little space. Taste this, Brian."

Coughing a little for the rib injury took him in his lungs every now and again, on the sharp point of his *ryting* Thorhall Gamlason thrust a roasted gobbet of bear's flesh toward Brian.

"Try it," he said, pressing the morsel upon him. "One bite, and you will not be able to get enough of the meat."

Brian's gorge rose at the very thought of eating. Nevertheless, he did what Thorhall Gamlason urged him; and, once again, his companion proved to be in the right of it. The bear meat was delicious. Brian could hardly wait to chew it, so ravenous was he become on a sudden.

"Steady now," said Thorhall Gamlason, laughing. "Not too much all at once, or you will be sick again. Try the water now."

When Brian's hunger was a little appeased, he sank back beside the cubs who even now went right on sleeping. Thorhall Gamlason watched him a little less anxiously than before, though anxiety was by no means gone from his eyes.

"Do things look better now?" he asked.

"Much," said Brian, yawning.

Thorhall Gamlason clapped him on the back.

"Good!" he said heartily. "Skjold, the shield-hero, father of our viking race, he who took bears in his cradle, could not have done better than you did against the great bear! Eric will be pleased with the prizes you bring him."

"No, Thorhall," said Brian. "It was you who were the hero there, not I."

"I?" asked Thorhall Gamlason, and his voice rang darker than his dark wolf's face. "I? It is not so. I am a caitiff who have slain a brother against my oath."

After that there was no conversation between the two of them for a long while. Brian felt sorry. But he did not know what to do. At last he broke the awkward silence.

"How long," he asked uncomfortably, "have we been thus in the cave?"

"A week," said Thorhall Gamlason briefly. "Or, it may be, a week and a day. One loses count in the darkness and snow. But it can be no more than a fortnight to Yule now. We must be on our way soon if we mean to keep the Yule feast with our comrades of the *Mariasuden*."

Thorhall Gamlason did not see fit to add that, if they were to win back to the Vinland settlement at all, it must be now. For their food was dwindling, and Brian was much too weak to help him hunt. He thought he might be able to live out the winter in the cave by himself; but never with two to feed and warm.

"I am ready to start," said Brian, struggling to get to his unsteady feet.

Brian's gesture broke the ice again.

"Not just yet, comrade," said Thorhall with a laugh, gently but firmly pushing him down again. "Even Sigurd Dragonslayer had to nurse a wound. Besides, it is still snowing. In two days, perhaps. But no sooner. And even then, only if you are much stronger."

The great weariness came over Brian once again. But this time there was no faintness with it. The cave shrank farther and farther away. He felt himself dropping off to sleep through hundreds and hundreds of feet of swathing snow.

It stopped snowing at last on the day before they left. But by then the snow was so deep underfoot that the going turned out to be very heavy. Moreover, when Brian stood up for the first time, he discovered that his right ankle was so badly swollen that it was useless; and that his left knee, too, had been severely wrenched. He had no memory of either injury, as it happened— but it must have been when the bear plucked him from the cave wall. Luckily nothing was broken. It all meant, though, that for the first stages of their journey, anyway, Thorhall would have to pull both Brian and the bears on the sledge. The lake was fast frozen over now so that it was not necessary to pole the raft again. That, at least, was a comfort.

Thorhall Gamlason wrapped the sleeping balls of brown bear fur in their father's warm pelt and placed the living bundle in the sledge beside Brian. He did not think they would waken. But, as an added precaution, he looped withy ropes about the right hind leg of each bear cub and attached these loosely, so they would not chafe, to the back runner of the crude sledge he had built. The frozen bear meat he set at Brian's feet under the lashed shields, the ax, and the great spear. When all else was in readiness, he slung his bow on his back and asked Brian to see to it that his crossbow was ever on the cock.

Thorhall Gamlason had not bothered to take such precautions on the journey out to the skerry. Brian looked at him narrowly.

"Why?" he asked.

"Because," said Thorhall, throwing the sledge rope over his shoulder and begining the weary trudge. "Because there were other men on the island not long before we came. I saw the pit they dug—for the bears probably, and it seems they caught the she—and the pitch pine knots they burned. We must be very wary not to blunder upon them. I have long known there were

men in this new land to which we have come. I have seen their
trail often. But it has always been a cold trail until now."

"Perhaps they will be friendly," said Brian, troubled in mind
by what his comrade told him.

"Perhaps," said Thorhall Gamlason with a barking laugh. "But
I do not think it is ever wise to rely on strangers' friendship. Do
we mean friendship to them?"

"I hope so," said Brian, more troubled in mind than before.

Brian began to think then on the copper-colored warrior with
the feather in his hair whom he and Leif had seen on the forest
trail that morning of their land-taking. It was on the tip of his
tongue to tell Thorhall Gamlason of the man. But he remembered
Leif Ericson's prohibition and kept silent. He had time, as the
sledge moved with painful slowness through the deep snow and in
and out of the endless rows of trees, to think much on that man
with the skin so different from his. Perhaps, he said to himself,
despite the way that Thorhall Gamlason laughed at the notion,
these new world folk would turn out friendly in the end. It had
been that way with the *fir-gorm*—the blue-skinned men, as the
Irish called them—who came from Africa and whom he used to
see at his great-uncle, the *Ard Rí's,* court. It was true these men
had been slaves and so tried to curry favor with their masters.
But he had liked these dark people very much for their good tempers and their sense of fun. It might be that the red men, too,
though they did not look at all the same, would turn out to be
as kindly. Nevertheless, he kept one finger on the arbalest, and
his eyes roving from side to side, as the sledge glided over the
crusted snow. It was cold now in that deep forest. A chill wind
began to whine down from the north.

That same night, before the moon rose, Brian looked up at
the North Star, wondering to himself if Grainne, too, looked on
their star at this same moment. Thorhall Gamlason noted the
direction of his gaze.

"You watch the Bear stars, Brian?" he asked him bleakly.

"No," said Brian. "I watch the North Star. I leave the Bear
to you. Those stars are yours."

"Once, perhaps," said Thorhall Gamlason sadly. "But no
longer. I may claim the Bear no more."

He bent to the sledge lashings to make sure all would be in
readiness for the morrow. At last he stood up straight again.

"It is not good for a man to be without a star," he said.
Brian said nothing to that. What was there to say?

On their fourth day out from the Bears' skerry, proceeding still
at a snail's pace because Brian's knee and ankle were so slow in
mending, the two of them came upon the Skraeling encampment
in the ravine. It was, they came to judge, not a permanent encampment at all; but a spot where the same war party, which had
killed the she-bear, had made a stopping place till the snowstorm
was over. These Skraelings, who, as we learned later, were hundreds of miles from the great lake of their people, had improved
that forced encampment of theirs by raiding two neighboring
villages with profit. There would be many scalps to hang in the
warriors' lodges according to their vile practice, when they got
back; and no fewer than seven captives to torture at the stake.
But, since this was enemy country they still trod through, they
decided these captives would have to be disposed of before they
left the temporary camp. Even at that, the Skraelings thought the
captives would provide good sport.

While, crouched at the head of the snow-choked ravine, Brian
and Thorhall looked on in horror, the hellish game was played
out under their eyes. The captives did provide the best of good
sport while they lasted, never crying out under the tomahawks—
we found out later that this was the name of the Skraeling war
ax—that were hurled at the stakes to which they had been bound
naked in the cold, never wincing when the burning pine splinters
were forced under their finger nails. When this grim play was
over at last and the sated captor Skraelings all asleep except for
their sentries, Thorhall Gamlason whispered once in Brian's ear
before he took up the sledge rope once again, this time to walk all
night in order to put as great a distance as was possible between
the two of them and the red men.

"Well," he said, grinning in the snow-lit dark. "We know one
thing now, at least. We know what to do if we come upon any
of these new world men."

Brian started in the sledge as something shook down some
snow upon him. He drew his *ryting* half out of its sheath before
he saw what it was. It was a white owl that swooped soundless
overhead, its golden burning eyes fixed upon him and Thorhall.

Thorhall Gamlason, looking up at the bird, showed his teeth in
a soundless laugh.

"In this land," he said, "Odin has owls instead of ravens. But here as elsewhere he keeps his wolves without change."

Carefully Thorhall settled Brian in the sledge again; and took up the leading rope. It would be well, he thought once more, that they put some miles betweeen them and these Skraelings before morning. He only hoped that the new world warriors were not going in the same direction. For there was no hope whatsoever of covering tracks in all this world of whiteness, unless, of course, it snowed—and then they could not win through to the Vinland settlement for another reason. But luck was with them. They saw no further sign of the Skraelings. As he trudged forward in the cold night, it came into Thorhall Gamlason's mind that he would like to try his fortunes in war with these same red warriors. It would be a new kind of sport for a Jomsburger and, he would go bond, a good one.

The necessary skirting round the Skraeling encampment—they made it in a wide circle—added another half day to their long journey back. Again Brian held his peace about the other red warrior he and Leif had seen. It was a pity. Things might have been different in the end, had he felt free to speak. But he did not feel free. When Leif Ericson commanded, we men of the *Maria-suden* obeyed.

So ends my account of what Brian and Thorhall Gamlason told me of their quest after the great bear. The rest of their story I saw for myself. But I shall have somewhat more to say of Thorhall's bitter powder later on.

The first night of our great Yule feast was at its height in Leif Ericson's cabin when, just before midnight, the door burst inward without warning and a man sprang into the firelit room, coat all frozen, wolf-gray hair matted with sleet. The feasters drew their knives and Steinn the *stafnbui,* who believed in trolls, cried aloud. But Thorhall Gamlason—for it was he—only grinned and tossed the gigantic bearskin he was carrying onto the table in front of Leif. Hunbogi Ale-Head's eyes bulged at the size of the shaggy pelt.

"What kind of bear is this?" he asked, awed, and gasping in his awe.

"A large one," said Thorhall Gamlason, still grinning. "Brian has the cubs outside. This one could not walk by himself, so I had to carry him."

After we had borne in Brian, who could not walk well even now though his splinted arm was mending nicely, Thorhall Gamlason sank into a chair Hunbogi had contrived from deerskins slung on elk horns even as he had seen chairs made back in Norway.

"It was a long walk," he said. "And we met with scant hospitality. I need food and drink now—much, much food, and more drink."

Never had the crew of the *Mariasuden* seen Thorhall Gamlason get drunk before—though often had they seen him drink deeply. When, hours later, it came time to go to bed in the Yule dawn, he could not make his way to the ship's shed where he laired.

"Bed him here for once—before the fire," said Leif Ericson, "though it is against his Jomsburg oath."

"What odds?" asked Thorhall Gamlason, though Leif did not think he had been listening. "I have breached one article of my faith in slaying the bear. I may as well breach another one."

That was our only Christmas in Vinland without the comfort of the Mass.

As Leif Ericson enjoined, I set down the skerry in my chart as *Bjarney*, the Bears' Island. It was Thorhall Gamlason's further suggestion—and Leif was quick to agree—that the lake itself where the skerry was be called *Hunavatn* or Bearscubwater. For he had become very fond of those cubs he and Brian had borne home from their quest.

Brian's ankle and arm healed perfectly in time, though the wrenched knee left him with a little limp that prevented his running as swiftly as before—Leif Ericson said, with a laugh, that he would never catch the Irish maid now. It was not Brian, however, about whom Leif had to worry in earnest. It was Thorhall Gamlason who brooded on the bear he had killed. Men noticed that, from this time on, he went back somewhat to his moody ways, dwelling apart from the others, and not speaking much. Brian told Leif of the red men's encampment and what had gone on there. But Thorhall Gamlason said nothing of that, either. Nor did Leif Ericson say anything to him. Again this was a mistake, as it is easy to see looking back. But when was hindsight not better than foresight?

Leif had something else to worry about, too. As was to be expected, the men began to be restive without their women. Svein Haldorson put the matter in a nutshell one night as we all sat about the fire.

"I used to say," he said, blue eyes twinkling in his fat red face, "in the days when I knew no better, that a woman was good for a man only two times in her life. When she was in bride-bed and, again, when she lay in her grave. I would say now she is also some good in between, now and then. My old woman, who is a long way from both bride-bed and grave, would be right welcome to me at this minute."

It was now Leif told the men—what he had already told the council—of his plan for taking the *Mariasuden* back to Greenland in the spring before Thorfinn Karlsefni came out with his three ships. They were content enough since, as he pointed out, it would mean he could bring back more of their women, including some who were betrothed as well as wives, than had been first thought. Thord Thordarson alone did not cheer up at this prospect. For, being neither married nor betrothed, he could expect no assuagement of his woman-hunger unless Leif were also to bring out some unhandfasted girls, a thing Leif did not yet see his way clear to doing. Like Thorhall Gamlason, Thord Thordarson, too, went apart in the evening and talked to no one. It came into my mind, watching him, that we might have trouble with Thord before we were through. Leif thought so also, as did Thorvald Ericson.

So our first winter in the new land wore on to spring; and it came time to get the *Mariasuden* ready for sea once again. For the space of his absence, Leif Ericson appointed his brother, Thorvald Ericson, captain in his stead, with Steinn the *stafnbui* second in command. This business of Steinn's preferment over him, as it turned out, became still another grievance on the part of Thorhall Gamlason who thought he had been unfairly passed over in this matter.

But, though it gave him little satisfaction, it should be said that Thorhall Gamlason's slaying of the bear was long remembered throughout all the northern lands. That, and his drawing of the sledge through the winter forest. Men said in after years that not even Grettir Asmundson ever did a greater feat than this one.

CHAPTER TEN

DEATH AND LOVE

MANY YEARS HAVE I LIVED ON THIS EARTH NOW; AND, IN THAT time, I have seen much of the doings of men and women in both love and death. It comes into my mind, after all this waste of time over which I have journeyed, that love is much like death. It has no times or seasons as have the other things of man. It comes to all alike. No man can say it nay. And, once it takes possession of a heart, fear and shame leave that heart. For love that is, in its origins, of God will do anything to attain its object even to the flouting of the law of God. Yet, in the end, love tampers with law at love's peril so that there is much strife between men because of love.

But if love be like death, death is not like love. For love is a goddess, when all is said and done, and death no goddess at all, but a fleshless woman putting everything into her gaunt troll's belly, ever beset by a thirst that can never be quenched so long as time parches us. In the end, I know, love wins over death. But that end is a long time coming. Meanwhile death's sway stretches far as we of the *Mariasuden* found it come to pass in Vinland.

Leif Ericson sailed for Greenland at the end of March, taking with him twelve men, which was as scant a number as he dared risk this dangerous venture with. These were the Irish Vikings: Rafn and Steinof Humblepie; the two from Scotland: Gunnbjorn and Floki Ravenson; for the others: Bolli Holluson, Thorgils Bollason, Thorstein the Black, Viga-Thorlak, Bjorn Korekson, Illugi Tomcat, Bolli Blacksark, and Hauk Erlendson. That left resident in our Vinland camp Thorvald Ericson as captain; Steinn the *stafnbui,* his second in command; Thorhall Gamlason, Brian, Tyrker, Hunbogi Ale-Head, Hallbjorn Half-Troll, Onund of Trolleskog, Asgeir Aedikoll, Thorleik Eldgrimson, Thord Thordarson, the brothers Alf and Ornolf, Sveinn Haldorson, Thori Englandsfari, and myself. The tally came to twenty-nine altogether. Our company had been thirty-one strong on the day we weighed anchor at Ericsfjord for our journey out. Then Ari Marson had deserted and Ran had claimed Thorstein the White. But all in all, I thought, we had done as well as could have been expected—and much better than might have been feared.

It seemed to me that Leif had made a good division of responsibility, all things considered. The young, as was fitting, went with him. Those who stayed behind with us were—with the single exception of Thord Thordarson—stronger in experience and responsibility. For ours was the grimmer lot, alone against the forest and the unknown. Brian, of course, was a special case. Given the political situation involving his great-uncle and the viking power in Ireland, it was safer for Leif to keep the lad in Vinland.

Leif had thought twice about Thord Thordarson, however, as he explained to Thorvald Ericson. In the end, he would have taken him with him in the *Mariasuden* but for one thing. The slightly built Thord had developed a hacking cough over the winter. He ran a fever mornings and evenings which left him listless in between. Leif hoped it was not the beginning of the wasting disease which consumed the lungs. He said he had seen too many good men slowly bleed to death that way. So Thord Thordarson stayed behind with us, though he was the only man, neither married nor betrothed, Leif left in Vinland.

All the rest still lacking wives went with him. Thorhall Gamlason, of course, was neither married nor betrothed, though he had gone with women many a time in his day. But it was too late to do anything about this now. What woman in her senses would take Thorhall the Hunter any more? Yet Leif, setting sail, had more than one foreboding in Thorhall's regard.

On Leif's own side, the twelve men sailing with him were all good sailors, Bolli Holluson and Thorgils Bollason being the most skilled of all. Their seasoned presence under him would almost balance the fact that Steinn the *stafnbui* would not be sailing on this voyage. Leif had two things in mind in Illugi Tomcat's case. As Thori Englandsfari had to stay behind because his injured leg still unfitted him for life on shipboard, so Leif would like Sveinbjorn, the Hafgrimsfjord leech, to look at Illugi—I think Leif was proud enough of his own leechcraft but that, at the same time, he would not want Illugi to come to grief through any fault on his part. Also, as he told us, it had come into his mind that Illugi should sail back with Thorfinn Karlsefni on his return trip.

It would make things easier all round if Thorfinn should have the benefit of a pilot who was making this hard voyage for the third time.

So the choice was made; and we men of Vinland abode by our leader's choice. On a crisp clear day in spring, the sea as still as a blue brooch on a maiden's breast, the *Mariasuden,* Brian's two bear cubs aboard, weighed anchor for her eastward crossing. Those of us left behind seemed cheerful enough as the long ship, dragon sail spread to the wind, the Blessed Lady smiling from the prow, sailed with the tide out of our Vinland lake. But, underneath everything, our hearts could not help sinking a little. It would be lonesome for us if Leif Ericson's brave craft should never return. This new land of ours was a wondrous land indeed. Day by day it twined itself about our hearts. But it was not home yet. We had no women and no children in our midst.

Thorvald Ericson voiced what we all felt. Standing on the strand, watching the swift ship now round the distant promontory, he smote the strings of his crooked harp and sang very low as if to himself, but so clearly that we all could hear:

> *"Fare thee well, Mary ship!*
> *A good faring to the homeland!*
> *And a quicker return!"*

Out on the open sea Leif Ericson and the *Mariasuden* both fared well—I set this down here from what I learned much later on. King Helgi, Sigmund's great son, he who wedded the shield-maiden, Sigrun, had as steersman of his hero ship a man named Leif when he sailed against King Hoddbrodd. That first Leif was, in days of old, the best of seafarers in all the northern lands. But he was not so great by half as our Leif, the son of Eric. The Mary ship swam the swan road. Her sharp keel ploughed the field of the seal. And the long days and weeks passed.

Back in our Vinland camp things did not fare so well as aboard the *Mariasuden.* The bad times set in almost as soon as Leif Ericson departed. First the clear weather broke and was followed by several weeks of chilling rain. There was nothing for the men to do but sit in the cabins and mend their war gear.

Hunbogi Ale-Head's cabin was cheerier than the others since Hunbogi, at least, had no difficulty staying busy. From morn till night his workroom was shrill with the keening cry of swords and spears set to his whirring grindstone. The noise was like an old Irish mother mourning her dead son in Gaelic, as I once said with a laugh to Brian. Brian thought it sounded even more like the fairy woman, Aibhinn, the banshee of the Dal gCais, who dwelt in the haunted rock of Craig-liath, and who cried in the night whenever one of the *Ard Ri's* line came to his end. Hunbogi, who was hagridden by fears of trolldom, did not find this kind of conversation very much to his liking. Sveinn Haldorson fore-gathered with him, however, so that there was also plenty of the ribald sort of merriment he preferred.

Alf and Ornolf found much to do, too. During the winter they had managed to fish through the ice. But, for the born fisher-man, ice fishing is at best no more than a stopgap. Now that lake and river were open again—with the camp so short-handed, Thor-vald Ericson would not let them try their luck in the open sea as yet—they had gone back to fishing almost every day, though it was still a week or so off the time when the fish would begin biting really well. In the evenings the two brothers repaired their tackle and talked of fish again. It has been my observation in life that fishermen offer no one very much trouble—unless, of course, it be the fish they take.

Tyrker made copies of my charts—he proved a most apt pupil —and staked out certain vines which he had transplanted the preceding autumn. Thorvald Ericson fashioned additional strings for his skald's harp and played with the great wolfhound who had taken to living now in his cabin. Bran was happier these days than he had ever been before. Physically he throve apace. His coat, which Thorvald Ericson combed until it shone, was thick and lustrous. His great chest gave out a church bell's bour-don when he bayed on the trail. Twice, during the past winter, had Bran taken an elk. Once, when Leif foraged far afield with Thorhall, hunting, the huge dog had cut out and pulled down the coursing leader of a wolf pack. He stood a full thirty-seven inches at the collar now; and, when he reared on his hind legs, he towered high over a tall man. Thorvald Ericson made a song about him which he called *Bran's Hunting*. This was a good song, I mind me, and I knew it by heart once. But now it has gone clean out of my mind.

Brian, too, I think, made out more than a little better than the ruck of his comrades. For if love is a tyrant who binds, she is also a goddess who frees. He had Grainne's lovely face to think on;

and the promise of her coming before many moons were out. He said to me he thought, if Leif were only willing, that the two of them might fare together in marriage before the end of the coming year.

In the meantime Leif Ericson had left instructions that, so soon as the frost was completely out of the ground, we should build a large new cabin to house the unmarried women who would be coming with him in his and Thorfinn's ships. Old Thorleik Eldgrimson had charge of this. Brian kept a watchful eye on the building. It was clear to me that, in his own lover's mind, he had appointed just where Grainne's bed-closet would be situate. As soon as the first violets poked their small blue faces out of the thawing ground, he made a little nosegay and, when no one was looking, placed it on the pine floor. In the morning old Thorleik, walking over the part that had been built, wondered where those flowers had come from. But he said nothing. Steinn the *stafnbui* might have cried troll. Thorleik only smiled to himself. As for myself, I, too, kept my peace. There are some things even comrades do well not to jest about.

As for the other men—this time all but Thord Thordarson who was now too ill to care much what was going on around him— they thought on women, too, and with a sick longing that kept their tempers on edge and their tongues' rough edges foremost. They tried to keep darkness at bay by drinking it down whenever they could. But that only worked for a while. After the drink had worn off, the darkness came back blacker than ever. Besides, the beer supply was running low. Steinn the *stafnbui* kept what was left under jealous lock and key, doling out only a limited measure at and after each evening meal, and none at all during the days.

Thorhall Gamlason was by far the worst of all. He, who had been a fable when it came to holding in liquor, had been more or less besotted ever since the Yule feast when he came back from the Bears' Skerry. Moreover, he now sat apart, sodden and morose, and held conversation with no one except to snarl at Steinn whenever it came time to put the ale under lock again until the next evening. The *Mariasuden* was long gone from its winter shed. But Thorhall insisted on sleeping in that dank place anyway. For the first time, instead of animals, he had taken to carving men out of his walrus ivory. It seemed to Brian, when he thought on the matter, that the little people Thorhall now fashioned were like the new world savages the two of them had

seen in the ravine. He did not ask him, however; and Thorhall
said nothing one way or the other.

I thought Brian might well be right in his judgment; for the
tiny figures were not unlike the single Skraeling I had seen coming down the summer trail. One thing was clear about those
images whoever they may have been intended to represent. They
were being modeled out of hate, not love. The whole matter made
Brian, who had come to know Thorhall Gamlason better than
any of the rest of us, very uneasy. He spoke of it to Thorvald
Ericson and myself. Thorvald confessed that he, too, was worried.
But, he added—and I had to admit that his objection was reasonable even if it did not satisfy me—what more could we do but
wait, and hope, and keep close watch?

Now we fixed this same watch so that one of the five of us—
Thorvald Ericson, Brian, myself, Steinn, and Tyrker—might keep
a wary eye on Thorhall Gamlason at all times, each man a day at
a stretch and, turn about, a night, too, when next his time to
guard came up. It was very hard to do this without Thorhall's
finding out; and, in the end, he slipped through our loose fingers,
anyway. It was on one of my watches that I found out the secret
of the powder Thorhall Gamlason called "gods' flesh."

He had gone down one of the trails which we now knew had
been made by Skraeling feet. When I came upon him, pretending
great surprise the while, he was bent over a spot where violets
grew, putting something small into his leather scrip.

"Well, Thorhall," I said, dissembling as best I could, "so you
collect wild flowers in the spring. Let me see what you have
plucked this time."

Thorhall Gamlason got to his feet sullenly.

"Since you must know," he said, baring his teeth in a wolfish
grin in which there was even less of mirth than usual, "this is
what I cull."

He opened the wallet for me.

"So," he said bitterly. "Now you know my secret—much good
may it do you!"

There was nothing in the scrip he bared but five or six of the
ugly growths children call toadstools: slug white and mottled,
glistening with damp. I knew that the mushrooms, which resem-
bled these poisonous things, were esteemed a great delicacy in

Frankland. But toadstools! They had been known to slay the careless cook who mistook them for something else.

"What secret do you mean, Thorhall?" I asked him, honestly puzzled.

"Do not pretend, Thrand Thorbergson," he said in ugly wise. "Now you know what gods' flesh is and where it grows. Why else should you spy upon me thus?"

"Why else?" I said quickly, content enough that he should have made this mistake if it would only serve to hide my real purpose in following after him.

But I was staggered all the same. So this vile trash was the divine powder I had sniffed that Twelfth Night in Thorhall Gamlason's cabin! Well was it said that the devil was the ape of God. Like most other wickedness in this fair world of ours, when all was said and done, this, too, was a wretched secret.

"All the berserkers know of these," said Thorhall Gamlason, making a clean breast of things. "We taste them before battle, and they make us like wolves or bears. The plants can also be used for other purposes, as you well know. You will say nothing of all this, Thrand Thorbergson? It is one of the Jomsburg mysteries— one of those we held dearest of all. I am the last of that old fellowship, and I would not want it said in days to come that I held that honor so cheaply as to have given this same secret to the world."

"I shall say nothing, Thorhall," I said.

"Swear then," he said to me. "Swear by the *Jomfru* Maria." So I swore by Mary Virgin. He had to be content with that.

Nor did I say anything, either—not even to Brian or to Thorvald Ericson. But I set this all down in the log where Tyrker read it when he made another copy of the record. He, too, said nothing to anyone. But the two of us together showed the passage in question to Leif Ericson when the *Mariasuden* came back from Greenland, I thinking that, in this way, I could both keep faith with my captain and not breach the oath I took.

Tyrker, who was versed in matters of this sort, told me that the toadstools probably accounted for the *berserksgang* which was the fury that overtook berserkers in battle, making them foam at the mouth, howl like wolves, and bite on their brazen shield rims—it should be remembered, though, that Thorhall Gamlason himself, last of the berserkers, always fought in utter silence. The little southron also said that the followers of Hassan

did much the same thing in Sarkland. Only the drug they chose
to chew was called hemp or hashish.

Since I had tasted once of this abomination, as Tyrker had
never done, another thought came into my mind then. I thought
that this was how Thorhall Gamlason—or so men said—was able
to talk with Thor. But I said nothing of this to anyone, not even
to Leif Ericson or to Tyrker.

So the long days and longer nights dragged on until the terrible
May morning when it became clear that none of us had kept close
watch enough on Thorhall Gamlason.

I was awakened, in my cabin which was also Brian's, by Thorvald Ericson's gently tugging at the sleeve of my night rail a half
hour or so before day dawned.

"Get up, Thrand," said Thorvald Ericson quietly, speaking in
my ear. "Rouse Brian. But try not to wake the others. We have
trouble on our hands. Great trouble. If it can be settled at all, I
think it can be better settled if the whole camp is not aroused. It
is mere chance I saw what I just saw when Thorhall Gamlason
went into his cabin."

Thorvald Ericson's face was white and serious in the dawn
light. Never had I seen him look so much like his brother Leif.
Swiftly I slipped on my clothes and, Brian with me, followed
Thorvald Ericson out into the silent compound. No one stirred in
the Vinland encampment—except for the birds who had some
minutes before begun their morning song. Luckily Steinn the
stafnbui was on sentry duty. Thorvald made a sign to him to be
silent. There would be no problem there, I thought. Steinn, when
he had to be, was quiet as a tomb. The rainy weather had broken
at last and a beautiful May come in its stead. There was a fresh
scent of flowers in the paling darkness. Just inside the second
palisade, where the builders had been careful not to disturb them
last fall, some bushes flared golden in the light that had now
begun to tremble on the point of dawn. It was a morning for life,
not death. But it was death that had come with us to Vinland.

The trouble Thorvald Ericson spoke of lay in Thorhall Gamlason's cabin. When we broke in the door, I saw that Thorhall had
a woman with him—a woman, moreover, who did not wish to be
with him in any way. At first glance I knew she must be one of
the savage people Brian and I had seen with Leif on the far-off
morning of Leif's land-taking; and, later, Brian and Thorhall,

as they made their way back from their tryst with the bear. Even though, at this moment, her sobbing face was contorted into a mask of horror and loathing, it was clear that this Skraeling was very young and very beautiful; straight as a Skraeling arrow and fresh as this May morning itself. Her skin was a smooth breathing copper; her gleaming hair blue-black; her slanting eyes as shining dark as ripe black cherries. There was an ugly smear of blood on her right cheekbone; and the print of a bloody hand on the shoulder of the soft-cured white buckskins she wore as a dress. It came over me, with a sudden thrill of revulsion, that the hand was Thorhall Gamlason's.

If he did not possess the habit of authority that belonged by nature to his brother Leif, and his father Eric, Thorvald Ericson's mind was very quick. He saw at once the trouble a woman's presence would create in our camp. He understood just as vividly the danger of creating a breach between our Vinland camp and the people to whom this woman belonged.

"You have touched this woman?" he asked Thorhall Gamlason without any beating about the bush whatsoever.

"I brought her here to my cabin," said Thorhall Gamlason sullenly, "if that is what you mean by 'touched.'"

"That is not what I mean," said Thorvald Ericson. "I think you know what I mean. So I ask you again: have you touched this woman, Thorhall?"

"And if I have, what then?" asked Thorhall insolently.

"We shall have to go into the matter in that case," said Thorvald Ericson. "But you have not yet answered my question—a plain question and an easy one, Thorhall. I repeat it. Have you touched this woman?"

"No," said Thorhall. Then he grinned. "Not yet, at least. But she is mine to do what I please with when I so choose. She is mine according to the old Jomsburg law."

"We are Christians here, if you are not," said Thorvald Ericson. "This is not Jomsburg. Jarl Eric destroyed that nest and—though I never said this before—it was well that he destroyed that eagles' eyrie. No, Thorhall, this is Leif Ericson's camp, and I command in Leif's absence. Where did you come upon the woman?"

"On the promontory," said Thorhall Gamlason. "I—"

"Whose night was it to watch?" asked Thorvald Ericson, wheeling to look at me.

"Tyrker's," I said to him, and stopped. I think the same thought came to the both of us: that Tyrker, who had not drunk much for a long time, had chosen this night to quench his drought.

"No matter," said Thorvald Ericson after a moment. "We must dree our weird now. You were saying, Thorhall?"

Thorhall Gamlason grinned at me to show that now, at last, he understood what secret it was I trailed down the day I came upon him with the toadstools in the forest. When he chose, he could look most sinister, that old Jomsburg wolf of ours.

"I was saying," he said, "that I took the girl in fight as a man who follows Thor is wont to do—as, for that matter, if they are only honest about it, many Christians are wont to do, too. But I will not quarrel over that point now. I took her in fair fight, and that is what counts. The eight comrades who were with her sleep their last sleep now under their boats of mooseskin."

"Eight!" said Thorvald Ericson, aghast, and I could hear Brian, too, catch his breath in horror. "You killed eight of them singlehanded!"

"It was not such a feat, after all," said Thorhall Gamlason, shrugging. "Six of them I took in their sleep. The other two, the ones that woke, I slew in open combat. I think one of these last must have been the girl's husband—or else her brother. Her close kinsman, surely, judging by the way she struggled while I slew them."

Thorhall Gamlason grinned in real admiration at his captive. Never had I seen a more terrible look of hatred for anyone than the look I saw on the savage girl's face.

From Thorhall's story it was easily possible to piece together what had happened. He was returning to camp, after midnight, from a hunting expedition which had carried him far afield when he had come upon what seemed to be three hillocks on the shore nearest the sound but farthest from our settlement. Only they could not possibly have been hillocks. Hillocks did not have a habit of springing up overnight like so many toadstools. Besides, there had been no such knolls in evidence when he had last passed that way only twelve hours before that. Creeping closer on his belly, so that he should make no manner of noise, Thorhall had satisfied himself that the mounds were actually three boats fashioned of skin with three people asleep under each one—eight men and this woman whom he had brought back to his cabin, after slitting the throats of six of them and killing the other two in hard hand to hand grapple. Thorhall Gamlason noted somewhat grimly that bringing the woman back to his cabin had been no easy task. She had bitten and scratched him. Also, she had screamed a good deal at first.

There was a pause after Thorhall finished his story. Thorvald Ericson and Brian looked on the woman who looked back at them, the terror and loathing never leaving her face so that her eyes were slitted and her mouth wrested into a kind of square. I found I could not look upon her face after that first glimpse, so shaken was I by shame and a kind of despair.

"But why kill them at all?" asked Brian after a space.

"So that they might not take back the news of our encampment to their people," said Thorhall Gamlason in some surprise that this should not be at once evident to everyone. "You must know, if anyone does, Brian, the kind of devils these people are in war. For you watched them with me from the head of the ravine. And we are far too few to fight against a whole village— maybe a kingdom even. From what I saw and felt our weapons are better. But they must have many, many more than we."

I remembered the lone warrior I had seen that day with Leif; the red feather in the blue-black hair. And my mind wavered, for a moment, between fear and horror. Then I came back to myself. What Thorhall Gamlason had done was wrong from any point of view.

"Perhaps these savage folk know of our whereabouts already," I said to him.

Thorhall looked at me in real perplexity.

"How may that be?" he asked. "I left none alive to carry the tale."

Then, at last, and because we thought Leif would want Thorhall to know now, I told him of the man we had seen on the forest trail. Anger and chagrin convulsed Thorhall Gamlason's face.

"In this case," he said with passionate intensity, "what I did may have been a mistake. I did not know there had been others of these earlier so close to our encampment. But how could I tell? This is not my mistake alone. I should have been told about this! Why was I not told?"

"It was Leif's decision," said Thorvald Ericson wearily. "At the time it seemed the right one. But I agree with you that, in the upshot, it does not seem so now. You should have been told. It is too late to amend that mistake. Where are these dead men now?"

Thorhall Gamlason's mood changed at once; and not for the better, either.

"Why, where should they be?" he asked, grinning his crooked grin. "Where they fell, I suppose. Unless, of course, they have since got up and walked away. But I do not think that very likely. I am going back there after a space. They are safe from wolves at this time of year, I think, till nightfall. But no later. I should not want them spoiled, you know. I should like to keep their heads in salt. To take six of them, even in sleep, and two others waking, now seems to me no little exploit."

For the first time I wondered seriously if Thorhall Gamlason were going mad. Or if he had been mad for some time and no one had noticed it. Perhaps it was the gods' flesh once again. His pupils were strangely dilated. The wooden bowl lay on the table. There were fresh toadstool stems in it, the upper parts of the pulpy fungi gnawed away.

"We shall go there at once," said Thorvald Ericson sternly. "Now—long before nightfall. And we shall lay those dead warriors in howe, even as it is fitting warriors should be laid. If time allows, we shall even build cairns over them so that later on, if they become drows—as seems likely, since they were violently slain and without their fault—they may not walk."

"I fear no drows, Thorvald, even if you do," said Thorhall Gamlason, the same strange smile on his face. "But this maid of mine, though she is no drow, may do a little walking if we do not watch out—right over our stockade and so back to the people to whom she belongs. If I am not to have her, no one else shall, either. In that case, it is well we kill her at once. Otherwise she is sure to escape sooner or later. She is like a wildcat no one can watch."

Thorvald Ericson's face had set like iron now.

"We must risk that," he said. "No one shall slay this girl while I command in Leif's camp. There has been enough killing this day—and more than enough, too—as it is. But I will set close watch upon her—and we shall see if she shall escape."

"This is a matter of war decision," said Thorhall Gamlason stubbornly. "In a matter involving military policy, like this one, your will alone may not prevail. We must call a council of war."

Thorvald Ericson's dark face seemed to lighten a little. It was as if he were unexpectedly relieved of a burden that had been pressing too heavy on him.

"I agree," he said—and I think that now his words were as wise as any Leif might have spoken. "I agree that we should call a council—and at once, too. But let it be a council that is of peace, not war. Peace is superior to war. So is a Thing superior to a war council. So let this council be a Thing—our first Thing. I think that, if Leif were here, he, too, would convene a Thing. This issue goes far beyond a matter of war alone. It calls for a supreme Council. And, by the law of the north, the Thing is our supreme Council—supreme even over the King. Do you agree?"

Thorhall Gamlason shrugged. What he considered technicalities were always matters of pure indifference to him. What he did not see was that this was not a technicality at all. It was a thing of political life or death. It could tip the scales toward either tyranny or freedom.

"Call it what you will," he said. "So long as it be a council where each man's voice is equal."

"Then do you see to it, Thorhall, that the men are roused," said Thorvald Ericson. "And let them assemble by the mound in front of Leif's cabin. And, Brian, do you break out the raven banner atop the mound. It is rolled in wadmal in Leif's great chest. Here is the key. Meanwhile I shall guard the girl so that she may not flee."

Sleepily the men tumbled out of bed to the sound of the *lur* as Thorhall Gamlason blew it hoarsely in the Vinland dawn. Steinn the *stafnbui* went off sentry duty, and Onund of Trolleskog replaced him. Onund was to have his vote, of course. From where he stood on guard, spear in hand, he could easily hear the proceedings; and, when the vote was taken, declare his intentions as well and freely as the others. By a show of hands, Thorleik Eldgrimson, who was the eldest and who had had experience of many Thing meetings in both Greenland and Norway, was elected Lawman. Then, when all his comrades were assembled and all else was in readiness, Brian broke out the great banner with the raven on it which Grainne had stitched with her own hands.

The first Vinland Thing was open.

It seemed to me, who had seen several other Things so far in my life—for Thorberg Skaffhogg, my father, had some small reputation as a Thing speaker—that these proceedings of ours

went off with amity and expedition, even if with some slight
degree of technical irregularity. I have since heard it said in Ireland that, when we are not marauding or sailing the world's seas,
we Norsemen make the very best of lawyers, even those of us
who are not trained to that arduous game. I think that Irish saying is very true, as the people of Duke William's Norman *vik*
are even now proving all over again in Harald's England.

Thorhall Gamlason began his case by arguing for one of two
alternatives, the same two alternatives, as it happened, Thorvald
Ericson, acting as camp leader, had previously said nay to. These
were: either that he should have the girl, in which case he would
assume complete responsibility for her safe-conduct. He had
broken mares in his day, he added with a sinister expression at
which my blood ran cold. He thought he could go bond for the
savage maid's docility after a day or so. If this privilege, which
he had won in fair fight, were denied him, then he stipulated that
the girl be killed outright—and at once—as a danger to our camp.

Thorvald Ericson, fighting against Thorhall Gamlason before
the assembled Thing, based his arguments in the girl's behalf
mainly on what King Olaf Tryggveson and Bishop Sigurd liked
to call *Kristenret,* or the Law of Christ, which stood above all
other man-made laws. Thorhall Gamlason, who showed an unexpected quickness for legal debate, countered this argument with
a closely reasoned demonstration that the issue now before our
Thing was an issue of state alone, not of church, whether the
church in question happened to belong to Asa-Thor or Christ.
This, I noted, was a point which seemed to impress several of the
hearers. Tyrker, for one, nodded assent; and Hallbjorn Half-
Troll. Hallbjorn, we were to find out later, had his own ax to
grind here.

In answer to Thorhall, Thorvald Ericson now insisted that this
line of argument, if valid at all, would hold good only in case of
actual war which always suspended peacetime arrangements; that,
if it should turn out to be an issue of war in the bitter end, then
this was the result of Thorhall's own rashness; and that the girl
should not pay so heavy a penalty as losing her life for the fault
of another merely because he happened to be the accuser of her
innocent self. Even Odin, he added, stood for justice. If Thorhall
Gamlason wanted to invoke Thor or Odin, let him. The old gods
would stand against him in this present case. As for this business
of war or peace, Thorvald Ericson denied either that it was a

matter of war at all yet, or that it must necessarily become a matter of war. Here, he reminded our assembled Thing that, because of the fact we were newcomers and guests in this strange land and not yet settled inhabitants thereof, this was all the more reason why, in common prudence, we should try to keep clear of a war that would be sure to crush us by sheer weight of superior numbers.

With a sardonic look addressed to Thorvald Ericson, Thorhall Gamlason, on his side, next insisted that responsibility for any mistake in policy involved in his slaying of the savage folk must lie with Leif, Steinn, Thorvald, Brian, Tyrker, and myself, all of whom had been privy to the existence of these dangerous neighbors and had not informed the rest of us about them—and this, Thorhall insisted, was the action neither of comrades nor of sensible men. It was possible, he freely admitted, that he had made a mistake in slaying the savages; but, if so, the fault could not possibly lie with him. For the sake of argument alone, let him grant, for the moment, that Thorvald Ericson was right in his insistence on the necessity for their avoiding war at this time. That was precisely why this girl must die so that there might be no evidence of any sort left to tell her people what had gone on in the matter of the nine missing savages. Again Tyrker and Hallbjorn Half-Troll nodded assent; and this time, Ornolf, too, seemed to be with them.

With a sinking heart I realized that the tide was running against Thorvald Ericson. The rest of our company had become wroth inside because they had been kept out of the secret that there were other men, besides ourselves, in this new land. Thorvald dared not raise other arguments from either reason or expediency lest Thorhall Gamlason cunningly turn these, too, against him to the certain ruin of the blameless captive. He had invoked necessity; and, in return, necessity had smitten him squarely in the face. Then, without warning, where one might have least expected it, our cause and Thorvald Ericson's gained a powerful ally.

Sick-faced and wan, Thord Thordarson, who had been sitting huddled in a blanket for all that it was a fresh May morning, got quickly to his feet, a spot of hectic red burning bright on either cheek. With all eyes upon him he flung out one thin arm in the girl's direction.

"Look on her well, comrades!" he said, coughing his racking

cough the while, though the sun shone warm and full now. "She
is a soft and pretty maiden, is she not? If we freely vote to slay
her, have you thought who is to do the butchery?"

The savage girl, who had been placed next to Thorleik Lawman, shrank away when our Thing, as one man, turned our heads
to look at her. If the gesture had been planned to attract sym-
pathy, it could not have worked as well. She looked as lovely as
the morning and as defenceless as a limed song bird. And, somehow, she seemed to know that Thord Thordarson had spoken up
in her defense. For a swift instant her white teeth gleamed at him
in a shyly attractive smile. It was then, I think—if one can ever
put his finger on the exact moment—that the blind bow boy
launched his arrow straight at Thord Thordarson's heart. As it
happened, it was a Skraeling arrow. But I have not heard that,
in love, a Skraeling arrow flies any the less surely and straightly
than a Norse one.

There was a long pause then, during which no one spoke; and
in which Thorvald Ericson almost dared to hope again. Hunbogi
Ale-Head was the first to break silence.

"By God!" he said, his great face flushing. "Thord Thordarson
has the right of this! I, for one, will not play executioner. I make
war on men, not women."

"Nor I!" said Alf.

"Nor I!" said Ornolf, though I thought he spoke a little more
reluctantly than his brother.

On our side, no one said anything. For we had never so much
as dallied with the evil notion that the girl be slain.

Thorhall Gamlason laughed his barking laugh.

"I will do it, then," he said with an ugly grin. "I may as well
bind the Hel shoes on her pretty feet as on those of her eight
fellows."

"Of course, Thorhall," said Thord Thordarson, and there was a
sneer on his handsome, haggard face. "Of course. It was to be
expected. It is ever Thorhall Gamlason's way to hunt, day in, day
out. He will slay this pretty Hlin for us even as he would slay a
little bird on a bough above our heads."

Thorhall Gamlason's face became contorted with rage. It used
to be said of him that, in his berserker days, his cheeks turned
red as blood in anger, then pale as winter grass, then blue as any
dead man's livid cheeks. Though I had known the man for many
moons now, never had I seen him thus. The stories were true.

His face did go those furious colors. Now they did so again. It seemed to me, looking on, that Thorhall had no need to traffic in the evil fungi—it took no gods' flesh to send this old wolf into a murderous frenzy. I thought now he might even fall in a swoon as happened to those unfortunates who suffered from the falling sickness. But, after one interval of spasm, the old berserker controlled himself again.

"If you were not a sick man, Thord, with whom it would not be honorable to fight," he said in a dead voice that was even more terrifying than his rage, "you would go to holmgang with me for that insult."

"I will go to holmgang with you whenever you wish, Thorhall Gamlason," said Thord Thordarson, his voice, too, expressionless. And, strangely enough, this time he did not cough once.

For all that Thord Thordarson had been sick so long, it might have come to deadly shield play then and there except that, at this point, seeing his chance to bring this matter to a good conclusion, Thorvald Ericson intervened.

"Time enough later for the reddening of swords if the two of you so choose," he said swiftly. "For the moment Odin's eagles must wait a little longer for their hero supper. Let us deal now with this matter we still have in hand. I think we have deliberated on it long enough. It is my mind now that we put it to a vote. We have much work to do before nightfall out on the promontory. Graves must be dug for the dead, and cairns raised over them while the light holds."

Now Thorvald Ericson was commander in his brother's camp. But in our Thing he was but a member of the Vinland company, an equal among equals. So he looked up at Thorleik Eldgrimson, deferring to the Lawman's verdict on this motion of his. Thorleik Eldgrimson bowed courteously in return; then bent his old head in the direction of Thorhall Gamlason.

"Thorhall Gamlason," he said. "As a plaintiff in this action, you have further rights in the matter of argument, if you so choose to exercise them. Is it your will, too, as well as Thorvald Ericson's, that it should now come to a vote?"

"I am willing," said Thorhall Gamlason, the resentment against Thord Thordarson still most apparent in his rasping voice. If he had more arguments to present, it was too late now. The gall in his throat almost choked him when he tried to talk.

Thorhall Gamlason was right to feel anger against Thord

Thordarson. The man's eloquent few words and even more eloquent gesture had tipped the scales in favor of the new world
girl. In a show of hands the verdict went for her twelve to three,
only Hallbjorn Half-Troll and Onund of Trolleskog siding with
Thorhall. In his capacity as Lawman Thorleik Eldgrimson, of
course, did not vote. But it was quite clear, from his expression,
when the verdict was rendered, that he, too, approved the girl's
cause.

It was further agreed, before our Thing broke up, that the
girl should sleep in Leif's cabin, which was empty, until the captain of the *Mariasuden* returned. By that time the new building
set apart for the unmarried women would be finished, and she
could move in with Grainne and what other maidens came with
Leif and Thorfinn Karlsefni. To guard against the possibility of
escape, the cabin doors and windows were to be fast bolted at
night. During the day the maid was to have free range inside the
first and second palisades, but not without them. Thorleik Eldgrimson, as the eldest and presumably the most prudent among
us—the only one, moreover, beyond the age of temptation where
women were concerned—was appointed to have conversation with
her daily in order to instruct her in the Norse tongue as well as
to learn a little of her language himself.

When Thorleik failed at this latter task, it was turned over to
Thord Thordarson who, though he continued to improve from
day to day, was not yet well enough to take on other work. As it
happened, Thord showed an unexpected gift for tongues. It was
possible, though, that the goddess, Freya, who shared this month
of May with Mary Virgin, may have aided him a little. For it
was soon clear to all eyes that there was the beginning of love
between Thord Thordarson and the Skraeling maid with the black
cherry eyes. It was clearest of all, I think, to Thorhall Gamlason
whose wolf's face grew grimmer whenever the two of them,
Thord and the girl, spoke together.

Other eyes than Thorhall's cold gray and Thord's level blue
ones turned in desire toward this comely savage maid; and not all
of them were as clean of heart in intention as Thord was. Hallbjorn Half-Troll, who had voted for her death, began to act almost as strangely as Thorhall Gamlason. Thorvald Ericson remembered that there had been some talk of Hallbjorn's having
trouble with his wife back in Greenland; and he worried accord-
ingly. In the evening, when the ale horns passed around, Hall-

bjorn more than once muttered his mother's old saying against
loose women:

> *"On turning wheels were shaped their hearts,*
> *Their fickle hearts and fitful minds.*
> *There is the death of men in their eyes' keen arrows."*

It did no good whatsoever to point out to Hallbjorn that the
savage maid was no loose woman. Had she been a loose woman,
Thorvald Ericson once angrily said to him, she would have gone
with Thorhall Gamlason in the first place. Thorvald Ericson
thought he knew, he said to me, what ailed Hallbjorn in this
matter. He desired the girl for himself; and this was his way of
denying his desire to his own mind. It was true, nonetheless, in
the end, what Hallbjorn said: the savage maid was appointed to
be the death of more than one among us.

What bothered Thorvald Ericson even more, however, than
this lust of Hallbjorn Half-Troll's for the girl was that, from
the day of the Thing on, there was bad blood between Thord
Thordarson and Thorhall Gamlason. The handsome stripling took
once again to practicing the swordsmanship for which he was
famous. Men thought that, if the wasting sickness in him continued to retreat as the fine weather advanced, it would one day
surely come to holmgang between these two enemies. In such a
case, despite his age, Thorhall would probably be the favorite.
For Holmgang-Bersi had never yet lost a bout at holmgang; and
many were the men he had killed. There were some, though, who
thought Thord Thordarson could turn out to be the winner in
the end. The old wolf grew older. There was always a first time
for losing as well as winning. Thord's sword arm was quick, if
slight—and was it not fortified by love besides?

On her side, the savage girl appeared well enough satisfied with
her lot. On her own offering to do so, she became cow-girl for
the camp—the cow Leif had brought with him in the *Mariasuden*
had calved after our arrival; and so there were two cows for her
to tend. If, as Leif intended to do, either he or Thorfinn Karlsefni
brought a bull this time, the cow would freshen again; and the
camp need never be without fresh milk. Meanwhile the new world
maid took care of these grazing kine. They had frightened her at
first with their lowing. But now it seemed as though she were
very fond of these strange animals she had met for the first time
in the camp where she found herself captive.

Thord Thordarson, who had begun to speak her language more than a little now, found out that in her own tongue the girl's name was Little Maid. So now we Norsemen had a name for this little Skraeling. We called her Meyla. Thorvald Ericson began to feel happier about the situation. Now that the men had a name for our visitor, friendliness grew in the camp once again.

So, in the short space of one day, Death and Law had come to Vinland with Love close behind, helping to fulfill this beautiful land that so far wanted other impress. But it had not been a good sort of Death—if Death can ever be said to be good. And Thorvald Ericson, though he said nothing about it to anyone but me, feared that this Love might well bring trouble in its train. Even, he added grimly in his skald's way, as it often did under the best of circumstances.

I think that Brian alone thought little of this new world maid whom Thorhall Gamlason had brought into our midst. His desire for Grainne stayed shining constant as the North Star by which Leif Ericson and Steinn the *stafnbui* had taught him to sail and on which, nightly, he looked, confident that Grainne, too, looked on it while he did. More and more often as the slow days lagged by, he said to me that he wondered which long ship would put in first within our Vinland lake—the one that bore Grainne's fair self, or the one that bore her lovely image rising from the prow.

CHAPTER ELEVEN

THE GARDEN

ONE MIGHT SAY THAT THIS FAIR NEW LAND WE CAME TO WAS
all garden; and yet had it not a garden. A land needs a garden for
completeness. It was Grainne who brought us our garden when
she came with Thorfinn Karlsefni in the first of his ships.

It was Leif Ericson's *Mariasuden* which sailed first into harbor,
the Blessed Virgin, decked out afresh in clean blue and gold paint
by the loving brush of Inge priest back in Ericsfjord, still stooping in gracious benediction over our Vinland lake which, by right
of discovery, was her lake as well as that of Leif and his men.
Only, unlike ourselves, that loveliest of all earth's ladies wanted
nothing from the land except that it let her love it along with
her Divine Son Who was all Love. The *Mariasuden* had been
gone, all told, thirteen weeks, four and one half days. It was
good to see our bonny ship back again and to know, besides, that
in a few short weeks, at most, we should have a priest in Vinland
to hallow our comings and goings.

For Thorfinn Karlsefni, and Sira Inge with him, Leif said,
would be close on his heels, provided the weather held as well as
it had up to now. He had the men build great beacon fires nightly
on the promontory of Keel Ness so that the cape could be seen
miles out at sea in case Thorfinn's ships made their first Vinland
landfall by night instead of day. That he might be the first of us
to sight the vessel bearing Grainne, Brian slept in his skin bag
out on the promontory at night and, during the day, kept watch
from the crotch of a tall oak that grew inside the camp stockade.
Leif and Thorvald Ericson worried a little about the savage folk
when they thought of Brian sleeping alone. But they did not want
to say the lad nay.

Leif was also conscious that these beacon fires represented a
certain measure of risk after he had listened to Thorvald Ericson's account of Thorhall Gamlason's dealings with Meyla and

with the eight savages who had been slain. But it was a risk that
had to be taken all the same. He could not chance the possibility
that, even with Illugi Tomcat on the lookout, Thorfinn Karlsefni
might overshoot the camp. As for Meyla, now that Leif was
back, it would not be fitting that she live in his cabin any longer.
Luckily the women's cabin was now complete. We set apart a
comfortable corner of it for the new world girl—as it happened,
just next to where Grainne was to live until the time came for
herself and Brian to fare together in marriage.

Onund, Asgeir, and Hallbjorn—Hallbjorn, I thought, less than
his two fellow Eastmen—were somewhat disappointed that Leif
had not brought their wives with him in the *Mariasuden,* leaving
them, instead, to follow in one of Thorfinn's ships. Leif had
wanted to keep his own craft clear for the heavy lading he bore.
Two new red cows heavy with calf, and a bull. A he-goat, a she-
goat, and a kid. Many farm tools to work the fertile soil of Vinland. Bale upon bale of wadmal. Five spinning wheels, and the
tools to turn new ones with. Barley in abundance from Papa
Stronsay where the monks had been more than generous. Barley
seed, too, and wheat seed in plenty. Iron for Hunbogi Ale-Head's
forge. Squawking fowl in wooden cages and three crimson-
crested roosters to squire these same dames.

It had been an easy trip, on the whole, both ways. Six weeks
going and six weeks, five days, coming, with five days at Ericsfjord and an extra day and a half for the stop at Papa Stronsay.
It had been easier going over than coming back—which, Leif
Ericson said with a laugh, could be taken as an omen one way or
another, he did not know which—for the prevailing winds blew
in the direction of the homeland. There had been only one bad
moment during the whole journey when, on their way to Papa
Stronsay, they had been blown a little off the *Mariasuden's*
Orkney course and, near Swona, had come a bit too close for
comfort to the awful Swelkie maelstrom where, on the sea bottom, forever ground the magic quern that made the sea so salt.
But, since in the end they had managed to come off so luckily,
Leif was glad now he had seen the Swelkie and lived to tell the
tale. It would make another good story for a winter evening
when the north wind blew and the ale horns went round the
hearth ingle. What, he asked us, was so cozy as a braw tale with
the fire bright and the wind keening outside?

Leif Ericson brought back much news from Greenland. Some
of it was domestic. Old Eric had been ailing of recent months.
His eyes were dull, though they lighted up merrily enough at the
sight of the cubs Leif bore with him. Sveinbjorn, the leech of
Hafrsgrimfjord, when he came to look at Illugi Tomcat and pro-
nounce him the better for Leif's leechcraft, had said it was Eric's
age and that there was nothing much to do about that. It was, he
said, the vigorous ones like Eric who had a habit of going quickly
—the thin-blooded ones might linger on for years and years, and
much good it did them! Eric would be luckier in the end.

After his talk with Sveinbjorn, Leif had come to an agreement
with his mother, Thorhild, that, if anything should happen suddenly to Eric, she would lay the old man in howe but delay the
funeral-ale till he and Thorvald could attend it, no matter how
long it might take for them to get this news and sail from Vinland. Leif then left a clean set of my charts with Freydis' husband,
Thorvard, who promised to make the Vinland voyage and bring
the news in case old Eric died. This meant, of course, that their
troublemaking half sister, Freydis, would most likely set foot
within the Vinland encampment, as she had long desired; and
neither Leif nor Thorvald Ericson, when Leif told him, liked
that prospect overmuch. Thorvard, for all his wealth and seamanship, was a poor-spirited fellow who could not keep Freydis quiet
—he would be lucky, Thorvald Ericson said grimly, if he did not
one day find himself murdered in his bed by one of Freydis'
lemans. But, awkward or not, it could not be helped. Old Eric of
Ericsfjord must be laid in howe and honored in death as became
the sons of the greatest *hersir* in all Greenland. All his life, after
a turbulent youth, the great Greenlander had been energetic, wise,
openhanded. The lady Thorhild, whose piety grew apace month
by month, still worried about his stubborn clinging to the old
gods. But Leif had talked again with Bishop Sigurd; and he no
longer had any anxiety over this. There was time yet for Eric to
change. If he did not, Bishop Sigurd said, his fidelity to the old
ways would not be remembered against him in the free courts of
heaven.

The rest of the Ericsfjord news was of somewhat better cheer.
Gudrid, Thorfinn Karlsefni's comely wife, was with child at last.
Her time would come upon her in the autumn after Thorfinn's
vessels had already dropped anchor in Vinland. So, at first, both
Thorfinn, her husband, and Leif, her brother, when he heard the

news, argued with her that she should stay in Greenland where leeches and skilled midwives were close at hand, and not risk the long ocean crossing. But Mistress Gudrid had refused even to consider such a plan. And, in his heart of hearts, Leif Ericson said to us, he had been glad. It was well, he thought, that a birth should help fulfill this new land of ours. He hoped that it would be but the first of many. His own son by the lady Thorgunna throve amain, though the Greenland nurse, who had the child in charge, thought it was still a year or so too early to bring out the babe without a mother to care for it.

The political news, Leif said, was more disturbing. While he spoke of it, Leif kept a solicitous eye on Brian to see how the lad was taking it. For it concerned his Irish kinsmen nearly. Except for the men of Leinster, who still held out against what they considered a Munster usurper, all the native Irish now recognized Brian of Munster as *Ard Rí*—the first time in many reigns there had been an undisputed High King ruling over the island. From the Norse point of view, this meant, of course, that the disorder and disunion on which the alien power in Ireland depended for its survival was being healed by Brian; and that the Viking kingdoms in the north and east of Ireland would soon be seriously threatened. So Sigtrygg of Dublin, the jarl against whom King Brian had first breached the truce, was organizing a great hosting against him. It was even possible, men said, that the great Danish King, Sweyn Forkbeard, would throw in his lot with Sigtrygg.

The fourth day after the *Mariasuden* had dropped anchor in our lake, Thorfinn Karlsefni sighted *Furthustrandir*. It was just after dawn when the three ships he commanded first saw Wonderstrands' white beaches. By midafternoon they had rounded the promontory where Brian, who had now taken to watching there by day instead of from his oak crotch, glimpsed them from afar —and I beside him, as it chanced, for I had borne refreshment to him from the camp, not wishing him to grow peaked because he took so little notice of food and drink nowadays.

Thorfinn Karlsefni's ship, like Leif's, had a maiden for figurehead. Grainne stood in the prow, her fair hair streaming out behind her as Thorfinn's oarsmen rowed hard against the stiff head wind that blew cool from shore. Only Grainne's kirtle was not blue, as was the Virgin Mother's. She wore a saffron-yellow gown which was the royal Irish color as well as the color of the torch borne by the pagan god of wedlock whom the scholars in her father's court called Hymen. It lay sweetly close upon her in the wind stream, molding her firm breasts and lithe limbs as if some great artist had cast a goddess all in breathing gold. She saw Brian waving to her even before the sharp eyes of Illugi Tomcat, who stood beside Thorfinn's *stafnbui* on the forecastle deck, espied him.

Illugi sent out the afterboat so that Brian and I might come aboard. As the small craft pulled away from the long ship and toward the shore, the sun tipped those flashing oar blades with liquid silver. Half in a dream, Brian climbed over the gunwale. So Grainne had come to him at last—more beautiful even than he or I remembered. I think he could not believe it now that it had finally happened. Yet it was so. With his own eyes he had seen his beloved; and she was goodly to look upon.

Thorfinn Karlsefni and Mistress Gudrid—who, I could see, was far gone with child—greeted us most kindly. Almost as if she were a stranger, Grainne gave a shy hand to the lad. Thorfinn was bubbling over with the surpassing merits of a new compass —a magnet floating on a bowl of water—which he had bought from an Iceland trader who, in his turn, had had it from an Arab merchant he had met in Spain at the court of the great Sarkland jarl, Abd-ar-Rahman II, Emir of Cordova. He wanted to show Brian how to read it at once and was more than a little put out, at first, when the lad seemed absent of mind. Then Mistress Gudrid whispered something in his ear and Thorfinn, who had not quite forgotten the days of his own courtship, laughed a little before he took Brian by the arm and spoke to him aside.

"Here, lad," he said with rough good nature. "Time for such things as compasses later on. Talk to your lass by the stern. No one can overhear you there. I will speak of the compass to Thrand Thorbergson here who has a taste for such things."

Then, when the long ship had settled down again and everybody else had gone about their business, except for Thorfinn Karlsefni who could not leave off speaking of that blessed compass of his, Brian took Grainne in his arms and kissed her on an eager mouth until he bade fair to stop her frightened breath. Under the spangling early light the dragon wake stretched out behind us like some fire drake's glittering tail. The sun burned hot on the blue water. Sea mews, circling, cried overhead. It had been a long time for the two of them. But the wait was over now.

"Oh, Grainne mine!" he said almost brokenly.

"Dear Brian!" said the girl, her deep blue eyes shining in the morning light.

Grainne had not greeted me yet. But I could not find it in my heart to be wroth with her. It is not often in life that even lovers have their hearts' desire in their hands as these twain now had.

Thorfinn Karlsefni's heavily laden vessels were not able to drop anchor before sundown because of the tide. Not counting Illugi Tomcat, who belonged by rights to the first Vinland settlement, Thorfinn had brought with him seventy-four more settlers, including himself. With Leif's twenty-nine our combined number, men and women together, came to one hundred and three souls, a good round figure for a colony just beginning. In addition to the human freight, Thorfinn bore with him rich store of goods of every sort—Inge priest, who looked rounder and pinker and sugar-piggier than ever, even had books, ink, and parchment in his crowded sea chest. This pleased me almost more than any thing else. For my supply of ink and parchment was already beginning to run low.

Sira Inge would not so much as sit down to dinner that evening—and he was a man who fancied his dinner, too—before he had blessed each boundary and building and pointed out to Thorleik Eldgrimson exactly where he would like his new stave-church to be reared. Then, in the handsome vestments which Bishop Sigurd had sent him from his episcopal see as a parting gift when he left Greenland, and which he now donned for the first time, Inge priest celebrated Benediction atop the Thing mound before Leif's cabin. The whole colony attended the service even down to Skraeling Meyla—except, of course, for Thorhall Gamlason who watched the foreign ceremony from afar, leaning on his great halberd-shaped spear and grinning sourly the while.

So, in still another measure, was this fair new land of ours fulfilled. This time with incense, soft candlelight, sacring water, and the clear chiming music of a little bell that sounded over our lake each time Inge priest lifted up the body of Christ in the golden monstrance that was also the gift of Bishop Sigurd.

Afterwards Leif's men feasted the newcomers—some of whom were their own wives and so triply welcome—on long wooden

benches knocked together for the occasion by Thorleik Eldgrimson's busy hammers, since no single one of our cabins, not even
Leif's great one, would hold near that number at once.

As the slow summer days drew on toward autumn, throughout
what was left of July and through all of August and September
waxed and waned and waxed and waned again white moons of
magic for those lovers. Brian played the licensed fool that all
true lovers seem to all others but themselves. A lover must adore
his beloved. It is the first law of his existence. I do not think
Brian ever forgot the first morning when he saw Grainne wash
her heavy gold hair. He had splashed water over his own face at
the water butt outside our cabin, then gone with me, at Leif
Ericson's request, to the women's quarters to fetch Meyla to Leif
who wished to question the savage maid about certain things now
that she had learned a little of our Norse tongue. Sira Inge had
consecrated me deacon now. So it seemed to me no longer fitting
that I deal with women unless there was someone else along with
me at the time. Meyla, as it happened, was in the inner room when
we knocked.

"Come in," she said in her curious and appealing accent.

So Brian entered the room with me, his crisp-curled hair still
wet from the butt where he had dipped his head. Grainne was in
the inner room with Meyla. She had just finished washing out
her hair and now was combing it with great flashing strokes that
struck gold sparks from the heavy mass under the morning sun.
As if forgetting for what the two of us had come, Brian bowed
to Grainne, and asked her as if he were under a spell:

"Will you lend me your comb, Mistress?"

With a little smile, as if she liked and understood the courtly
game, Grainne handed him the comb. Looking at her the while,
he ran it through his wet curling hair so that the water drops
spattered them both a little, then handed it back.

"Thorvald has taught me a little of the tricks of *rímur*," he
said. "And I know somewhat already of our Irish bardry. Listen,
lady, while I praise your hair."

Never once stopping her plaiting of the golden tresses, Grainne
listened while her beloved declaimed softly to her in the dust-
grained summer sunlight:

> *"On Grainne's head the hair*
> *My Irish Hlín is combing*
> *Is worth all Olaf's gold,*
> *Is worth all Olaf's shielings.*
> *Not for all Norway's wealth,*
> *Not for rich England's treasure,*
> *Would I yield up a tress*
> *Of that which is my pleasure.*
> *Love forged the silver arrow*
> *To pierce each shining braid—*
> *And pierce me to the marrow*
> *With looking on the maid!"*

Grainne's hand faltered a little in its deft arranging of her braids. Then she picked up the silver arrow from her table and drove it swiftly through the topmost tress as if in answer to the challenge in the song. Meyla clapped her honey-colored hands.

"Pret-ty, Brian," she said, bowing to him—and I think the Skraeling maid understood a good deal more of this song than she did some of Thorvald Ericson's. "Pret-ty, pret-ty."

I had noted before that, when the Irish made their songs, they liked to rhyme the line-endings. When I pointed this out to Thorvald Ericson, he said it was true of the Welsh as well; but that their rhymes, being inner, were even subtler in effect.

Meyla and Thord Thordarson were with Brian and Grainne a good deal these days. Between Grainne and Thord the savage girl was learning Norse rapidly—even with Brian Grainne spoke Norse only nowadays. Grainne herself picked up not a little of the difficult new world tongue; enough, at any rate, so that she was able to tell Brian the native names of those flowers and animals which were new to him. Meyla was also of great assistance in bringing Grainne to those hidden parts of the woodland where grew the loveliest wild flowers.

At Leif Ericson's order the guard on the savage girl had now been relaxed. Meyla came and went as she chose now without any constraint whatsoever; and showed no sign of discontent. For, as Leif truly said to Thorvald Ericson and myself, we could not keep watch over the girl forever. If she really wanted to escape, sooner or later she would find a way. But, if she were treated as a friend and equal, it was quite possible she would wish to stay of her own

free will, especially since Thord Thordarson also dwelt here; and
Love, if it laughs at locksmiths, knows how to forge its own
massy locks. Leif said he looked to see a wedding between the
Skraeling girl and Thord at the time of the Winter Nights, as
October twenty-third and twenty-fourth are called back in our old
Norwegian homeland. This was a favorite time for lovers to
make their first faring together. Leif thought that, so far as he
was concerned, it would be a good marriage. He did not think
Inge priest would object, either, since the savage girl seemed
drawn to the way of Christ. But he was afraid that Thorhall
Gamlason would not think it quite so fitting; and he looked for
some trouble from that quarter. Even as things now stood, it
seemed to me Thorhall took Brian's growing friendship with
Thord Thordarson very ill. But so far the old berserker said
nothing, only keeping apart more and more, biding his time in
sullen silence.

Now Grainne had it in her mind to plant a Mary Garden on
the small island in our Vinland lake. She had brought many seeds
and rose slips with her from Greenland which would not bloom
until the following spring at the very earliest; and then only if
she had great good luck over the winter. Meanwhile she did what
she could with the new world blossoms, some of which were
exceeding fair.

These same Mary Gardens had become very well known now
in Italy and Frankland, Sira Inge told me, though, he thought that
this Vinland one of Grainne's might very well be the first in the
entire North. They had them commonly in England as well as
Ireland. The one Grainne knew best grew in an Irish monastery
near her chieftain-father's *dun*. It was a kind of Eden garden
within the greater kitchen garden where the monks grew the many
herbs they brewed in their herbals. For this monastery was known
far and wide for its lore in leechcraft. Men came there from all
over Ireland and the outer islands to be healed of their stubborn
wounds and of hurts suffered in battle that would not otherwise
mend. Grainne never named this monastery to me; and I did not
ask her. But it comes into my mind, now that it is too late to
ask, that it may have been the monastery of Rath Aed founded
by Hugh the son of Brec.

A garden, the old Sacristan had taught Grainne, honored God
even more than it honored His Mother. If it were well designed
and neatly tended, always kept well weeded and featly mended

whenever the wind beat down the blossoms' swaying heads, a garden reflected God's attributes. Its unity mirrored the Creator's Oneness. Its sweet proportions stood for the justice, harmony, and peace of the Trinity. Its beauty was God's own greater beauty shining through each leaf and flower. He said that she must always remember a garden was a church where God dwelt all the year, even in winter when the stems were sere and brittle. And a Mary Garden was this church's Lady Chapel, the green, leafy bower given over to the honor of God's dearest creature, His Mother, Mary Virgin.

It was really surprising how many of the flowers Grainne had known in Greenland, Ireland, and the outer islands had their counterparts here in this new land. There were enchanting newcomers, too, for which she had no names—she supposed, though, she said to me, that Mary would have names for them up where she sat forever in the courts of heaven. So it did not matter, provided only the flowers were beautiful; and Meyla could be trusted to see to that. Meyla knew the whereabouts of every flower growing in the forest. The Skraeling girl's slim brown fingers could prise out their roots so gently—always taking care to leave a sufficiency of earth about them—that the fragile things suffered not at all in their quick flight from the mossy nooks, where they had first come into life, and the Mary Garden to which they were now transplanted. Sira Inge, who approved of what Grainne was doing, had carved a small Virgin in wood and painted it expressly for the little island garden. Thord Thordarson, who knew somewhat of masonry, then mixed the lime and built the wall against which the Holy Maid and her Babe were set by Grainne's loving hands.

What time he could steal from his duties about the Vinland colony, Brian had taken to spending with Grainne on the island. I went, too, whenever I was invited, for I did not think this kind of recreation—it was Mary's Garden, after all—would in any wise breach my sworn service to Mary's only Son. Sometimes Meyla and Thord Thordarson came with the three of us; and we would make a small feast of it, for the afternoon and evening, spreading our supper cloth on the clean, sweet-smelling grass. But mostly they walked in the woods alone, as became their lovers' time of life; or else paddled over the lake waters.

It was Meyla who had showed Brian how to build one of the light skin boats her people traveled in—the three boats Thorhall

Gamlason had found out on the promontory had, by Thorvald Ericson's command during the afternoon of the Thing hearing, been placed inside the cairns with the dead bodies of their slain masters. In this leaf-light craft of moosehide the two of them, Brian and Grainne, paddled over every inch and cranny of the lake to find still newer and more beautiful plants and flowers for the garden. Brian liked to help Grainne arrange the new flowers Meyla had pointed out to her. Scarlet columbine and lavender-blue wild geranium of a sort that did not grow at home either in Ireland or Greenland. Lily pads with golden flower cups for which he built a tiny pool just in front of the wooden Mother and Child. Orchises. Heather with shiny white bells chiming in the eye of the beholder. A clump of crimson-centered silver stars for which Grainne had no name as yet, since Meyla could not remember, for once, what her people called it. Inge priest who came to bless the bower when it was done—if it could ever be called really done—said that Eden Garden, which was in the beginning, could have been no more beautiful than this lovely Mary Garden of Grainne's tender fashioning.

It seemed to me that Grainne's garden—for it was hers, too, as well as Mother Mary's—was like Eden Garden in still another way. The animals came to her, unquestioning, as to Mother Eve. Fawns. Raccoons with black masks for muzzles. Once a great stag stalked stately off even as Brian and I approached. Grainne's witchery with the smaller woodland dwellers beggared belief. Birds perched on her slender fingers when she let them. Rabbits came and ate from her hand. She could sit still, and a striped chipmunk would leap upon her shoulder and suffer itself to be lightly stroked. When she first saw this sight, Meyla said that Grainne must be a near kinswoman of one of the gods of her people, Pau-Puk-Keewis who, in ancient days, had gently petted the chattering creature and left the print of his god's fingers on its glossy fur—which was why this little new world squirrel always wore a black gleaming stripe on its sleek back. I could not help thinking that in one way, anyway, if in no other, Grainne and Meyla were very like that Thorhall Gamlason whom the two of them hated so bitterly. For all three of them believed that every living thing deserved respect for its special fashion of life, whatever it might be; and had its own place, however small, in the great plan of things. The trouble was that all too often Thorhall Gamlason did not extend this belief of his from the four-footed things whom he cherished with all his might and main to the two-footed beings with whom Fate, as he would say—I should rather say Providence—had appointed that he live out his dark life.

For Thorhall Gamlason mooted mischief, as he sat brooding in his cabin and in the *Mariasuden's* shed, ever honing his halberd's edge, waxing bowstrings that needed no more wax, they were so strong and pliant already.

One late August afternoon Brian and Grainne brought me with them to their island to see a new flower for which even Meyla had no name. Already there was a breath of fall in the air. I mind me how Grainne had a fright that day from the one animal with whom she did not live in amity. She had just stooped to arrange some bog rosemary a little more to her taste when a black snake, which had been lying coiled in the heart of these flowers, hissed its ugly hiss and slithered across her wrist. Grainne screamed a piercing scream. It was all Brian could do to comfort her. A cloud seemed to have come across the sun. It was colder there in the garden on a sudden. It seemed to me our afternoon was spoiled.

Perhaps, like the Serpent of the First Garden on whom Inge priest had preached a sermon the Sunday before, that snake had been some manner of omen. For there is a concord in nature, all things hanging—as once, in the beginning, they danced—together. For when, at sunset, the three of us paddled back to the encampment, it was to find that our colony's peace had been shattered from within. In the middle of that afternoon what Leif and Thorvald Ericson and I had long been fearing had come to pass. Thorhall Gamlason had appeared, dressed in the blue doublet that meant he wished to fight, and challenged Thord Thordarson to holmgang on the lake island where Grainne's garden grew in honor of the Mother of the Prince of Peace. According to his bitter lights Thorhall Gamlason was a fair man. He had waited thus long before giving out his challenge only because he did not wish to fight a man weakened by illness. It seemed to him now that Thord Thordarson had come round far enough from his sickness to be ready for this weapon play.

When Thord Thordarson, never hesitating a moment, accepted that challenge, Sira Inge Skakkeson had protested to Leaf that holmgang was against the law of Christ. Leif Ericson had said that he could do nothing about it. Holmgang was one of the ways of our fathers—whether good or bad was beside the point at the moment—and things could not be changed all at once. As matters stood, if two men appointed holm-tryst according to proper form, even as these two had done, he could not stop them. One thing Leif could insist on, however. According to the old law of holmgang the victor might demand from the vanquished whatever he pleased. If, Leif said, Thorhall Gamlason should come off the victor in the morrow's contest, he might not demand Meyla of Thord Thordarson because Meyla was not Thord's to give. The new world maiden was the guest and ward of our whole community and would be protected as such, so long as Leif was captain. Thorhall Gamlason looked black at this saying of Leif Ericson's. But he said nothing. Then it was appointed that he and Thord Thordarson should go to holmgang after sunrise on the island in the lake.

Steinn the *stafnbui* was to serve as second for Thorhall Gamlason; and Hunbogi Ale-Head as second for Thord. Neither of these men had any stake in the contest. They were chosen because it was the opinion of Leif's company that they would see to it there was fair play on both sides. That same evening Steinn and Hunbogi oversaw the setting up of the lists, measuring out the hide, five ells square, on which, according to the ancient custom of our northern duel, the contestants were to take their stand after the shield smiting was finished—if, of course, this holmgang went that far. Some of these duels were decided on the first or second blow. It was not at all uncommon for Thorhall Gamlason to slay his adversary at the first pass. Hunbogi and Steinn then went on to trace out the three lines, of a foot's breadth each, around the hide, set up the four hazel posts, and placed the six shields in readiness—each man was allotted three shields apiece with a shield-bearer to hold them for him. In this fight, Steinn would hold for Thorhall; and Hunbogi for Thord.

According to the rules of holmgang, if the fight did not go to a finish, the contestant worse wounded would be adjudged the loser and would be bound over to pay the victor three marks of silver in holm-ransom in addition to whatever other request the winner might wish to make. Whoever fell in death on the holm, all his inheritance, supposing there were any, went to him who had done the felling.

Thord Thordarson, who had gained strength steadily all summer, proved a good match for the old berserker when they met in combat on the lake holm next morning. Each one of them spoiled three shields for the other so that they had to fight it out upon the hide with the short swords that are specially reserved for holmgang. Then the berserker fit came upon Thorhall Gamlason for the first time in many years, though I am sure he had not tasted of the evil gods' flesh on that day. Perhaps it was that his bear *fylgja* had come to him again after months of absence. Though it was not his usual fashion, this time he bit the edge of his smiting blade and growled like a bear.

Thord Thordarson stayed cool the while. During one of Thorhall's bearlike lunges, Thord wounded him on the sword wrist and the right shoulder—this was the worst hurt either of them had yet received. In return Thorhall Gamlason sliced away Thord's right cheek and thrust him through the fleshy part of his upper arm. Up to this point it would have to be adjudged an even bout. But, on the fourth exchange after the spoiling of the shields, Thord Thordarson's old trouble came upon him. He began to cough and spit blood. As marshal of the lists, Leif Ericson acted then. He stepped in and stopped the duel, awarding Thorhall Gamlason the agreed-on three marks of silver.

His blue doublet all spotted and blotched with his own blood, Holmgang-Bersi hefted Thord's coins, grinning wolfishly the while. They were round white *dirkim* coins of purest silver according to the coinage that was then current throughout the North. Thord Thordarson had been a long time amassing that much treasure. But it might be said of Thorhall Gamlason that he did not have overmuch regard for money.

"If I may not have the girl," he said, jingling the coins up and down in a horny fist, "then you may keep them, Thord. It is enough for me to have won—and to have spoiled your maiden's face in so doing."

Then Thorhall Gamlason threw the money straight into Thord Thordarson's maimed face.

Thord Thordarson left the *dirkim* where they fell and walked off, his head hanging down. Leif, who knew somewhat of leech-craft, would have helped him with his bleeding cheek. But Thord shook off Leif's hand impatiently. He was ashamed at what had come to pass, even if men said he did not have to be. When the ale horns passed around that evening after supper, it was our

company's judgment that Thord Thordarson had acquitted himself very honorably in that day's holmgang. It was no disgrace
to have been bested by such a fighter as Thorhall Gamlason.
Moreover, there were even those who said—and I among them—
that, considering the odds and Thord's infirmity, he had come off
better than the winner, Holmgang-Bersi.

No one of us, or of Thorfinn's company, either, touched the
coins where they lay, though they were half a jarl's ransom in
worth. For all I know, they lie there in Vinland yet, covered with
earth and the rotting leaves of the years. It comes into my mind
that other men, one day far distant, may dig these up and wonder
how they came there. Thus it comes to pass, in our day, with the
old coins of Greece and Rome. I have myself found some of the
Roman kind in England. It would be fitting, too, that such a
thing should come to pass. For I think our Vinland faring belongs with the tales that have to do with the horse of Troy and
the wanderings of Aeneas.

But, if men praised Thord Thordarson for how he had fought,
they blamed Thorhall Gamlason more than a little for that he had
grudged Thord the new world girl. Hunbogi Ale-Head, who was
well content with his own plump wife now that Thorfinn Karlsefni had brought her out to him from Eric's Greenland steading,
was most outspoken of all.

"A man," he said, "has no call to go to another man's house
seeking better bread than is made of wheat."

Most of us nodded approval to this. But Thorvald Ericson only
laughed.

"There are two troubles with this saying of Hunbogi's," he
said, still laughing.

"Yes?" asked Sveinn Haldorson eagerly, for Sveinn dearly
loved a jape.

"They baked Meyla with rye and honey," said Thorvald Ericson. "Not with wheat—though I think not the less of her honey-
smooth flesh for that. Also, there is no bread of any sort—rye or
wheat—in Holmgang-Bersi's empty cupboard."

Thorvald Ericson began to pull then at his lower lip. He looked
at his brother, a mischievous glint in his eye.

"A thought comes into my mind now, brother Leif," he said.
"What if we were to mate Thorhall the Hunter with our sister
Freydis—after she is done with brother Thorvard, of course, as

she will one day be? They are well matched, those two. What do you say?"

Leif Ericson did not always engage in jesting such as this. But now he threw back his head and laughed aloud. It was a good thing to hear this son of Eric laugh. One liked to laugh with him always.

"I say it is a good idea, brother Thorvald," Leif said, still booming out laughter. "It comes into my mind, in that case, that we should one day have to lay the twain in howe at once. For neither one could get the better of the other."

It was well we laughed then, we men of the *Mariasuden* and of Thorfinn Karlsefni's three ships, however grim our laughter. We had not much reason to laugh on the morrow.

Next morning, very early, Steinn the *stafnbui* came into Leif's cabin, his face very grave. Meyla was missing from the camp—flown during the night—and Thord Thordarson with her. Leif Ericson supposed, he said, that Thord felt ashamed because of what Thorhall Gamlason had said and done after their bout together. He also supposed that Thord would feel he could not marry Meyla now after what had come to pass in that holmgang which, whatever Leif might say to the contrary, was really fought over her; and Thord had lost. Or, at least, Leif said to Thorvald Ericson and myself but not to the others of our company, Thord Thordarson would feel he could not marry Meyla before his present comrades. Before the men of her tribe, who had not seen him lose at holmgang, it might be different.

So, along with the rest of us—but in greater measure since the leader bears a greater burden of responsibility—Leif Ericson had two things more to worry about. He had to worry about Thord Thordarson's coughing his lungs out in the wilderness into which he had now vanished. Even worse, he had to worry about our Vinland camp, from which a comrade had now forever cut himself off, in the face of what might happen once the savage people learned, as they were sure to do, of its whereabouts and how it was situated and how many or how few it presently contained and what Thorhall Gamlason had done to eight sleeping Skraelings.

So still another new thing had come to pass in our sweet-smelling garden of Vinland. Within the space of a few short hours Treason—and Treason wearing the face of a well-loved companion—had, like a serpent, put out its forked tongue. This land was not Eden, we knew now, however beautiful its face. Where man was, it seemed, the same sad old story wrote itself again.

But the land was very lovely nonetheless. And it was hard to think of Thord Thordarson, whom we all knew and liked, as a serpent. I know that in her own heart Grainne blamed Thorhall Gamlason much more than she did Thord. The Irish maid still tended her Mary Garden as the autumn days drew on and we lit the fires earlier and earlier each afternoon. The fall leaves bronzed and fell from the Vinland trees in other coins of tribute than the silver *dirkim* coins which still lay where they fell. Yet it seemed to Grainne, grieving in her garden, that the blood of that holm-gang between Thord Thordarson and Thorhall had forever pro-faned the peace of Brian's and her island and the beauty of the Mary Garden Thord and Meyla had helped to build. The little animals appeared to think so, too. They came no more to Grainne's call.

It seemed to me that pride was the cause of Thord Thordar-son's fleeing: pride which is the primal sin. He could not endure to have lost that holmgang before the eyes of Meyla and his fellows. In an evil hour—for one should not sit in judgment on his fellows ever—I said as much to Grainne.

"Pride it is that has led to this betrayal," I said to her, the unction of self-righteousness like heavy whey upon my tongue.

Grainne flared out at that.

"Life is not so simple as all that, little deacon," she said spite-fully in answer—but there was woman's wisdom on her tongue all the same. "You will find this out, if you live long enough, Thrand Thorbergson. You will also find, I think, that life is often a choice between betrayals."

"That is right, Thrand," said Leif Ericson suddenly, though I did not think he had heard the two of us at our unseemly bickering. "I have found it so, at any rate."

Grainne was thinking of Thord and Meyla when she spoke. But I know Leif thought on himself and the lady Thorgunna. As for myself, I have proved my own point in bitter wise. For I had spoken out of wounded pride, not liking it that Grainne should care for Thord Thordarson so well. She had called me "little deacon" in her anger; and, in very truth, I had showed myself very little of a deacon on this sorry occasion.

The day after Thord Thordarson's and Meyla's disappearance
Leif Ericson ordered that a large boat be built—not a long ship,
a *karfi,* with six oars on a side; and that it be equipped, in addition, with four of the skin boats the savage people used. Brian,
under Meyla's direction, had already built one of these canoes, as
we later came to call them. It did not take long for me to copy
his—or to get the *karfi* finished, either. For I had built more than
one of these merchant vessels in Thorberg Skaffhogg's Ladehammer shipyards. A plan had come into Leif's mind in connection
with this *karfi.* But he kept his own council about it for the time
being.

In October Mistress Gudrid bore a fine son to Thorfinn Karlsefni. She had an easy birthing of it, God be praised. They called
the boy's name Snorri which was a great name in Iceland where
Thorfinn Karlsefni hailed from.

One more fulfillment, and one of the greatest any land can
know, had now come to the fair land of Vinland with the birth
of Snorri Thorfinnson. The good seed that had been sowed across
the sea in Iceland had come to harvest in the new world its sower,
Thorfinn, had chosen for his own.

CHAPTER TWELVE

VINLAND YULE

OF THE THREE YULETIDES WE SPENT IN VINLAND, I THINK OUR second was the one to be remembered most—by me at any rate. For it was then I saw the great foss which, if I had been like Thorhall Gamlason, I might have thought of, more than Thorhall's bear, as the god of this new land.

It may be, though, that Brian and Grainne did not remember this same Yule with that much joy. For they had thought, in the spring, to have fared together by Christmas. But now, with Thord Thordarson's treachery and the growing peril from the Skraelings, Leif Ericson had grimmer business on hand than the bride-ale of that twain.

This is what Leif Ericson had in mind to do with the *karfi*. Now that the savage folk were almost sure to find out, from the lips of Meyla, just where we were, and that, unprovoked, we Vinland strangers had breached the peace against the old Skraeling dwellers in the land, Leif feared much for the safety of our community. One hundred and three of us—no, with Thord Thordarson gone, one hundred and two, and twenty-four of these women at that—we could not hope to stand against a wilderness in arms. But perhaps these savage folk were not so many as we feared. Or, even if they were, perhaps there were portions of this trackless land where they had not yet settled. This latter possibility, Leif said to Thorvald, Thorfinn, Steinn, and Tyrker, with me to take it all down for the log, was something that had to be determined, one way or another, for the future weal of our Vinland settlement. It was, to be sure, as he was the first to admit, rather late in the season to be setting out on such an extensive exploring expedition as he now planned. But, with the *karfi's* shallow draught, he thought we would be safe enough, always providing we were careful to skirt the wooded shores and, if some given stream proved too shallow even for the *karfi,* to leave

the boat under a skeleton guard and take to the skin canoes. That
the colony, during our absence, might not be too short-handed,
Leif intended to take along no more than twelve men, including
himself. Twelve was the limit of the *karfi's* capacity, anyway.

Leif Ericson chose these eleven others for the expedition: Thorvald Ericson, Thorhall Gamlason, Sarkland Tyrker, Steinn the
stafnbui, Hunbogi Ale-Head, Svein Haldorson, Brian, Onund of
Trolleskog, Kari Englandsfari—Kari was now quite recovered
from his leg injury—Bolli Blacksark, and myself. We were all
seasoned travelers and accomplished foragers, too—even Brian,
Leif said to Thorvald and myself, must be considered seasoned
now after what had gone on last December in the great bear's
cave. Despite his wiriness, Tyrker, possibly, was a little old for
the hardships we might well encounter on the way. But that could
not be helped. Tyrker was a land pilot even as Steinn was a sea
one. We needed him to blaze a trail through the lakes and forests
over which we would be journeying even as we needed Thorhall
Gamlason to hunt for our expedition. Thorfinn Karlsefni wanted
to let us borrow his Arab compass for an added surety. Leif,
however, refused the loan, saying that he could not be responsible
for such a valuable instrument on a forced march—and he
thought there might well be more than one forced march to take
before our return. Who knew what might not happen in the interior of this unknown country?

During Leif's absence, and the absence of Thorvald, Tyrker,
and Steinn, Thorfinn Karlsefni was to command the Vinland community. Thorfinn had good men in his group. They were not all
Norse, as it happened. He had, in addition, a smattering of Goths
who are, of course, near cousins of us Northmen. If there were
any manner of attack, it was clear that the Goths would give a
good account of themselves. So Leif was not overmuch concerned
with the colony's safety unless the savage people should make an
onslaught in overwhelming force. But this was a risk which had to
be taken; and, in such a case, there was not much that could be
done anyway. An attack in real force, on the Skraelings' part,
could wipe out one hundred and two of us almost as quickly as it
could ninety. The palisades were strong, however; and, lately, we
had added a shallow ditch to these. In any case, Leif's plan to
reconnoiter the coast line and interior had become absolutely necessary, if we were to think of remaining in Vinland at all.

Our party carried a store of hard biscuit baked under Mistress

Gudrid's supervision, and a certain amount of cured venison as
well, both of these commodities carefully placed in the *karfi's* food
chest. Whatever Thorhall Gamlason's shortcomings in other respects, with him along to hunt, Leif was not really afraid for our
food supply. Tyrker urged him to take some of the newly vinted
wines in skins, saying that, if the weather should turn bitter cold
—and one had to be prepared for this even thus early in the winter season—then we might be very glad of that same red liquid
fire. After thinking this suggestion over for a little, Leif Ericson
said yes. He insisted, however, that Steinn the *stafnbui* be en-
trusted with the care of these wineskins. Smiling ruefully, Tyrker
consented to this unwelcome arrangement. I think that, without
asking his fosterling for the reason, Tyrker knew the why and
wherefore of that prudent rule.

It was a warm foggy morning in mid-October, just one week
after Mistress Gudrid had borne Snorri to her husband, Thorfinn,
when our *karfi* weighed anchor. Grainne, mantled against the dripping mist in a blue hood with a crimson lining, kissed Brian
good-by at the mooring ring. Her face was quiet, but I knew the
girl's heart must have been heavy. This might have been the very
morning of their faring together, she and Brian. Instead he journeyed without her into the unknown wilderness. As it happened,
Leif had some last-minute instructions for Thorleik Eldgrimson
whom he had left in charge of his part of the encampment—
always under Thorfinn Karlsefni, of course, whom Thorleik had
orders to defer to in any matter requiring a general decision.
While the two of them talked together, Brian had one last chance
to kiss Grainne farewell.

Under the woolly mist the lake and river were quiet as a mirror;
the ocean outside, when we rowed into it, almost as still. Not a
breath of air stirred. The *karfi's* wake was like a straight line
traced by a charcoal stick on some flawless glass. It did not smooth
out as far as the eye could see. But one could not see very far,
either, the mist lay so thick upon the motionless water.

I knew by now the sea that rims round Vinland; and somewhat
of her lakes and rivers. Now I was to know her forests: the strong
untamable trees that as yet endured sun and rain and snow and
wind and lightning stroke only, not the biting ax of man. It came
into my mind, of a sudden, that perhaps these giant trees would
not be our friends in every respect.

Once he has tasted their northern wine, I think a man can have a thirst for trees as he has a thirst for other things. Such a thirst comes over me now for the trees of Vinland as I remember them here in this Ireland that, though it is a sweet and bonny country, has so many fewer trees than that far land.

Westward the land was heavily timbered, with the thick forest growth coming down close to the shore. There were very many islands. But Leif's eye made out too many traces of human habitation to encourage further exploration, on our part, along that shore. We struck inland, then, four days after weighing anchor, and sailed up the mouth of a mightier river than any of us had yet seen or heard of. Tyrker, who had been in the land of the tribes that lies south and then east of Norway, said that not even the Rhine, where the dwarfs hoard the Niflung gold, was so lordly as this great stream. Dense forests burned their witchwood's many colors in the new world autumn. Along the river's edge they blazed; and, right beneath them in the river glass, burned other forests as beautiful as they. Some of these trees did not burn with the rest of their tall brothers and sisters. These were the pungent firs and fragrant spruces which grew higher even than the firs and spruces I had seen in the Finnish Mark. There were many animals, too, along this river. But, once again, Leif Ericson spied out the marks of humans. In fact, we twice passed savage villages in the night. Dogs barked at our passing. But no one else seemed to waken. On these occasions Leif did not let us ply the oars for fear someone might hear the plash. Luckily we were going downstream both these times, so that the *karfi* was able to drift with the sluggish current until we had put a full mile between ourselves and those sleeping villages.

After that we entered an enormous fjord where two dark rocks beetled over the water's edge, and the river opened out so wide that one might have thought the ocean was beginning again. The water was fresh, though, with no trace of salt in it. A little farther on, it closed in once more and again became an unmistakable river. An island lay in this same fjord with so strong a current running round it that the *karfi* was hard put to moor at a skerry just off shore.

Leif and Thorhall Gamlason paddled ashore there in a skin boat. There were so many eider ducks nesting on this island that a man could hardly set his foot down without cracking a bird's egg. For this reason Thorhall wished to call it Bird's Island. Leif

said it should be Strong Stream Island, instead, for the reason
that the ducks might one day go elsewhere, but the rushing current
would stay the same till the day of Ragnarok. So I marked it
down as *Straumey* in my lengthening chart. The fjord I wrote as
Straumfjord, or Strong Stream Firth, for the same reason.

The tide in the river was far stronger than any river tide Leif
Ericson had before encountered. The streams running into it were
full of fish. Our fishermen, Alf and Ornolf, were not along with
their lines. But Thorhall Gamlason, who rarely went fishing by
choice, still knew a trick or two where fish were concerned. He
had Kari Englandsfari and Bolli Blacksark dig pits, at high tide
mark, in the sand bars that stood in the mouths of most of these
streams. Then, when the tide flowed out again, we found flatfish
in abundance flopping about in the pits. When broiled over an
open fire in a rock hollow and then salted, these same flatfish tasted
delicious, though I am afraid Alf and Ornolf might have turned
up their own flat noses at this sort of fare.

Leif Ericson was more than a little puzzled just what to call
this land surrounding the great river. After thinking it over for
a long time, he finally hit on *Hóp,* or Landlocked Water. This
name, though, he was never afterwards satisfied with. Nor have
I ever thought it one of his better names.

It was up one of these *Hóp* streams that Thorhall Gamlason
came upon the dead savage. It was quite evident the Skraeling had
not been dead very long. For his flesh was still warm to the touch.
So Leif Ericson made us tread warily in the neighborhood of the
body, our bowstrings ready and our arrow nocks fitted to the
strings. There was a painted arrow through the savage's heart.
His whole scalp had been cut away, after the filthy custom of the
Skraelings, so that the veins in the dead man's head lay bare like
so many worms. A short-hafted ax lay useless by his side. Hunbogi Ale-Head tried its temper on a tree where the stubby hatchet
cut well enough. When, however, he next tested it against a rock,
the axhead snapped, which went far to prove Thorhall Gamlason's
statement, made on the morning of the Thing, that we Norsemen
had the better weapons by far. Hunbogi then tossed that ax disdainfully into the underbrush. It seemed to him, he said, that he
had little to learn from the new world armorers. Thorhall Gamlason had an equally poor impression of the crooked bow slung on
the Skraeling's back. On his side, Leif Ericson thought long and

hard on the dead man. It appeared quite evident, he said to us after
a space, that these savage folk fought against one another just as
often, if not more often, than feuding enemies did in our own
Northland.

Up to this point the weather had held mild and clear. Now, as
November began swiftly to wane, the forests looked winter-dark
by early afternoon, and there were light snows during the nights
which usually melted by noon, though it seemed to me, nonetheless, that day by day the snow lingered a little longer on the rocks
and in the hollows before it disappeared under the sun's weak rays.

One evening we moored off a bleak headland whence blew an
evil stench for a distance of a mile or so on either side. It had
begun to snow around dusk that day, and Leif Ericson would have
liked to go ashore where we might have built a fire instead of shivering on board in our chill skin bags. But, because of the bad smell
and of certain trampling heavy noises we could hear on the headland, he thought it more prudent to stay on the *karfi*. Next morning a cold dawn light revealed the source of both the stench and
the trampling noises. The headland was black with herd upon herd
of caribou which had made one huge dung heap of it.

Not liking the look of things, Thorhall the Hunter shook his
shaggy wolf's head a little at the sight of all those caribou. He
said he had seen herds of reindeer much like these huddling together in these numbers once before when he had hunted in the
Rús long years agone. It meant a long hard winter with game
scarce. We would be sucking beechwood by spring, he said grimly
to us, and glad we had such poor fare to stay our hunger. So it
was his opinion that, perhaps, we had better begin thinking of
getting back to our Vinland encampment before a hard freeze
made it impossible to use the *karfi* any more. As for the caribou,
Thorhall did not even waste an arrow on them. He did not care
for reindeer meat himself, though, when pressed he could bring
himself to eat it. More importantly, it would be hard—even dangerous, possibly—to bring the game off the headland, such was
the press of the animals all around. If he were only a Lapp, he said
with a laugh, it might be different. One could sell reindeer skins
to Lapp wizards for a pretty price. They put enchantments on
them; and then they kept off steel better than chain mail itself.
No sword would bite on the man who wore a reindeer skin over
which the proper spells had been said by a Lapp wizard.

When Thorhall Gamlason said to Leif that he thought it might be better if we made up our minds to turn back now, Leif said he thought so, too, on the whole. But our *karfi* had now entered a lake so huge it was like some great inland sea. It was easy to get out of sight of land upon its spacious reaches. Now that he had come so far, Leif the Lucky wanted to try his luck still further and to find out where this same lake led to. So he gave orders that we should push on a little longer.

It was the afternoon after we left the caribou headland that the Skraeling brave, into whose country our *karfi* had now advanced, picked up our trail. This was something Grainne learned long after from Meyla when she spoke to the savage girl once more. But I set it down here for the sake of order and clearness. He was hunting along the shore by himself, many miles from his tribe, when the strange boat—never had the Skraeling seen one so wondrous large—came nosing in to land in some dried reeds that rustled as the first early evening snowflakes fell lazily through them. He watched while the large-framed bearded men with the fair hair came ashore.

While we sat about our fire, that Skraeling crept closer, wriggling on his belly in the snow, and listened to our outlandish talk. He could, of course, understand nothing of what we were saying even though, among his tribesmen, he had some reputation for knowing tongues. In addition to his own language, for example, he could also speak some Algonquin, which is distantly related to the tongue he had been born to. But these newcomers interested him greatly all the same. He could not help wondering, Meyla said, how one or two of those fair scalps of ours would look alongside the blue-black ones already hanging in his lodge. If possible, he meant to trail us when we left, even though the snow would make the task difficult. He thought his tribe, the people of the Bears, would be very interested in strange folk such as we were.

So, every day and night from now on, an unseen shadow drifted in the wake of us twelve men as we penetrated farther and farther into Skraeling country. We did not lay eyes on it until Yule Eve. But I think we felt it. I know I did, for one—and Thorhall Gamlason. Sometimes the short hairs would prickle on my neck. I would wheel round at once. But there would be no one to see or hear. For these Skraelings can drift along a trail as still as wood-

smoke in gray dusk when mist and evening merge with it so that
no one can tell for sure where smoke begins and twilight leaves off.

A kind of madness had taken possession of this Leif of ours,
the son of Eric of Ericsfjord. It was Yule Eve again, our second
in this new land, and, driven by his desire to know what lay just
beyond, Leif had pushed down the chain of lakes until now he
could push no more, unless he wanted to abandon the *karfi* altogether and go on walking overland in the bitter new world winter.
For a week or so longer, perhaps, this great new river we had just
now come to with the mighty rock bastions towering on either side
—it was the second of the greater rivers we saw in this new land—
would continue to take our skin boats. Then it, too, I was sure,
would freeze over solid; and the thick ice would stay locking the
waters till spring.

But, strangely enough, no one of us said nay to Leif in his im-
prudence. Not Brian, for all that he had Grainne waiting for him
in our far-off Vinland camp. Not Thorvald Ericson, not Thorhall
Gamlason, not Sarkland Tyrker, not Hunbogi Ale-Head. Not
Svein Haldorson, not Onund of Trolleskog, not Steinn the *stafnbui,* not Kari Englandsfari, not Bolli Blacksark—and this Bolli
loved his comfort more than most men. Least of all Thrand Thorbergson of Ladehammer, for a fury to know more of what lay
before us had seized upon and shook me as I had once seen Bran,
our wolfhound, shake a rat. And we were rewarded in the end, I
think—Great God of Hosts, Thou Who poised the waters in the
beginning, were we not rewarded? Once in my life have I gazed
upon the All Father's unleashed powers unveiled in their naked
strength even as Moses saw them in the thunder of Sinai mount.

Thorvald and Thorhall, who did not always see eye to eye on
every matter, could have walked to the end of the world to see such
another sight as this one we now gazed on which must surely have
been far and away the greatest foss in all the world. This mightiest of fosses fell, with a thundering roar that shook the rocks
around it, sheer over a precipice and into the deep gorge between
whose walls the lordly river ran. Leif Ericson and we, his men,
could hear that rumbling as far as a mile downstream. Knowing
that some large waterfall must lie ahead, we had moored our *karfi*
on the north bank of the river. But we had not bargained, in our
wildest dreams, for a fall so gigantic as this one. What a foss!
Even to see it was a foretaste of Valhalla, Thorhall Gamlason

said, gazing up into that white thunder. I would not have said Valhalla. But I knew what Thorhall meant all the same. When he first laid eyes on it, Leif knew that it was journey's end for us at last. We might carry our skin boats round the cataract, but never the *karfi*. Not even the mountain trolls who lived above the Sognefjord in our old homeland could make a portage such as this one would have to be.

There had been no snow for some four days now. But the polar air had a keener bite in it. Like a white-shagged aurochs the great foss made its humped bison leap into cold space. The spray froze on our skin coats even as we watched those tons and tons of water fall in a long green wall of glass that shattered into white shards of broken crystal at the foot of the waterfall. It was as if this giant foss were an ice-smith on an enormous scale. Every twig and tree trunk, every rock and jutting piece of earth was armored in a bright ice-mail against which the winter sun splintered its endless spears of glancing light. It was almost as if frost giants had sculpted great chessmen out of an ivory more precious than walrus ivory. Icicles three times longer than narwhal tusks—four and five and ten times, even—fanged the rock platforms near the brink. Since childhood had I heard around the winter fires of Jotunheim and its ice palaces. Here they were before my eyes.

Because it was the day before the feast of Yule again, the holy night on which the white Christ had first come to our world as a Babe, Leif Ericson gave order that we broach the last of the wineskins which Steinn the *stafnbui* had managed to husband, at great odds, in the *karfi's* food chest. There was no more biscuit at all and but little dried venison left in the locker. But Thorhall Gamlason had had good luck that same morning with his bow and arrow, bringing down a buck as well as three brace of ptarmigan. If Leif would only permit a fire after dark, we would be able to feast well into the night with all this fresh game and with what remained of the wine. Leif had been very cautious about such beacon blazes ever since we left our Vinland lake—unless, of course, we stayed aboard the *karfi* where a savage attack would have to come by water, and where, moreover, the *karfi's* twelve oars, six on a side, could easily outrun any skin boat the savage folk might launch against it.

Thorhall Gamlason looked questioningly at our leader.

"It is Yule Eve, Leif," he said. "Shall we chance a fire?"

For even Thorhall celebrated Yule, though his celebration had naught to do with the Incarnate God who came a Babe to Bethlehem that is in Judaea.

Leif Ericson squinted at the low gray sky where the snow fleeces hung heavy on those dirty bellwethers that were the winter clouds.

"Not yet," he said. "But very soon. It is already dark enough, though the hour is still early, so that we could be seen for miles. A little later, though, I think it will come on to snow. If the snow is only heavy enough, we may enkindle a fire without much risk."

Thorhall Gamlason laughed his short barking laugh at that. But he spoke low so that only Brian and I could hear him.

"If snow will keep the savage folk in this night," he muttered, "then we shall have snow—much snow. I can take care of that much, at least—I and the red-bearded one, my patron, he who makes the weather for good or ill."

So, while the rest of us looked on, half angry, half amused, but never doubting for a single instant the efficacy of Thorhall's actions, the old berserker walked widdershins for snow, crooning a song to Asa-Thor, his patron—to Thor, old god of weather. I think it was on the tip of Leif Ericson's tongue to say Thorhall nay. But, in the end, he held back; and I think he was right in so forbearing. It was, after all, a very little spell Thorhall was this time making. I did not always approve of Thorhall the Hunter's doings. But I did not think the white Christ, who made this snow, would mind thus much white magic which was, moreover, being worked in honor of His own Birthday. I said as much to Thorvald Ericson.

"You think it is Thor, Thrand, who sends this snow to us?" he asked, a strange look on his dark face. "I think it was going to snow anyway."

As Thorhall the Hunter walked backward for the third time, the first large flakes began to fall, twisting lazily out of the sky. Soon there was enough of the frail white stuff to creak underfoot. Looking up, one could no longer see the North Star. Looking off to the side, one could make out no more than a whitened ghost of a tall ice tube where, during the afternoon, frothing bubbles had been breaking through an air hole in the ice. Now these bubbles had frozen round their rims like so many silver balls and had built up into a thin ice cairn of better than ten feet in height. Even as we looked on, this silvered tube vanished behind a mov-

ing curtain of flakes. The air grew rawer. Hunbogi Ale-Head
and Bolli Blacksark, both of whom had been badly frostbitten
back in Norway, stamped their feet and buffeted themselves
about the shoulders with crossed mittened hands.

"I think it is all right now," said Leif Ericson, looking up into
the sheeted air, the snow standing white on his cheeks and eyelashes until he looked like some winter gnome. "We can build
the fire in safety now."

Afterwards, when the venison haunch was finally done to a
turn, and the trussed birds were brown and crackling on the
sharp-pointed spits of wood sticks that Kari Englandsfari and
Svein Haldorson slowly turned, Leif Ericson gave the word that
the drinking should begin, starting with the health to Christ
which, he said smiling, Thorhall Gamlason should lead.

It was an old joke of Leif's, but none the worse for being old.
Like wine and good acquaintance, good jokes age well. Thorhall
the Hunter grinned an appreciative grin.

"I am willing," he said, "always provided that I be accorded
the longest draught."

Steinn the *stafnbui* passed the hairy wine skin to Thorhall
Gamlason. Now it was an old rule, in this kind of drinking, that
Steinn should count to a certain number, long or short depending
on the amount of drink there was, while each man drank from the
skin in turn. This time he did not count while, so long as his
breath held out, Thorhall drained a draught as long and deep,
it seemed to me, as the one Asa-Thor quaffed in Jotunheim from
the giant's horn, not knowing it was really the bottomless sea he
drank. It was new wine Thorhall drank, vinted only that autumn
past from the blue grapes of Vinland that had the silver frost-
breath misting their purple-regal skin. It was good wine, though,
even if a trifle too new—as good as we got back in Norway,
and much better than any pressed in Iceland. Sarkland Tyrker
knew what he was about with grapes as well as with trail blazing.
I think our men began to like wine almost as well as ale; and it
had this advantage over ale that one could carry it more easily
on a journey.

"A-h-h!" said Thorhall Gamlason at last, setting down the
skin and wiping a gray-bearded mouth with the back of his hand.
"Not so good as Papa Stronsay ale, I still say. But good enough,
at that. So I drink your toast, Leif. *Skoal! Skoal* to the Baby
Christ!"

It seemed to me that Leif Ericson was very amused at the order Thorhall had seen fit to observe in this matter.

"So!" he said with a smile. "It is drink first, then the health afterwards—eh, Thorhall? Do you begin a new custom for us thus?"

Again Thorhall Gamlason showed his teeth in a grin that was far from unlikable. Yes, there was something to be said, after all, for that old Jomsburg wolf of ours.

"It was a bargain, remember, Leif," he said, still grinning. "I paid even as we agreed. But, as becomes a good merchant, I paid only after delivery of the goods agreed upon."

After that, beginning now with Leif Ericson and ending with Brian, who was the youngest of us, the rest of our band drank the Yule health to Christ. Whenever they traveled, Leif and Thorvald Ericson wore silver cups, chained to their girdles, which they had bought once from a Varangian who, in his turn, had looted them lawfully when, after the death of one of the Greek emperors in Micklegarth, the imperial treasury had been given over, as was the custom, to the Varangian Guard to plunder.

We feasted late then. Before the fire burned down all the way, the snow was inches deep and still falling. One could no longer see the star Archer overhead, he who was Orvandil, Bowman of the gods; nor the moon which had arisen an hour before midnight. Hunbogi Ale-Head grew mellow on Tyrker's red wine. With his skilled hands he swiftly molded a little snow troll, and set him up for all of us to admire.

"Look!" he said. "We have a Nisse for Yuletide!"

Thorhall Gamlason dipped a playful forefinger in the lees of Tyrker's wine and daubed a red nose on that white Yule goblin.

"It is plain to see," he said to all of us by way of explanation, "that our Nisse drinks too much."

An hour after midnight the snow fell off somewhat, though it did not leave off falling altogether. Going apart from the fire to relieve myself, I came suddenly face to face with the watching Skraeling just as the moon came from behind a cloud. It would be hard to say which of the two of us was the more surprised. The startled savage froze into immobility. I looked full into his eyes. They were oval-shaped and dark like the eyes of the Eastern folk who live farther away than Sarkland even. But they were northern eyes, too. As northern as my own; narrowed from much gazing on snow trails in winter, and on the arrowing wakes of skin boats during many summer paddles.

The new world man wore buckskins with fringes to them. These buckskins were so white it would be hard to see him against the snow. He had a hatchet at his belt; and a crooked bow slung across his back. For a long instant the two of us stared at one another, measuring one another more as fellow humans than as warriors, speaking with our eyes across a gulf of difference. Then the savage's right hand crept slowly to the stone ax at his girdle. But, remembering what night this was and Whom I served, I raised my own right hand, palm outward, in token of peaceful greeting. Uncertainly, the savage's hand let go of the ax haft. Then the moon went behind a cloud once more. The wind shifted. A sudden gust blew a glittering powder of snow between me and the Skraeling. Under cover of that little snow squall the red man slipped away.

I went quickly back to the smoldering fire round which most of our men now slept in their bags of fur-lined skin. Steinn the *stafnbui* was on guard. Making a sign to Steinn, I roused Leif then, and told him and Steinn what I had just seen. Leif nodded his head, alert, masterful. He was a leader among leaders, that son of Eric! Never have I seen one to match him!

"We must go back to the *karfi* at once," said Leif Ericson to us, speaking low. "Rouse the men, Steinn. If the river is still navigable, we will raise anchor so soon as it is dawn. If it is not, we must leave the *karfi* and begin walking. Wake them as naturally as possible, Steinn—as if you were not really waking anybody at all. We are being watched. So we must pretend to be what we are not for a little. Just before we leave, we will throw more logs on the fire and lie down again for a minute or so, so that the watchers will think we mean to spend the rest of the night here."

Leif Ericson turned to me then.

"As for you, Thrand Thorbergson," he said, and it was as if war *lurs* were sounding in my ears while he spoke. "I wish you and Tyrker to stay behind here. Do not let yourself be seen— Tyrker is good at disguise. It is something one learns, he says, in Sarkland. If the red man follows us, you will follow him. If he does not move at once, stay until he does. We will take the charts with us. With Tyrker along, you will not need them—my *fóstri* has eyes in the soles of his feet. We will leave you as much food as you can carry. Tyrker hunts well, too, at need; and an arrow is quiet so that the red man need not hear. I might say kill him, if we were closer to Vinland. As things stand, it is too dangerous to try. A day or so before we reach our Vinland settlement, see if you can rejoin us by a forced march round the Skraeling. It is a post of great peril I give you and Tyrker, Thrand Thorbergson. But it is a post of great honor, too. Godspeed!"

While Leif Ericson was still talking to me, Steinn roused the other men at once, quietly, efficiently, as if he were not doing anything of the sort. Then, after a deliberate space, the ten of them slipped away so carefully that the Skraeling, trained tracker that he was, was, for once, deceived. In the morning he would realize his mistake when there would be nothing before him in the chill light of dawn but a blackened spot where the fire had been.

So it happened in the morning even as I had hoped. Tyrker and I, burrowed into the snow behind a great boulder, looked on while the Skraeling examined what was left of our encampment. It was bitter cold now. An eager wind had begun to drive ice down the rapids. Then the shivering brave in the white buckskins, with the single blood-red feather in his scalp lock, noted the Yule dwarf Hunbogi Ale-Head had sculpted in the snow. Thinking it was the god of us Norsemen—and so it was, in a certain sense, even of me—he aimed an angry kick at it, then hopped in pain, nursing a moccasined right toe. I laughed to myself. We had done well to let Hunbogi carve out the little god. And he had served us well, too, us Norsemen who had left his service for the service of One far greater and better than he. It was so chill the little Nisse had frozen hard as ice this Christmas morning in the one thousandth and fifth year after the Incarnation according to the flesh, by the Holy Spirit, of Christ Jesus God, Second Person of the Most Holy Trinity, in the blessed womb of Mary ever Virgin.

The Skraeling did not begin his grim pursuit right off. Instead, so soon as the sun rose higher, he climbed to a table rock alongside the great foss and there kindled a fire. The snow had stopped altogether now. A black plume of smoke rose into the still blue air. Crouched in our snow burrows, the two of us looked on, munching a ptarmigan bone from our scant store of food.

"He calls his people," said Tyrker. "This is a dangerous game Leif sets us—eh, Thrand?"

"Yes," I said proudly. "But my heart rises to it. It is the kind of game a man should play now and then."

"My heart rises, too," said Tyrker with a little laugh. "Though it may be that I will come to this game once too often. Well, a man can die but once; and we all owe the Norns a death."

The Skraeling settled down to wait. In the end, he waited two full days. But his people did not come. Instead came a great still cold, so piercing bitter it stiffened the hairs in our nostrils. We shivered in our skin bags as did the Skraeling in his buckskins. For the winter smote the two of us alike, both hunter and hunted —though it would be hard to say which of us was hunter and which hunted.

The great white cold settled down over this land. The waters froze all round the snowy shores of the two great lakes this river joined together. The ice became so thick at the head of the great foss that only a bare trickle of water came over the lip of the fall. Then that, too, froze; and the giant foss was bridged with a bridge of shining ice so that, for a wonder, one could walk upon that white mass of frozen water. It was a pity, I thought, that Thorvald Ericson could not have stayed to see it. He would have thought of ice-trolls caught out after sunset and turned into ice-cliffs by the wand of the enchanter sun. These were bubble-blowing trolls, too. Where Leif and we others had seen the air hole, the frothing bubbles continued to float upward from the ice cairn. When the sun glanced off the many-colored globes, they gave back rainbow glints. It was as if each bubble carried a tiny Bifrost, which is the bridge of the Aesir, over which walked tiny gods into a Valhalla of crystal magic. Perhaps we came near to paying with our lives, Tyrker and I, for that same godlike sight. But it was worth it. Though my old blood runs thin these latter years, I should give much to see that river and that foss again.

We lay out that Christmas night under the stars of Yule. I do not know what Tyrker thought on. For myself, I thought on the Mass Sira Inge Skakkeson had that day celebrated for our Vinland company. Orvandil the Archer and the Great Bear hung like bright lamps overhead. But they did not burn so bright as had another smaller star one thousand years ago. For the twelve nights of Christmas we watched those stars, Tyrker and I, from the warm depths of our skin bags. We did not have the Mass of Christ this holy season; and that was a loss. But we had the stars even as the Magi had them; and that, I think, was a gain. Every Christmastide since then I become a watcher of stars again, journeying in spirit with the Kings on their camel backs—and, if the truth be told, with the far-off Vinland self that used to be mine in the days of my youth.

On the morning of the third day the Skraeling gave up his fruitless waiting. It was not overdifficult for him to pick up Leif Ericson's trail in all this telltale snow. Our comrades' tracks led straight to the skerry on the north bank of the river where the *karfi* had been moored. The *karfi* was gone now, as it happened. But, as I watched the new world warrior with grudging admiration, it seemed to me that the brave did not worry about that small detail. As Meyla told Grainne later, he knew the route our boat would have to take in order to return to the point, hundreds of miles north of here, where he had first come across the track of us strange white men, almost two months ago now. Besides, he thought he would be able to make almost as good time as the Norsemen he tracked—in the end, even better, perhaps. For, despite our comrades' head start and the charts I had prepared for them, the Skraeling knew the country much better than they. And it would be slow going for that great wooden canoe in these winter waters. The Skraeling also realized one other very important thing: that soon the Norsemen would have to abandon their boat altogether and proceed on foot. To balance this, there was one thing he did not know: that we twain followed after him even as he followed after the others of our company. And Leif had been right—Tyrker had learned his tracking trade very well indeed in Sarkland.

The Skraeling was right about the *karfi*. On the fourth day of their journey back the ice pack had become so heavy that our comrades had had to leave their boat behind for good and all— we saw it abandoned in the snow, and our hearts, Tyrker's and mine, were heavy as lead at the woeful sight. But, luckily, they had made very good time up to this point, being by then once again in the first great river, so that it was easier to find their way now that they had been forced to take to the land. Unluckily, however, this was the selfsame day the brave, as he had hoped would happen, fell in, at last, with a wandering war party of his people, twenty-five strong.

So that terrible stalk began, twenty-six against ten—and, on our side, two against twenty-six.

I have been a man of peace these many, many years; and I

thank God daily on His Mass altar that it never fell to my lot to slay any man. But I am glad, nonetheless, that I had a chance to prove my mettle in that grim old wager with death that Tyrker and I made. It comes into my mind, as I ponder this matter, that God has not set His face against fighting so much as against evil. Did He not approve the fight of Michael against the dark angels when they laid an ambush for His holy feet?

CHAPTER THIRTEEN

THORHALL'S FEAT

I CALL THIS PART OF MY VINLAND CHRONICLE THORHALL'S FEAT for the reason that, of all the great feats Thorhall Gamlason accomplished in his day, this one was the greatest, being greater even than the killing of the *Bjarney* bear.

Quite some few days before the time Leif Ericson had counseled us that we should rejoin him, Tyrker and I took it upon ourselves to make our forced march by night around the Skraelings. This was because, from certain signs, we thought those new world warriors were preparing to make a sudden onset against our comrades; and we wished to warn Leif while there was yet time. In the upshot it was well we did. We rejoined Leif and his men on the afternoon of the second day after we began our march. After that our party quickened its pace, sleeping no more than three hours a night. The Skraelings closed the gap again. But, since they had to do it all at once, the effort weakened them more than it weakened us. I have often wondered since what the Skraelings thought of our party's having gained two men. The thought comes into my mind that now Tyrker and I make another story to tell about the Skraeling campfires.

That forced march of Tyrker's and mine was no little thing. For what this is worth, it must be reckoned the greatest of my exploits. But, on this level, I am in no wise to be accounted among the heroes of our old Vinland faring.

Since the time Tyrker and I gave over our stalking of the Skraelings, Thorvald Ericson was the first among us to catch sight of those stalkers stalking us. It was toward evening when he glimpsed them; and it seemed to me that, once they let themselves be seen—for otherwise we would never have seen those forest ghosts—they made no further effort to hide themselves. Rather was it as if they wished our party to see them in their full strength. When, on Thorvald Ericson's information, Leif called a council of war, Thorhall Gamlason did not appear too surprised at Thorvald's report.

"It is a good tactic," he said approvingly. "I have noticed many times before now that some peoples like to fight even as the animals they track fight. This is true of the Lapps in the Finnish Mark; and of the Samoyeds who live north of Eric's Greenland. From what little I have seen of these savage folk, I think it is also true of them. It may even be that they pattern their methods after those animals. The way we are being stalked now, for example, is the way the wolverine stalks the moose which outweighs him by many hundreds of pounds. Night after night, day after day, the great clawed creature follows the greater horned one, making no move to attack until the moose's will to live dies in its breast, and it almost begs the wolverine to devour it. Then, and only then, the wolverine moves in for an easy kill."

Thorvald Ericson did not like Thorhall Gamlason's image.

"I see what you mean, Thorhall, and you are right," he said, finicking as only a skald can finick when words are in question. "But your likeness is false, for it would make us greater in weight than the Skraelings and we are manifestly not as great. It seems to me we are, so far as poundage is concerned, more like a rabbit than a moose."

Hunbogi Ale-Head smiled a grim smile at that.

"Rabbit or moose," he said, "I think we will be no easy kill. It is true we may all die in the end. But I think our will to live is not likely to die before our bodies. I know that I, for one, do not intend to beg these dusky wolverines to devour me."

One night, just as dusk was falling, without any warning the savage war party charged the men they had so long been stalking, crying out a sobbing, high-pitched war cry as they did so. Steinn the *stafnbui* and Leif Ericson were on guard while the others of us made ready for our evening meal, each of us having our weapons within easy reach. But this was not the way to best a war-tested party of Northmen such as we were. This Skraeling tactic never, from beginning to end of our Vinland wars, offered us much trouble. As it turned out, it was not hard for us to beat off that first screaming assault. And, at the end of the skirmish, we found that we had gained something we had not expected. We had at last a name for these adversaries of ours who screamed when they charged.

"How like you our Screamers now?" asked Leif Ericson, wiping the sweat from his forehead, though it was very cold in that January forest. "I think I have met better fighters in my day."

"I, too," said Bolli Blacksark.

"And I," said Kari Englandsfari.

So, from this time on, we men of Vinland called the new world folk the Skraelings which is Screamers in the Norse tongue. I know I have been calling them by this name all through my chronicle almost. But, anyway, this is how the name began. It made things less terrible, somehow, thus to have a name for the enemy.

Leif Ericson did not know just when it was the Skraeling stalk finally left off, since there might be days at a time when we pursued did not so much as lay eyes on our pursuers. But, after three straight days had gone by without any sign whatsoever of the savage stalkers in our rear, Leif almost dared to draw a breath of hope. When the fifth morning dawned, still without hide or hair of the Skraelings, he was sure this absence of the enemy was no mere feint. For reasons of their own the savages had melted away into the snow-covered forests of this winter-dark North. Grainne learned later from Meyla what had happened. The reason was that this particular war party had, six days before, crossed the invisible border line of their own Skraeling country. A day's march beyond their own territory, the Skraelings abandoned the chase. It was not their custom to leave their villages in winter for longer periods than this. For they had many enemies, among the other Skraeling tribes, who did not scruple to wage fierce war on their women and their children.

With the pressure of that terrible stalk relaxed at last, we men of Leif's could now make better speed overland even though, without the *karfi,* it was a much wearier time going than coming. This was the end of January. We had now been absent from Vinland since the middle of October. So the men became feverishly anxious to get back to the settlement—most particularly those with wives and, though he had no wife as yet, not least Brian, from whose mind Grainne was never absent an instant any more.

Even at that, however, we had another month's hard slogging before familiar landmarks began to turn up. On the first day of March we were within an hour's stiff marching of the Vinland lake, when we saw the savage council fires smoking on the hill tops that overlooked the lake beach where Leif Ericson had built our cabins.

Thorvald Ericson was the first of us to spy out that ominous smoke against the pale blue winter sky. A terrible cry broke from his lips. For who of us could tell whether they were council fires or the smoke of burning cabins?

"The Skraelings!" said Thorvald Ericson, growling deep in his throat. "They must be besieging our cabins!"

Thorvald did not add—"or burning them!" He did not have to. That grisly thought leaped at once into the mind of every on-looker among us.

Though we were still miles away from the encampment, we were just breaking into a dead run when Leif Ericson stopped us with a shout of command.

"Hold!" he said grimly, once he had our undivided attention and order had been restored in our broken ranks. "We will advance now in single file—in single file and in silence. To rescue, to avenge, or to join the slain. God grant that it be to rescue! But, if it be to join the slain, in this latter case let us sell ourselves as dearly as we may."

No more than an hour later, the twelve of us silently defiled out of the unbroken forest wall at a point where a steep hill sloped down to the beach on which our cabins stood. As one man, all twelve gave vent to a long sigh of relief. However else it went inside the palisade, however desperate otherwise the plight of the defenders, one thing, at least, was clear. The raven flag on the yellow ground still flew bravely from the hillock in front of Leif Ericson's cabin. That much, anyway, we could see with our own eyes. We could also see that the situation was desperate enough.

The savage besiegers must have been five hundred strong. But they had not yet breached the stockade defenses. Their tents were pitched within a half mile of the cabin moat, well out of arrow shot on the part of the besieged. Lances, with pennons attached, stood fixed in the ground in front of each Skraeling tent. Even as we watched, a company of the savage bowmen, their faces painted with stripes of bright paint, deployed to the left of us— they did not see us, however—and, one after the other, shot flaming arrows on to the cabin roofs. At once the defenders swarmed out to extinguish the fires. One of these was a heavily built woman whom I could recognize as Hunbogi Ale-Head's wife.

"My old woman is still busy about her housework, I see," said

Hunbogi, looking on the situation with a cool professional eye—
but there was pride in his voice, too. "Well, our comrades will
not lack for water to put out those fires, anyway. Even if the lake
is frozen over near shore, there is plenty of snow for the purpose."

Thorhall the Hunter placed a mittened hand on Leif Ericson's
right arm. It seemed to me, when I heard him speak, that the
odds were great against any plan which might have come into his
mind. Nevertheless, Thorhall Gamlason always fought best against
great odds. I could tell that a berserker joy kindled now in his
old bear's heart—wolf's face, perhaps, but bear's heart summed up
Thorhall.

"Well, Leif," he said, jerking his right thumb in the direction
of the painted braves. "It seems to me this day we shall have good
hunting. An idea comes into my mind now. But there is no time
to describe it. May I try my idea?"

"Try it, Thorhall," said Leif Ericson, "whatever it be. Desperate plights demand desperate remedies."

Thorhall Gamlason was not wrong about that day's good hunting. In the rolled pack where he kept his extra arrows and his
sleeping bag, Thorhall always carried the pelt of the great Inuit
bear he had killed outside the cave on *Bjarney*. This had been
easy enough while we still had the *karfi* to sail in. But it had been
more than a little irksome on the overland march; and more than
once I know that Leif had wondered if he ought not command
his huntsman to leave that bearskin by the way. I think Leif was
glad now that he had not yielded to that impulse as he watched
Holmgang-Bersi prove he did not bear his totem-name in vain,
and that it was not for naught his *fylgja* was reputed to be a
great bear.

Thorhall Gamlason put on the shaggy pelt so that the bear's
head came down over his own head, and he had to look out
through holes where the old Inuit's eyes had been. As it was,
Thorhall was quite tall and broad-shouldered. Even so, it was
amazing how much he seemed now like a real bear. This bearlike
effect was increased when he sat down on the spear-shaft of his
heavy halberd-spear where the slope was steepest and iciest, the
point of the spear toward downhill where the Skraeling bowmen
were ranged, the battle-ax over his right shoulder as he sat thus.

"Give me a start, Thrand Thorbergson," Thorhall said from
his spear-sledge, speaking to me through the animal's blunt

muzzle. "Then, when I am well on my way, do you and the others follow me as swiftly as possible. Who knows what may be fated for us even against such a number as there is below there?"

Despite myself, I could not help starting a little, though I had seen that pelt almost daily for the last fourteen months either spread on the wall of Thorhall Gamlason's cabin or, lately, rolled in his pack. It was as if Old Silver lived again even as I had seen him in the vision wrought by Thorhall's gods' flesh; and, what was more, as if he had somehow learned to speak as a man speaks, while all the time preserving a bear's growling voice. It was not altogether pleasant, either. Nevertheless, I mastered the sudden crawling of my flesh and, with Thorvald Ericson at the bear-man's other shoulder, helped push Thorhall carefully down the snowy slope till he began to gather speed of himself and shot beyond our grasp straight toward the cluster of savage bowmen who, intent on their fiery archery, did not mark what was going on in their rear.

The first the Algonquins knew—these Skraelings were Meyla's people, and hence of Algonquian blood—of what was happening was when, aroused by a growling, snarling noise growing ever louder behind them, they looked back. Hurtling down the icy slope at the speed of an avalanche came a gigantic bear sitting on a spear, a huge ax over his right shoulder. Then he was upon them, growling horribly deep down in his bear's throat, sinking the ax in the brains of the first bowman he smashed against, transfixing the next but one with a spear through his belly. Then the uncanny bear-thing was all the way through their ranks and, before the scattered warriors could regroup, had turned like a flash of summer lightning and was on them again with that terrible ax upraised to slay some more. In blind panic the Algonquins broke to the rear. Even as they did, we other eleven men of Vinland charged full against them down the slope, shouting whatever war cries came to mind in the heat of conflict.

Like Thorhall Gamlason, Hunbogi Ale-Head, though he had been a good Christian for some two years now, called on Thor.

Thorvald shouted: "Olaf forever!"

Brian found the name of the great Munster King, his grand-uncle, on his Irish lips.

"*Ború abú!*" he cried aloud in the ancient Gaelic war slogan of the house of Brian.

As for me, I called on Michael, the warrior archangel, he who forever stands at the Father's back with his flaming brand in readiness.

It was too much for the Algonquian braves. One of their medicine men, as Grainne later learned from Meyla for us, got it into his head that the Bear god of their ancestral foes, the Skraelings of the country round about the great foss, had come down from his high mountain and was advancing against them at the head of the whole Bear nation. The panic of their priest took hold on the other warriors ringing the stockade. In pell-mell confusion, they, too, scurried first one way, then the other.

But Thorhall the Bear was not done with his battle play even now. The lake side of our Vinland palisade was protected to a large extent by the lake waters themselves which had already begun to thaw out during the warmer days. Nevertheless, a resourceful group of these new world fighters had had it in mind to invest that water side of the stockade by paddling a huge ice floe up to the very verge of the palisade wall. Thorfinn Karlsefni had seen what was going on from inside and had a strong force ready to repel the boarders. But, with all the pressure on Thorfinn's front where the invading force was heaviest, to say nothing of the distraction caused by the fire arrows, things might have been touch and go if it had not been for the diversionary action Thorhall Gamlason now fought.

The Algonquian boarders on the floating floe noted the ungainly bear-thing with the ax and spear, waddling to the shore's marge on its hind feet until it came close to a place just opposite the great floe which was as smooth as glass underfoot, and far more slippery. As it neared the edge, the bear creature increased its clumsy speed and, from a running start, leaped over the dark water between the shore and the moving floe right on to the green-shining ice-block, snarling fearsomely the while. It landed on all fours; and, so great was the force of that leaping rush, it slid along the floe from one end to the other, bowling over warrior after warrior in its resistless course till only one of the braves was left on the ice pack.

I marked that this brave did not panic like the others. He was a slight man, painted like the rest of his comrades, and, again like them, wearing winter buckskins. But he had blue eyes which grew large in sudden recognition as Thorhall Gamlason's slide came to a stop. I knew him then for what he was: our comrade and our traitor, Thord Thordarson in Skraeling war paint. Thord threw down in Thorhall's path the shield he carried which, with the sword at his side, was the only thing he seemed to have kept from his former life. Less than six months had passed since Thord had deserted from our Vinland camp. But so deep had bitten the chagrin of that holmgang day that, it seemed to me, he was become an Algonquin, in so far as he could, inside and out, almost as if his Norse past had never been.

Thorhall Gamlason, under the bear's head, recognized Thord in that same instant. He cast back the pelt and stepped forth clad in the familiar black doublet. Even now I doubt if the Skraelings could tell what had happened. All they knew was that now there was another man on the floe where there had been none before; and that the fearsome bear was gone on a sudden.

"Holmgang-Bersi!" said Thord Thordarson, great hatred, but no fear, chilling his voice.

"So, Thord," said Thorhall, grinning. "So we come to holmgang once again. You are the first who ever lived to come against me twice. Had I only known when I dressed this morning, I should have worn my blue doublet."

Thorhall's blue doublet was, of course, locked up in the sea chest within his cabin, and had been all the months of our absence from the settlement. But Thord Thordarson could not know that. Nor did Thorhall Gamlason really lie in this great brag of his. It was only a duelist's manner of speaking.

"I do not mind," said Thord Thordarson, drawing his sword and balancing it in his right hand. "You are well enough dressed for what I have to do with you."

Then Thord Thordarson cut swiftly at his old enemy. Thorhall Gamlason parried the sudden blow with his halberd-spear.

"Our weapons are unequal," said Thord Thordarson, breathing lightly as if the wasting sickness no longer afflicted him at all. "You should have a sword. Would you care to borrow mine?"

"A spear will do, I think," said Thorhall Gamlason, suddenly launching the heavy halberd at his partner in that strangest of all holm-trysts. The spear passed through Thord Thordarson's chest and out his back. He began to cough up clots of blood at once, for his right lung had been pierced in passage.

"Yes," said Thord after a space, sitting down for very weakness on the floe that was slipperier than ever now with the blood that had been let. "As you say, a spear will do. It seems broad

spear blades are back in fashion nowadays. But you could not
have done it with a sword, Thorhall."

Thorhall Gamlason caught his enemy as he slumped backward
to the ice.

"No, Thord," he said with gruff generosity, for he was ever a
free-minded wolf. "You are right. I could not have done it with
a sword. As a swordsman you were ever peerless. I say that
freely here—without compulsion or constraint. I say something
else, too. I was at fault when I flung those *dirkim* pennies in your
face, Thord. It is I, as much as you, who, in the end, will have
destroyed the colony."

It was a moment of vision on Thorhall Gamlason's part. So far
as any of us could tell the die had not yet been cast for us to go
or stay. But Thorhall knew already and, I think, Thorvald Ericson. Not Leif, though. It was Leif's way always to hope to the
bitter end. That is another reason why I think he belonged to
the time that was coming and they to the time that was already
past.

"I am sorry about that betrayal, Thorhall," said Thord faintly.
"If I do not live long enough to tell Leif, do you tell him for me."

By now the floe had drifted up to the water-postern of the
palisade and was knocking gently against the wooden door. Thorleik Eldgrimson, who had watched the combat through a loophole
and who, I remembered, used to be oar mate of Thord's aboard
the *Mariasuden,* opened the postern at once; and careful hands
drew in Thorhall and the dying Thord. By now Thorvald Ericson and myself had launched one of the skin boats left behind
in their flight by the terrified Algonquins. We entered on the very
heels of Thorhall and the bloodstained burden he bore.

"Lay him down carefully," said Thorhall Gamlason, strangely
tender for once. "I think he is going fast."

Mistress Gudrid's was among the faces that pressed about the
dying man. Thord waked once more, before the end, and hers,
I think, was the face he saw first as he swam up out of the white
mist that was closing in on him forever. At any rate, he groped
with his hand on the pine floor beside him, as if he had something
there he wished to give her. When, at last, giving over the useless
search, he brought up an empty hand, it was all sticky with his
own fast ebbing life's blood.

"Why is your floor so wet, Mistress?" he asked her with some-

thing of his old gay smile. "For shame! You are not so good a
housewife, it seems, as you used to be when I once knew you."

"Thord!" said Gudrid, her voice choking. "How white you
are!"

"Few grow fairer by wounding, Mistress," he said, and the
smile was ghastly now. "Especially by wounding such as Thorhall
Gamlason doles out. But tell me, Gudrid—you used to be my
friend?"

"I am still your friend, Thord," said Gudrid softly.

"Then let my wife, Meyla, have me when I am dead," said
Thord. "You would not want to bury me under the raven banner.
It is not fitting that a traitor should be laid in howe beside his
comrades who have fallen in battle. If he chooses, I should like to
have Inge priest say a prayer, too, over my corse. And—
Gudrid . . ."

Thord's voice could barely be heard now. Gudrid put her ear
down close to his.

"Yes, Thord," she said. "I will do as you say."

"There will be a child in the summer," he whispered. "If it
were possible, I should like Thorfinn Karlsefni to foster him."

Gudrid, I was sure, did not think Meyla would ever agree to
this. I also think she saw no point in saying so to Thord.

"If it is possible, it shall be done, Thord," she promised.

No one spoke of all those standing around the dying man. His
laboring breath was loud in the stillness.

"One more thing," he said after a long space.

There was only the poor ghost of a voice left in him now.

"Yes, Thord," Gudrid said, her hand on his head. She shook
her own head sadly, and made sign to us that Thord's head was
growing cold.

"Give Holmgang-Bersi my sword. It is a good sword," he said.
"A sword can do no treason, however its owner may have dishonored it."

"Yes, Thord," said Gudrid.

Thord Thordarson did not speak again. After a little while,
Thorfinn Karlsefni's wife got up and covered his face.

I had thought on Thord Thordarson many times since his
treachery. But always had I thought on him either as a traitor
or a comrade. I had not remembered how slender of frame he
was, nor how handsome, nor that he was but a boy, next to Brian
the youngest of all our company.

While Thord Thordarson was dying inside the postern door, Thorfinn Karlsefni had directed a sortie in force against the disorganized Algonquins. The upshot was total victory for our Vinland camp, with no fewer than fifty of the new world men dead or dying on the field, and but six of the Greenlanders, chief among these one of Thorfinn's best men, Thorbrand Snorrason. Two among these dead were Goths who had come with Thorfinn. No one was dead on Leif's side, though Hunbogi Ale-Head had an arrow through his left arm which Leif drew out, then washed the arm and packed it with healing herbs. As it turned out, the arm mended nicely after that. Along with his other luck, Leif was lucky in leechcraft, too.

That same night Leif Ericson held a general council. It was his opinion, as well as the opinion of the majority, that, despite the victory, the position of our colony was very grave. We all knew in our hearts that, after the new world men had licked their wounds a while, they would be back. Leif offered it as his thought that another exploring expedition should be sent out in the spring, striking east this time. He did not add that, if that should fail to bring back a certain kind of news, it might well be that we should have to abandon our hard-won outpost in the new world. But he said it to me and to Thorvald Ericson, his brother. If it should ever come to pass, Leif said, that we had to leave, then we would surely one day come back. It might take many years, but we would come back in the end—and, if not we, then others like ourselves.

Brian did not attend this war conference of ours. We all knew the boy and his betrothed had other things to take care of. It was Grainne's task, too, to help Mistress Gudrid with the laying out of Thorbrand Snorrason, Thorfinn Karlsefni's man, and Thord Thordarson—as for the dead Algonquins, we intended to leave them to the ministrations of their fellows. One savage warrior had been taken prisoner. He would be our go-between with that message. Grainne remembered enough of Meyla's tongue to be able to tell the young Algonquin both this and what had been determined on in the matter of Thord Thordarson's body. Thord was to be carried to a point three-quarters of a mile from the stockade gate, just where the forest began and the beach ended, and there laid down after sunrise. Then the Norse bearers would withdraw, and the Algonquins might pick up this dead comrade of theirs who, of his own free will, had asked to be given back to them in death even as he had chosen to be theirs in life. It would be as well, finally, that they picked him up at once, for, as they well knew, there were many wolves in that forest. Grainne also said, on her own side, that she sent Meyla her dearest love and wished her the best of fortune when the birth-time came upon her. After that the captive was turned loose.

In the morning, from the stockade platform, I, together with Brian and Grainne, watched Thord Thordarson's meager funeral-ale. When, on our part, the Vinland bearers had withdrawn, there was an interval during which nothing at all happened—the Algonquian bodies had been carried off earlier under cover of darkness. Then, quick as sandpipers on wet sand, a small band of savage folk came swiftly out of the snow-covered firs and caught up the dead man. One of them—a slimmer person than any of the others but, I noted, somewhat fuller about the girdle than before—lingered behind the others. She fluttered a red cloth toward our palisade, as if she thought someone might be watching there, pointed down to the snow where Thord's body had lain, and then she, too, was gone into the waiting winter woods that, in a few short weeks, would wake to another spring.

Later that morning, covered by Thorvald Ericson and Thorhall Gamlason with drawn bows in their hands, Brian went out to where the girl had pointed. In the trampled snow, carefully shaded from damp by a cover of sweet-smelling bark after the fashion of the Skraelings, lay a soft pouch of buckskin. Inside was a brooch, a flying eagle worked in blue beads of the sort Meyla had called wampum, this same blue figure standing out in relief against a background of other beads in white. Brian gave it to Grainne for whom it was apparent this gift had been intended. Her eyes misted over with tears, Grainne told us that the strong-winged bird was the totem of Meyla's people. I marked that this ornament was never absent from Grainne's breast after that.

As it happened, there was something hidden under the brooch which even Brian did not see, though he had been the first to finger the cunning gewgaw. Nor did Grainne show it to him, either, until much later on. It was a sort of map of the Mary Garden's island with an arrow drawn on it pointing to a certain tree under which, in happier days, the five of us—Brian, Grainne, myself, Thord Thordarson, and Meyla—had used to hold our little feasts. Grainne kept that tryst which Meyla had appointed without telling anyone till it was over. It was then she found out all the matters we did not know about the Skraeling's stalk after us—a captive Meyla's folk had taken in battle against the Bear Skraelings had told all this to Meyla's people. Grainne was much criticized in the camp for running this risk. But, in my heart, I knew she had done what was right. There are some things which are above tribe and the color of one's skin. I think that fast friendship between Grainne and Meyla was one of them. Sira Inge Skakkeson thought so, too, when I put the matter to him. Inge priest grieved much over the Skraeling girl's going back to her people. For she had gone far down the road that leads to the white garment of Baptism. And now she would go no further.

Game grew very scarce in the final weeks of winter, even as Thorhall Gamlason had foretold; and the people of our colony had to tighten their belts more than a little. The Algonquins did not come back. But both Leif Ericson and Thorfinn Karlsefni were sure they one day would. Much more happened in that winter which I do not have space to set down in my account, even though, by rights, it belongs to the saga of our Vinland faring. It was said, in after years, that Njal's son, Skarphedin, might have equaled, but that not even Grettir the Strong could have surpassed Thorhall Gamlason's double feat of the sledge-spear and the ice floe.

So the long second winter passed for our Vinland colony. And the second spring began. It was not to be a good spring, as it happened.

CHAPTER FOURTEEN

AVE MARIA, SAVE US FROM EVIL . . .

IT IS A WISE SAYING THAT GOOD CHRISTIANS SHOULD NOT PRY too curiously into the womb of time to come. For, besides that those secret parts of the future are reserved for God's eye alone, one would not be able to sustain coming hardship if one knew it too far ahead. It is not true, as some philosophers maintain, that foreknowledge would spare man much evil. Foreknowledge would only plunge him in deeper misery since the decrees of Providence are immutable. He would know, then, the sickness he could not heal. No one can cheat the Norns.

I think the famine which came upon us in our second spring proves the truth of what I say here. It was a bad time. Even fat Svein Haldorson grew melancholy as the flesh dwindled on his bones and his moon cheeks hung flapping like the dewlaps on dog Bran. But even then Svein had a merry saying to explain why he was no longer merry.

"For," he said with a shrug that made us laugh again, "it is guts carry heart, not heart guts."

Sleep is food in time of famine. But this holds true only in time of peace. Now that road, too, was closed to our starving selves. With Algonquins prowling in the forests, sleep could easily have been death. But we endured. We became as scarecrows, we men and women of the Vinland colony. Praise God, we stopped short of becoming skeletons.

As the spring advanced, game fell off so badly that even Thorhall Gamlason, who liked nothing but meat and bread and ale, was constrained to stay his gnawing hunger with fish. In this same department of fish, Leif Ericson's people seemed to fare somewhat better than did Thorfinn Karlsefni's, perhaps for the reason that Alf's and Ornolf's prowess with line and tackle was so much greater than that of any of Thorfinn's fishermen. Mistress Gudrid, too, who freely shared her cooking secrets with her brother's folk, was a sovereign preparer of fish; and, like most good cooks, never above benefiting by new ideas. Tyrker, for example, taught her a trick or two about cooking with wine as it had been done in the Greek Emperor's kitchens in Micklegarth.

Afterwards, as the great hunger bit down even more firmly than before, Leif Ericson found it necessary to share Alf's and Ornolf's catch of fish with Thorfinn Karlsefni's people. Nobody grumbled at this arrangement. For there was much liking between our two parties. Mistress Gudrid was a little reluctant, however openhanded her dealings with her brother's folk, to share her cooking secrets with the wives of the Goth seamen who liked to eat apart from the rest with their husbands. Thorfinn Karlsefni insisted that she do so, nevertheless; and, after a time, she gave in with good grace.

One lucky thing was that the Vinland grasses continued to grow in great plenty so that our cows had good grazing always. Our bull was a willing lover, too. The cows freshened. We were never without good milk and butter. We never wasted the leftover milk, either. Under Mistress Gudrid's direction, our dairymaids made *skyr* which is a kind of sour milk curd not unlike a soft cheese. One made this by pouring all the unused milk into a well-scalded wooden barrel, then, somewhat later, drawing off the whey by pulling a bung in the bottom of the barrel. Not everyone liked this *skyr*. But, when bread grows scarce, hunger is always the best of sauces.

Our sugar supply stayed good, too. For Meyla had taught us the Skraeling trick of tapping maple trees in spring for the golden sweet stuff they stored up. So, if for a while we did come to sucking beechwood as had been Thorhall Gamlason's grim foretelling, we had enow of this precious maple honey with which to flavor it.

Food was not our leader Leif's only worry—nor, indeed, even his main one. I found him brooding more and more over the problem of the savage folk, and making what arrangements he could against the day of their return. In the March assault against the stockade the *Mariasuden's* shed, which was not very close to the stockade, had been unaccountably overlooked by the Skraeling attackers. It was clear that we could hardly count on their overlooking it a second time. So Leif directed that a new shed be constructed within the water confines of the palisade. This called for a great deal of work on the part of his men since Thorfinn Karlsefni's party had, on its own side, to build no fewer than three sheds for their own long ships, a task which involved extending the water side of the palisade as well.

Then there was the important matter of building a second *karfi* for the expedition that was soon to sail east even as we had sailed west the fall before. This new expedition, it had been agreed, was to be under Thorfinn Karlsefni's direction, though he did not see fit to go with it, as Leif had gone with ours the preceding autumn. Instead Thorfinn set Ulfilas, one of his Goths, a hard-bitten, shrewd campaigner, as captain of this *karfi*.

Ulfilas took with him three of his fellow Goths, four Greenlanders, two Icelanders, and two Eastmen from near Vik in Norway. One of these Eastmen turned out to be very quick at new tongues—he even knew a little Latin, Sira Inge told me once, and there had been great admiration in the priest's voice when he mentioned the thing. For this reason Grainne took him in hand and taught him what little she knew of the new world language which Meyla had used. The Norwegian made great strides in a very short space with this crabbed Skraeling tongue.

The *karfi* sailed, after Inge priest had celebrated a solemn Mass for its safety, on the second day of April. No one of us looked for its return before October at the earliest. But, as things turned out, it never came back at all; and there was no tongue to tell of what had befallen these twelve good men and true of Thorfinn Karlsefni's company—unless, of course, one could believe what Thorhall Gamlason said he saw in a vision in the middle of September.

I do not know what to think or say about this so-called vision of Thorhall's. But I set it down here as well as what Thorhall told us he saw in this vision, so that wiser heads than mine may make up their minds for themselves about the matter.

This is the way it all came to pass. Ulfilas' eldest brother had been a fellow Jomsburger with Thorhall in the old days of that famous fellowship. He had died in the final great battle that had dissolved the Jomsburg brotherhood, the same battle, as it happened, from which Thorhall Gamlason himself had come off scotfree. So, for old times' sake if for no other reason, Thorhall Gamlason was more concerned than ordinary when the days stretched out and the second *karfi* continued to put in no appearance. Finally he resorted to something the Lapp shaman had taught him how to do many years before when he had first learned how to dance for good hunting and to eat the gods' flesh before battle. It was only the third time, he told us, that he had attempted this especial practice. For it was a very difficult thing to accomplish, and not unattended with danger—though Thorhall was not a man to make much of danger in itself. Before he tried it, he asked me if I would venture to snuff the gods' flesh once more and see if my luck still held at scrying. But I had had enough—and more than enough—of that same unholy business.

For three days and three nights running Thorhall Gamlason shut himself up fasting in the old disused shed that had earlier housed the *Mariasuden;* and, during that time, asked that his name be not so much as spoken in the settlement, since the speaking of his name might have the bad effect of calling back his spirit from where it would be sent during the divination-ordeal he had now to undergo. So it was done, even as Thorhall Gamlason had requested. Then, drawing back into memory certain of the spells the Lapps long ago had taught him, Thorhall sent his *fylgja* forth—I put this all down, remember, even as he said it happened—to find out what had befallen Ulfilas' party. At the end of the three days and nights, Thorhall came out of the shed again, pale and wasted-looking, and told Leif Ericson what his *fylgja* had seen in his stead. It was not a pretty tale he had to tell us.

Ulfilas and his eleven men of the *karfi,* turning west again, had forged far into the land. They had there come into communication with one of the savage tribesmen. That one of the Eastmen with Ulfilas, who had learned a little Algonquin from Grainne, was able to make himself understood by this man of the new world people. But only with great difficulty. He turned to Ulfilas at last.

"Cut it on the rune stick," said the Eastman—it comes into my mind now, though I do not remember the names of many of Thorfinn Karlsefni's people, that this one's name was Sverker. "The red man says these are the Minnesotas—whatever the Minnesotas may be. He says the tongue I use is Algonquin—very bad Algonquin, as it happens. Himself he calls an Ojibway."

Even as the Eastman spoke, an arrow took him by the throat. The Ojibway had not been alone. Of the twelve comrades of the *karfi,* Ulfilas the Goth was the last to die. Before he did so, he took nine tribesmen with him as companions of his Hel-ride. When the moon rose over the fir trees, Ulfilas, feathered arrow in his lung, crept to the rock skerry where the *karfi* was still burning. From the corner of one dimming eye, he caught a glimpse of what seemed to be a great bear near the skerry. It made signs of sorrow with its paws, as if it grieved for what was happening. It also appeared to Ulfilas that this bear bore the eyes of his brother's Jomsburg friend, Thorhall Gamlason. It was a strange portent; but he was too weak to think much on the matter. Before he died, with the point of an unsteady sword the Goth scratched on the mooring stone:

> *We, twelve men of Vinland—four Goths, four Green-*
> *   landers,*
> *Two Icelanders, two Eastmen—on a journey west from*
> *   Vinland,*
> *Came thus far in our questing.*
> *Ave Maria, save us from evil . . .*

That was what Thorhall Gamlason's *fylgja* had seen on the skerry where the Goths and the Norsemen died. Leif Ericson, when he heard, did not know what to believe, though he inclined to think the *fylgja* spoke truly. It was obvious to all—to me, not least—that Thorhall Gamlason spoke in good faith; that there was no intention to deceive on his part. I do not think, for example, that he, of all men, would have put that part in about the Blessed Virgin, if he had been inventing. But what, I said to myself, if the *fylgja* were deceiving him? Or if, without knowing it, he were deceiving himself? I put the riddle to Inge priest who said a *fylgja*—if it existed at all—was devil-sent, and no one should respect its communications. Then I asked Sira Inge if the devil would speak so respectfully of his enemy, the Virgin; and he had no answer for that.

At any rate, Sira Inge Skakkeson did not stick to say many Masses for Ulfilas and the other eleven comrades of the *karfi*. For, as he said to me, though he did not voice this thought aloud to the rest of us, sometimes the devil spoke truth in order to deceive the further. Thorfinn Karlsefni, on the other hand, put no faith whatsoever in the *fylgja*. I do not know what Thorvald Ericson thought. It was ever hard to read his mind.

But all this of which I have just written happened in September. Before that time many other things had come to pass.

As the famine grew worse, Thorhall Gamlason began to suffer in his own way. Even though, on the night Leif Ericson's *karfi* had anchored off the caribou headland, Thorhall had predicted that game would be very scarce that winter, he had not expected the dearth to last this far into the spring. His pride as a hunter, I think, was therefore hurt. Also, Thorhall Gamlason did not care for fish, except the fish be whale; and, for fear of the Algonquins taking them unawares, Leif refused to send out even one of our four long ships after whale, and this in spite of the fact that we had sighted more than one of the great fish off the promontory where the *Mariasuden's* damaged keel had been set up for a sign. So once again Thorhall turned his dark mind to the shaman magic he had learned among the Lapps. And this time he called on Asa-Thor, even as it had been his wont to do in the old times before what he thought of as all this Christian jugglery had come into the North.

When Thorhall Gamlason had finished with his verses to the red-bearded god, his patron, he cut them on a rune stick with a spouting whale carved atop it and went apart from us others for a period of three half days. At the end of this time Leif Ericson grew concerned about his huntsman and sent out myself and Hunbogi Ale-Head with a small party to search for him. We found him, in the end, on Keelness, lying out on a projecting crag, looking up at the sky, eyes staring, mouth and nostrils agape, mumbling something our party could catch well enough, as words, but could not understand.

"Well?" said Hunbogi Ale-Head, a little disgusted. "What nonsense is it now, Thorhall?"

Thorhall Gamlason stared at him vacantly. But the dreadful emptiness began to leave his face.

"Well?" said Hunbogi a second time.

This time it appeared that Thorhall Gamlason understood him. He waved one languid hand in the direction of the promontory tip. There was a stranded whale—a rorqual—still breathing on the beach.

"It is the flensers' turn now," said Thorhall Gamlason, pronouncing each word separately and with great difficulty as if he were just learning to speak all over again. "I have done my part, I think—I and the Red-Bearded One."

Thorhall Gamlason smiled his old crooked smile at this same

saying of his. When next he spoke, it was as if to himself. But we all of us could hear him just the same.

"Did not," he said, "Thor once more prove more helpful than your Christ? This is the reward for the songs I made for him. Seldom has the Red-Beard failed me in my need."

Despite the objections of Inge priest, who said it was an unholy fish, Leif Ericson—and Thorfinn Karlsefni, whose skepticism was shaken for once, agreed with him—gave orders that the rorqual should be flensed. There was enough meat, when the flensing was finished, to tide us over what remained of the famine. In the upshot even Sira Inge, whose belt had looked sadly shrunken these latter days, ate his share of roasted whale steak, and with a will. He had insisted on first blessing the cooking-pots, however. Leif Ericson saw no objection to the priest's so doing. For his part, he said, blessing or no blessing, he welcomed that whale.

The rorqual was cast up on the promontory late in June. It was already the beginning of July when we heard the first Skraeling drums beating in the hills. After that, Leif Ericson appointed guards for the lake as well as for the stockade itself.

It was during the same week, when the Algonquian war drums started throbbing in the hills, that Thorvald Ericson came to the conclusion that he was fey. For three nights in a row, he heard an ax strike against the wainscot partition of the bed-closet in which he slept. The third night this happened, Leif and I were with him, and heard the death-knock, too. The three of us had been sitting up late in Thorvald's cabin, Leif and Thorvald discussing what our strategy should be when the Algonquins struck again—for we thought in terms of "when" now, no longer "if"—and I taking it all down for our log. When we had finished this lengthy business, Thorvald offered the two of us some wine in his silver cup. Then he brought out the ivory chessmen in their otterskin bag; and, while he played a game with Leif, I sat there and looked on. It was then that the death-knock sounded on the wainscot.

Leif Ericson looked questioningly at his brother when the ill-omened noise was repeated a second time. A strange smile played over Thorvald's face.

"So you, too, hear it, brother Leif," he said. "And you, Thrand Thorbergson, deacon that you are. This is the third night now that ax has knocked. It comes into my mind now, my brother and my friend, that the witch, Gefjon, was right. It is fated that I am to end my life on the shores of this new land. Well, I am content, when all is said and done. Every man must die once, and no man may ward off death when his time is come. No man may escape the lot appointed for him. Gefjon saw it all from afar—I think there are few things stronger than the ancient spells by which that witch saw. Death alone is stronger. I am fey, brother Leif."

"Love is stronger," said Leif Ericson, his eyes far away, thinking, it may be, on the lady Thorgunna.

"Yes," said Thorvald Ericson. "It is true that love is stronger. Every skald knows that. But that is still another reason why I know now I am death-bound. Do you still mind the maid, Rannveig, daughter of Alfgerd, the West Firth leech?"

I could tell that Leif remembered the pretty maid, Rannveig, very well; and I had heard enough of her and Thorvald Ericson's story to know how Thorvald then felt. The two brothers, Leif and Thorvald, and the maid, Rannveig, had been children together. There had been some talk, when she became a maiden, that she and Thorvald would fare together in marriage one day. But it had all come to naught. For the maiden had died untimely young of the spotted sickness that had carried off so many, old and young, in Greenland that year; and even Alfgerd, her wise father, had been unable to help her, though he helped many others. It seemed to me now, from the face he wore, that Leif had not thought on Rannveig for many years; and that he was surprised, besides, that his brother still remembered her. I wondered now if Rannveig had been the reason why Thorvald Ericson had never married, even though he liked women well enough, and women liked him passing well. It was no secret that, so far in his lifetime, Thorvald had slept with many a woman—and some of them other men's wives. But never had he thought to fare with one in marriage since Rannveig's passing.

"You think of Rannveig often?" Leif asked his brother.

"She is never long out of my mind," said Thorvald simply. "It is as if her grave-ale were yesterday."

"Never have you told this to me before," said Leif, disturbed.

"No," said Thorvald. "Nor would I now, either, were it not that I know myself fey. But, if you were a skald, you might have guessed it from my songs, Leif."

They played no more at chess that night. As Thorvald Ericson swept the ivory men back into their otterskin bag, he laughed a little.

"Death wins all games at last, Leif," he said. "Hugger-mugger are we jumbled into his bag: kings, queens, bishops, pawns. There is no skald among these pieces, as it happens. But, when the time comes, the skald goes into the bag, too, for all that, more than most, the skald has mocked at death."

I set down next what Thorvald Ericson told to me next morning when he came to rouse me for my lakeside watch. For it was my turn to play sentry once again. It is a strange story he told, as you shall see. Do I believe it? Yes, I think I do, though you, it is very like, may not. This is why I believe it. It seems to me the old gods had dominion for so long in our Northland that they would not go forever without making their presence known to someone who, like Thorvald Ericson, had ever loved and honored the old ways.

This, then, is what Thorvald Ericson told me. After the chess playing it had been his turn to keep watch on the lake. As was the great hound's custom always, Bran spent the night hours watching with his friend, stretched out beside where Thorvald stood. Our lake this night was drowned with summer stars. Thorvald fixed his eye on where the constellation, Orvandil the Archer, swam in the dark moving mirror of the water. Suddenly the hair stiffened on Bran's neck. Thorvald Ericson could feel it bristle, he told me, under his probing fingers as he stroked the dog. So he knew he was not sleeping. Then Bran growled a menacing growl. In that same instant Orvandil's bright star bow was shattered by a boat's keel crossing it. The shards of splintered starlight trembled in the water. At once Thorvald sprang to his feet and challenged that midnight craft. It did not stop. Instead it came swiftly and silently toward him across the sleeping lake.

"Stand!" Thorvald Ericson had said, leveling a deadly arrow straight at the boat's pilot.

He could now see that there was an old man in the little skiff which he propelled, standing upright in the stern, by means of a single long oar. The old man's flowing beard was white. He wore a cape and a broad-brimmed hat pulled down low on his forehead. He was very tall, and broad-shouldered beyond the make of men as Thorvald Ericson knew them.

"Stand!" said Thorvald Ericson a second time. "Stand! Or
I shoot!"

Still the boat came swiftly forward, noiseless as a shadow.
Thorvald launched his arrow then. It bounced, harmless, off the
old man's breast and fell, clattering, to the boat's single thwart.
Yet, from what Thorvald Ericson could see, the ferryman wore
no manner of corselet. Then at last he knew that what he dealt
with on that midnight Vinland lake was not mortal flesh and
blood. He dropped the bow thereupon and picked up the ax, pre-
senting the cold iron at the phantom's breast. For he knew it
was said that even a drow could not prevail against the power
of cold iron so presented. The ferryman laughed a grim laugh
at that and turned back the flap of his hat to reveal that he had
but one eye. Howling a single howl at the sight, Bran stretched
out again on the lake shore, his quivering nose laid to the ground,
his great frame trembling all over. Thorvald Ericson knew now
with whom he had to deal. It was Odin, Father of gods and men.

"So you know me now, Thorvald Ericson," said the ferryman.
"There was a time—and not so very long ago as mortal time
is measured—you would have recognized me sooner. But never
mind that. It is enough that, at the last, you acknowledged who
I am. I come not for everyone. I come for heroes and I come
for skalds. Before three days are out you, who are already a
skald, will also be a hero. I came for Sinfjotli, and I came for
Egil. It would be enough if you were no more than a skald, for
the mead of poetry, which is my mead, was won from the yore
depths by the first skald to the everlasting profit and great good
of both gods and men. But you will be a hero, too, Thorvald
Ericson, before this week is out."

Bran raised his great head and growled a little at this. The
old ferryman laughed again.

"I will take the Irish dog with me, too, when I come for you,"
he said, "though by rights the great hound belongs to my fellow,
Angus Óg, and not to me. He is a good dog, Thorvald Ericson,
this Irish Bran of yours."

About this time, Thorvald Ericson told me, he began to feel
himself again. He was of the breed of men, I think, who, when
they find out they are fey, feel as if they had quaffed a heady
draught of good wine. Some of his skald's old impudence returned to embolden him.

"It is a small boat for so heavy a purpose, this craft of yours,"

Thorvald said then to the ferryman, measuring the slight bark with an appraising eye.

"You will find it is heavy enough for the purpose," said the old boatman with another laugh, but, Thorvald thought, not an unapproving one. "It has carried Sigurd and Sigmund in its day. It will carry Njal and Grettir, too. I think it will do for you and your dog, Thorvald Ericson."

Then, even more quickly than it had come, that strange boat was gone, still noiseless as a shade. One minute, Thorvald said, it was rocking gently on the dark wavelets raised by its own gentle passage; the next minute it had disappeared. But the little ripples of its sudden passing still troubled the dark tableland of water, breaking the star shine into a thousand quivering lances of broken light.

Thorvald Ericson had rubbed his eyes then. He said to me again he wondered if it had not all been a dream, even though the dog, Bran, still trembled where he lay, and the long lake circles still lipped the pebbly Vinland shores—yet no air had stirred through the listening pines and firs. Thorvald Ericson had strained his ears to hear the better in that quiet night. The drums were beating in the hills again. It seemed to him, he said, that their rhythm was grown a little more insistent now.

Next morning, after he had talked to me, Thorvald Ericson told Leif that he thought the Algonquins would attack within the next three or four days. But he did not say why he thought so, and Leif, his brother, did not ask the reason, even though he must have wondered in his heart. As it happened, I knew the reason well enough. But my lips were sealed on this head even from my leader, though Thorvald Ericson had not pledged me to silence. I could not help myself. Ever since Thorvald had known himself to be fey, he had gone about his business differently from other men; and there was a strange authority now investing what he said and did. For the first time he had gained, I think, the habit of command. It was as if Thorvald the skald had, almost overnight, become Thorvald the champion.

CHAPTER FIFTEEN

DEATH OF A SKALD

MUCH AS I LOVED THORVALD ERICSON—AYE, AND THORHALL Gamlason, too, if the truth be told—I know that the greatest difference of all between them and Leif was that they believed in death and he in life; that they lived so as to make a good death, in the end, and he so as to make a good life. Now I know that this difference is partly the difference between the old man and the new one. It is also, I think, the difference between the joyous hope that is Christ and the sad acceptance that is Odin. But it is, in large part, a matter of men's natures, too. Leif Ericson could not altogether help being Leif Ericson for good or for ill—in his case it was mainly for good. They twain could not help being what they were, either, for ill or for good—and it was not all ill, in their case, by any means.

But, whether it was their fault or no, they were wrong, Thorvald and Thorhall; and, whether it be all imputed to his merit or not, Leif Ericson was right. Think how, all about us unto this very day, men wonder at death most steadfastly and most stubbornly refuse to believe in it for themselves even when its fleshless jaws are already gaping. It is not all folly, this denial of mortality on man's part. It is the blood remembering what was in the beginning and, through Christ, shall one day be again. Birth is not the greatest wonder really. Death is. For we sons of Adam were born to live, not die. And live again one day we shall, and forever, even Thorvald Ericson and Thorhall Gamlason who, while they yet lived, did not believe in life.

There lies the cream of that great jest. I want to be there to hear the two of them roar out their old Viking laughter over this life that never ends as they drink deep of those ale horns of eternity that shall never empty out no matter how hard and long one quaffs from them.

On the second morning after that same night the Algonquins struck at high noon, which took us Vinland folk almost completely unawares, for we had expected this first attack of theirs to come during the dark hours, not realizing that these savage folk could move as silent and unseen through noonday as through midnight woods. As it happened, this same onslaught would have been a total surprise, had not Brian and Grainne, with myself, been on the lake island during the later hours of that morning. Grainne had been tidying up her Mary Garden, pinching back the pansy faces, setting to rights the ragged edges of her pleached walk. While Grainne weeded in the morning cool, I copied out some psalms from a Psalter of Sira Inge's to which a Frankish monk had set the music. Brian amused himself meanwhile by shooting arrows at a tree stump. He was practicing with a longer bow than his favorite arbalest since, in case of a savage attack, Leif Ericson had said that he wanted his bowmen to have a farther range than a crossbow could afford—in the first stages of the battle, anyway. If it came to hand-to-hand fighting, in the end, then the arbalest, which was most effective at close quarters, would be called on to do its part.

On his twentieth shot, or thereabouts, Brian's bowstring broke with a dull twang. He had not brought along a spare string, which, Leif said later, had been very careless of him. But that could not be mended now; and, as I thought at the time, no harm was done. For it was not the turn of either of us two to be on guard against the savage folk. He dallied with his betrothed in her Mary Garden. I wrote down King David's sacred song. With a little laugh, then, Brian set aside the bow.

"Well, Grainne mine," he said, chewing a spear of fragrant grass. "I would you were an armorer for a quarter of an hour—but no more. My only bowstring is snapped."

"If it were important," said Grainne lightly, never bothering to look up from her gardening, "perhaps I could make you a string."

"It is important, Grainne," said Brian on a sudden, a new edge rasping his voice that, but a moment before, had been all play. "For the love of Christ, make me a new string, if you can—and quickly. The safety of our whole colony depends upon it!"

Warned by Brian's change of voice, I looked up at once from my copying and saw the Skraelings on the farther shore, opposite the stockade. In another two minutes our Vinland lake would be black with their skin boats. But so far no one in the stockade seemed to have taken the alarm.

"If I only had a string," said Brian swiftly to me, "I could shoot a fire arrow to warn the colony."

"Strike your flint then," said Grainne, speaking as swiftly as he, for now she, too, had caught sight of the Skraelings. "I will make you a string."

The girl put up her white arms then and quickly unplaited one heavy strand of the golden hair that wound in a soft rope round her head. With the scissors at her girdle she cut several long blonde skeins and deftly wove them into a bowstring. Meanwhile, with his flint, Brian fired a small pile of dried chips on the path, brought them to an instant blaze, thrust in an arrow till it flamed, fitted the arrow nock to Grainne's twisted hair which she had already slipped over the bow, and arched a burning shaft into the stockade. As luck would have it, the flaming arrow fell on the wooden roof of an outhouse next to the sentry's mound. I saw that one of Thorfinn Karlsefni's Goths was on guard. He looked up, open-mouthed, and saw the war flotilla already on the lake. Seizing the *lur* beside him, the Goth wound the alarm on it.

The three of us were already on the lake, Grainne and I paddling furiously, Brian with his finger ready on the golden bowstring, when we saw the raven flag break out from the hillock in front of Leif's cabin. But we had not much time in which to congratulate ourselves on this good fortune, for a single Skraeling canoe, with three warriors in it, two to paddle and one to use the bow, had seen us and put out from the main fleet in order to cut off our boat. If the three of us had the advantage of a slight head start, to balance this the pursuing canoe had three warriors to man it, while one of our paddlers was the maid Grainne. It was true that the three of us should, by rights, reach the shelter of the palisade a little before our stronger pursuers. But, some short time before we did so, we would be well within arrow shot. I marked Brian eye the narrowing distance between us and the Algonquian canoe. Out of the corner of my own eye I could see the straining muscles of the Skraeling paddlers, and hear the guttural grunts they gave vent to at each powerful stroke. They were getting closer every half second. Even so the odds, I thought, were against Brian's hitting a moving target at that distance. Nevertheless, despite the distance still separating our two craft, Brian decided he would have to chance a long shot. If it had failed, he said to me later, he thought that no one of us would have reached the stockade alive.

While Grainne and I redoubled our strokes, Brian put a second arrow between his teeth and fitted still a third one to his bow.

"The boat is all yours now, Grainne mine and Thrand," he said to us between clenched teeth. "Only keep the craft on course and steady, while I shoot."

Then Brian launched the first of his arrows. It took the Algonquin bowman full in the throat when his arrow arm was already drawn back to the full. The Skraeling fell across the low-slung gunwale, capsizing the frail skin craft. Even as he did so, Brian's second and third arrows found their deadly mark. The second entered the right arm of the foremost paddler; the third pierced the chest of the paddler behind him. These, I judged, were probably not fatal wounds. But they had achieved their purpose. That war canoe and those paddlers would fight no more that day.

"I have killed my first man, Thrand," said Brian in a tone of wonder. "And I have wounded two others. Yet I feel no more moved than if I had winged a rabbit."

The stockade gates swung open to admit us on the water side; and were as swiftly closed again. The siege of our Vinland colony had begun.

The lives of all of us had that day poised on a single tress: a golden tress from the maid Grainne's head.

Some of the Algonquian enemies had come by land. But even more had come by sea, paddling from the south, past Keelness, and up the tidal river into our lake. The river and lake were covered with their skin boats now. From each canoe waved war pennons on the tops of lances that had been painted blood red. We men of Leif Ericson's and Thorfinn Karlsefni's displayed our own red shields in angry token of war to match those Algonquian battle lances.

The invaders had war slings as well as crooked bows, both of which weapons they emptied against the colony defenders so soon as they came in range. But, in the main these missiles fell harmlessly within the stockade. It was different, however, with another kind of missile which the Skraelings next made use of. This was a great heavy ball, as large around as a sheep's belly, which they set upon a pole, then bent the pole, and hurled the ball inside the palisade where, with a deafening noise, it fell upon Thorleik Eldgrimson's cabin, smashing the roof to flinders.

The black bull Leif had brought with him from Greenland, on

the *Mariasuden's* second voyage, was tethered next to Thorleik Eldgrimson's cabin. At the noise of that hideous death-ball, the animal became terrified. It was in a bad enough mood to start with, anyway. For it had been some days in rut, and nothing had been done about this need. Now, rearing and champing and pawing the earth in front of it, it burst its bonds and rushed, bellowing, to the door of the stockade. Leif Ericson, who had been directing a file of defenders near the gate, thought of a trick when he saw the red-eyed bull. If a Skraeling maid like Meyla, he said to us later, had been frightened of a cow, he thought it likely a Skraeling warrior band might well be frightened of a bull.

"Quick!" said Leif Ericson to Hunbogi Ale-Head who fought beside him at the stockade portals. "Open the gate, and let the animal through!"

Hunbogi Ale-Head did so. The first wave of Skraelings was just beaching its canoes on the shore near the palisade when the frenzied animal burst upon them. Their scrambling panic was, if possible, worse than when Thorhall Gamlason had played the great bear on the ice floe. Convinced, most likely, that here, at last, in this fearsome monster the like of which no man had seen before, was the white man's true god, the Algonquins turned tail in terror and fled, pushing off their skin boats once again and paddling frantically back to the hither shore. Leif Ericson, who had been looking on with Hunbogi Ale-Head, was almost weak with laughter at the sight.

"It is better than fighting horses in the games at Ericsfjord," said Leif at last, leaning against the rough stockade wall till his fit of mirth was spent. "Go out now, Hunbogi, and bring in our good bull. He shall have three cows to firk for this."

His wild anger abated, the foam-flecked animal came in again, as meek now as if he were a newborn lamb and not a bull in rut.

"They will recover soon all the same," said Thorhall Gamlason who had laughed almost as hard as Leif, looking out after the vanishing canoes. "And then they will be all the angrier for their great shame. What are we to do now, Leif?"

"One cannot always have a plan," said Leif Ericson. "Sometimes, as now, one must just wait and see. No more. What do the besieged ever do, but just this?"

Our Skraeling foes did not return that day. Nor yet that night. But we defenders, who could see their campfires ringing the beach

and hear their low war drums beating in the hills, knew that we
were not done yet with these new world folk. In the morning
the attack began anew. This time the Algonquins used different
tactics. They had invested the lake island where grew the Mary
Garden. From this vantage point they arched fire arrows onto
the roofs of the colony cabins. The fires were easily put out by
the defenders, however, for the water supply was inexhaustible.

"These Skraelings will have to do better than this, if they
want to win over us," said Leif with a grim laugh. "Eh, Thorvald?"

"Yes, Leif," said Thorvald Ericson, the strange withdrawn
smile on his face again. "The Norns will appoint things as they
choose."

Leif Ericson did not know it, of course, but his brother Thorvald was thinking then that, not the Norns of whom he just
spoke, but Odin, Lord of Battles, had appointed this same day
as his death day. I knew it, if Leif did not. For he had told me
so that morning; and nothing I could say to the contrary could
make Thorvald Ericson change his mind on this same head.

Looking back afterwards on that day, men said that Thorvald
Ericson had borne himself as if he, not Leif, his brother, were
captain of the colony—though Leif Ericson, as was his wont,
had fought well, too. No one would gainsay that. At the council
of war held that morning in Leif's cabin, which was attended by
Leif Ericson, Thorfinn Karlsefni, Thorhall Gamlason, Thorvald
Ericson, Hunbogi Ale-Head, Steinn the *stafnbui,* and the captain of Thorfinn's remaining Goths, Thorvald gave it as his
opinion—and, acting as scribe, I duly set it down even while he
spoke—that he should lead a sortie in force against the Algon-
quin-held lake island because it had become apparent that the
colony's single chance of beating off this new Skraeling attack
was either to kill or capture the Skraeling chieftain who had
taken up his stand on that same island. If he were killed, the
Skraelings' discipline might be disorganized. If, on the other hand,
he were taken captive, he might be held as a hostage and, some
time later, even as a bargaining point. Even this might not be
enough, Thorhall admitted, to save the colony in its present desperate plight. But, barring a better suggestion, he thought it
should be tried.

"But why should you lead this sortie, Thorvald, and not Leif?"

asked Thorhall Gamlason with one of his wolf's growls. "Or, if Leif does not see fit to lead it, why should not I?"

"There are two reasons," said Thorvald Ericson to him. "First, it is my own plan, and not Leif's or yours. Leif knows the other reason. He will tell it to you, if you ask him."

Even while he spoke, the strange withdrawn smile came upon Thorvald's face again. Thorhall Gamlason turned to Leif.

"My brother thinks he is fey," said Leif Ericson by way of explanation. "So think I, too."

Thorhall Gamlason looked at Thorvald Ericson with great respect, never questioning that he was fey.

"In that case," he said, "it is well that you lead the sortie. But I still have another question to ask. How is this sortie to be accomplished? We have not nearly enough skin boats for such a purpose."

"What have we to do with skin boats?" asked Thorvald Ericson contemptuously. "We are the people of the *vik*. We shall use one of the boats of the *vik*. What say you to the *Mariasuden*, Leif?"

But Leif Ericson balked at using the *Mariasuden* for the enterprise—for two good reasons. He said he thought Thorvald's idea was a good one and a soldierly one, too; but that, if it could in any way be avoided, he did not care for sending anything that had to do with the Saviour's Mother into battle where blood was sure to be let on every side. Also, he did not like to risk one of the larger ships. If any were to be sacrificed, surely it should be the smallest boat of all. Of course, Leif added quickly then, the chances were that, if the venture succeeded—and it gave every promise of so succeeding—there was no real reason why any of the boats would have to be sacrificed. Then Leif turned to his brother-in-law, Thorfinn, to ask his opinion, since the boat he proposed using, in place of the *Mariasuden,* was Thorfinn Karlsefni's property.

Thorfinn Karlsefni said he had no objection to such an arrangement, so long as he and his men had a part in the venture. So it was arranged that his party should supply fifteen of the thirty men Thorvald Ericson would need. These were selected by lot, as were Leif's fifteen, though, for the greater good of the colony, Thorvald Ericson insisted on excluding certain leaders from the draw. Those excluded, after a warm debate on this subject, were

Leif himself, Thorfinn Karlsefni, Hunbogi Ale-Head, and Thorhall Gamlason.

Thorhall Gamlason, however, vigorously objected to his being banned from Thorvald's sally on what seemed to him the reasonable ground that he was not fated to die at the hands of these savage folk. Consequently, if he went along, the colony would be taking no chance of losing its hunter. Thorfinn Karlsefni was impatient of what he considered such foolish talk, and said so bluntly in Thorhall's teeth. But the argument had great weight with Thorvald Ericson who at once withdrew his objection. As it turned out, we had wasted precious time in this dispute. For the luck of the draw excluded Thorhall Gamlason anyway.

The lot fell on one of Thorfinn Karlsefni's Goths—after the dead Ulfilas this Ulf was the very best of these Goths, and they were good men—two of his Eastmen, four Icelanders, and, for the rest, men of Greenland. On Leif Ericson's side, the Norns decided that, in addition to Thorvald Ericson himself, Brian, Bolli Blacksark, Illugi Tomcat, Thorstein the Black, Hauk Erlendson, Asgeir Aedikoll, Steinof Humblepie, Floki Ravenson, Hallbjorn Half-Troll, Onund of Trolleskog, Svein Haldorson, Sarkland Tyrker, Thorleik Eldgrimson, and myself should go a-viking against the Skraelings. Both Tyrker and Thorleik Eldgrimson were adjudged somewhat old for such a sortie. But, since the lot had chosen them and since they were also bent on going, there was nothing at all to be done about this. Besides, as Thorleik Eldgrimson said with a grin when the issue first arose, a venture like this would fare none the worse for having an old wolf or two along.

There was a little talk, at first, that I, too, should have been excluded from the draw. For my comrades knew that, as an intended priest and one already in the diaconate, it was not seemly that I should be put in a position where I might have to take human life. But, because the old Adam was still strong in me, I felt deeply shamed when all this was pointed out.

"Remember," I said to them, "that as yet I am but a deacon. I do not mean to shrink from killing, if it be necessary, in this war that has come upon us. And it is known to all that I draw as straight a bow as anyone in all our settlement."

"Let Thrand Thorbergson go," said Thorhall Gamlason suddenly when I least expected it. "There is no loyaler comrade in the colony."

Thorhall Gamlason's championing me warmed me as I did not think I could have been warmed for such a reason and from such a quarter. I would not shirk my duty, I said to myself, whatever came. But I prayed in my heart, nonetheless, that it would not have to come to killing on my side. Christ heard my prayer. I wounded more than one man before the sun set on that same bloody day. God be praised, no arrow of mine tasted a fellow mortal's lifeblood. It is much to be thankful for, I think; and I so return thanks to God each morning and evening prayer time since that far-off day.

When everything else had been settled, Thorvald Ericson said he meant to take the great hound Bran along with him on the ship. I alone of all those there knew why. I was afraid god Odin's ferry would be full that night.

At first all things went well. We put up the shield rack on the long ship, red shield faces turned outward; then rolled the craft from its shed and down to the water's edge, three men on a thwart, two to row, and one to shield his fellows further if arrows should come arching over the shield wall. This third man had heavier mail on than the others. But our mail was heavy enough at that. I mind me yet how the steel rings over the quilted jacket weighed heavy and chafed in the summer heat. Once off the island itself, there would probably be no need to row any more—all thirty could serve as bowmen then—until the tense minutes when we would run the boat up on the beach.

Those new world men, who held the Mary Garden island, seemed never to have seen a long ship before. The gilded dragon on the prow, especially, struck them with dismay so that, while the surprise was still fresh, they were fatally laggard in returning the first heavy Norse fire. Several Skraelings went down to death in this arrow storm. I noted again that Brian was become a deadly shot. One of his arrows went through the right breast of a huge copper-colored warrior. Then Thorvald Ericson, standing exposed to enemy fire in the *stafnbui's* place, gave orders that we run the ship up on that portion of the beach which was nearest to a certain cave mouth on a cliff-side overhanging the water. It was there, from the pennon flying before the cave, Thorvald judged the Skraeling chieftain had set up his standard.

The Skraelings had not expected this great war canoe with the dragon thing on its front to come dashing up on the beach. There

was, consequently, a long minute, after the keel first grated on
the shingle and our men came tumbling over the gunwale on to
the island, in which nothing happened at all. There was utter
silence everywhere except for the summer insect song. Standing
beside Thorvald Ericson, I felt the sun burn hot on my chain
mail. It came into my mind, on a sudden, that I had loved this
fair land of Vinland passing well—better even than I knew until
this minute when death's presence made sharp my eyes and ears.
It came into my mind, also, standing there beside him with the
Skraeling drums beating all about us in the hills, that Thorvald
Ericson loved it even more passionately, perhaps, than any of
the rest of us; and that no land can ever be fulfilled without
skalds to love it as Thorvald did. I remembered now that he had
hoped one day to set up his homestead on that headland where
the *Mariasuden's* first keel had been established for a sign.

"I should like to build my home here in this pleasant spot," he
had said to me as we rowed past it on that day, two years before,
when we made our first Vinland landfall. Now, with the wind of
Skraeling arrows in our ears, Thorvald Ericson turned to me
and smiled.

"Do you remember, Thrand," he asked, "what I once said to
you about Keelness? When all this is over, tell it to Leif, if I no
longer can. I would like to set up my last home there."

I thought I knew what he was thinking now; and it came into
my mind that perhaps he had been prophetic when he spoke that
day off Keelness. He could—or I could for him—ask Leif to
bury him there. I looked at the man beside me. Thorvald's eyes
were far off as he gazed on distant horizons no other eye than
his could see. Then the Skraelings, whooping, came pouring over
the beach in a red flow of painted bodies; and the spell was
broken. Time began its reign again for Thorvald Ericson.

"All men wearing heavy mail," said Thorvald quickly, barking
out his commands, "take their stand in the van on the shore before the ship, taking care to ward their faces with their shields if
the Skraelings open fire. Let the others remain behind the shield
rack here and rain arrows upon the enemy till I direct them to
charge—if, that is, it has to come to a charge. It may be we shall
escape that. I and Bran together will try to break this Skraeling
line. If I get through, I will do my best to take the chieftain, alive
or dead, from his cave mouth—if I am able, it will be alive. If I
fall in this attempt, Thorstein the Black is to have the command.

If he falls, the captainship passes to Bolli Blacksark. If Bolli also falls—for this is like to be a bloody day before we are through—then do what Ulf the Goth bids you."

Here Thorvald Ericson stopped, pulling at his lower lip. A crooked grin came upon his face.

"If you can understand Ulf's accent, that is," he said to us, still grinning.

A roar of laughter went up from the men. For Thorfinn Karlsefni's man spoke Norse as if a large potato were burning his German mouth. The Skraelings paused, puzzled. I think they wondered what manner of men were these who laughed in the jaws of death.

"Let no man speak a word during the fight," said Thorvald Ericson, taking up his directions again. "Except for a war cry here and there. That way all may hear what the leaders command."

Then Thorvald Ericson turned and ran to meet the advancing line of Skraelings. It was a thin line in depth because it fanned out so widely in order to envelop the flanks as well as the middle part of our long ship. Thorvald had counted on this, which was why he ran straight toward the center of the attackers. On their part, the Skraelings were not expecting a single warrior to attack them so rashly. So he broke through without much difficulty in the beginning, slaying two of the Algonquins as he did so with two blows from his war ax. However, a third warrior, directly in the path of his rush—a gigantic Skraeling with corded arms as thick as most men's thighs—proved himself cooler than his fellows. He saw what Thorvald meant to do, and waited for him to come near. Then he raised the thrusting lance he carried and was on the point of launching it straight at his enemy's unguarded front when, growling, Bran sprang upon the Skraeling, tearing out his throat with one great snap of his jaws.

The huge warrior wore a stone dagger at his girdle. As he went down into the final darkness under the hound's strong teeth, he plucked the knife from his belt and sank it up to the haft in the great dog's back. It found Bran's heart. The dog set up a long-drawn shuddering wail such as I had never heard before. I knew it was Bran's death cry.

But Thorvald Ericson, though he must have grieved much more even than we, could not stop now to aid the hero hound. If this venture of his were to succeed, he must forge on. I watched him run, never once breaking stride as he went; and it was as if the pounding heart would tumble right out of my heaving chest while I watched.

"So," I said to myself, "Bran goes before to wait at Odin's ferry even as the midnight visitor said. It comes into my mind that Thorvald, too, will prove faithful to that tryst."

An arrow came winging through the air to fix itself in Thorvald Ericson's left arm. He snatched it forth as he went, exultant that it had not been his sword arm which that Skraeling shaft had stung. Blood ran down his corselet in a bright red sheet. But he never faltered.

The cave mouth, where the chieftain's pennon flew, overhung the lake at a height of some forty feet or thereabouts. There was a grass plot in front of the cave onto which a very sure-footed person might leap down from above. We saw now that it was Thorvald Ericson's intention to do this and to take the Skraeling chieftain by surprise by coming on him from out of the air. But two Skraeling warriors, anticipating this intention of Thorvald's, ran after him at great speed. From the corner of his eye, Thorvald Ericson saw these coming. Casting away his shield as he ran, he slipped his short sword into his left hand, took his ax in his right, and leaped down on to that grassy strip. As luck would have it, the Skraeling chieftain saw nothing of that puma leap. He was just beneath Thorvald when he jumped, thus breaking his fall. With the side of his ax, not the smiting edge—for, as he had told us, he wished to take the chieftain alive, if it were at all possible—Thorvald struck the stunned savage heavily over the right ear, rendering him unconscious but not killing him.

Thorvald Ericson scrambled hurriedly to his feet then, to greet the first of his two pursuers who came hurtling through the air to land beside him and the chieftain, his knees buckling under the impact of the flying body. Thorvald smote that Skraeling on the back of his neck, this time with the striking edge, severing the spinal cord at that point, and at once sprang aside again, as the second of the pursuing warriors dropped over the ledge, striking Thorvald between the shoulders with his stone knife. The blade drank deep of his life's blood, but it was clear Thorvald Ericson knew in his heart that he had not got his death wound yet. There was no time for him to turn, though, and use his own ax. The sword in his other hand was worse than useless at such close quarters. So Thorvald dropped to the ground, rolled over quickly, and tried to topple the Skraeling into the water. The trick worked all too well. As the Skraeling tumbled over the edge, he caught Thorvald in his powerful clutch, and the two of them, thus locked together, fell like plummets into the lake below.

It was evident to all of us that Thorvald Ericson had lost a great deal of blood by now from those two terrible wounds. But, even though he must have felt himself weakening second by second, the shock of the cold water, smashing his body as he dropped through layer after layer of healing coolness, revived him for a time. Unfortunately the savage, with whom he now found himself locked in death grapple, was unwounded altogether, and a strong swimmer in addition. So when, lungs bursting, the two of them shot up to the surface again in a burst of silver bubbles that starred the sun-shot green depths, Thorvald Ericson was the first to tire. Yet, since not even now was he fated to enter Odin's ferry for a little space yet, he bethought himself of a ruse.

The savage was not wearing loose nether stocks such as we Norse clad ourselves in; nor even such a kilt as the Irish and Scots wore into battle. He had on to cover his nakedness, after the fashion of these Skraelings, no more than a breech clout fastened with a deer sinew. Even so, Thorvald Ericson thought the trick he had in mind would work. With a sudden tug he pulled the clout down around the brave's feet, trammeling them so that he could no longer kick his feet in swimming. Letting go of Thorvald, the Algonquin bent double in the water then, trying, with his two hands, to free himself from the muffling loincloth. It was then Thorvald sank the single weapon he had left—the *ryting* at his belt—up to the bone haft in his enemy's breast.

There was no need to do any more about the Skraeling after that; and it was as well. For Thorvald Ericson was now weary even unto death, and growing steadily weaker, moment by moment, from excessive loss of blood. Sluggishly he crawled up on the dry shingle and lay there, for several minutes, half in, half out of the lake, looking indifferently on the death throes of his enemy. Just offshore, where the water happened to be very deep, the Algonquin was going down another time. Once more he came up and once more he went down. Then he did not come up any more. Only his shoulders and his breechless buttocks showed above the surface. The water swashed over him several times. He turned over again, and his face came uppermost even where, a moment before, his breech had been. The mouth and eyes gaped open. It seemed as if he were grinning about something.

Thorvald told me later that he heard a scratching noise then from the projecting ledge far above him. He knew at once what must be happening up there. The chieftain was recovering from the blow he had been dealt. Painfully Thorvald sat up and looked about him. Everything would be in vain, and he would die for naught, if the chieftain should escape now. Then his wandering eye came to rest on something; and he knew what further thing he had to do before this feat he had set himself was finally accomplished. Beside him, off to the left, there was a steep path leading up from the shingle to the cave mouth. Setting his teeth, Thorvald Ericson began that terrible climb.

With painful slowness, drawing breath with difficulty at every step, on all fours he crawled up the path to the top. The Skraeling chieftain was standing on the grass plot, lurching like a drunken man from side to side. Calling up one last reserve of strength from he knew not where, Thorvald Ericson crept behind the Skraeling and stunned him anew with a heavy blow from the war ax he had just picked up from where it had dropped on the ledge during his struggle with the Skraeling who had drowned. Then, taking the Algonquian chieftain from the grass plot onto which he had fallen a second time, Thorvald dragged him by his heels down to the little beach below the cave mouth where he had caught a glimpse of a skin boat half hidden in some reeds.

It was at this point we lost sight of Thorvald Ericson. After long minutes had passed we looked at one another, one question in our eyes. Perhaps the time had come now for Thorstein the Black to take over the command. I was the first of us to note the skin boat moving unsteadily over the lake to where our dragon ship had been beached. I aimed a careful arrow at the single paddler, thinking, even as I did so, that it would not be a hard shot, then withdrew my arrow finger from the string, not believing what I saw. Yet it was true. It was Thorvald Ericson in that boat, white-faced and breathing hard. And he had the Skraeling chieftain with him!

Willing hands pulled Thorvald and his unconscious captive over the gunwale on the lake side of the ship so that the two of them would be protected against the rain of Skraeling arrows which now began anew. Walking with difficulty over the tilted boards, Thorvald Ericson made his way to the *stafnbui's* place again.

The attackers saw him now; and the chieftain with him. A yell of angry shame went up from the front ranks of the savage bowmen. The arrow rain slackened. For the Skraelings did not wish to chance killing their chief.

"Push off in order now," said Thorvald Ericson faintly, but clearly enough so that all of us could hear. "We have what we want—and more even. The Skraeling chieftain lives. He will be a valuable hostage if it ever comes to parley between our two peoples."

The dragon ship began to move away from the lake island and back to the stockade. Slowly at first, then more quickly, as the oar beat picked up speed. A wild surge of joy came over me of a sudden. Could Odin have been wrong? I knew Thorvald's wounds were severe. But they were far from mortal. Had Odin's midnight visit been a dream then, and the ax knocking on the wainscot no more than a delusion? Thorvald Ericson said he was fey. Yet had he not died! But it was wrong for me to rejoice so. The gods do not like mortals to joy overmuch.

Whether Odin's visit should have been adjudged a dream or not was a matter Thorhall Gamlason, Sira Inge Skakkeson, and Thorfinn Karlsefni—to name but three members of our Vinland company—might differ on. A moment after this no one of the three of them could have argued that Thorvald Ericson had not been fey. Even while, from his *stafnbui's* post, Thorvald leaned down to inquire if any of his men had been yet wounded in the melee, a lone arrow flew over the gunwale and between two shields to stay quivering in his armpit. I thought, from the look of things, that it had gone through his lung.

Thorvald Ericson laughed aloud before he said anything. Then he took the arrow in his hand and drew it forth. The shaft came away from his flesh easily enough, but the head stayed lodged deep inside him.

"I answer my own question," he said then in a conversational tone of voice, and I knew at that he, too, had been wondering if what he saw on the midnight lake had been a dream. Then, raising his voice and holding up the arrow as if someone looked down on it from above, Thorvald spoke again.

"You were right, Odin," he said. "And I was foolish to doubt you, were it only for an instant. I shall keep tryst with you at the ferry when you call—and it comes into my mind now that you will call very soon. But till then we have no more to say to one another, you and I, O Lord of battles who always deceivest. I have forsworn you for Christ. As the bright Aesir go—and they do not always go well—you are good, old Odin. But my Christ is better than any of the Aesir."

We, his comrades, looked on, never speaking a word while Thorvald Ericson had his say out. Then he sat down carefully on the *stafnbui's* thwart as if he wore a fine new robe and wished no spot of cooking grease to soil it before he came to the King's high banquet.

"It is best we row back now to the palisade," said Thorvald Ericson almost casually, as if nothing more were at stake than an afternoon's pleasure cruise in the King's fjord back in Vik. "It is possible, I think, that I may not have very much time left. If darkness closes my eyes before I see Leif, my brother, again, do you remember this, my comrades. If we prevail against the Skraelings, on the day of my grave-ale I wish to be borne to that headland where once I had it in mind to build my home—though I told no one but Thrand Thorbergson of this desire. For even then I knew in my heart it could not come to pass that I should ever build a shieling on Keelness. Perhaps, though, it was truth that came unbidden to my tongue then. For now, I think, I shall dwell there for a space in the kind earth. There shall you bury me and plant a cross at my head and at my feet. It is called Keelness now. Let it afterwards be called Crossness forever—in memory of me and of the deed I this day did in Vinland."

It was not a long distance at all from the lake island of the Mary Garden to the place of our mooring stones. But some time before the dragon ship reached this harborage, Thorvald Ericson had fainted dead away.

"Bear him on his shield," said Thorstein the Black, even as our craft docked. For to Thorstein, even as Thorvald Ericson had directed, the leadership had now passed.

Thorvald roused a little as we laid him on his shield—it had to be the red shield opposite the *stafnbui's* thwart on the shield rack, for Thorvald's battle shield had fallen on the island as he ran. Onund of Trolleskog, Sarkland Tyrker, Hauk Erlendson, and Steinof Humblepie were the men who did that shield-bearing.

"You will bring Bran, too?" Thorvald asked in a faint voice. "I would that dog Bran slept beside me on Crossness."

"We will go back and get the hound, Thorvald," said Thorstein the Black, swearing a great oath before us that he would do so with his own hands before nightfall. And Thorstein kept that oath, too, though not all oaths get kept. So Bran sleeps by Thorvald Ericson now in the cairn beneath the promontory pines.

The rain of arrows from the lake island had fallen off almost to naught now. It was as if the savage folk were waiting to see what we men of Vinland would do with their chieftain. That captive Algonquin had regained his senses now. Thorstein the Black gave orders that his hands be pinioned behind him, but that otherwise he be treated respectfully as became a chieftain.

Leif Ericson met our little procession at the stockade gate. He unfastened the strap of his brother's helmet and stroked the damp hair with gentle strokes. The dying man smiled up at him. I noted with a twinge of pity how red the helmet crease stood out against Thorvald's dead white skin.

"Array me in my best byrnie, Leif," said Thorvald. "Place my shield at my feet and my sword at my head. Then cover me over with my holiday cloak—the one King Olaf dowered me with two Yules ago. Up to my waist cover me, but leave my face and arms free. It is thus I would like to bid farewell to my friends."

Very quickly we set up bolsters on the green turf clothing the mound that grew under the raven banner, and skins and soft robes over the bolsters. It was cool in the shade of the great banner. Thorvald Ericson looked like a champion lying there in his war gear. No one approached while Sira Inge Skakkeson, stole awry over his chain mail, shrived the dying man and put the sacred wafer to his lips. Then, one by one, the people of our colony filed by, those who knew Thorvald best saying least. Leif said nothing at all. He only stood looking down on his brother, holding him by the hand.

"Farewell, Leif," said Thorvald Ericson. "We have been good friends as well as faithful brothers for many years now. When you have Masses said for me, bid the priest remember Rannveig Alfgerdsdatter as well. She was a fair maiden, and her memory should not perish from the Northland."

"I will," said Leif, stroking his brother's hair again. But he could say no more than that.

Thorvald Ericson smiled up at his brother. Weakly, with a wandering right hand, he gestured to the sky and trees and water of Vinland.

"It is a good thing, our Vinland," he said. "It comes into my mind now that men shall hear and say much of it in years to come; and that it shall wax great above other lands of the earth. It is hard for me to leave it thus, Leif—and to leave the *Maria-suden*. Never have I known a ship like the *Mariasuden*. Remember me to Thorhild, our mother, Leif. And to old Eric, our father, if he yet live when next you touch Greenland. Never had sons a better sire than Eric of Ericsfjord—though I must say he has not had much luck with sons. You are the last of the three of us, my brother."

One after the other we filed by the dying warrior, our comrade. Mistress Gudrid his sister. Thorfinn Karlsefni his brother-in-law. Sarkland Tyrker who had known him when he was a boy. Thorhall Gamlason.

Thorvald grinned a troll's crooked grin at Thorhall Gamlason. It came into my mind, as I watched, that Thorvald, too, like Thorhall, had loved the old ways that were passing. He, too—though not so much as Thorhall Gamlason—had gone on half believing in the Vanir and the Aesir, though, at the end, he had declared once and for all for Christ, as I had heard with my own ears. When all was said and done, I think Thorvald Ericson understood Thorhall Gamlason a good deal better than most others did these changing days.

"Odin's eagles drink dark wine this day, old friend," Thorvald Ericson said to the huntsman. "But it is well, all in all. No man lives one night more than the Norns have granted. Now Hel waits for me out on the promontory. But I go to her not all unwilling. It comes into my mind that the best of days are over, and that we have seen those best of days together, you and I. Never could I expect to find another lord like Olaf Tryggveson. So I am content, old friend. Do you bind the Hel-shoes on my feet for me in memory of the old customs we have known and honored together in our day."

Thorhall Gamlason laid a light finger then on Thorvald Ericson's wounds.

"Only by the hard road of weapons manfully used," said Thorhall, "can one gain entrance to the world of the gods. There will be no need to mark you with a sword dint after, Thorvald Ericson, as is done to lesser men to cheat the eye of Odin. The gates of Valhalla swing wide for heroes such as you."

After that Thorhall Gamlason went apart from us others, his

face working. He clenched his right hand into a ball and smote it hard against a stockade post.

"Thorvald had a great heart," he said, his gray wolf's face still working. "How great these latter-day men will never know —for there is more in the heart of man than money can buy."

Then Thorhall Gamlason looked over to where the Skraeling chieftain stood erect against the palisade, his hands pinioned behind him. I followed his gaze, and my own eye was suddenly taken by the dark face of our captive. Now there, I said to myself, is another one who understands the old ways—as well as Thorhall himself does. As well as Thorvald Ericson did, and better than Leif or Hunbogi. The terrible thought came into my mind, unbidden, that in the bad old times, on the day of Thorvald's grave-ale, we would have cut the Viking blood-eagle on the Algonquian chieftain's back, thus insuring that we sent a kingly servitor, wearing his badge of servitude graven in his flesh, to Thorvald in Valhalla. It was the sort of thought that was sure to have come into Thorhall Gamlason's mind, too. But I did not worry, knowing that, with Sira Inge Skakkeson at his elbow, Leif would never consent, however tempted to take so base a vengeance for the killing of his brother. Nonetheless, I could not keep from watching Thorhall Gamlason. After a little space his hooded eyes came back, brooding, to rest on the Algonquin. The Skraeling caught his glance this time and stared proudly back, black eyes looking into blue.

"He would not cry out, that one," said Thorhall, musing to himself, but aloud, as it happened, so that I heard. "I wonder . . ."

Then, despite myself, I feared suddenly that devilry might yet be let loose among us.

Brian was one of the last to stop beside this man who had been the first of all Leif's company to befriend him on that night, when all this great adventure had its beginnings, back in Olaf Tryggveson's great hall.

"You are become a man now, my Irishman," said Thorvald Ericson, smiling, and his voice was so faint now one had to strain to catch it. "It comes into my mind that I will play no more in the play of swords. It would be a pity, I think, to take Skrymir with me into the dark howe. I would wish you to have my sword, friend Brian—it is a skald's sword, after all, and of all of us you are closest to a skald—now I am going. Leave me my good shield, though, that I may not stride naked across Bifrost. And,

Brian—cherish well the little Hlín. I tell you this for the sake of Rannveig whom I would have cherished, had fate so brought it to pass that we twain fared together in marriage. Time does not wait upon our pleasure, Brian mine. Do not delay too long your faring together, you and the maid Grainne."

When we had all gone by, Thorvald Ericson lay there quiet for a little space. It was thought he had already passed over the gods' rainbow bridge when he sat up suddenly and spoke aloud in a strong voice.

"It comes into my mind," he said, "that Ragnar Lodbrok made a death song in the snake pit. Bring me my crooked harp now that I, too, may laugh at death as Ragnar did."

After we brought him his harp, Thorvald Ericson fell silent again. Then he ran his fingers lightly over the strings and began his song, musing at first.

> *"Gold passes,"* he sang.
> *"Kinsmen die.*
> *Die we, too, in the end.*
> *One thing only dies never—*
> *The bright name one wins for oneself."*

The dying man's voice grew stronger and stronger as the verses rolled out into the Vinland air.

> *"In the shield play we struck!*
> *We hewed with the sword!*
> *The bowstrings sang when the harpstrings were silent.*
> *Our shields we lifted in Ericsfjord,*
> *Our helms we donned in Dublin Bay,*
> *Our byrnies we gashed in grim Hlimarek,*
> *With the brides of the gallowglass laughing lay.*
> *With the sword we smote. In Caithness firth*
> *Fell on our shields a hard cold rain.*
> *In the morning fell those Scots on the earth,*
> *With our spears we reaped the field of the slain."*

Thorvald Ericson's voice was strongest of all now.

> *"But today I glutted the raven god,*
> *Today on Skraeling blood I trod.*
> *Today I brought to the Skraelings bale,*
> *And tonight I drink of Valhalla ale!*

Tonight I drink Skoal to the Aesir tall,
The Disir invite me to Odin's hall.
I fly with the shield-maids high in the sky.
Life's hour has struck. Laughing, I die!"

The harp slipped from Thorvald Ericson's nerveless fingers.
Inge priest, in stole and amice, anointed the dying man with the
holy oils which I held for him on a salver tray. Thorvald opened
his eyes again at the feel of the sacred unction. They seemed as
if deep sunken in his head. The eyes were shadowed and the nose
looked sharp.

"Pray for me, Inge priest," he said, "and for the maid Rannveig Alfgerdsdatter whom, it may be, I shall see again—I do not
know, though, for, even with the holy oil upon me, I find it hard
to believe that we do not go down into darkness in the end. But,
however it be, in the end all else is vanity, even my songs. See
to it, son of Skakke, that they set up the crosses over me out on
the promontory."

There was a long silence during which Thorvald Ericson did
not speak at all. But we could hear his labored breathing in the
hush. Then he raised his head again for the last time.

"Let that headland be called Crossness forever," he said. "Do
you see to it, Thrand Thorbergson. Set it down thus on your
chart."

Then Thorvald Ericson died. He had not been dead an hour—
Mistress Gudrid and her women were just done with washing
and streeking his corse—when Bran was laid beside him. Thorstein the Black had fulfilled the great oath he swore before us
in Thorfinn's ship.

Men have said that, when the women washed Thorvald Ericson's body to prepare him for the grave-ale, a wise-woman among
them cleft open his breast to see what sort of heart he had with
courage such as he showed on the lake island that day; and that,
when this wound was made, it was seen, to everyone's surprise,
that his heart was small, not large at all. But there is nothing in
this same tale, though it has been widely told in many places.
And, if there were, what difference would it make? It was a
skald's heart, that heart of his, and the heart of a hero. Men did
not look soon to see again the like of Thorvald Ericson. For the
race of skalds was already dying in the North. As it happened,

I had known the last and not the worst of them—and the first to help fulfill that lovely land where now he lies asleep.

It comes into my mind now, as I think back upon those days, that a skald is not the least of the things it takes to fulfill a land.

We people of Vinland were not able to hold Thorvald Ericson's grave-ale just then, though things promised well with us against the Skraelings at first. Through Grainne it was possible to come to parley with those savage folk who held the lake island. These said they were ready to give up the siege of the colony in return for their chieftain whose name, so far as Grainne could make out, was something like Avalldamon. But the other and larger Skraeling host—the one pressing upon us from the direction of the tidal river—was under the direction of another chieftain called, once more so far as Grainne's ear could determine, Avalldidida; and these would not consent to such a truce. It seemed there was some sort of enmity between the two chieftains who had made common cause against the invaders but were otherwise at odds.

During the parley with Avalldamon's people, Avalldidida, who did not consider himself in any way bound by what Avalldamon's people said or did, attacked suddenly in great force. In this new and bitter fighting Leif Ericson was badly wounded, but not before we had once again cast dismay into the Skraeling ranks by still another device altogether new to them: the use of a fire ship which wreaked havoc on their shore installations. Not only were our weapons better, as Thorhall Gamlason and Hunbogi Ale-Head had always said—our tactics were, too. But the Skraelings were as brave as we; and they had overwhelming numbers. It bade fair to go ill now with our Vinland encampment when, without warning as is the way in life, the tide turned in favor of us defenders.

Two new dragon ships, shield-racks in place, came rowing swiftly up the river, taking the Algonquins in the rear. It was Freydis Ericsdatter, Leif's sister, and Thorvard, her husband, bearing news of the death of the old *hersir*, Eric of Ericsfjord. With her, but in their own ship, sailed two Icelanders, men of the East Firth, brothers named Helgi and Finnbogi who had met with Freydis Ericsdatter in an evil hour for both them and us. Counting women, these newcomers were close on eighty people

altogether; and, for all the Skraelings could tell, they were no more
than the van of a great fleet of war canoes. The Algonquins were
thrown into a panic by the unexpected reinforcements. As was the
fashion of those new world folk in matters of warfare, they
melted away like snow in spring.

With Leif Ericson hovering between life and death for days,
a great gaping wound in his head, responsibility for Thorvald
Ericson's grave-ale fell to his two sisters, Gudrid and Freydis of
the crooked heart, who were like the two sisters of the fairy tale,
from the mouth of one of whom came diamonds and from the
other toads. As it turned out, my own heart had been prophetic
when it warned me the day I watched Thorhall Gamlason look
on the Skraeling chieftain. It was indeed the blood-eagle Thorhall
had thought on then; and it proved fatally easy to enlist Freydis
in his evil design, even though, as luck would have it, Freydis had
never cared overmuch in life for the brother she now chose so
terribly to honor in death. This Freydis was, I think, the dark-
est soul I have known in my day. If Thorhall Gamlason was of
the party of Odin and Asa-Thor, Freydis Ericsdatter was of
Loki's and Wolf Fenris' faction.

Sira Inge Skakkeson spoke out loud and long against this plan
of Thorhall's. But Freydis stopped his mouth—and my mouth,
too, for I could not stand against her long. Hers was a twisted
mind from her girlhood—ever was she a trap and a snare set
for the feet of men. Thorfinn Karlsefni and Mistress Gudrid were
opposed, as were Steinn the *stafnbui* and Hunbogi Ale-Head. But,
in the main, Leif's men, too, as well as better than half of Thorfinn's supported Freydis and Thorhall in their project.

So, on the day of the grave-ale, even while Inge priest was
speaking the last words of rest over Thorvald Ericson's cairn, on
the very tip of that promontory where the two crosses had now
been raised Freydis Ericsdatter and Thorhall Gamlason had a
blood-eagle cut on the Algonquin chieftain's naked back. Most
of the colony looked on, laughing—I set it down here to our
shame. Mistress Gudrid was not present, though, nor Thorfinn
Karlsefni; nor yet Brian and Grainne. They had set their faces
toward the stockade so soon as the service for Thorvald was
complete. If Sira Inge and I were there, it was only to pray.
Someone had to pray on that day of horror.

Thorhall Gamlason did the grisly work himself. With his own
two huntsman's hands he broke the ribs away from Avalldamon's

backbone and wrenched out the lungs until they lay like red wings on the Skraeling's body. Not once did the Algonquin cry out during the torture. But as he died, uncomplaining, more than a few of our colony sickened at the sight and crept away to think on the dark deed they had cheered so loud but a little space before.

Long after Thorvald Ericson had been laid in howe and the Skraeling, Avalldamon, sent to Valhalla beside him, Sira Inge Skakkeson and I stayed out on that promontory, kneeling together and praying that Freydis' and Thorhall Gamlason's dark doings bring not ruin upon all the rest of us.

When he regained his strength at last, after lingering in the shadows for weeks as a result of the fearful blow the Skraelings had dealt him, Leif Ericson brooded long over what had happened while he lay unknowing in his deathly swoon. He said to me, lying there wan on his pallet, red beard and hair unkempt, that this deed of Thorhall's and of his sister Freydis was the real beginning of evil for our Vinland colony. Thorhall Gamlason and the Skraelings together had brought war to Vinland. But Freydis' crooked mind it was that let in the cruelty which debases man worse than war. In a little space she would bring in foul murder, too, as we were soon to learn. But this was destined to come later, on a winter's day which would see Helgi and Finnbogi and all their people lying stark on the cold turf of our doomed encampment. The awful deed, as it happens, does not belong to my saga of the *Mariasuden's* Vinland faring. For, by the time it came to pass, Leif Ericson and I with him, together with most of our folk, had sailed in the *Mariasuden* for Eric's grave-ale. But, in its own way, that same ill-starred act played its own terrible part in bringing down the Vinland colony forever. So I note it here and pass on at once. For I do not like to think even thus much on this Freydis Ericsdatter who had, of her own free choice, taken on the white garment of Christian baptism as Thorhall Gamlason had not.

The new land had known death and birth and treachery before. Now it knew war as well; and the terrible cruelty war brings in its train. It would have to wait a little for a marriage. But it would not have to wait very much longer for this first and— save one other—best of man's fulfillments. Remembering Thorvald Ericson's dying injunction, Brian, with Grainne's consent, appointed October's Winter Nights for their first faring together. These same Winter Nights, which were celebrated at the time of the hunter's moon, were then but a few weeks distant. There was time and to spare for Mistress Gudrid and her seamstresses to make a wedding gown. They had sewed Thorvald Ericson's shroud on shorter notice.

Krossaness I set it down in my chart. *Krossaness:* the Head-land of the Crosses. Out on that promontory, which had been Keelness first and was now Crossness forever, Thorvald Ericson slept under the two crosses, the great wolfhound, Bran, at his feet. Or if, at times, he woke a little, it was because the Algon-quian war drums began beating in the hills again and did not give over their beating night or day.

CHAPTER SIXTEEN

THIS LAND FULFILLED

OF ALL THE GREAT LESSONS LIFE TEACHES THIS ONE, I HAVE come to know, is the most important and includes all others: we come into this world for one reason only, to learn to love. If we do not learn easily, then must we be taught; and the teaching and the learning of this same lesson can be very hard indeed. It is much easier for some than for others. It is easier, I think, for women than for men. For women love with a grace as men cannot. As it happened, it was easy for Brian and Grainne; and it was in them I first learned to the full what I now set down here for all to read. They took love as a gift with open hands that gave even as they took. They were the lucky ones, they twain, who did not have to learn. They knew without being taught.

They looked, on the Vinland morning of their marriage, like lord Adam and lady Eve standing for their nuptials in the Garden that was in the beginnings. When I gazed upon them there, it was as if I looked into some mirror pool of Paradise and the comely faces of the prime parents looked back at me serene and strong. In them, as in a costly glass, shone the great ancestry that was theirs and is every mortal lover's, if only he or she remember to claim it.

Yes, on a marriage morning, we mortals are kings—and queens, too, for I must not forget that this was the marriage morn of Queen Grainne as well as of King Brian. It comes into my mind, for the thousandth time, how strange it is they two should have gone on to become King and Queen in earnest.

As our third summer waned, Leif Ericson came to a reluctant conclusion, one arrived at only after many wrestlings with conscience and much agony of heart. It was one he did not quite know how to break to the colony. So he spoke of it, at first, to no one but Steinn the *stafnbui*, Hunbogi Ale-Head, Thorleik Eldgrimson, his brother-in-law, Thorfinn, and myself. He said to

303

us that he thought now that, for the present at least, we must abandon this Vinland outpost of ours in the new world. His reasons were clear. The Algonquian pressure was increasing daily. Council fires ringed all the hills, flames by night, smoke smudges by day, and the war drums beat without ceasing. Behind the Algonquins lay those Skraelings who were the people of the Bear. Beyond the Bear Skraelings, he supposed, lay still other tribes. Most likely, if we could only travel the length and breadth of it, this fair new land was inhabited by tribe upon tribe stretching almost farther than the mind could compass.

Leif Ericson went on to offer other arguments. By now, he said, Thorhall Gamlason had communicated to all the company the finding of his *fylgja* in the matter of the second *karfi,* the one captained by Ulfilas the Goth, the one which had not returned. Perhaps one should not be willing to accept this uncanny—and, it might well be, unholy—kind of information. Nevertheless, even if Thorhall were self-deluded about the second-sight of his *fylgja,* it was probably all too true that Skraeling tribesmen lived to the west of us as well as to the south and north—and what matter in the long run if their names were the Minnesotas or something else? In any case, he wound up his argument, as matters stood at present, the people of the new land were far too many for the Vinlanders. And our withdrawal could be temporary, too. Someday we Vinlanders could return.

Though he said nothing of the matter of the blood-eagle, I think Leif had a bad conscience over the slaying of the Skraeling chieftain, Avalldamon. He had lain in a swoon, during that time, it was true, and so could not be held accountable by anyone. But I know he blamed himself for that dark deed because Freydis Ericsdatter was his sister and Thorhall Gamlason his man. I think there was one other reason, too, for his looking shamefaced, though even on this head Leif Ericson had no real reason to be ashamed.

I think Leif, who was the greatest of realists, knew in his heart that it was not likely he would ever return. Someone else from the older lands someday, perhaps. But never Leif the Lucky, son of Eric, new master of Ericsfjord. Leif was become the Greenland *hersir* now. His brothers were both dead: Thorstein Ericson first; now Thorvald, who slept forever out on Crossness. It was clear that the last of Eric's sons should stay at Brattahlith and take care of his inheritance. There was his aging mother to think of. There was his young son by Thorgunna. There were the tender fortunes of the Christian Church he had set up so recently in Greenland under King Olaf Tryggveson and Bishop Sigurd. Perhaps, I said to myself, Leif would marry now, and rear a family, as became a great *hersir* who did not wish his line to die out. When, in a few months, he would set sail in the *Mariasuden* for Eric's grave-ale, I did not think Leif would again come back to Vinland. It might be, though, his sons would. Or the sons of his sons. But never he.

Leif Ericson told us he meant to stay through Brian's and Grainne's wedding, though. They were his charges in a special way. He thought he owed that much to the fosterling he had taken from Olaf Tryggveson to foster in the great King's place; and to the fair prisoner Olaf's men had taken in war. Since the wedding would not be held until the Winter Days, which fell on October twenty-third and twenty-fourth, he would have to remain in Vinland over this winter. No prudent captain—and Leif Ericson was a very prudent captain—would risk his long ship so late in the autumn on such a voyage as the eastern crossing could so easily turn out to be at that time of year. I thought to myself it would be much better that he stay over the winter, anyway. It would take that length of time, and more, so to order the affairs of the colony that the remaining colonists—supposing there were any who might wish to remain—would have the best possible chance of survival.

When Leif Ericson opened his mind on these heads at our September Thing, there was, naturally enough, great disappointment; but no particular surprise over his decision. For everybody who gave any thought to the matter at all had assumed that Leif would now return to take up the Greenland hersirship in his father's place. Both Thorfinn Karlsefni and Freydis Ericsdatter, however, thought it would be a great pity to abandon so promising a project as the Vinland colony had already bidden fair to be—and this in the teeth of the fact that there was no love lost between the two sisters, Gudrid and Freydis. So they proposed to Leif that he release to them his rights in the Vinland landtaking for certain agreed-on monies that would result from the sale of the timber cuttings in the Greenland and Iceland markets, one half of these same profits to go to Leif year by year without his having to venture anything in the cutting and haulage of

the wood. It was a fair enough offer, all men said; and Leif
was glad to accept it, provided that, in addition to that arrangement in his own regard, a certain share should also be paid over
to those of his party who would choose to abandon their holdings
in the colony and return to Greenland on the *Mariasuden*.

As we were soon to find out, something else came into Leif
Ericson's mind at this time regarding the disposition of one of
Thorfinn Karlsefni's boats—that smallest one it was, the one
Thorvald Ericson had used in his attack on the lake island. The
chances were, he thought, that if Thorfinn Karlsefni and Mistress
Gudrid stayed and some of their people chose to return, the canny
Iceland merchant would not care to keep an idle boat in Vinland;
and would be something more than willing to sell it for a reasonable price. But Leif said nothing of this idea of his just yet. It
was somewhat later before he spoke of it even to me, though I
set it down in this place for the sake of order.

A poll was taken, then, of the colony's preferences in this business of going or staying. It turned out that all the people who
had come with Freydis Ericsdatter and Thorvard, her husband,
as well as those who had voyaged with the brothers Helgi and
Finnbogi, wished to chance their luck in Vinland. So, with the
exception of five, did all of Thorfinn Karlsefni's people. On the
other hand, all but three of Leif's folk voted to return to Greenland. Brian and Grainne were among those returning. Only these
two had it in mind to go back to Ireland, not Greenland or Norway. After that, if things worked out, they said they might wish
to return to Vinland. There was no difficulty over this decision
of theirs. So far as Leif's people were concerned, their Irish
comrades were free people and could choose for themselves. The
political troubles involving King Brian of Munster and the Norse
leaders in Dublin were someone else's business, not ours.

A very strange thing came to pass even as our Thing broke
up. The afternoon, I mind me, was a fine one, though hazed over
a little by the faint blue smoke the autumn earth breathes forth.
Onund of Trolleskog saw the ferlie first, though, perhaps, it is
wrong to call this thing a ferlie since it was a thing of nature,
after all.

"Look!" he called out hoarsely. "There are Skraelings in the
sky!"

Over the tall Vinland pines strode taller Skraelings across the
autumn haze. Taller than Jotunns they were, filling the sky, strid-

ing in single file into the blue distance, crooked bows slung on their giant backs. Some carried pennons on war lances. They were painted for war and their chiefs were splendid in feather headdresses. Like images seen in water they shimmered into dimness and became clear again.

"It is the *fata morgana,*" said Tyrker to me, but, despite himself, his voice sounded shaken. "I have seen it often in Sarkland. I saw it once on the Straits of Messina. But never so clear as this."

I, too, had seen it, when I paused to think. Even in Norway one saw the mirage on hot summer days, if there were water somewhere near, glimmering in the distance. Yet there was something strange in this sight all the same. It was almost as if we men of Vinland had been sent a sign.

Leif Ericson kept his eyes fixed on those awesome sky warriors till they faded from the air before us. When they were altogether gone—and not before—he spoke to the Thingmen who had not yet disbanded.

"It is a mirage," he said. "No more. Yet I think we will double our sentries on this night."

Then, as the Thingmen dispersed, Leif Ericson spoke again to me.

"I think also," he said, "though I do not say it to the others, that we do well to leave Vinland, Thrand. I do not say it to the others, but I say it to you. These sky Skraelings are but images of real Skraelings—smaller ones—marching miles away. But it comes into my mind that they are also the spirits of the land warning us to go."

Leif Ericson was right, I know. Yet Thorvald Ericson, his brother, and Thorhall Gamlason, who was so much less wise than he, would both have had other thoughts about those great warriors in the sky. They would, I think, have wished to stay in Vinland all the more. I do not know that I should even think such a thing. But it comes into my mind now that, in some ways, those old adventurers were more resplendent and more noble than this new merchant. This marks the only time I was ever disloyal to Leif Ericson even in mind. It troubles me to set it down here after all these years—it troubles me both for him and for myself. But the truth should be told always.

Now that I have written down what I have written, another thought comes into my mind unsummoned. Can it be that what, all these years, I have thought of as "truth," is, in this case, something quite other? That I feel as I do feel, on this point, because, like Thorvald Ericson and Thorhall Gamlason, I, too, belong more to the old than I have realized?

About a week before the time set for the bride-ale, Leif Ericson got, through Grainne, some additional tidings as to the Algonquin strength. He told me himself of these matters. But I was to glean most of the details years later from the lips of Queen Grainne when the two of us were already old.

Grainne had taken once again to spending a good deal of time on the lake island in her Mary Garden which she had set to order after the Skraelings withdrew from there—and this despite the fact that, after the defeat of Thord Thordarson in holmgang, she had thought never to go there again. Brian, as it happened, did not go with her quite so often as before. This was at Grainne's own request. She wanted, she said, to spend a certain number of these last hours of her maidenhood in prayer before the Virgin's image which, for some reason or other, the Skraelings had not seen fit to touch. It was safe enough now, Brian decided after he had talked the matter over with Thorhall Gamlason and Steinn the *stafnbui*. For the lake was well guarded day and night; and, besides, if the Skraelings came in force again, they would have to come down the tidal river from the sea. The forest side, near where the lake island stood, would not permit a large number of warriors moving in secret all at once.

Nevertheless, our net of guards was not so finely meshed but that one slim Skraeling—two, in point of fact—managed to swim through. I tell this part of the tale even as Queen Grainne told it to me when we twain were old in body but as young in memory still as if we were but new come from Vinland shores. I have noted many times, as the years keep passing, that it is the body ages only, never the heart. Does not this prove against mockers that the soul will never die? But again I maunder on, which proves sufficiently that the mind decays if the heart does not!

As she prayed that October morning in her Mary Garden, a shadow fell across Grainne's own shadow. She looked up swiftly, affrighted. There was no need to feel any fear. It was Meyla, and she bore with her a young infant on a little board that was strapped to her straight back. The baby's skin was as clear and copper-colored as his mother's; and his eyes were slanted like the sloe-dark eyes of Meyla's people. But they were also as blue as Grainne remembered Thord Thordarson's to have been.

A great wave of love went out from Grainne then toward her Algonquian friend and the fatherless child.

"What a beautiful child!" she said, getting to her feet at once, and bending over the baby.

Meyla put a slender brown finger on Grainne's lips at that.

"Speak softly, Grainne," she said. "It is not wise anyone should know that I am here."

Then, when it seemed that it was safe to talk, Meyla's eyes glistened in merriment—there were those among us, I know, who used to say the Skraelings were dour. But, except for Meyla, we knew them only in war. I can bear witness that Meyla laughed more than most of us Norsemen.

"I hear," said the Skraeling girl, "that you are getting married, Grainne—and to Brian. Is what I hear the truth?"

Grainne nodded with a little smile.

"So the story is true, then," said Meyla, never making it known, however, where or how she had heard the story in question, nor did Grainne ask her. "It is good, I think, my Grainne. Your Brian is kind of heart and valiant of mood. I bring you two presents for your bride-ale—and one piece of advice. Here!"

The Skraeling girl held out a woven basket of fragrant grasses. It was filled with ten little earthen pots.

"Open one, Grainne," said Meyla eagerly, showing her white teeth in a smile.

Grainne opened one of the little clay pottles. It was brimmed with golden honey as clear of hue as yellow wine.

"For your moon of honey," said Meyla, smiling again. "May it be as sweet! Thord told me of these moons of honey when the two of us first fared together. The sweet stuff is clover honey —Thord showed me how to make a hive. My people had no bees till Thord brought them."

The Skraeling girl pointed upward then to where a waning moon floated, pale and misshapen in the clear air of a blue morning sky.

"Look!" she said. "My people say it is good luck to see the moon by day. It is shaped like a hive now. Tonight the stars will swarm round it like bees bringing sweetness for your moon of honey. When the new moon lies in the old moon's arms, you shall lie with your beloved."

With a little pang, Grainne remembered then the bee-skep of twisted straw Thord Thordarson had brought from Greenland with him. He must have taken it with him on his flight from our Vinland camp. No one else in the colony had tended bees; and there were no honeybees in this new land. It came into Grainne's mind how odd a thing it was that, because of Thord, the Algonquins had honey while the Norse had not.

"There is another gift, too," said Meyla. "A more important one. I have it here in my buckskins."

The other gift was a blue wampum turtle.

"Take it with you on your moon of honey," said Meyla, very serious now. "Never let it be absent from your person. Never, Grainne! I have a reason for saying this. So long as you wear it, it will protect you and whoever is with you. My people will not touch the bearer of the turtle. The people of the Bear would, it is true. For the turtle is not sacred among them. But we are many moons' marching from the borders of the Bear country."

Then, Grainne told me, Meyla's eyes grew very troubled. The Skraeling girl looked down at the flowers in the Mary Garden as if she did not know what to say or how to say it. Even as she tarried, not speaking, there came a faint *brum-brum,* as if a Skraeling drum had just been no more than brushed with fingers near to where the two friends sat together. Grainne paled at the sound. For she thought at once that the Skraelings must be on the island again. Meyla looked at her.

"It is not what you think, Grainne," she said. "It is only *Sek-sah-ga-dah-gee,* the bird we have named Little Thunder-Maker because his call is like summer thunder. See! I will rouse him for you."

Meyla went over to a wild apple tree and gently shook one of the branches. At once a ruffled grouse flew out of it with a rushing *chir-chir,* but not so fast but that Grainne caught sight of the beautiful bird's hazel-brown eye glinting as bright as a cut topaz. Laughing, Meyla came back and squatted on her haunches, Skraeling-fashion, opposite Grainne.

"No, Grainne," she said, becoming sober at once. "It is not our drums—not yet. But they will come again, as they came with Avalldamon, our dead chief, whom Thorvald Ericson took from this island, single-handed, in a deed that is told now round our camp fires. He was a great warrior, Thorvald, and I am very sorry he is dead. For he was a good man and my friend. I am afraid many more good men will die soon, both on our side and on yours. Unless—"

Then Meyla paused again, as if she did not know how to go on. Grainne waited without speaking. Finally the Skraeling girl raised her head and looked squarely into Grainne's eyes.

"This is very hard to say, Grainne," she said at last. "But it must be said between you and me—both because we are friends and I do not wish you or yours to come to harm, and because we belong to different peoples and I would have my people prevail in this quarrel, not yours. Very soon, Grainne, even the blue turtle will not protect you any more. My people do not wish your people here in this land of ours. It might have been different, I think, but there is too much blood between us now. So they mean that you shall go—and, if you do not go, they mean to kill you. All of you. The tribes are meeting now—including many who have been warring on one another. We are very many in number, Grainne."

The Algonquian girl looked up at the crimson foliage that was slowly dropping, with tiny rustling noises, all around them.

"As many as the red leaves still on the trees, Grainne," she said, pointing upward. "Tell the others what I have told you. Tell the golden-beard above all. For he is both wise and good. I do not wish your people to die, if it can be helped. The Bersi, yes. He is not a good man. The others are, though—yes, even those who looked on while Avalldamon died. For our people would have looked on, too, if it were the golden-beard who was dying at the stake."

Before those two fast friends parted for what the Irish maid knew must be the last time, she asked to hold the Skraeling child in whose little veins now mingled the blood of mortal enemies.

"While Thord was dying, Meyla," she said, rocking the child back and forth in her arms, "he asked Gudrid to foster the baby. Would you wish it?"

Meyla's dark eyes smoldered like two live coals.

"Never!" she said passionately. "He belongs to me and to my people! I loved Thord as a woman loves a man, but he was not of my tribe as this child is. The child will be a great chief among us. Among you he would be no more than the half-blooded son of a traitor."

Grainne sighed a little, though she recognized the truth in what

Meyla had said. Then she smiled as the child yawned in her face, showing that he already had a single little tooth.

"If I can do nothing more," she said, "let me give him a present for his tooth-fee. Among us, when a child cuts its first tooth, his kinsmen give him the present of a ring and a sword."

"He has his father's sword," said Meyla as proudly as before.

Yes, the babe had its father's sword. When the bearers carried Thord Thordarson to the forest marge, they had, on Leif Ericson's instruction, placed the sword he dishonored by his side. I was glad we had done so when I heard Grainne's tale. It is good to think there are two Norse swords still in Vinland: Thorvald Ericson's in his cairn and Thord Thordarson's somewhere in the deep forests.

A strange smile, not altogether lacking in cruelty, had come on the Algonquian girl's face when she thought on her husband's sword. Now, after a space, as Grainne gazed troubled at her, it softened a little.

"But I will let you give him a ring, Grainne, if you wish," said Meyla. "It will be a great treasure for him in later years. And, so long as I, his mother live, I will be able to look on it and say to myself: *This did Grainne, my friend, give to my first-born son.*"

There was deep emotion in the Skraeling girl's voice. Moved almost beyond her powers, Grainne stripped a gold ring from the second finger on her right hand. She had had it of her father as her own teething-portion many years before. It writhed in upon itself as do the serpent letters in the Irish manuscripts.

"What is his name, Meyla?" she asked, slipping the golden circlet on the Skraeling girl's slim finger.

"He has none yet," said Meyla. "But I think now I know what I shall call him in memory of this day."

"What is that?" asked Grainne.

"*Sek-sah-ga-dah-gee,*" said Meyla softly. "Little Thunder-Maker. It is a good name for a warrior, I think. He will take another one himself the first time he goes down the path of war. Till then it will do well enough."

The tears came into Grainne's eyes then. She said no more. The two girls took leave of one another silently at first. Then Meyla spoke one last time.

"Good fortune, Grainne," said the Algonquian girl, finally breaking from her friend's embrace. "I shall think of you often here in the forest. Do you think of me in your own land and on the sea. But, Grainne—do not tarry too many more moons in these woods of ours. After the moon of honey will come the moon of blood. My people mean to make an end of this danger."

That same night Grainne told the "golden-beard," as Meyla had called Leif Ericson, of her conversation with the Skraeling girl. I was in Leif's cabin at the time, working over my charts with him. He looked very serious at what Grainne had to say. But I think he was hardly surprised.

Grainne placed the blue turtle and the pots of honey with her other possessions in the new cabin she and Brian were to share until the time came for the two of them to sail from Vinland. Her needle and loom had been busy almost two whole years against this time when she and Brian should finally fare together in marriage. She had made two kirtles with long linen sleeves: one for everyday and one for ceremony. She had also sewed five fringed aprons for wearing over these kirtles. The brace of fur-lined cloaks in her goodly cedarn chest—one blue, one deep scarlet in color—she had not made, as it happened. Mistress Gudrid had given them to her on two different occasions; and they were handsome as well as very costly. Mistress Gudrid had, besides all this, also dowered her with a warm felt hood for traveling in bitter weather. Grainne had, in addition, no fewer than ten shifts and as many nightrails. Her hose were richly embroidered. The elaborate headdress, which she expected to wear from the day of her bride-ale till the time came to go upon her bier, was ready and waiting, starched and stiffly goffered, for the appointed day— I mind me now that she did not wear that matron's crown upon her bier, after all. She wore a Queen's crown instead. But who of us, on the day of that Vinland bride-ale long ago, could have foretold such an end? The gold band on her head was her own, however—it had come with her from Ireland where Olaf Tryggveson's men had taken her on their autumn viking years before.

Brian did not have nearly so many goodly clothes as Grainne— except for two mantles which were very costly and which he had brought with him to Greenland from Olaf Tryggveson's court at Vik. His shirts and hose, though clean enough, were beginning to look more than a little threadbare. It was clear Grainne's needle fingers itched to be at them, though she knew—and, if she did not know, Mistress Gudrid reminded her often enough—it would not be seemly for her to touch them just yet. So she had to content herself with weaving and sewing new ones which she would bring with her as part of the wedding gift she would make to Brian on the very morning of their bride-ale.

Meanwhile preparations for the bride-ale, which Leif Ericson had pledged himself to give at his own expense, went on apace. Thorhall Gamlason ranged far afield, hunting daily for deer and wild fowl to deck the festive board. He took with his arrows many of those red-wattled birds with the great fan-tails which we had come to prefer to all the other Vinland fowl. Chickens were plucked and white loaves baked. Leif set aside many barrels of the good ale we had brewed from the Papa Stronsay hops. In her own still-room, Mistress Gudrid brewed gallons of the metheglin for which she was famous, using pound upon pound of the precious maiden honey she had brought with her from Iceland, flavoring the sweet drink with rosemary, marjoram, mace, cloves, cinnamon, and many whites of the plumpest eggs her brooding hens were then laying. There would be enough, and to spare, for those of our company who wished to partake of this honeyed draught. Gudrid knew that most of the men, who do not have the same sweet tooth that women do, would not touch the mead which, besides, was already going out of fashion except in the remotest country districts. But the women relished it, if the men did not. And, as that wife of Thorfinn Karlsefni said to me, flushed from working in her still-room, why should we not have a honey drink in honor of this moon of honey?

The day of Brian and Grainne's bride-ale was so golden fine, the sky so bright a blue, the new world air so like wine, that Sira Inge Skakkeson said it must be Saint Martin's Summer come upon us at last. The raven banner was flapping its soft thunder overhead in the brisk autumn breeze even as, habited in the surplice Grainne had sewn for me, standing forth before that congregation on our Thing mound, I spoke my first sermon.

"Dearly beloved in Christ," I began, starting with a Latin quotation, for I was very proud of the Latin Sira Inge Skakkeson had begun to teach me. "I begin with a Latin text from St. Jerome's translation of the Sacred Scripture: *Ecce, nova facio omnia.* Those are Christ's own words and they mean: *Behold, I make all things new.* That is what our dear Lord's Incarnation, His coming to earth, was for: to make all things new even as they were new in that first Garden which was the earthly Paradise. You will remember, I think, that our Lord's first miracle was a miracle He worked at a bride-ale: the bride-ale of Cana which is in Galilee. That was a first wedding, too. For, since man fell in the Garden, there had to be a new beginning—a second first wedding, as it were.

"Now all good weddings are like these two first weddings: the early one of Eden and the later one of Galilee. Today you twain, dear Brian and dear Grainne, go again into the Garden to drink that best wine which blushed red at Cana when our Lord looked upon it as a lover looks upon the unveiled face of his beloved. Our own sweet land of Vinland, this white and gold October day, is like a garden in very truth. Thanks to God's grace, to King Olaf Tryggveson, to our leader, Leif, the son of Eric, and, not least, to our priest, Sira Inge Skakkeson, the wedding room of Cana has been set up in this fair new land of ours. As at those two first weddings, there are three persons involved in this great sacrament which all you guests, our dear comrades here assembled, now honor with your presence. Brian stands for lord Adam: Grainne for the lady Eve; and Sira Inge Skakkeson for God Who is the witness, for God Who gives the woman away that she may cleave to the man and become one flesh even as it was appointed in the Book of Genesis. But neither God nor Sira Inge, acting for Him, confer this great sacrament upon you, Brian and Grainne. It is the one sacrament of all the seven sacraments you confer on one another: the woman on the man and the man on the woman.

"So, since you are the celebrants, not I, I say no more. For today is your day, not mine. Today is your day, and no one else's. No other voice but yours should break the Garden's silence from now on—yours and, perhaps, the song of birds."

Since the weather was favorable and our colony still had no hall great enough to hold all the residents at one time, the bride-ale benches had been set up on the grassy turf before the Thing mound. Brian sat on one of these, his groomsmen with him. These were Leif Ericson, Thorhall Gamlason, Hunbogi Ale-Head, and Steinn the *stafnbui*. Because Grainne was fatherless and belonged to Mistress Gudrid's household, Thorfinn Karlsefni sat on the opposite long bench in her father's place together with certain members of his household. On the cross bench sat Grainne herself with Gudrid and the other women in attendance on her.

At the great feast following the ceremony, which Inge priest had performed with great dispatch, Grainne took her proper place between the bridesmaids on her left, and the bridesmen on her right. There Brian gave her her morning-gift and the linen-gift which was also customary—what these were I can no longer call to mind. After he had finished, the giving of gifts on the guests' part began.

Thorfinn Karlsefni gave the pair a costly ivory chess set with pegs thrust in the pieces so that they could be used on shipboard during the rolling and pitching that was always brought on by high waves. A silver ring was inset in the board. The chess bag itself, which was of soft-cured buckskin, had a gold ring set with gems going over the drawstring so that the deer thongs which closed the bag could be pulled through it. Other gifts were similarly valuable. People waited with impatience to see what Leif Ericson would offer, since we all knew he bore a special responsibility in this matter and had, besides, a reputation, like his father before him, for being very generous. I must say Leif in no way disappointed our expectations.

When the proper time came, the Vinland captain stood up before our company, wearing his new crimson cloak, his fair beard combed so that every golden hair curled in its fitting place.

"This is a good lad, this Brian of ours," Leif said approvingly to us all. "And his Grainne is as good a woman. Look at the two of them, comrades! Brian makes as straight and tall a bridegroom as Brage, Odin's son, himself. The maid seems so fair in her bride-ale crown she might have come from Alfheim where all the many daughters King Alf begot were of the elfin race that is fairer than all other races except the race of the *risir*. They are a princely pair, our Brian and our Grainne. A princely pair deserves a princely present. What shall this present be, people of Vinland?"

I marked that Thorfinn Karlsefni smiled here to himself as Leif Ericson paused in his speech. Thorfinn—and no one else but Gudrid, his wife—knew what his brother-in-law had in mind. For Leif had spoken to him only the night before about selling one of his boats, and he had been in entire agreement.

Leif Ericson looked directly at Brian then.

"Will you, Brian," he said very quickly, "trust me enough to surrender what small rights you have in the Vinland timber cutting on my promise that the gift I now give you will more than compensate for the slight loss you will suffer in this timber matter?"

I could tell Brian was a little embarrassed.

"Of course," he said, flushing under his fair skin. "Of course, Leif."

"Would you also surrender this notion you have of going back to Ireland?" Leif Ericson asked him further. "The gift I have in mind will make it well worth your while to do so."

I could tell from Leif's tone that he but tested Brian in play. But Brian took him to be in earnest, even as Leif intended that he should take him.

"No," he said, flushing all over again. "On that condition I can accept no gift. I say to you what hero Finn once said to the woman of the *Sídhe* who wished to take him with her to the Country of the Young: *I give you thanks for what you offer. But I would not yield up my own country of Ireland if you proffered me the whole of the world and all the Tír-n-an-Óg beside.* I am sorry, Leif, if I offend you by this answer. Your brother, Thorvald, would have understood."

"So he would, Brian," said Leif Ericson, kindling to the memory of his brother. "Let me not offend you, either. For I but jest here. I am no such curmudgeon as to attach conditions to any gift I give. Behold now!"

Leif Ericson swept his arm then in a spacious semicircle toward the lake side of the palisade.

"I give you the ship that Thorfinn sold me yestereve!"

The smallest of Thorfinn Karlsefni's three vessels, the trig fifteen-thwarter that Thorvald Ericson had sailed against the Skraeling, Avalldamon, made a brave show now as it was rowed from its mooring stone up to the stockade postern, its gaping dragon head freshly gilded, spreading a snowy new sail with bright red stripes upon it like a banner against the Vinland sky.

"The ship is yours, Brian, to have and to hold," said Leif Ericson. "The ship is yours, but what is in it belongs to Grainne. For in Ireland a woman must have a bride-price from her man equal to the amount of his first year's income after marriage; and you twain are Irish. I give this to Grainne in your stead. The wares are hers to sell wherever she wishes—in Vik or in the Orkneys or in Irish Hlimarek where there is a great fair every year. With the proceeds she may buy a middling estate on which to set up housekeeping."

We guests all gasped at Leif Ericson's generosity; and well we might, too. That same cargo—as well I knew who made out the bill of lading—was priced at thirty long hundreds of wadmal which, measured in money values, came to something under twelve hundred ounces of pure silver. No greater gift had been given within men's memories in all the Northland. Men said it had been done in honor of both King Olaf Tryggveson and of the old Greenland *hersir* for whom Brian had helped to get two new bears. This was true enough, so far as it went. But I think Leif Ericson also did it for his own honor, too, and for that he wished to make a lordly gesture toward this fair land he would soon leave forever, at this, the first wedding we men of Vinland held in the new world he had discovered in his good ship, *Mariasuden*.

Then the feasting began again; and all men drank heartily to the newly wedded pair, toasting them both in ale and in beakers of Tyrker's red wine, as well as—if one chose—in brimming bumpers of Mistress Gudrid's best metheglin. I think that everything seemed like a dream to Grainne, even as it does to most maids on their wedding morns. When, later, the dancing started, and Leif Ericson claimed her for the second dance, she shyly whispered her thanks to him beneath the merry squealing of the Hardanger fiddles that two of Thorfinn Karlsefni's men, Aslak Sverkerson and Bolli Mord, had brought with them from Norway. It seemed to me the maid looked truly queenlike under her bride-ale headdress.

Only two at a time may go into the Garden; and no other may accompany them. So what I set down here about that twain's moon of honey was told me long afterwards by the lips of Brian and Grainne themselves. It is an odd thing, now I come to think on it. Brian told me his part of the tale while we yet tarried in Vinland. Queen Grainne said naught of this until the year before she died, when King Brian had already been some years dead, and she and I were old. Yet did she, after all that space of time, remember many things he had forgotten in a month. For those are the different ways of man and maid. And, even as a little girl with her doll is already a woman, so is an old woman, remembering, still a maid.

When Leif Ericson said, at the bride-ale gifting, that Brian was like Brage, Odin's fourth son, and Grainne like one of the bright elves of Alfheim, he spoke no more than truth. It seems to me—and I have married many a couple now in my long day—that, in the first strong moons of their true love, mortal lovers are like gods and goddesses in the ancient stories. Nor was this my thought alone, I remember now. The thought came to Brian, too, he told me, when he watched Grainne sleeping for the first time, that there was something in the old tales, after all. Here was Etain in the *Tir-n-an-Óg;* and he was Angus Óg, god of youth, lord of love, master of the colored birds.

It had been Grainne's fancy—and he had not been unwilling—to spend the first night of their moon of honey on the lake island where she had planted her Mary Garden when she first came to this new land. The two lovers paddled over in a night of softest silver—for the moon, as Meyla knew it would be, had been full that week—their skin bags for sleeping packed in the skin boat's prow. Where the wavelets rolled on the pebbled beach, the breaking waters showed snow-white in the light of the moon, as if the great round planet were sheathing and unsheathing a blade of silver in the scabbard of that autumn lake. It was a warrior's figure and a skald's as well, this figure of the sword and sheath, said Brian to me later, after his skald's fashion. For was not he a thrusting blade and his beloved a supple sheath for love? That again, I think, is the way of the man. He remembers the images he made where she remembers the things that happened.

At dawn those lovers bathed together in a morning lake that crisped with little lancing golden waves. The fine weather of Saint Martin's Summer held as they paddled up the tidal river into the forest heart of Vinland. The great trees blazed overhead now like the tall archangels one saw painted above the high altar in the church at Olaf Tryggveson's Vik where Brian and Grainne had gone to Midnight Mass on that Yule Eve when first they met; or else like the Irish parchments they had seen in their childhood that were stiff with gold leaf and crimson color. All the leaves had turned now. Yellow like the Niflung gold. Scarlet like rubies from that far Micklegarth which in the Greek tongue is Constantinople. Strong russet like the leather pouches of kings' messengers. Only the evergreens stayed green, and the willows that, even thus late in the year, still trailed their emerald mermaid tresses over the dreaming water. They slept one night in each other's arms under the shelter of just such a fairy tree.

At one point in their journey the river and the sea came so close together that one could smell the sea salt with one nostril and the wood musk with the other. Lying quiet by the sleeping Grainne's side, it came into Brian's mind that the sea was a man and the river a woman; and that the darkness of these surrounding woods belonged to the natures of both man and woman. The sea air thrust through his eager senses like a sword. The river wound its subtler way into the very tendrils of his yearning heart. The sea was a hero, sworded, bucklered, strong with thrusting spear. The river was a goddess. The river was Grainne as the sea was himself. He woke his beloved to tell her of this wondrous discovery. But, before he was able to finish telling, Grainne had stopped his mouth with her soft kisses.

They saw the Skraelings only once; and that time the blue wampum turtle served them as well as Meyla said it would. They were just crossing a forest glade to collect brushwood for their evening fire when they came suddenly upon the two Algonquins—a young man and woman like themselves. The Skraeling warrior at once slipped the stone ax from his belt, and raised it to throw. Before he was able to, however, Grainne had plucked out the blue turtle from where it rested between her breasts and held it up before her, saying, at the same time, one of the Algonquian words of greeting which Meyla had taught her. The Skraeling dropped his striking hand then. He smiled, as did the woman with him, his wife, who looked so much like Meyla, yet was not Meyla. Grainne and Brian smiled back. Brian made signs that the four of them eat together, pointing to the great cock pheasant, dangling from his belt, which he had killed late that same afternoon. So the four lovers, two of them red, two of them white, broke bread together in the autumn glade that would be a winter glade so soon instead.

This part of Brian's tale—for it was Brian, not Grainne, told me this—always saddened me more than a little. This is the way it might have been, I used to say to myself. We might have thus dwelt in amity side by side, we and our Skraeling brothers. But it was not to be. Will those who come after us—and the Skraelings who come after them—be any wiser? I wonder. But I am not hopeful. They, too, will be men even as the Skraelings and ourselves were men. Perhaps only in God's holy mountain will lion

and lamb ever lie down together again—or should I rather say
lion and lion? Of all the men who ever were only One was a
Lamb; and He was sacrificed because He was our Lamb.

When the round moon rose over the firs, the brave made signs
to Brian and said something in Algonquian. From what Grainne
could make out, he was telling them it would come on to snow
very soon. Brian nodded his head to her in agreement.

"The Skraeling is right, Grainne mine," he said. "All day I
have thought there was snow in the air. It felt this way when
Thorhall Gamlason and I were on *Bjarney* questing for the bear.
We will turn back in the morning."

The Algonquins left them before midnight. The threatened
snow did not begin until late in the next afternoon. But by then
Brian and Grainne were well on their way back to our Vinland
encampment. They had dallied, as became new married lovers,
paddling out. Paddling in, they did not dally, as became married
people with important matters on their minds. So it did not take
very long to return, though there was something sad about this
journey back which they had not felt venturing forth. Man may
not linger long in the Garden. Someday, when time no longer is,
he will be able to. But that same time of timelessness is not yet
even for true lovers.

The Vinland camp was sheeted over with the season's first fall
of snow when the two of them stepped ashore from their skin
boat. The moon of honey had lasted, it seemed, no longer than
a tale told children over the fire before bedtime. But it had been
magic while it lasted all the same. Now life's other moons
stretched into the viewless future before them.

That third Vinland winter was a time of great cold and heavy
snows. But luckily our colony's food supply stayed more than
ample. The grain harvest had been good. Thorhall Gamlason managed to slay enough buck deer so that the venison hanging in
our larder was in no danger of running out. Despite the deep
snow that lay on the ground all through December, January,
February, and well into March, Thorhall was able to take a sufficiency of birds and rabbits whenever he went out with his bow,
stalking the game on snowshoes as the Skraelings did.

Thorleik Eldgrimson had tight-caulked Brian's and Grainne's
cabin against the wind and cold. No one, whose felling arm was
sound as Brian's was, could lack for firewood in a land timbered

so generously as this new world was. So Brian could well afford always to have a cheerful fire roaring on his hearth where I was always welcome as his oldest friend. This was a new kind of bliss that Brian now experienced with Grainne: the comfortable everyday bliss of bread and firelight; of pattern and good custom instead of ecstasy and excitement. It was the bliss of bears in caves, I described it to myself, in place of the joy of eagles mating high in air. Early in the winter Grainne felt new life stirring quick within her. After that, I think, she was so glad that her previous happiness seemed as nothing.

I was glad at the news, too; and all the rest of us who knew that twain. It comes into my mind now that the land, too, was glad in its own way as a land is always glad of birth and increase. Yes, the good land of Vinland had now its last and most miraculous fulfillment of all men's great fulfillments: the fulfillment of conception and plenishment; the fulfillment of the womb's firm-fleshed living fruit. But this child, I said sadly to myself, would not be born in Vinland. If Brian's plans held, his and Grainne's babe would be born in Ireland, the land of their fathers. This great land, the land its father and mother held so short a space, would not fall to the child's inheritance.

We had a quiet winter all in all. For the Skraelings kept the war arrows tight sealed in their quivers. It was as if they waited on our going, till then preferring truce to war. For they had learned to respect our Norseman's prowess in battle. I am afraid their holding back gave Freydis Ericsdatter's men, in especial, a false sense of being safe. Thorfinn Karlsefni knew better, it was true. But mayhap even he hoped that from now on our colony would be left in peace and quiet. It was not so to be.

On the first day of spring, Mistress Gudrid, acting for our whole colony in this same matter, set a firkin of fresh butter on top of the Thing mound so that the sun, returning to earth, would know it was welcome among the settlers. Not even Sira Inge Skakkeson, who had mellowed much since he left King Olaf's court at Vik, saw anything wrong in a custom which, in any case, he hardly thought of as being pagan, it seemed so natural and so proper to show one's gratitude thus to the source of earthly light and growth. It was on that same day we men of Vinland rolled our four ships out of their sheds—two to go and two to stay—and down the rollers into the lake.

Brian had given great thought to a name for his *knorr*—did I think to say before that this boat Leif had gifted him with was a *knorr*? For that is the kind his craft was, larger than a *karfi*, but not so large as a full-fledged long ship; not so large as the *Mariasuden*, either, which was the largest *knorr* Thorberg Skaffhogg had ever built in the King's shipyard at Ladehammer. Brian did not care at all for the name Thorfinn Karlsefni had used, which was *Marten* after the name of the fur-felled beast. In the end he decided he wished to call it the *Grainnesuden*. But Grainne would not hear of any such thing. She insisted that it be the *Synnovesuden* after the sweet Saint of the Selje men whom she and Brian had seen sleeping in the cave. So, since women know how to get their way in this as well as in other matters, the *Synnovesuden* it was in the end. Inge priest, most happy to be able to keep his hand in, carved a fine figurehead for it which, except that the cloak was green not blue, looked not unlike Sira Inge's graceful Mary head for the *Mariasuden*. Once again Thorhall Gamlason growled against displacing the old dragon figure. But folk had grown used to Thorhall the Hunter's grumblings at last. No one paid much attention to him this time.

Now I come to what is almost the saddest of all our days in Vinland—yes, even though we were going home, and I was going home to my heart's desire which was the attaining of Christ's priesthood. Our withdrawal was, each one of us knew in our hearts, a defeat; and a retreating army is rarely a joyous one.

The *Mariasuden* and the *Synnovesuden* sailed from Vinland side by side on the first day of April. Brian carried the people from Thorfinn Karlsefni's party who had chosen not to remain in Vinland, as well as Leif's Irish and Scottish vikings, since it would be easier for him to give these passage to their homes than for Leif Ericson himself. Counting Brian himself and Grainne, that brought his crew to the number of fifteen, and of these fifteen two others, besides Grainne, were women. Leif Ericson did not consider this number enough to work the ship properly, especially since Brian would now be making his first voyage as commander. So he proposed sending Thorleik Eldgrimson, Hunbogi Ale-Head, and Svein Haldorson, seasoned veterans all, to the *Synnovesuden* to sail with Brian as far as Greenland, at least. At this point, much to most people's surprise—not really to Leif's or mine, however, nor to Brian's—Thorhall Gamlason offered to sail with Brian and Grainne in the place of Svein.

Brian accepted gladly. For that old sword-wolf, from enmity in the beginning, had come to love that Irish pair passing well; and they him, though I think that sometimes, when she looked upon her husband together with Thorhall Gamlason, remembering Gefjon, there was a kind of chill misgiving about Grainne's heart. I know there was about mine.

So the division of the crews was made. Sira Inge Skakkeson went with Leif after many heart-searchings, for he did not like to leave our colony—which was no longer ours but Freydis Ericsdatter's and Thorfinn Karlsefni's now—without a spiritual director. But he had to make his report to his ecclesiastical superior, Bishop Sigurd, at Vik. He went, much troubled in heart, promising to send out another priest, so soon as one was ready—which might be a good long time, since we were sorely in need of priests all through the Northland.

On the day of our departure Grima, Onund of Trolleskog's old mother who had come out with Leif Ericson on his second voyage and now returned with him, sang—though she took due care not to let Inge priest know about this—for a favoring wind. Whether it was the result of her song or no—I cannot say—a following breeze escorted our two vessels down the tidal river to the sea. There the wind changed a little. But, on the whole, the winds blew in our favor all during that eastward crossing.

As it happened, I thought it my duty to go with Leif, my captain, not with Brian and Grainne, my friends. When we three spoke our farewells till Greenland, Brian said to me he felt very sad, leaving his cabin and the great forest that stretched beyond his cabin. It was like a trumpet call, though, he also said, to set foot on the pitching deck of one's own ship and, for the first time, to be able to call it one's own. In her turn, Grainne told me that she felt saddest bidding farewell to the Mary Garden she had planted on her first coming to this fair new land where she had been so happy and which she now must leave—most likely forever. Neither Leif nor Brian would ever admit it might be forever, I mind me now. But Grainne did. For the woman is ever a greater realist than the man. There was one great consolation I could point out to her on this especial head. If it was good-by to the Mary Garden, it was not good-by to Mary. The Mother of God traveled with her children in both ships. She would be waiting for Leif when the *Mariasuden* moored in Greenland. She would have come before Brian and Grainne into Ireland.

A porpoise met us in the tidal rip where the river flowed swiftly into the sea. This, I found out later, was considered a very good omen by Thorhall Gamlason who, during the eastward voyage, carved for Grainne in token of this meeting a lifelike porpoise in wood which she still had in her possession when I first came to her court years later. That same night, as the *Mariasuden* beat by the promontory where Thorvald Ericson lay buried under the two wooden crosses, a great fire shot up on the headland, though there was no hand apparent to light it. Perhaps it was an oak kindled by lightning hurtling out of a cloudless sky. This happened sometimes. All I can say is that, in my homeland, we called this light the hero's light. Wherever it came from, it befitted the skald who slept under that lonely cairn.

As the flame soared to the sky on Crossness, Leif Ericson, who was at the *Mariasuden's* helm, locked the tiller and gazed into the darkness behind him long after the strange fire had burned down. Then he did what I had seen him do once before when he kept his tryst by the lady Thorgunna's Hebridean grave. He cupped his hands and called into the lonely dark.

"Farewell, Thorvald!" Leif cried with a great cry. "Farewell! I go without you, my brother, to our father's grave-ale. But ever shall I remember you where you sleep in the new land!"

On the second day out our two ships, which till then had sailed together by agreement, passed great snow-covered fells; each snowy mountain edge cutting a sharp white cantle out of the pure blue of the sky. Sky and mountain came together there like shield meeting sword in never-ending, passionless exchange. It was there above all that I knew how much Leif Ericson had yielded up in deciding to abandon Vinland. But fate is ever stronger than man.

Our two ships parted then, to keep tryst next in Ericsfjord. It seemed to me—though this must have been no more than a fancy—that the lady Synnove curtsied to maid Mary, and the lady Mary to maid Synnove, as we went our separate ways.

The *Synnovesuden* touched briefly at Ericsfjord to drop off Hunbogi Ale-Head, Thorleik Eldgrimson, and Thorhall Gamlason. It was the parting of the ways for those old comrades. Brian and Grainne took the western way to Ireland, even as I was to follow them as far as Iona within the year. Leif Ericson and Thorhall the Hunter took the northern way of the old Norse sea

road. For such as Thorhall Gamlason, who had been of the Jomsburg fellowship, the eastern way into the *Rús,* the way that ended
up in the Greek Emperor's great Micklegarth, which the men of
those parts called Constantinople, was still open; and, for a time,
Thorhall Gamlason pondered going down that road. But at last
he made up his mind to stay in the North with Leif, even though
he knew full well that, with Eric the Red dead, the old ways were
passing fast and that things would be quite different now in
Ericsfjord.

When Thorhall Gamlason clasped Brian's hand in farewell, he
grinned his old crooked grin.

"Well, Irishman," he said. "When things began with us in Vik,
I did not expect them to turn out this way. But I am glad we
end such fast friends. Gefjon, who was right about Thorvald
Ericson, was wrong about one thing, anyway. You did not have
to bury me, after all."

"He may yet," said Hunbogi Ale-Head who was standing by.

A chill ran down my spine at that. I do not know if either
Brian or Thorhall heard their comrade. I think Leif Ericson, who
heard, was very angry. The both of us considered Hunbogi's jest
ill-timed—if it was a jest, for Hunbogi, who was troll-ridden,
rarely jested about such serious things as omens. But neither of us
said anything.

"Farewell, Brian!" said Leif Ericson, embracing him. "Farewell, Grainne!"

"Farewell, great captain!" said Brian, moved as I had never
seen him moved before.

"Farewell, Leif!" said Grainne, her blue eyes swimming with
tears.

We did not bid farewell to one another, I and that twain, my
friends. Our three hearts were too full for that. I watched the
Synnovesuden out of sight, Brian standing in the *stafnbui's* post.
Grainne fluttered a kerchief from the prow. My heart told me
we should meet again. God be praised, it told me truly.

Years later Grainne told me how she and Brian made their Irish
landfall, by design, off that part of the Irish coast which King
Brian of Munster held against both the Norse power and the
power of the Leinstermen, his enemies. The *Ard Ri's* terri-
tories grew year by year. For his fortunes waxed even as King
Sigtrygg's waned. He made his namesake grandnephew very wel-

come. He was courteous to Grainne, too, for, besides that she was his near kinsman's wife, he remembered her father well.

With the profits from the *knorr's* cargo, Grainne was able to buy her husband and herself a farm steading of twelve cows, twelve oxen, and six horses, to say nothing of sheep, chickens, and pigs. King Brian gave his grandnephew another horse—this one a blooded war-charger, saying that a *destrier* like this, as the Frankish knights had taken to calling war-horses, was necessary nowadays. For a great war was surely coming. Brian shrugged his shoulders and accepted the gift. But, as was the way with women, Grainne feared in her heart that the King was right about this.

Brian did not sell the *knorr* Leif Ericson had gifted him with, as Grainne had sold the cargo. A cargo, he used to say, is to sell, but a ship is to keep. He used the craft for coastal voyages; and, as these first years passed, he grew moderately rich as a trader, though trading did not sit so naturally upon his shoulders as it did upon Leif Ericson's. For, in many ways, these Irish among whom I have made my home, for all their cleverness—and they are very clever—belong to the old ways more than do my people.

As one year succeeded the next one, Grainne had, besides the wooden porpoise Thorhall Gamlason had carved for her, one other thing to remind her of Vinland—and of Olaf Tryggveson's court before that. This was a white cat, the descendant, several generations removed now, of the white kitten that had been so friendly with Bran, the giant wolfhound, who slept his Vinland sleep now at the feet of Thorvald Ericson on Crossness.

So the slow moons waxed and waned with them and gradually grew into years. As their family flourished around them, Brian and Grainne tasted of the sacrament of daily fulfillment and found it good. It was good in a different way from the way in which Vinland had been good. But it was very good, nonetheless.

Yes, they were well content with their quiet lot, that twain, and would have stayed content. But the Norn sisters carded other wool for them upon the spindles of destiny. As Thorhall Gamlason used to say, and Thorvald Ericson, fate is stronger than man. It behooves me to add to Thorhall's saying that Providence is as beneficent as it is strong. Yet, because we men walk in shadow during life, the face this compassionate minister of God's unsearchable intentions turns on man often appears doubtful.

CHAPTER SEVENTEEN

THE HEBRIDES: GOOD FRIDAY, 1014

OLD BRIAN OF MUNSTER'S POWER CONTINUED TO GROW THROUGH-
out the next few years after his grandnephew's return to Ireland;
and, as this King's star rose in the western seas, that of Sigtrygg's
waned. The Leinstermen still held out against King Brian's authority as *Ard Ri* of all Ireland. But he gained allies elsewhere,
even in the ranks of those vikings—and they were no longer few
—who had taken upon themselves the yoke of Christ. Jarl Sigtrygg's cards were not all played out, however. If the new Christian power rallied to Brian Boru's standard, so did the old pagan
power to Sigtrygg's.

It is too much to say, perhaps, as some chroniclers are now
proclaiming, that the foreigners of the Western World were up
in arms against Boru. But it is all too true to say that secret gold
from Sweyn Forkbeard, the great Danish sea King, had bought
for Sigtrygg mercenaries from England, France, the Low Countries, Scotland, and the Hebrides, as well as recreant gallowglasses
from parts of Ireland itself. For the first time in over forty years
the seas around Ireland and Scotland were black with the dragon
ships of the vikings. Once again, as in other centuries, Irish and
English Mass prayers ended with the old fearful ejaculation:
*A furore Nordmannorum libera nos Domine! From the fury of
the Norsemen, deliver us, O Lord!*

We used to pray this prayer daily on Iona; and much it pained
me thus to pray against my blood brothers. I had not seen any of
my own people since Bishop Sigurd made me priest two years after
the *Mariasuden* came home from Vinland. Norway was sealed off
now by these new troubles, and Iceland and Greenland, too—
though neither of these latter lands took any part in the quarrel
between Sigtrygg and Brian. As it happened, the sea road was
still open to the Hebrides where, every Good Friday, Leif Ericson
came to pray and do penance on the lady Thorgunna's island.
My abbot granted me permission for the journey there. I ap-

pointed tryst with Leif, by messenger, over the winter; and, so soon as the spring seas were open, sailed to the Hebrides in a *karfi* whose master I knew.

It was good to tread the planks of a ship again. We reached Thorgunna's island in good time at the beginning of Holy Week. Leif Ericson was there before me. He made me very welcome. Of all his crew only Thorleik Eldgrimson belonged to the old days which I remembered.

There were so many dragon ships abroad that year, Leif Ericson told me, that, for the first time since his return to Ericsfjord from Vinland seven years before, he wondered for a while whether or not he should journey out on the *Mariasuden* when he made this yearly Lenten pilgrimage to do penance by Thorgunna's grave. Perhaps, he had thought, it would be better to take a *karfi* this one time rather than risk the lordly ship that was his dearest treasure for the triple reason that it was the first ship in all the Northland to be vowed to the Mother of God, that in it he had discovered the fair country of Vinland which stayed in his memory like a song, and—last but by no means least—that it had been the gift of King Olaf Tryggveson. Then Leif had put aside that thought as unworthy of the great Greenland *hersir* he was known to be.

I knew that Leif Ericson had taken no part whatsoever in the many political quarrels which, since Olaf's death at Svolder, had rent the Northland. When he was not out on a merchant voyage, he kept his fleet of long ships as dry as newly woven fishing creels under the awnings in their sheds. But he would not stay off the seas for anyone, though he never courted trouble, either—and woe betide the maurauder who dared assault the *Mariasuden* while Leif Ericson stood in the *stafnbui's* post. So, in the end, he had sailed for the Hebrides as usual, so soon as his Greenland harborage was free of ice.

Now, as it happened, Thorleik Eldgrimson, who was very old and had not been out on the seas since his return from Vinland years before, had had what seemed to Leif an unaccountable desire to go along on this trip. Leif had said yes to Thorleik because, except for Hunbogi Ale-Head who managed Brattahlith now for him, Thorleik was the only one left at Ericsfjord of our old Vinland company. The others either had scattered, or else had their own smaller farms to care for. When I asked after Thorhall

Gamlason, Leif told me that, restless as any old wolf, Thorhall had stuck it out with him for several years, whiling away the time by going out with the Inuits after musk ox, seal, eagle, gerfalcon, even an occasional polar bear. But, when one has been an old berserker, one never loses his taste for stalking that biggest game of all, which is one's fellow man. So, when Sigurd Jarl declared his adherence to Sigtrygg's federation against Brian of Munster, Thorhall Gamlason had joined that pack of desperate adventurers under Sigurd's banner.

As things turned out, Leif's fears for the *Mariasuden* had been needless. He met far fewer craft than usual—and hardly any dragon ships at all—on this journey to the Hebridean island where the lady Thorgunna slept away her twelfth year in the quiet earth under the great cairn. It seemed to him that every long ship in the outer islands had sailed to Dublin Bay for the onslaught against King Brian. Never had Leif seen the isles so deserted. Only old men and boys stayed out that Lent in the Hebrides and the Orkneys. But it suited him far better than if there had been a busy stir. For, as was his wont in Lententide, he came into these western seas to pray and do penance, not to chaffer.

For the very first time, his young son by Thorgunna came with him—his only son, as it happened, now in his twelfth year. For Leif Ericson had not married, as I thought in Vinland that he might.

The old chief, Thorgunna's father, was ten years dead; and his eldest son, who liked Leif Ericson passing well, held sway in his stead. When the two of us met, Leif and I, in this chieftain's shieling, I knew, looking on him, that I, too, had grown old. For we see ourselves best in our friends' eyes, not in our own mirrors. But if Leif the Lucky and myself looked somewhat older, Thorleik Eldgrimson looked as ancient as some withered apple-john that has lain in a loft over two winters. He was toothless, too; and his gray eyes were bleared.

"Greetings, Sira Thrand," said Leif to me. "It gives me much pleasure to see and speak with you after all these years."

"It gives me much pleasure, too, Leif," I said.

Thorleik Eldgrimson said nothing at all.

Though she had been dead for twelve long years now, and though he was growing old, the lady Thorgunna was never long

absent from Leif Ericson's thoughts. Once again, on this Good
Friday as on every Good Friday since the *Mariasuden* had come
back from Vinland, during the six weary hours our Saviour hung
upon the cross Leif kept lonely vigil by Thorgunna's cairn in
penance for the wrong he had done the dead woman so many
years before, and for the eternal peace of his and Thorgunna's
souls. He kept it alone, too, though I had offered to go with him
out on the promontory. So, while old Thorleik Eldgrimson wandered off about his business, I kept vigil by myself in a village
church built after the Irish fashion. For this island, too, had
lately become Christian along with the other islands of the Hebrides. Since Leif had said he would come down again from the
headland about the fourth hour of the afternoon, I made a point
to meet him on the causeway that led over the moor into the village where the chieftain kept his shieling. I saw him coming at a
distance even as I walked out onto the long fen bridge. I thought
he walked a little more stiffly than of old; but perhaps that came
only from kneeling so many hours on hard stone. His golden
beard had become flecked with gray. His calves were a little more
shrunken than they used to be in the days when he led us men of
the *Mariasuden* against the Skraelings in Vinland. But, all in all,
I thought Leif Ericson still a man of imposing figure; and there
was great authority in his mien.

Much to Leif's surprise, for he had not expected to meet him
in this out-of-the-way place, Thorleik Eldgrimson, wrapped in a
shepherd's tartan, also awaited him on the long bridge. A burn
flowed out of a thick forest here under the rough-hewn causeway.
Except for the burn's busy chatter, there was no sound on the
moor beyond the dull striking of a cottar's rammer as he tamped
fast the sods on the outer wall of a white-washed cottage which
stood out on the moor a hundred yards or so from the far entrance of the causeway. Just before Leif came upon the causeway, the man was finished with his work and off again to that
end of the village where the fishermen kept their low huts. He and
Leif met at the far entrance to this bridge in the middle of which
we other two were waiting.

Again I noted how utter the silence had now become, with even
the rammer's thud now silent, except for the burn's never-ending
brattling over the brown stones. No bird sang in the hush, which
was strange, considering that the spring was already so far advanced and, besides, had not been cold, and that that most haunt-

ing of all northern songsters, the cuckoo, made her home in the
Hebrides. A mist began to rise from the moor now. I shivered
on a sudden, and wished I owned Thorleik's tartan.

"Whose house is that?" Leif Ericson asked the cottar, pointing
to the shieling.

"Dorrud's," said the man, shouldering his rammer.

"Who is Dorrud?" asked Leif then.

"Who is Dorrud?" asked the cottar with a dry sort of laugh.
"Why, Dorrud is—Dorrud. I can tell you no more about Dorrud
than that, except that, if I were you, I should not linger about
Dorrud's house after the sun is set—nor while this mist is rising,
either. Dorrud pays me well for my work. I ask him no questions."

"Why should I not linger?" asked Leif Ericson.

"It is not chancy," said the cottar. "Is there a better reason than
that?"

"The man is right about Dorrud's house, Leif," said Thorleik
Eldgrimson, as the cottar trudged off to the village.

Leif Ericson looked down at his old friend; and I looked with
him. For there had been a strange tone in the old man's voice.

"What do you know of Dorrud, Thorleik?" asked Leif.

"Enough," said Thorleik. "Those of us who remember somewhat of the old ways that are passing have heard of Dorrud and
his house."

Then Thorleik Eldgrimson shut his old lips and would say no
more. Leif had told me that, as the man had grown older, he had
begun to take great pleasure in the interpretation of dreams.
Though this kind of interest is not at all uncommon in the Northland, it had made Leif Ericson uneasy sometimes. For he thought
it belonged a bit too much to the bad old times when old women
used to sit their Thor chairs and look into the future. I was
more than a little afraid now that Thorleik had been up to some
of these uncanny tricks again. After his two short sayings about
Dorrud, the old man had withdrawn once more, huddled into his
tartan on the causeway, his rheumy eyes vacant, as if he heard
something but did not see. Only there was nothing to hear at all
on all that empty silent moor; and nothing to see, either, except
for the mist that, in a matter of minutes, had become very thick.

"Hearken!" said Thorleik Eldgrimson suddenly, even as our
eyes searched the moor. "Listen to the hoofs drum, Leif!"

Perhaps there was something to hear, after all. Listening, I

could catch the soft thunder of horses' feet. Closer and closer they
came, twelve steeds in all, mailed women sitting those saddles,
riding swift and, except for the steady hoofbeats, silent out of
the rising mist; black as crows their flowing mantles against the
spear-gray of the moor. After the dead stillness of the afternoon, a chill wind began to stir; and the light grew dusked, though
it wanted some hours yet till evening. The twelve shield-maidens
dismounted, still without speaking, and went into Dorrud's house,
leaving their horses on the moor close up to the wall of the
thatch-roofed cottage. It was no dream, for all it seemed so
dreamlike. I could hear the cropping noise the horses' jaws made
as they champed the coarse grasses growing by the wall.

"What do you here, Thorleik?" asked Leif Ericson.

Thorleik Eldgrimson gave him a strange smile.

"I wait the twelve maidens," said Thorleik, still smiling that
fearful smile. "Even as you await one. My twelve maidens have
come to me. Did Thorgunna come to you this time, Leif?"

"Who are the maidens?" asked Leif Ericson, disregarding the
question which, had Thorleik Eldgrimson been a younger man,
he would have resented as unwarrantedly insolent.

Thorleik Eldgrimson did not answer.

"Who are these maidens, Thorleik?" I asked him in my turn,
though it came into my mind that I already knew the answer.

Thorleik Eldgrimson looked straight at me then, his rheumy
eyes no longer hooded.

"Do you not know, priest?" he asked. "You heard Thorhall
Gamlason and Thorvald Ericson name them over more than once.
They are the Valkyries. Today is the day of Clontarf."

"Clontarf?" said Leif, manifestly puzzled.

I was as perplexed as he. Except that Clontarf was a place near
Dublin, where trading ships moored, the name meant nothing to
me. It is thus fate's hammer first falls on the eardrum, making
no sound.

"What is Clontarf?" Leif asked Thorleik Eldgrimson.

"It is Thor's doom, and Odin's," said Thorleik Eldgrimson.
"It is the end of the old North that was. I saw it all first in dream
back in Ericsfjord. It is why I wished to come with you on this
trip, Leif—that I might be near Dorrud's house on this Good
Friday."

"But why?" Leif Ericson asked him. "Why, Thorleik?"

"You shall see," said Thorleik, "if you so wish. But it is not wise so to wish. I am old. It will not bother me overmuch. I cannot answer for you, though, Leif."

Thorleik Eldgrimson got off the causeway rock where he had been sitting and went over to a window slit in Dorrud's house through which he peered, Leif close at the old man's elbow. The heart pounding hard in my breast, I followed the two of them. Inside the twelve shield-maidens sat about a loom with men's fleshless heads for weights and warriors' gut strings in place of the warp and woof. A great sword—and an ancient one, too—was the treadle they trod; an arrow the batten they beat. As they wove they sang:

> "*Wind we, weave we*
> *The web of arrows.*
> *With dead men's marrows*
> *We spin the war.*
> *We spin the lot fickle*
> *For Sigtrygg mickle;*
> *For Sigurd Jarl*
> *And Brian Mór.*
> *Who win, who lose,*
> *Valkyries choose.*
> *Valkyries pour*
> *The cruse of war.*
> *Let him who listens*
> *At Dorrud's door*
> *Hear and remember*
> *For ever more."*

Then the shield-maidens pulled that awesome web down and into twelve pieces, each one holding onto the portion which came away in her hand. After that, they came out the door again, mounted their horses and rode away, six to the south, the other six to the north. Thorleik Eldgrimson waited until the soft thunder of hoofs had died away. Then he turned to Leif.

"Dare you go in with me, Leif?" Thorleik asked, while the odd smile started to play over his wrinkled face once more.

"Am I not your captain?" said Leif Ericson, half angrily, half proudly; and now it was as if he did not see me, though I stood close beside him. "What you dare I dare!"

Thorleik Eldgrimson pulled open the low door and, stooping, went into Dorrud's house then, the two of us upon his heels. The peat burned red upon the hearth. Old Thorleik took another turf slab and put it on the fire. The flame flared up at once.

"Look into the fire, Leif," said Thorleik. "It is this I came from Ericsfjord to see."

There are pictures to be seen in any fire, if one stares hard enough upon the crumbling embers. The pictures in this fire were different. They were of real things just then taking place, brought close by witchcraft. It was not lawful for me, a priest of Christ, to look on this warlock's fire. I turned my head away and prayed but not until it was as if those pictures came nearer. It was as if the bloody field of Clontarf, whereon Brian Boru, *Ard Ri* of Ireland, was breaking the Viking power forever in the West, came into Dorrud's house that dark Good Friday afternoon. Once the fire sank low even to vanishing. But Thorleik Eldgrimson threw on another pile of turfs and it flamed out brighter than before.

Until sunset the two men watched, never speaking, while I prayed a half room's length away, and, hundreds of miles distant, two great armies fought and died. Then, even as the sun began to sink, Jarl Sigurd died from a spear wound; and, just after him, his enemy, old King Brian, fell under his banner, struck down by the ax in Jarl Brodir's hands. But, though he was dying, the pagan gods died with him; and the Christian cause triumphed. The Irish drove the Norse into the sea. The sorcerers had not lied to Jarl Brodir, after all, when they promised that, if only King Brian fought on Good Friday, he would surely fall. Only, as was their fashion, the dark powers had cheated him in the very act of granting his desire.

This was at Clontarf which lies between the Liffey and the Tolka, bounded on the north by Tomar's Wood and on the south by the whelming sea whence came these sea kings into Ireland four hundred years before. Three hundred battle banners flew and fell between Grangegorman and Glasnevin while I prayed there in the dark house of Dorrud.

"Look, Thorleik!" said Leif Ericson suddenly, clutching the old man's arm. "Those men before the shield rampart around the dying King! It is our Brian, Olaf's fosterling! And Thorhall Gamlason!"

However it was this came to pass I do not know. I think Thorleik and Leif saw true that afternoon. But I tell this tale not as they saw it—for I stopped my ears and eyes and prayed—but as Brian told me much later when he, too, had become King. I draw, too, upon the memories of some of the soldiers who were with Brian that day. For he was ever shamefast about himself, that grandnephew of the *Ard Rí* who had been my friend.

For anyone who had known him back in Vinland days, I think it would have been easy enough to tell Brian at Clontarf, though he had grown older and though there were dark blood smears on his cheeks. For he fought bareheaded after the reckless fashion of the Irish who scorn the protection of helms. Perhaps it would not have been quite so easy to make out Thorhall Gamlason, unless one knew beforehand that he had once again taken to going into battle, as the Jomsburg vikings used to, clad in a bear sark. It was as if the two edges of Thorhall's sword were aflame there on the field of Clontarf. He dealt death on all sides of him when he broke the shield-wall around King Brian and rushed, ax raised, to where the dying *Ard Rí* lay. Then another Brian was in his path; and the two old friends and enemies knew each other at once.

"Stand aside, friend Brian!" said Thorhall Gamlason. "I have no quarrel with you. I fight for Jarl Sigtrygg against the Munster King."

Brian shook his head sadly.

"I am very sorry, my old friend," he said. "Brian of Munster is my liege. I owe you my life. I owe him my honor. I will not stand aside—not even for you, Thorhall Gamlason."

Under the bear's head, nodding on his casque, Thorhall Gamlason drew back bearded lips in the old grin Brian knew so well.

"Then, friend Brian," he said, raising his sword, "we shall have to see, we two, if witch Gefjon was right or wrong when she made her prophecy about the two of us so many years agone."

Thorhall Gamlason aimed a heavy blow at Brian with his two-handed sword. Parrying arm crooked within the shield handles, Brian warded that blow with his buckler. Then Thorhall made to smite with his ax. Even as he did so, he bared his right side for a moment. A moment was more than enough. Stepping aside like one of the rope dancers of Sarkland, Brian sank his sword deep in Thorhall Gamlason's side. The old berserker stood erect an instant, leaning a little on his sword. Then, wavering from side to side, he slowly toppled to the ground. Brian caught him in his arms with a low cry of grief. The shield wall had regrouped itself now, after Thorhall's break-through. So the two of them were well protected from the melee which still raged outside.

"Is it Thorvald Ericson's Skrymir you still wield, Brian?" Thorhall Gamlason asked him, coughing. "I think it no disgrace to yield to Thorvald Ericson's great blade."

"Yes, it is Skrymir, Thorhall," said Brian, trying vainly to stanch the red flow of blood with a strip of his yellow sleeve—yellow, the *Ard Rí's* royal color, which all of King Brian of Munster's men wore when on his service.

"It was ever a good sword, Skrymir," said Thorhall Gamlason between coughs. "Mine is a good sword, too, though this time yours has prevailed. But I am not so generous as Thorvald, Brian. I do not think I will give you my sword. I will take it with me to Valhalla. Perhaps the old gods there will still look with some favor on an old swordsman like myself for whom there is no place anymore in this new order of things."

"Do not talk of dying yet, Thorhall," said Brian, distracted. "I will get you a leech—the best leech on Clontarf field, Ailill, King Brian's leech."

Thorhall Gamlason looked over his shoulder to where, but a few paces away from the two of them, the white-bearded Brian of Munster lay dying under his *Ard Rí's* standard. Norse helmets, with curving aurochs' horns upon them and boars' crests in gleaming bronze, littered the field about him. Thorhall Gamlason noted the strewn helms and nodded approvingly. Brian of Munster had wrought well while he still stayed on his feet. This had been a good King Jarl Sigtrygg had fought against. It was no disgrace to be beaten by such as he.

"Your leech has not done his royal master much good, I note," said Thorhall Gamlason sardonically, turning back his head. "No, Brian. It is the old, old story we warriors know so well. No man may fight against his doom. No fighter lives till evening whom the fates mark down at morning. I was doomed longer ago than that, as you well know who remember the bitch, Gefjon, in Olaf Tryggveson's great hall. I should have known I was fey this dawn when the two ravens flew above me all the way from the long ships to Clontarf field. It even came into my mind, as I marched, that one of them had the eye of Olaf's wish-maiden, Hjlod, in her mantle of crow's feathers. But I am glad it is you who slay me, Brian mine. Do you remember the old promise you made me back in Vinland where we fought the bear together, you and I?"

"I remember well," said Brian, his heart full. "I will give you honorable burial, Thorhall—as honorable burial as any warrior upon this field."

Then he looked at Thorhall uncertainly.

"You still cling to the old ways, Thorhall?" he asked. "You do not wish a priest?"

"Yes," said Thorhall Gamlason. "I still cling to the old ways, Brian—else would I not be here when I might be home by the fire in Ericsfjord. The old ways are best for me, though it comes into my mind now that they may not be best for every one. I learned that night of storm aboard our *Mariasuden* that the lady Mary had great power. It seems her Son, the white Christ, has even greater power. For he has this day prevailed over my patron, Asa-Thor. But that makes no difference to me. Ever has the Red Beard been my friend. I will not desert him or Odin now."

Thorhall Gamlason swooned away after that. Brian thought him already dead when he opened his glazing eyes one last time.

"Let it be you, Brian," he said, the death rattle already throttling loud in his throat, "who bind the Hel-shoes on me. Salute the Hlín, your Grainne, for me. Tell her to bear more sons like their father so that the house of Brian may stay strong in the West."

Then Thorhall Gamlason died. King Brian of Munster, *Ard Rí* of Ireland, sank fast just after, even as the sun went down on that field of blood. The priest signed him with the sign of the Three-in-Power and touched the holy oils lightly to his temples.

"Four hundred years ago they came first to our shores," said the *Ard Rí,* dying. "Now they go hence forever. Praise God mine was the arm that drove them forth!"

As the sun went down and darkness reigned over the field of Clontarf, the last turf flickered on Dorrud's hearth.

"Before God!" said Leif Ericson, swearing a mighty oath. "It warms my heart to think those twain were our comrades aboard the *Mariasuden!*"

But Thorleik Eldgrimson wept, as only the very old can weep. For he had loved them both; and, besides, he did not like to see the passing of the old ways.

That was the last time I saw Leif Ericson, the captain of the *Mariasuden* on our great Vinland faring. I am glad I knew a man like that one in my day. Men say his son by the lady Thorgunna was a good man, too, though not equal to his father in all respects. But men cannot always judge these things for sure. It is only God can search the hearts and the reins of the creatures He has made.

It was not only in the Hebrides there were portents that Good Friday. In Svinafell, in Iceland, blood fell upon the priest's vestments as he raised the host in the act of consecration. It seemed to still another priest, at Tvaattaa, that the altar before him opened out into the depths of the sea; and in the sea he saw terrible things so that it was long before he could go on with his blessed Mass. So it also went in Caithness, in Orkney, in the Faeroes, in the Southern Isles. I have heard that a man named Brand saw the Valkyries on Birsay even as we had seen them on Thorgunna's isle. On Ronaldsay a man named Harek fell in with the ghosts of Sigurd Jarl and his men who took him into the hill with them; and he was seen no more. Jarl Gilli, who had, in the end, stayed home and not joined Sigtrygg's hosting, was visited in a dream by a despairing messenger who bore him tidings of that evil defeat. So it came to pass through all the Northland on that day. The old gods were going, the old things were breaking, the old order was passing forever. I, too, though I should not have, mourned to see it go.

There is but one thing more to set down, and I am done. Brian told me this in his last sickness when, lying on his King's bed, here in Dungarvan, he thought back over the happenings of his life and talked to me, his counsellor. In the time left him his thoughts dwelt much on Clontarf field. He told me most of all of Good Friday night, when the battle was done.

Late that night, in the cathedral at Dublin, where they had sung the *Te Deum*, Brian sat, still in his blood-rusted mail, thinking on the old friend on whose dead feet he had that day bound the Hel-shoes on the field of Clontarf. Before the solemn victory ceremony, which was just now over, the great sails of Sigtrygg's and Sigurd's defeated flagships had been borne into this minster and there hung up, in Christ's house, as trophies of Christ's victory over Asa-Thor. Brian looked up at them hanging like banners in the nave. Other Norse sails were hung up there, too, like great flags: purple sails; sails snowy white with bands of red and green and blue; sails with scarlet serpents wriggling over them. They still smelt of salt and far horizons, those sail-flags; and, as

Brian gazed upon them, his heart, he said to me, was not so much jubilant in the glad knowledge that the viking power in Ireland had been this day smashed forever as sad with the sorrowful thought that the day of these proud vessels was almost over. For he had sailed farther into the West than other men in two such ships as these: the *Mariasuden* and the *Synnovesuden*.

A cold wind keened down the aisles, stirring the midnight flags, dimming the candles of triumph. Brian fell to remembering how, years back, he had sat while just such a wind—it was a winter wind, though, not a spring one then—blew over King Olaf Tryggveson's stave-church at Vik; and how he had thought the wooden church that creaked and gave with the gale was like a ship sailing into the northern night. It came into his mind that this greater church he sat in now was very like a ship, too—a ship that, he thought, would go on to spread wider sails than the world had yet known.

Again the great cloths moved above him. One sail was not there; and Brian was glad in his heart that it was not there. He was glad Leif Ericson's *Mariasuden* had stayed proudly aloof this day of blood as became a ship that wore the name she wore; a ship, moreover, that had seen so much more than other ships had seen—and he, too, had seen it all from her decks!

For a long time Brian sat there in the key-cold minster, thinking on Thorhall Gamlason, the old friend whom he had slain, and praying for his defiant soul. Then, at last, he got stiffly to his feet—for his wounds were cold and needed dressing again—and walked down the steps to where his shivering gilly held the great charger Brian of Munster had given his grandnephew. It was a good steed, this Irish horse of his; as good a horse as the *Synnovesuden* was a ship—the Norse *Synnovesuden* which he still kept in a shed back in his steading where Grainne waited and prayed this same night.

Rain had begun to fall in the darkness. The gilly hoped his master would have sense enough to put up, this one time, at an inn instead of riding all night. But Brian shook his head. Time enough, he said to himself, to sleep tomorrow and the next day and the days after that. If he rode all night again, he could be with Grainne and the children in the morning. Wearily he climbed upon the horse's back and signed to the gilly that they should start. Despairingly the gilly dug numbed heels into the sides of his nag.

The two riders passed the field of Clontarf on their way. The ravens were busy, and the looters, too. But Thorhall Gamlason lay quiet in the Irish earth, his sword and buckler in his hand. Brian blessed himself and said a prayer for that follower of Asa-Thor who had stood stanch for Thor on the day of Ragnarok.

The thrushes were just finishing their morning-song when Brian came into his hall where Grainne, kneeling on the hearth, smoored the fire with her own two hands.

"You are welcome, my lord," she said, rising, the anxiety going from her eyes. They kept the courtly usage always in the presence of servants, those two. It was only then that Brian knew how tired he was. He thought that he could sleep till doomsday's trumpets rang.

Things changed after Clontarf. Very slowly; but they changed. And I have watched them change still more in the half a hundred years since then. Even in the farthest North, things changed. Thor was forgotten—or almost so, for the Lord of Thunder will never altogether pass out of men's minds in those upland fells where he came to birth—and Njord, Lord of the Sea. Even as Manannan mac Lír and Angus Óg were they forgotten. St. Clement, the martyred Pope of the first days of the Church, he whose symbol is the anchor, took Njord's place for the fishers and sailors of the Northland. Stave-churches sprang up everywhere. Mary Gardens were planted in each town and village. Olaf Haraldson, who came next in line after Olaf Tryggveson in the long list of our Norse Kings—though the usurping Jarls, Eric and Haakon, stood between their reigns for sixteen years—died at Stiklestad, even as other kings had died before him. But, unlike most other kings, when his body was borne to Nidaros it was placed over the high altar; and Norway had, at last, a patron saint as well as a king of the great line of the Fair-Haired.

There will be other changes in time to come. But other eyes than mine will have to see those things and other pens set them down. My race is almost run.

How I came to Brian's and Grainne's court, on the eastern shore of Ireland between Dungarvan and Cloyne, after they became King and Queen, first as friend, then as counsellor, and always as priest, is still another story which I cannot tell here. For, however dear it may be to me to think on, it does not belong to my tale of our Vinland faring.

So I lay down a tired pen now at the last. My work here, in this kingdom where I have so long made my home, is all done. The new King of Dungarvan likes me well enough. But he does not need me, as did his father and mother. It is time—and more than time—I went back to Iona where, though the abbot is as new as our new king, I am always needed. One is never not needed in God's house where all is order and coolness and light and the great comfort of prayer. Here also, it is true, I have the Mass. But a younger priest can say Mass for this court now. There I am the Mass and the Mass is me because my fellows know of me, as I of them, that I am Christ and He is me.

In the end, life uses one up and casts one aside even as a worn-out javelin or a blunted arrow or a broken pen gets cast aside. Only the lover is never rejected—and a priest, too, always remember, must be ranked among the world's lovers. A lover is like a rose that buds and blooms and drops its petals. But those petals are not lost. They are picked up and pressed between the pages of the Book of Life by the great Lover who made all roses in the beginning. Death is no more than that for lovers: an aromatic sleep from which they wake, refreshed, for love.

But since all flesh is stubborn, however old, I think the arrow must sometimes yearn for the airy arc of its flight and the javelin remember the clean whistling wind of its passage against the blue sky. I know I remember such things. I cannot help wondering now how it stands with Vinland where, in time to come, there will be other stories told of that fair land. . . .

It comes into my mind now, as I lay aside my quill, that, across the ocean, far in the west, Leif Ericson's cabins crumble slowly back into the earth. It must be that the wooden crosses, too, have fallen down by now on Crossness where Thorvald Ericson sleeps his sleep with Bran till Judgment Day. Does brushwood grow all over the hillock now where his cairn still is—for stone, at any rate, lasts somewhat longer than wood? Does no one at all remember now what happened there so long before? And what of Meyla's son? Lives he still, a blue-eyed chieftain among those dark-eyed Skraelings, who, long since grown into manhood, has begotten sons and grown great in council with no one to reproach him for his father having been a traitor? There must be much to tell of him, too. But all that belongs to the many, many sagas that never get written down, though they well deserve the writing and the telling after.

Meanwhile I am sure of this one thing. That land still waits: forest and river and mountain and lake. Spring leaf and russet tree. Loon and salmon and deer; and, far out on the grassy plains where Leif had never gone but which Meyla told us of, the great herds of hairy oxen, their humps growing fat with the sweet grasses of the endless plains. Year after year, that land waits and grows ever more comely. And the Skraelings hunt and fish and fight and smoke the strange fragrant herb the older lands know not of—but Meyla did, and told us of it.

Yes, the land we called Vinland waits. It was ours for a time. But I know now we were not the land's. One has to belong to the land before the land can belong to one. There was not time for that with us. Someday it will be different. Someday this, too, will come to pass. Someday I think another *Mariasuden* will sail those western seas again.

Meanwhile I think on the moon at evening laying her broad silver targe on the waters, shielding the sweet land behind; and on the sun at morning holding up his broader golden buckler on those same dear waters, warding the strong land throughout the day.

It is very beautiful, that land, waiting, through the long centuries, its next fulfillment.

A NOTE ON HISTORY

"ONE MAN'S TALE IS BUT HALF A TALE," SAYS SKAPTI THE Lawman to the assembled Thing in the *Saga of Grettir the Strong*. If that was true of Viking doings in Grettir Asmundson's day in 1014, it is far truer today in 1958. I am afraid that, at a distance of nine and a half centuries, my own story of Leif the Lucky and his voyage to Vinland is but the hundredth part of a tale. Part of this results, of course, from the devouring tooth of time worrying the bone of tradition. Part of my problem is also caused by the deliberate selectivity of fiction. For I have, of malice aforethought, coalesced and transposed details from the various Vinland sagas, making, for example, Thorfinn Karlsefni's ships arrive while Leif's is still in the New World. The melodrama of Freydis, Leif's murderous sister, has been eliminated. The role of Thorvald, Leif's brother, has been elongated; and Thorvald himself has been somewhat gratuitously endowed with skaldship. Thorhall the Hunter is made more emblematic than he probably was, even though Thorhall, saturnine worshiper of the old gods, was emblematic enough at that.

As for the pair of Irish lovers, whom the sagas know only as Haki and Hekja, runners extraordinary, the bare fact of their identity is quite historical. It is true they are here romanticized—not, I hope, too implausibly so. They are also allotted a historical dimension which makes them politically symbolic. I must, in addition, confess an act of viking depredation all my own. The greater and lesser sagas have been rifled for contributory detail.

God Thor and certain other members of the Aesir get a pretty good run for their money; but there may be some measure of demurral over the proportions I give the Christian thing in this story of mine. Nevertheless I make bold to defend my action here even down to the probability of Leif's ship, which goes unnamed in the Vinland sagas, having been christened with a Christian name. The basis for this same probability is all down in the

sources even if the nineteenth century which, unlike Leif, seemed
to prefer Thor to Christ, did not wish to recognize the fact. The
few anachronisms are all deliberate. They are never off by more
than a decade or so; and this, in an age when the wheel of change
turned ever so slowly, means nothing.